HOT TO GO

KRISTEN BAILEY

Storm

This is a work of fiction. Names, characters, business, events and incidents are the products of the author's imagination. Any resemblance to actual persons, living or dead, or actual events is purely coincidental.

Copyright © Kristen Bailey, 2025

The moral right of the author has been asserted.

All rights reserved. No part of this book may be reproduced or used in any manner without the prior written permission of the copyright owner.

To request permissions, contact the publisher at rights@stormpublishing.co

Ebook ISBN: 978-1-83700-174-3
Paperback ISBN: 978-1-83700-176-7

Cover design: Emma Rogers
Cover images: Shutterstock

Published by Storm Publishing.
For further information, visit:
www.stormpublishing.co

ALSO BY KRISTEN BAILEY

Sex Ed
Five Gold Rings
Textbook Romance
We Three Kings

Souper Mum
Second Helpings
Has Anyone Seen My Sex Life?
Can I Give My Husband Back?
Did My Love Life Shrink in the Wash?
How Much Wine Will Fix My Broken Heart?
Am I Allergic to Men?
Great Sexpectations

*For those kids in Year 10 French
who asked me to dedicate a book to them.
This is it.
Just don't actually read it.
Merci beaucoup.*

PROLOGUE

Suzie

It's too hot for sex. I should have just said that before he pulled his shorts down and got his knob out. It's not just hot, it's hot-in-England hot which means that it's all anyone can talk about. *Isn't it boiling? I can't cope in this heat. I swear the pavements are melting.* You see, this country is not built for weather this extreme. We're built for rain, grey and temperate conditions, light coat weather. When we're this hot, we melt like witches in Oz. Middle-aged men start cycling around with no tops on, cans of beer in one hand; everywhere sells out of fans; people start announcing that it's hotter than it is in Spain and resurrect the word *scorchio*. I am those people. I'm usually saying that word as I peel my sticky thighs off a pub garden bench where I've gone on the hunt for shade, Pimm's and ice cubes I can put down my bra.

So yes, sex in these insanely hot temperatures was not our greatest idea. We may both expire on this sofa in a giant sweaty heap.

'You with me, babe?' Paul asks me, beads of perspiration on his upper lip.

'It's too hot for this, eh?' I tell him, trying to summon up a smile as if I may be enjoying this.

He laughs but he still grinds away at me. Obviously not too hot for him, then. Any sex is good sex for Paul.

But such is the way with sex with someone you've been with for many years. The sex is sometimes exceptional, but you also have your fair share of failed attempts, stolen fumbles, moments where you're not quite there but crack on with it to be a good partner. And there are times where you fall off the kitchen table because you had three ciders and have to run to the sink to throw up. (We laugh about that now but I was off work for a week with a bruised coccyx.) I don't want to use the word routine but that word can be a comfort. I like the intimacy with Paul. I like the orgasms and how I still find his brown eyes dreamy, how I love tracing a finger alongside the curve of his chin.

On this balmy spring evening, I liked the spontaneity and laughter at first. I was bogged down with marking and all the madness of the end of a busy school term, and he suggested we order a Thai. The app told us it would take thirty-five minutes. Paul joked about what we could do to kill the time. I mean, I could have got through at least four reading assessment papers.

Instead, I'm here, unable to tell if my thighs are sweaty from arousal or the heat. We really should invest in a proper fan. Lindy at work has air conditioning. I look at Paul. He can tell I'm not quite in the room. Why is his face so pink? He's the same colour as a boiled frankfurter. I bite my lip trying not to laugh.

'Here,' I tell him. I stop proceedings, removing my dress and bra completely. If I am completely naked then this might work better. He seems excited by the prospect and we part for a second so he can hop around, kick off his shorts and stand there to take a breath and put his hands on his hips. It's a call for me to be impressed by his gym-honed body and dick being half-mast, but all I can see is how matted his chest hair is, like seaweed washed up on pier pilings. I would joke but he looks so proud and I know that if I call this off now, he'll be grumpy and hurt. I'm not sure I can do sweaty and grumpy. Maybe it's best if I don't look at him. I turn around, resting my arms against the back cushions of the sofa. I can't lie – the cold air passing from the fan against my buttocks is a relief.

'Oh, yes...' Paul murmurs, surprised that I would want to attempt more than one position during this quickie. I'm just doing this as it'll mean less of our body parts will be touching. He pushes up against me. Christ, even his penis is warm. Can penises overheat? It might weld itself inside of me. I won't come like this. He rarely reaches around to assist in this position. I'd do it myself if I had the energy. Let's just get this done. And for a moment, as I stare into the wall in front of me, I wonder if that's what I should be thinking when another human being is physically inside me. All couples have this, no? Just sex to fill a void. Did I just refer to my vagina as a void? I'm glad he can't see my expression right now. That's not a good sound either. It's a dual rhythm of slapping and a sound not unlike someone walking through a swamp. That's not sexy.

'You OK, babe?' Paul grunts.

I need to let him know I'm enjoying this. I moan a little. 'Yes, just like that...' Now is not the time for a tutorial. I need to feed the ego. I know I should sometimes state my needs a bit more, but right now I don't have the patience or the desire. No one wants orgasms when it's this hot, we want to stand in front of the fridge. Now that's an idea. Sex in front of the fridge. The lighting would make my boobs look outstanding.

'Babe, I'm close. So close...'

I moan again. Thank fucking god. I'll need three pints of water to rehydrate after this.

'Are you close?'

Haven't even left the depot, lovely. 'Hmmm... yeah, it's so good.'

I can tell he's close because he's picking up speed, like a car engine in full throttle. Why do I lie? I should be honest. I'll tell him after. I'll turn it into a joke. We'll laugh at how my tits left sweat patches on the sofa cushions. It's one of those little things you put up with in a relationship. Occasional selfish and unsatisfactory sex, annoying relatives, the way they hog a duvet.

Ow! He just slapped my arse. I'm not quite down with that. But yet again, I fake some sense of enjoyment. To be fair, he does this too. He sits through romcoms in the cinema. He agreed to Thai even though he still gets wigged out by noodles. It's called compromise. It's what you do in a long-term relationship. We should repaint this wall.

'Aah, yes... yes... yes... you absolute...'

Please be a good word. I'm begging.

'*Beast...*'

What? Is he referring to me? Or was he talking to himself? Or worse, his penis? He withdraws from me, leaning over to put an arm around my midriff and kiss the side of my neck. I'd trade the last nine minutes for that lone kiss, the breath on my skin, his fingers tracing my hips. But he moves away quickly. I flip over to regain some sense of composure.

'Heads up,' he says, and I scramble my arms around to catch the tissue box he throws in my direction. I hate it when he does that. I can't catch things. He knows this too. 'To clean yourself up.'

This is romance. 'Beast?' I question him, hoping I don't sound hurt.

He chuckles to himself, pulling his shorts on again. 'Not you, obviously.'

'Well, that's a relief. I mean, I need a wax but I was saving that for...'

'Christmas?' he jokes.

'So funny...' I retort. I was actually saving it for our summer holiday next month so I could time and plan my regrowth without too much itchiness and stubble. I put my knickers on and go and stand in front of the fan. 'Grab me a Fanta from the fridge?'

Paul disappears. I need a shower. Maybe after we've eaten we could go to the beach? We live five minutes from the sea and everyone is at the beach after work during this early heatwave. It would be a welcome reprieve to just run into the sea, submerge and cool off. I feel an ice-cold can at the back of my neck and close my eyes. We should have started with this. That feeling, that relief is sexy. I grab the can from him and hold it to my forehead before opening it and downing at least half. Paul watches me curiously.

'It was too hot for sex,' I tell him, putting the can down and sliding my dress over my shoulders. I twist my dark brown hair to the top of my head into a loose bun.

He makes a face. 'This isn't hot. When I lived in Dubai, it was forty-two degrees,' he informs me.

'You had air conditioning...'

'Methinks the lady doth complain too much,' he says, winking.

'The lady doth worry about expiring before her time.'

'I can think of worse ways to go...' he says.

I'd rather go in my sleep, to be honest. The doorbell chimes through the house. Well, I know the food is early because that sex did not last thirty-five minutes. I get up, watching as Paul shifts his gaze to his phone. I hope he's looking at buying us a new fan. In the hallway, the cool of the tiles against my bare feet is welcome and I open the front door.

'Oh, I think I've got the wrong house?' the delivery man says, casually looking at the number on the door and back at me in confusion. I have sex face, don't I? I'm dishevelled and pink.

It could also be because I didn't put a bra back on, but I've been out in worse. I chased the bin men in knickers, a T-shirt and UGGs once.

'No, that's possibly for us... number thirteen,' I tell him. 'Are you... Sajeed? Code is 5672.'

He nods curiously. 'It's just... last time, you... I mean... it was a different lady. Maybe a housemate or sister? The girl with the red hair.'

I pause for a moment to think about the people who've been in this house, the food we've had delivered. A different lady?

'She works at the gym, an instructor maybe?'

'The gym?'

And in a split second, Sajeed's eyes meet mine and we share the same realisation. His expression changes to distraught. 'Must have been a different house,' he says, trying to backtrack.

It might be too late for that, Sajeed. He hangs his arm out, urging me to take the food so he can run away. I stand there and stare at it for a while. There was someone else in this house, someone who wasn't me? A woman?

'When was this, Sajeed?' I ask him. My face is frozen. A breath is stuck in my body, struggling to escape. I cling on to the door to steady myself, the heat from outside hitting me like waves.

'Last week maybe?' he says. 'Seriously, I think it was a different house. All these houses look the same. Maybe it was your neighbour?' He points to the house that shares our pathway.

My neighbour to the left is an eighty-four-year-old lady called Marjorie. She has no teeth and a flip phone so I know there's no way she's getting Uber Eats.

He looks to his left and right. Sweat runs down his temples. 'Yep. Definitely a different house. Maybe even a different street. I deliver a lot of food in this neighbourhood.'

But unfortunately, his sad eyes tell me different.

'Was it Thursday, Sajeed?' I ask, trying to control the shock from bursting out of me. I was on a teaching course in London. Overnight.

He doesn't know how to reply. 'Miss... I...' He hangs his arm out again. *Please, just take the food.*

'Babe, problem?' Paul says, popping his head out of the kitchen doorway. Sajeed doesn't hang around. He puts the food just inside the door and takes a light jog down the pathway.

Paul peers around to look at him running off then looks back down at his phone. I bend down and pick up the food and turn to look at him. I think he's on TikTok. Really? I take a long hard breath.

'He just got confused. He remembered delivering here last Thursday,' I say, trying to wrestle with my emotions and gain the upper hand in this situation. 'Another woman was here.'

Paul stops and looks up at me. It's a silent, panicked look. A face once full of colour, drained. His shoulders fall, a hand goes to the air as if he's about to try and explain.

You absolute dick.

'Heads up,' I say, casually, but I put all my emotion, all my rage into my arms and throw the takeaway at him with all the force and energy I can muster. Pad Thai, papaya salad and little crispy prawns rain through the air. *I can't.*

It really is too fucking hot for this shit.

Charlie

'What on earth is that on your face?' Patricia, our head of religious education asks me, as we walk towards the school hall for the staff meeting.

A hand automatically goes to my face as she smiles broadly. Patricia is the sort of teacher you feel is in the bones of this place, a woman of indeterminate age, a woman of legend (she threw a Bible at someone's head once), and for some reason she's always had a soft spot for me, telling me I remind her of a young Alain Delon (yes, I had to Google him). It's been six months of growing out my facial hair and the teens of this West London school (like Patricia) have been quite unforgiving. I've been called everything from Mr Twit to Gandalf. The problem is I do feel pride in the fact I grew this myself, even though I am aware I am starting to look like a common variety cult leader.

'Not a fan then?' I ask her.

'I can't see your lovely face, Carlos.' She's also the only person in school who calls me Carlos because I teach Spanish and she thinks it's funny. It would be, except I don't look like a Carlos. To me a Carlos is someone with swag and casual hotness like Pedro Pascal. The only thing Pedro Pascal and I have in common is brown hair, conversational Spanish and a penchant for spontaneous dancing.

She fans herself down with her hands, her silver bobbed hair clinging to her face. I slow my pace down to walk alongside her, to try and appear gentlemanly, but really because when I'm kind she'll sometimes give me a mint humbug from her handbag. I love a mint humbug.

'It's fucking hot, isn't it?' she says, puffing out her cheeks. I take it she's not talking about my facial hair anymore. 'And it's only May. If it continues this way, I'll die in my little portacabin classroom.'

She's not wrong. I mean, I hope she's wrong about the dying part as she's the sort of teacher I think and hope would live forever, but the mercury hit thirty-three degrees today and after lunch, the classrooms had become a mix of water guns, body odour and moaning ruddy-faced children.

'I have started keeping ice pops in the staffroom freezer, you know?' I tell her. 'Help yourself.'

'Flavour?'

'I have a range, Patricia.'

'Well, I look forward to having a suck on one of them,' she

jokes, and I try to restrain my face from reacting. The banter is always crude and mildly terrifying with her. The sort that would see HR make us have a sit-down meeting. 'Are they big?'

'They're manageable,' I reply, and decide to match her game. 'You know, Patricia, I can't take it when you tease me and say we can't be together.'

'You're so right. I'd ruin you,' she says, cackling.

I nod, grinning. And, on cue, a boiled sweet comes out of her handbag, almost like a thank you for humouring her.

'You still with the painted lady from English?' she asks me curiously.

I look around nervously in case Krystal is in the vicinity. I know she won't take kindly to the comparison. She often refers to Patricia as a relic, so at least the animosity is mutual.

'They're tattoos. You make her sound like a circus sideshow,' I tell Patricia.

Patricia makes a face. 'She's all pierced and wears those big jumpers with the holes. It's like the moths have been at her.' Patricia wears a boucle suit to work every day with the same butterfly brooch, a low navy heel and a handbag. She looks like a First Lady in waiting.

'You disapprove?' I ask her, curiously.

'I'm just jealous, obviously. Plus she's the one dragging us along to this meeting in a heatwave. How long is it supposed to last?' she asks as we arrive at the school hall.

'Hopefully, not long...' I say, picking up some biscuits on a silver foil tray at the front of the room. They really know how to treat us in this place. I hand a Rich Tea to Patricia, not before feeling a hand on my arm. I turn to see Krystal standing there.

'Where have you been?' she asks, looking furious. 'I needed you here.'

'I was escorting Patricia,' I tell her. 'She was being very complimentary about my beard.'

Krystal runs her fingers through it and I submit to this obligingly. 'Isn't it giving millennial Jesus vibes, Patricia?'

Patricia grimaces at the reference. 'I was thinking more Tom Hanks in *Castaway*. Was it your idea then?' she asks.

'Well, I think he looks rugged and distinguished,' Krystal says proudly.

'It looks like a big seventies muff...' Patricia whispers out of the side of her mouth. Far from being offended I laugh and then choke a little on my biscuit. Krystal doesn't get the joke and we stand there stewing in this strange awkward face-off.

'Oh look, it's Bev. I need to have a word,' Patricia says to break the silence, putting an arm to mine and giving me a cheeky wink before taking her leave.

'Relic...' Krystal says as she's out of earshot.

'You could be a little kinder.'

'What does she know about grooming?' she scoffs. 'Her vag is probably covered in cobwebs.'

I baulk a little at the mean girl energy. Patricia is a teaching lifer. She's everything Krystal never wants to be. Teaching to Krystal is just a wage, a way to bide her time until she can quit, write earnest literature and win the Booker Prize. She is adamant that her nightmare is to be in the same school for all that time, stagnating in the same place. I stand somewhere between the two. I can never project myself that far into the future but I'd argue you can never stagnate in teaching because the kids change, they make every day different, they deserve our loyalty and good influence.

'I think the beard is hot,' she reiterates.

'Well, then that's the only opinion that matters,' I say to reassure her.

'Exactly,' she confirms.

I smile. Krystal leans into me, resting her head on my shoulder, waiting as other teachers fill the hall. It's one of those multipurpose spaces that can magically turn from an exam room into a gymnasium, or a stage for amateur productions of musicals where Mr Foster annually gets out his trombone. It's lined with world flags, motivational posters and heavy curtains that vaguely smell like Lynx Africa and cheesy feet.

'I'm so bloody nervous,' Krystal says, looking at me to give her some confidence. 'The computer hates me. No one wants to be here.'

She's right – it's Friday and all of us are desperate for a pub garden, but we've been called in here to take in Krystal's ski trip presentation, designed to try and persuade more members of staff to give up their holidays and get out on the slopes. Maybe looking at pictures of the snow will also provide some relief in this mini heatwave.

'It will be grand. You'll see... And I am sure the computer loves you.' I try to appease her by offering her one of my biscuits but she looks down at it, disapprovingly. She's a healthy sort. She'll read ingredients out to me while I'm downing a whole packet of Bourbons and tell me what the emulsifiers are doing to my gut health. It's always mildly naggy but I plough on. Nothing can put me off an economy biscuit.

'Oh my, have you seen Stan? That shirt is giving.'

I don't always understand Krystal, she occasionally speaks in youth talk. I look over at Stan's shirt. What is it giving? It's giving me a mild headache. Is she telling me I need to wear more paisley? With this beard? I'd look like I sell crystals and dreamcatchers on a market stall. But that's very Krystal; she's a free spirit, a bohemian creative. We've been together only for a few months but I can already see the couple she's trying to mould us into. It involves sourdough, wild swimming and this beard that I'm wearing.

'EVERYONE, can I ask you to take a seat?' Alas, it's our fearless leader, head teacher Warren. Warren is very by-the-book. He speaks in business lingo about standards and expectations and is the sort who looks like he might sleep in his suit. It's a tad uninspiring, but to give him credit I think he manages it all very well. The teachers all fall into place, taking their seats amidst the patter of light chatter. 'So, how are we all feeling?' Warren asks. He does this – asks us rhetorical questions but never waits for a reply. One day I hope someone heckles him. *The Year 9s hate us all, Warren! We can't believe we have to buy our own pens!* Instead we just all stare at him blankly. 'Krystal, I will hand over to you. Please.'

She signals over to me. Oh, help. I'm the lights man. I do as I'm told and shuffle over to the panels of lights. I pass someone yawning, that's not a good sign. Krystal worked hard on this. There are fonts she downloaded. I was forced to watch it many times.

Krystal positions herself at a lectern and begins. 'Hi... so I won't keep you, but I came here today to show you some of our ski photos from the trip last month to Italy. I was one of the many members of staff who went, and I can totally recommend it. It's seven nights including travel, a chance to really get to know lots of kids in our school community, bond with teachers, indulge in a fair bit of après ski...'

I look up at the screen and feel a surge of concern. I've seen this presentation many times so, as the words come out of her mouth, I know that what's on the screen is not what she prepared. What are these pictures? What I saw was a jaunty collage with graphics and a cursive font. This is a real mishmash of pictures, as if it's coming straight from her camera roll. Krystal's oblivious, her back to the screen. Do I say something? Interrupt her? I'm not sure she'd like that. She's just put up a picture of her cat licking himself. A few people laugh. She thinks it's because she's funny. I try to signal to her and she puts a thumbs up at me. She'll turn around in a moment and realise what she's done.

And then I realise what's happened. She's connected her phone to the laptop and it's just automatically playing photos from around the time of the ski trip. Photos on her phone. A clip comes up of her walking in the park, spinning around to show her affinity with fresh air, then there's a photo of a smoothie bowl, a saved meme, a selfie of both of us. This is back when... Oh, god. Turn around now, Krystal. Stop harping on about the coach journey. A few people laugh under their breath and she assumes them to just be rude, giving them evils.

I can feel panic rising up in me. I cough. Loudly. Because I know what's in her photos.

'And the school offers a voucher so you can buy all the gear you need.'

Please no. Krystal, please turn round. I see Warren rise from his chair to intervene. Krystal looks mildly annoyed. The next photos are selfies of the two of us at home. Crapping hell. No. I know what comes next in this sequence. I run-shuffle towards the computer and slam my hand on the keys. But I haven't quite made it in time. I look up at the screen where I have indeed frozen a still from a video rather than stopping it or moving it on. And there I am. Naked. Worse than that. Not totally naked. I look out into the audience to see mouths agape, eyes boggling. Patricia may very well expire.

And how exactly did you kill the head of RE, Charlie?

Thing is, before my girlfriend of mere months went on the trip, I was helping her pack. We were both a bit drunk and we were just fooling around with her thermal socks and goggles. And before I knew it, I was naked and dancing. With a thermal sock on my knob. I thought she took a photo. I didn't realise she had been filming. I didn't realise my knob had such impressive swing.

Stan with the paisley shirt has an expression on his face that's a cross between a snarl and a stroke. Krystal turns around and sees what's on display as I try, in vain, to get this massive naked image of me off the massive screen, watching members of staff turn to each other talking in whispers.

'What the hell?' she says, panicked.

'You were filming me?' I ask, desperately trying to shut down the screen.

She seems unapologetic, more insulted that I'm upstaging her. 'Why did you put that up there?'

'Me? Why the hell would I put that up there? Why has this computer just frozen?' My hands are just pounding at keys, pulling at cables. I guess it could be worse. I could be broadcasting this to the whole school via a live assembly on Teams.

'This is all your fault,' Krystal mumbles, shoving me aside and pressing ESC multiple times, to no avail. I look at her, shocked at her anger, her rage. 'You were supposed to get here early to help me set up. You know I'm shit at technology. Fucking idiot.'

I step back as if I've been slapped. How is this my fault? But I say nothing. Can we cut the power to this place? Whoever has their phone out in the second row needs to be rugby-tackled to the ground. Someone turns the lights on, and the ridiculousness of the situation kicks in. This is mildly funny, no? But Krystal's face says differently. I'm the one who should be feeling embarrassed, surely? I turn to my colleagues. Do I bow? Maybe I shouldn't. But instead, I stay glued to the spot, a thick sickly heat around my collar, not knowing whether to laugh, cry or throw up. And for the first time, I feel very grateful to have this stupid big beard so I can at least hide how awful I really feel.

PART ONE
MALLORCA

ONE

LONDON, JULY

Suzie

'Blow a bit harder, a bit more. It's still a bit flaccid,' Beth instructs me, pressing at the soft bits.

I giggle. I'm not sure I have the breath. It really is too hot for this, but I've raked through all my belongings and it seems that when I left Paul, I didn't think to bring a pump with me. I blow at strands of hair that stick to my face, wondering what shade of raspberry my face is as I puff out my cheeks. 'Is this hard enough for you, dear cousin?'

She gives it another grope. 'Perfect,' she says, as she angles the hosepipe over the paddling pool, filling it with one hand, a Cornetto in the other, sunglasses perched on top of her head. I like the way she has her skirt tucked into her knickers, ready to jump in as soon as possible.

'Where did you say you got this again?' I ask her.

'My neighbour may have given birth in it. She wasn't clear. Feels a little shallow for someone to have given birth in though.' We peer into it further, looking for what, I don't quite know. 'Think of it as a housewarming gift.'

'A used paddling pool?'

'Upcycled, Suzie. Let's put a posh twist on that...' I laugh as she splashes me with the hosepipe. 'And you're sure it's OK to do this here?' she says, looking around the communal garden space.

'I think it's so bloody hot, no one will care,' I tell her. I may be right about this. Since the early heatwave in May, the temperatures have risen to the point where no one really cares about self-respect or modesty anymore. I saw a man doing his big shop topless the other day – hairy man boobs out and no one even blinked. It's why I have no problem standing here in my communal garden, the road running adjacent to it, wearing a bikini top, denim cutoffs and a Mickey Mouse baseball cap. Maybe that's the theme of the last few months. Learning to care less about things. Over the road, a woman waters her thirsty plants and watches us curiously. 'It was this or we drink in my super-hot flat in the bathtub together with the cold tap on.'

She laughs. I made a joke. Three months ago, I often wondered if I'd ever be able to joke again. Perhaps I was destined to spend the rest of my days sad, scarred and serious. I thought the anger would sear itself into my veins and change me forever and it was petrifying. So, I ran. I extricated myself from Paul and all that grief, all those big emotions I felt. For so long, I'd invested my time and energy into my relationship, into our future, so I shifted that focus on to me. I moved on. I came back to familiar London, my hometown, and found myself a new ground-floor flat near a train station where I worry about the crime but love not having to carry my shopping up many flights of stairs.

And to keep moving, I gave myself projects, and it's the ridiculously small things that bring me joy now. I've bought window boxes and started to grow my own herbs, I've got new bathmats, I've painted my bedroom yellow which is admittedly like waking up in the middle of the sun, but was something Paul would never have allowed. Fuck Paul.

Beth dips a toe into the paddling pool and shudders with delight at the coolness of the water. She turns the tap off the hosepipe and does a little excited dance. I laugh at how much delight she is getting from this simple set-up of two camping chairs angled around a pastel striped paddling pool, with a cooler box nestled in the yellowing, dried-out grass. Such are the joys of a British summer – when the sun is out, we don't care what we look like, we're just desperate to get as much light and vitamin D as we can on our skin.

We both sit down on our respective chairs and place our feet in the pool, sighing with relief as we do so.

'Oh, Lord, that is perfect,' Beth says.

I exhale deeply. This isn't Brighton. When it was hot in Brighton, the sea air was soothing, the beach never far away, but I can't be near that place now without my heart hurting, without thinking of a place where I'd forged what I thought was a great love. So this is the next best thing to perfect. Summer in the city in my small postage-stamp garden where in the bushes, I think I spy an old microwave. I tilt my head to the sun, searching for light, hoping my heart-shaped sunglasses won't leave silly tan lines on my face.

Beth reaches down to the cooler box, retrieving two bottles of beer, snapping the lids off both. She passes me a bottle. 'Suze, we need to drink.'

'For the hydration?' I ask.

'No. That too, but we should toast the new job! Have you celebrated that yet?'

I take the bottle from her and shake my head, smiling.

'Then...' she says, clinking her bottle next to mine. 'Here's to my brilliant cousin, Suzie. Elle est une professeur magnifique. Oui, oui. Bien sûr...'

I laugh. 'Did you Google Translate that?'

'No,' she says indignantly. 'I remembered a little of my GCSE. But seriously, I am forever proud of you. You are going to be amazing at this. And we're going to be working together so I couldn't be happier...'

I pull a face, unable to handle the compliment. When I ran away from Brighton, I escaped from it all – including my job in a school where I'd been teaching French for six years. I hated Paul for that. Because to transplant myself into a new town meant packing some boxes. But I know that transplanting my career to a London comprehensive is going to be miles harder.

'Tell me about the bloke I'm replacing?'

'Keith – old, bitter, moving to Northern France to go fish and spend the last of his good years eating cheese, he tells me. You are a million times better than him.'

'And the bloke who interviewed me... head of department?' I ask her, taking a sup of my beer.

'Yes... Lee? Isn't he the loveliest?'

I nod. For me it was the kind smile, the floral shirts and the lilting Welsh accent. It certainly beat the interview I had in a North London school where the man started talking to me in French and in a blind panic, I told him I was happy to be his wife.

'I mean, I got that job on my own merits, yes? Did you put in a good word?' I ask her.

She scrunches up her face. 'I may have had a chat but Lee said you were by far the best candidate they'd seen. You were creative, engaging and personable... all the good buzzwords...' she says.

I kick a bit of water her way and she giggles.

'Really?'

'Really,' she says sincerely.

'Did he mention that I hugged him?' I ask.

Beth laughs, knocking her head back. 'No, you hugged him?'

He let on that I had got the job during the interview and, because I didn't want him to see the tears in my eyes, like an idiot I just reached over and grabbed the man to cross those professional boundaries and give off a far worse impression.

'I was overwhelmed by his kindness – I couldn't help myself. And then I jabbered at him about running a French club and promised I wouldn't be one of those teachers who takes the Fridays off sick before half term.'

'Hate those teachers...' Beth adds, laughing. 'And don't be the sort who puts little lines on their milk in the staffroom fridge to see if anyone's stealing it.' She puts her drink down temporarily to spray some suncream on her exposed thighs. 'Don't worry about the hugging. Lee will see it as a genuine show of emotion. And that's very you.'

I smile for a moment. In low periods of wobbliness, it's sometimes warming to hear words that raise you up and recognise who you are. Beth is one of five sisters, my cousins, who I grew up with in London in my formative years. And when I ran back here, they helped piece me together, like some sort of group project. Sanity and peace came from their sisterhood, and evenings helping me stalk Paul on social media and write him strongly worded emails about how our sofa was mine even though I knew we'd had sex on it and I didn't really want to see it ever again.

'Fancy another Cornetto? I bought a whole box,' I tell Beth, reaching into the cooler.

'A whole box just for us?' she asks.

'When I said I was making dinner, this is it,' I say, laughing. I reach inside the box and throw her a strawberry one. Top-tier ice-cream choice, if I do say so myself. I grab one for myself, peeling back the paper and licking the ice cream and strawberry sauce from the card insert. The sheer joy of it makes up for the fact that the soundtrack to this escapade in the sun is a Tesco delivery man who's blocking the road next to us and angering motorists. The sun is out though. We do not care. We're just going to sit here taking in the drama, sunglasses on, ice creams in hand. *I'll stick them yoghurts up your arsehole in a bit if you don't move that sodding van.* It's good to be back in London. It really is.

'Oh! Before I forget... Meg told me to tell you that you're coming to Mallorca,' Beth informs me, leaning forward in her seat.

'Mallorca?' I ask, glancing over. 'But that's Meg's big fortieth birthday party with all the sisters. I'm not a sister.'

She raises an eyebrow. 'You may as well be. Come with us. The villa she's rented is massive, apparently. There's room and the more the merrier. You haven't got a holiday booked, have you?'

I was supposed to be going away with Paul but I cancelled that without telling him, not really wanting to go on that holiday by myself. 'No. I was maybe going to stay here, do some tiling work in my bathroom.'

Beth does not look impressed. 'Well, now you're coming to Mallorca. We'll see if we can get you on our flight.'

'How long for?' I ask.

'Five days.'

'I'll need to... wax,' I say, searching for reasons not to go. I'm not sure why. Maybe out of politeness. I will need to wax though.

'Won't we all, hun. But look, you've already started your prep here, building your patchy base tan with me. Come. It will be fun. And I hate to say this out loud but, out of all of us, you need a bit of fun.'

She says that so sweetly, not in a mean way, but she's seen all that's happened to me in the last few months. Now is the time to start putting things right. I laugh. I like how she's so relaxed about this – just pack a bag, come on holiday. The fact is, I can, right? It's the summer holidays and I don't have to think about Paul or any of the responsibilities of being in a relationship. I can put distance between us and his interminable stream of emails trying to argue with me about how we split our savings accounts. I can just hop on a plane with my cousins and escape, again. For fun. Nothing more. That is a nice feeling.

'Can I...?' I mumble.

'Think about it? I'll tell her you said yes.' Beth beams, and I smile back.

I sit back in my seat. Maybe it is that easy. I'll have to find the bottom half of this bikini though. A holiday. That might be a good thing.

'There better be space in there for me, girl...' a voice with a strong West Indian accent rings out, emerging from around the corner. I turn to see my neighbour carrying a white plastic garden chair, wearing a large floral muumuu, a broad-rimmed straw sunhat on her head.

'You are just in time, Maureen. Come dip your feet in. This is my cousin, Beth, who's visiting me today. The teacher one I was telling you about...'

'Of course. Hello, sweetheart. God, it's bloody boiling, isn't it? I had to take my bra off so ignore me,' she tells me, dragging her chair along the grass and pitching it up next to us, kicking off her burgundy leather sandals to put her feet in the paddling pool. 'And you got Cornettos? Where'd you get those from? All the supermarkets are sold out. Show a lady some love, please.'

I smile and reach into my stash. 'Small Tesco.'

'Beautiful and clever.' Maureen is my nearest neighbour in this building, someone who burst into the hallway when I first arrived and asked me a million and one questions. She surprises me once a week with something she's acquired from the middle aisle of Aldi. In return, I paint her nails because I'm cheaper than the salons on the high street. I watch her dive into her ice cream and sit back in her chair.

'Oh, my days, look at you in your bikini with your perfect ta-tas,' she says cackling. 'Putting all us girls to shame.'

'Don't be silly,' I answer. 'You can get yours out too.'

She laughs. 'The people aren't ready for that, baby, the cars would all be crashing.'

Beth smiles. 'Yeah, your little B-cups don't get what we big ta-ta girls go through in the summer. Am I right, Maureen?'

Maureen holds her ice cream aloft. 'Solidarity, right there, sister. I sometimes have to lift mine and hold the underparts to the fan.'

We all sit there giggling. 'I got the job, by the way, Maureen.'

She beams. 'I had no doubt. My sunshine Suzie. If you hadn't, I'd have gone down that school myself and had words.' To get that sort of validation from someone who's known me only a few months makes me a bit emotional so I down some beer to keep the feeling to myself. 'You know they're doing those lunchboxes down in Aldi on special. I'm going to buy you one so you have something nice to put your sandwiches in come September. You want one too, sweetie?'

Beth smiles. 'I'd love one.'

She smiles and reaches into her bag to take out a paper fan and some sunglasses.

'Then I'll need to bring you back something nice from holiday...' I tell her.

'You're going away? Where to, baby?' she asks, fanning her face furiously.

'Mallorca. With Beth and her sisters.'

She nods approvingly. 'Amen to that. My girl needs some sun and sangria.'

'What can we bring back for you?'

'You find me some lovely Spanish man, please. Someone who'll know how to handle my maracas, if you know what I mean,' she chuckles.

And we all double over laughing in that little corner of our garden, drowning out the sound of people still arguing in the street, the sun beating down on us and our paddling pool, the ice cream melting so fast it drips down my fingers. I lied before. For now, this is pretty perfect.

Charlie

There are sounds that define a British summer. The hum of a lawnmower in the distance, people laughing in their gardens, kids screaming in joy as they don't have to be cooped up indoors and – probably my most favourite sound of all – the metallic jingle of an ice-cream van echoing through the streets, making my heart sing with nostalgia. I can hear it now in this empty house and there's still that part of me that perks up to hear that music. Is it close? Is it in my street? What's that tune he's playing? I head to my front room window in a wild frenzy and see the van whizz down the street. Hold up. I'm here. I have earned this. I slip on some sliders, whip off my suit jacket and grab my wallet, doing one of those uncomfortable jogs down the pavement to where they've parked up.

Oh man, it is scorchio. I can feel the heat rising from the paving slabs, the tarmac almost simmering. I bet you a fiver I'll see a TikTok of someone trying to fry an egg on the road in the next week. I roll up my sleeves and loosen my tie, getting a glimpse of my black work socks and my brother's Adidas sliders making a real sartorial statement. I'd perhaps care if I didn't see so many people emerging from their houses in a complete panic to reach the van before it moves on. The dad who's been sitting in his garden in football shorts and some mismatched T-shirt he found to keep things appropriate. The mum who's slipped on her trainers with the backs bent in. The kid in a swimming costume, running around like she's on holiday. This isn't the

Costa del Sol, lovely. It's West London. Make sure to dodge all the recycling bins.

I stroll up to the ice-cream van and wait patiently in the pretty long queue that has formed there, perusing the menu in the window as families in front of me choose which cones and lollies they all want. Do I feel like a child? I do. It's great. I want them all.

My phone rings in my pocket and I reach down to answer it. I don't even get a hello. 'It's bloody hot. It's too hot. I'm literally standing in the bank in the high street because they've got good air conditioning. They think I'm here to hold the place up, I've been stood in here so long.'

'Maybe you could withdraw some cash to keep up the pretence, Max...' I reply.

'It's why I'm calling you. I'm going to say big financial words every so often so they think I'm legit. Mortgage. Pension. Savings bonds.' I'm glad that the heat hasn't just got to me. It seems to have taken my little brother too. 'Where are you? Are you at home? I'm ringing to hear about the job thing. How did it go?'

'Got it,' I say, smiling.

'Knew it! There was no doubt. Happy?'

I stand there for a moment, the sunshine warming my face and I think I might be. A successful interview can do that, massage the ego a little, especially after the cock-sock incident ousted me from my last school. Not that I was fired but it wasn't pretty. After we managed to get that screen turned off, Krystal and I barely lasted a week, I had to attend several safeguarding welfare meetings and of course, because of the nature of schools, the rumour mill went into full action. *Sir had a blazing row with Miss in the hall! Sir shags socks! Sir has really low-hanging bollocks!* Two weeks later, I had handed in my notice and I went in search for another school in time for the next academic year.

'It's all good. New start.'

'And how are we celebrating?' he asks.

'Come round? We can get a takeaway or something?' I suggest.

'Can do. We need to talk stag do too. I've got your costume,' he tells me, far too excitedly.

I stand there looking at ice-cream van menus trying to summon up some excitement about this impending stag event. The fact is I've bought a plane ticket and I've even bought travel bottles of shower gel, but the thought still fills me with a tiny bit of dread. It's a very laddish stag taking place on Mallorca with eight of his closest friends. I fear it will just be an orgy of all-day drinking and pranks and, unfortunately, I now know that costumes will be involved.

'Are we really doing costumes?'

'It will be fun.'

'Is mine decent?'

'It's not the mankini.'

Well, that's a plus. I think. Though this means someone will be wearing a mankini. I hope it's not his plumber friend with the hairy back. 'Come over at about seven when everyone else will be at home? Bring something... cold...'

'Will do. Income tax, cash ISAs...' he says in an elevated tone.

I smile as he hangs up and I return to my place in the queue.

'I want that massive one with the bubblegum sauce and the sweets,' a boy behind me says. 'How much is that one?'

I turn to the side to see him and two other little boys count out their coins anxiously, doing quick maths in their heads. 'We're £1.50p short,' one of them complains. With their matching football shirts, I'm going to hazard a guess that these three are thick as thieves and potentially brothers. Oh, to be little like that again, when this van was the greatest thing in the world to have ever existed. I notice the eldest brother is in charge of the money, noting down choices and ensuring no one strays from the pavement. I relate to him instantly and smile, empathising with all that responsibility.

'We could just get the small ones then?' the middle brother says, hopping around as he chose not to wear shoes.

'The baby ones?' says the youngest.

I intervene cautiously. 'So that one – does it have a bubblegum in it too?'

'Yeah, at the bottom,' one of the kids tells me, looking pleased that I've leant on his expertise in ice creams. 'That one is the best but I like the Oreo one too. That one's got chocolate sauce and Oreo crumbs but they all get stuck in your teeth. Depends if you have a date later on?' he jokes with me.

'I don't actually,' I reply. 'I'm single. I got dumped.'

'Oh. That sucks. Was she a moo-cow?' asks the littlest brother.

I think that might be my favourite way that someone has ever described Krystal. 'Yup. Kinda.'

'Is that why you're getting ice cream?' the other brother asks me. 'To make you happy again?'

All the brothers look up at me. We're in this conversation now but I don't really know how to answer. Also, the dumping happened about three months ago in the immediate aftermath of sock-cock-gate, over a pretty savage text where she called me a waste of time. Yeah, I don't think they need to know about that. But pretty soon after the whole debacle, I realised Krystal was deeply self-obsessed, slightly toxic and not a very nice person, and maybe I should be aiming for more. For nice, at least.

'No. Actually, I wanted to buy this for myself. I'm celebrating...'

'On your own?' one of the boys asks, looking around for who

I might be with. 'That's a bit sad.' His brother nudges him in the ribs. 'Is it your birthday?'

'No. I'm celebrating because I got a new job today.'

This doesn't elicit the happy response I thought it would. I guess when you're little you don't get the thrill of these things but today, I went for a job interview and a man I'd never met before told me I was quick-thinking, knowledgeable and personable – all the buzzwords – and he offered me a position there and then, on the spot. It's a longer commute than my last school but it seems like a decent place, and I'm just glad to have a job to pay the bills.

'What's the job?' one of the boys asks me. 'Are you a businessman?'

'No, have another guess.'

'Accountant.'

'Are you telling me I look boring?' They don't reply. 'I'm a teacher.'

One of them steps back from me, like I may have just grown horns.

'What do you teach?' he asks me.

'Spanish.'

'Like Dora the Explorer?'

'¡Vámonos!' I say, putting on the accent of an eight-year-old Latina girl. This does not endear them to me, in fact, the family in front turn around and watch me curiously, one dad putting a protective arm around his daughter. It's the heat. Let's blame the heat. I must look ridiculous, sweat patches forming around my armpits and the tops of my shoulder blades. I undo more buttons on my shirt, hoping it doesn't start to look too indecent. There's a man further along down the queue in what looks like a string vest and I'm strangely jealous of him despite the fishnet tan he's likely to get on his chest and back.

'Don't grown-ups usually celebrate with alcohol?' the eldest brother asks me.

'I might do that later but I thought I would go with ice cream first.'

Again, they look a little unimpressed by me and my sad life. I can be fun. Really. The queue at the van moves forward and I find myself at the window, an older woman inside looking like she's ready to melt, a towel wrapped around the inside of her T-shirt collar, her face flushed. There was me thinking that selling ice cream might be a lovely and cool way to spend the summer months. Surely, you could just put your head in the freezer?

'What will it be, lovely?' she asks me. She leans forward. There's no polite way of saying this but the lady has a rather large set of bosoms and they sort of lean against the shelf of the window. I thought the man before me took an extraordinarily long time to choose his cider lolly. I try to be polite and look away.

'Can I get an Oreo sundae, please? They come recommended,' I say, turning to the boys behind me.

'Sure thing, sweets,' she says, winking at me. I never quite know what to do in that situation because you don't wink back, surely. She heads into a cupboard in her van and pulls out a large waffle cone. I watch as she fills it with ice cream and adds chocolate sauce, Oreo crumbs and more Oreos to the top. That's less a celebratory treat, more a one-way stop to diabetes.

'You've got quite the queue today,' I say, seeing it wind down the pavement.

'Oh, they love a bit of Madame Whippy...' she laughs. I look up at the name of her van. Mr Whippy is the customary name of the traditional British ice-cream man but I like how she's upgraded her name so it sounds fancier, if a little kinky. 'They come for the sauce.' I raise my eyebrows. 'My Biscoff sauce,' she says, quite liking that she has someone to banter with. 'The ice-cream men round these parts know nothing about sauce. And you should see my toppings.'

'I can see them,' I say, pointing at her sprinkles. She's got a load of them. 'I mean they're all on show.' What am I saying? I don't quite know what this is. I'm flirting with an ice-cream lady who I suspect is double my age and could very well eat me alive. This could be quite the rebound fling. I suspect she'd be a lot of fun but also keep me in Magnums over these hot summer months. I notice a wedding ring on her finger. Looks like there's a Mr Whippy, possibly a Monsieur Whippy. But the lady has impeccable sales skills, I can see why she gets this sort of business.

'How many spoons, gorgeous?' she asks.

'Just the one.'

'A man after my own heart. That's seven pounds, sweetie.'

I hand her a twenty-pound note and lean forward. 'Look after the boys behind me too. Don't say it was me or they'll think I'm weird. Any change you keep it for yourself, Madame.'

She stops for a moment. 'And he's a gentleman too. I'll come down your street again soon.'

'You come whenever you want.' I said that, didn't I? We'll blame the ice cream, the heat.

She laughs again at the top of her voice. 'Right, who's next? Oh, it's you three monkeys again. What am I getting you? Why aren't you wearing shoes?'

And as I carry my ice cream away, I smile to hear how she just turns on yet another persona for the next customer. And there was me thinking I was special. I put my spoon in my sundae and scoop out a giant mound of soft white ice cream. It is stupid how bloody excited this makes me. There's a toddler a few yards ahead of me doing the same, a flake sticking out of his cone, the ice cream all round his mouth, with exactly the same grin as me. Well done us. Aren't we lucky? I've got a new job. The sun is in the sky. I take another spoonful of ice cream until I get to my gate and see a figure lurking by the door. She turns, her hair scooped back into a messy bun, a bit too much flesh on show for a seventeen-year-old. She might as well just go out in her pants.

'YOU GOT ICE CREAM WITHOUT ME?' she squeals, completely aghast in the same way people should be about global warming and bad politicians.

'You weren't here, Brooke,' I explain.

'I am now.' She reaches over, helping herself to an Oreo and using it to scoop up some ice cream. 'Were you going to eat all of that by yourself?'

'Obviously not anymore,' I say.

'Too right. Sharing is caring, bruv. I almost passed out on the bus. It's so bloody hot.'

I look up into the sky one last time before we head inside, feeling the sun against my face. 'You complain too much.'

'Yeah, whatever. Why did you only get one spoon? And what's going on with your sweat patches? You're gross.'

TWO

Suzie

There's a bartender in front of me looking at my chest curiously. I know why and I think I might be spending a lot of time explaining this T-shirt today.

'It's the band, UB40.'

He looks at me a little sadly, not quite knowing what to think. We're allowed to like who we like musically but to him it's clear I don't seem to be in their usual fan demographic unless I'm being deeply ironic. 'Are you a big reggae fan then?'

'Oh no... I'm with that group over there,' I say, pointing to my cousins in the corner of this airport pub, all in similar T-shirts. 'One of them is turning forty. She be forty.'

He pauses. 'So I guess you'll be drinking a lot of red, red wine then,' he replies, chuckling under his breath, and I smile back. Well, at least one person got it but, as Lucy complained before, this is the last time we put Emma in charge of T-shirts because we're just walking around this airport like a group of adult fangirls. Looking over, it also seems that Lucy has torn her T-shirt in a bizarre Hulk style to make it as brief and revealing as possible, flashing a little too much perhaps. I'm wondering now if this might get us thrown out and denied an overpriced fried breakfast and a pint, but 'Pete' with his jolly paunch and greying sideburns seems good humoured about it all. He follows my gaze. 'She with you?'

'She is,' I say, grimacing but with a smidgen of pride.

'Sister?'

'Cousin. That whole table there,' I say, pointing to the corner. 'The five of them are all sisters and I'm the little cousin on the end.' I am what they've always called the honorary sister. I've tagged along to every birthday, Boxing Day buffet, wedding and christening – a frequent flyer in their family history.

He glances over smiling. 'Who's the birthday girl?'

'That's Meg, the eldest cousin. The one with the sunglasses, napping against the wall.' Looking wildly enthusiastic about the trip. Emma is beside her with her sensible mum bob holding a folder of travel documents. Then you have Beth (teacher; paddling pool gifter; Converse wearer) and Grace (accountant; seasoned traveller; wore flip flops to get through security quicker), both of them laughing wildly at something on their phones. And then there is Lucy, in bits of a T-shirt, denim cutoffs and Crocs (with charms) – I've never seen anyone more ready for a holiday.

'They look like...'

'Trouble?' I say, as he pours my final drink.

'God, no. That hen do over there is trouble. The one in the leg warmers and the wig has been on tequila since four thirty. We're taking bets on whether she'll actually get on the flight.' I turn to said hen do. It's an eighties theme, the alcohol is rainbow coloured and the veils are cheap and possibly a little flammable. 'What I meant to say is that they all look like they're having fun. I'm guessing it's just you girls? No families, kids?'

I'm growing particularly fond of Pete here with his barman telepathy. I nod.

'Destination?'

'Palma, Mallorca.'

'Classy and very pleasant this time of year. Well, I wish you a lovely time,' he says, handing me the card machine. I glance at the screen as I tap my phone to pay. *How much?* Yet there is something about an airport pub, serving us alcohol in the wee hours of the morning and a mediocre fry-up that is just part of the pre-holiday experience. You could be angry about it but instead, there is a frisson of excitement simmering away that an airplane is in the vicinity, an escape is coming. Just take my money.

'That's very kind, thank you, Pete...' I say, balancing the tray of drinks and carrying it precariously over to the table where all my cousins sit. The sun hasn't even come up and some of us are already having alcohol. Lucy claps and cheers my arrival.

'Gin and tonic for our birthday girl,' I say, handing out the drinks, watching as Meg rejoins us from her nap. 'OJ for Emma, bottle of Becks for Beth, white wine for Grace and vodka Red Bull for Lucy...'

'Absolute legend, Suze,' Lucy tells me.

'Well, least I could do was get the first round in – food is on order too.'

Grace puts her hands to the air silently to know bacon will soothe our tired souls too. 'Then can I propose a toast?' she says. 'Here's to Meg coming of age. Life, love and laughter.'

'That sounded like a shit sign someone would hang in their kitchen,' Beth jokes.

'Oh, do piss off. It's five thirty in the bloody morning.'

'Here's to Smeggy being the first of us to become officially old,' Lucy intervenes, taking a large sip of her drink.

Grace laughs under her breath. A bit of my pint shoots up my nose.

Meg glares over at her, parentally. 'Seriously, there are children on that table?'

Lucy looks over at said table. 'One of them is a baby. They won't care.'

'Until it's their first word...' Emma joins in.

'Which would be mildly hilarious,' Lucy turns to me. 'It's what we called Meg all the time when we were teenagers,' Lucy explains.

'It's what *you* called her,' Emma clarifies. 'Please stop it with the smegma talk so early in the morning.'

'Oh, do lighten up, Emma. It's her fortieth. We're on holiday.'

'You may be. But we're still on British soil. They can ban us from the flight for inappropriate behaviour... clothing,' Emma informs her, pointing a finger over her cleavage.

'Inappropriate? There's a girl over there in a fishnet dress. I can see her pubes poking out the holes.' Do we all turn around? Of course we do. Christ, it's like a sea urchin down there.

Lucy looks down at her top. 'Instead, I look like a desperately sad groupie of a band that peaked in the nineties.'

'The T-shirt is funny,' Emma tells her.

'It's not. I'll tell you what's funny though. I stayed at Em's last night and saw her pack. How many pairs of knickers did you pack for a five-day holiday? Fifteen.'

The sisters all laugh and I do my best to hold in my giggles.

'I travel prepared...'

'For having diarrhoea?' Lucy retorts.

'You're such a cow.'

'Mooooooo,' she says loudly, attracting attention from the tables next to us.

Emma takes a deep breath before getting up and walking away. To where, who knows? But it's to avoid a fully fledged fight with her sister in this harshly lit terminal building so early in the morning. I love this familiar banter, and the fact that Emma will eventually come back because what binds these sisters is more than just knicker talk.

'Are we doing shots yet?' Lucy asks, unperturbed by her sister's storming off.

There's a collective no, but I see the disappointment in her eyes and I put my hand to the air.

'SUZIE! Yes!' she says, pointing at me, scuttling off to the bar. There is a collective eye roll around the table but the truth is, I owe Lucy, big time. Back when the Pad Thai hit the fan (quite literally), she was the first person I called. I was floored, distraught and a big seething ball of emotion. Paul had cheated on me with someone he'd met at the gym. It was such a cliché and I felt like such a damn fool and had no idea what to do. Lucy knew. She got on a train to Brighton, she came to find me, she burst through my door and offered to defecate on his clothes. And she was the one who told me to come back to London. *Come back home, Suzie. London will look after you. We'll look after you.* I idolised Lucy and her four sisters growing up. They treated me like a surrogate little sister, and being an only child, they were a force to be reckoned with, strong female energy that was embracing, warming. They've always made me feel part of their gang.

'You don't have to do shots with her, you know?' Beth tells me. 'She can do that on her own. We can't carry both of you to the plane.'

'I could do just the one? Or toss it over my shoulder.'

Beth laughs. If Lucy saved me, then Beth and the others dragged me on their lifeboat. They saw a girl in need and revived her. Everything from temporary digs to financial advice; they were there, and I'll forever be grateful.

'Well, this is at least better than my hen where she waited until I passed out and put a fake penis tattoo on my forehead,' Meg says, plainly, watching Lucy as she flirts with Pete the barman while sneakily putting quite a lot of ketchup sachets in her pockets. There's always been a brazen confidence about her that is entertaining but, man, I wish I could bottle it.

Inhale it for all those moments you need to be a touch more badass. Her sisters watch her and you can see a collective look of pride but also questioning if it's too late to leave her behind.

'Thank you again, for letting me be here,' I tell Meg.

She swats away the compliment. 'It saves one of us having to bunk in with Luce,' she winks. 'You are family. This is where you belong.' I beam at her kindness. 'Plus, we need a touch of youth on this trip too. People to remind us how to party. We don't trust Lucy. Last time I went out with her, the shots were on fire and I nearly lost my eyebrows.'

I forget how the Callaghans are in a different stage to life than me – apart from Lucy, they're all mums and either married, divorced or living with someone. It feels like they're light years ahead of me in maturity – a place I wanted to be with Paul. I hate how he hurdles into my thoughts like that. Fuck Paul.

'Well, I can definitely do that,' I tell her. 'Plus, this is a celebration. Yesterday, I signed my contract,' I say, pointing at Beth who claps excitedly on my behalf.

'Work buddies,' she says, holding her drink to the air.

Grace puts a congratulatory arm around me. Signing that contract felt good, freeing. It means I'm still moving in the right direction, away from Paul, reclaiming my power.

'It's all good. New home, new job, new chapter…' I tell the sisters.

'And new wanger. Plenty of it in Spain, I'm sure,' Lucy adds, returning to the table.

Grace rolls her eyes, hitting Lucy round the head. 'Lovely. I am sure that's what Suzie needs.' She looks over at me. 'Ignore her, take your time. When your heart is broken, you don't need wanger to fill the cracks.'

Lucy cackles as Beth chokes on her drink. 'Her cracks? Grace, you filthy mare.'

Grace tries to look unimpressed without breaking into a smile.

Has the thought crossed my mind? The last four months have sometimes felt like some strange fever dream but sex and love has been lacking. So much so that there have been times where I have thought about jumping on Tinder, opening myself up again to the possibility of love. Is my fragile heart ready though? Maybe the safer option is daytime drinking, lying on a sun lounger, taking in all that vitamin D and admiring my tan lines each evening in the mirror.

Lucy continues. 'One thing at a time. We don't have to find you a boyfriend yet. Just lose yourself in...'

'Wanger?' I reply.

'Orgasms, intimacy with someone who's not a tosspot.' Lucy grabs on to my arm and rests her head on my shoulder. 'It's a holiday, Suze. A chance for regeneration, to find your mojo again. All that sun and heat, just lap it all up – let loose, go wild.'

'You make her sound like a farmyard animal on the rampage,' Beth tells her.

'A stroke and a pet, it's all you need,' Meg adds dryly, as we all laugh over our collective drinks.

'Ooh, we could all do yoni sunning?' Grace, Beth and Meg look curiously at Lucy. It's clear she's relishing the chance to have her sisters all to herself, without kids and partners tagging along. In the WhatsApp trip chat, all her planned suggestions included everything from quad biking to matching tattoos to a fire-eating workshop in the mountains.

'Explain,' Meg says curtly.

'We get our vags out for a sunbathe. It's good for you, gets all that light on the labia, it boosts hormone production and energy.'

I laugh under my breath whilst the sisters look on at her, unimpressed.

'No,' Meg says, firmly.

'Are you worried you can't find yours?' Lucy asks, cocking her head to one side. Meg shakes her head at the absolute cheek of it all. 'It would be a moment of releasing all our feminine energy and power into the world. Look at me, World, I'm forty.'

'I can just say that aloud. I don't need to have my legs akimbo and minge to the sun to prove that,' Meg argues. Grace and Beth lean on each other to control their laughter. 'There's no sunscreen factor strong enough for that. I don't want a burnt taco on holiday.'

'Who's burnt their tacos?' Emma says returning to the table, curiously. 'Who orders tacos at five in the morning?'

Grace is crying with laughter at this point.

'Oh no, Luce wants us to sun our lady bits on holiday so we can bond,' Meg tells her.

Emma stares at Lucy and then walks away again.

'It's your sacred space. You all need to recharge it, reconnect with your life force,' she lectures us. Grace and Beth stare at each other, eyes rolling to hear Lucy start to go all new-age on them. Lucy is just a freer spirit, she's pierced and tattooed and has never settled down, her focus simply on loving herself, her journey in life. We could all learn something from her. 'I just want you to use this space to let go a little.'

'I was planning to do that via cheap wine,' Meg informs us.

'But just... this holiday, don't do that thing where you walk around in a bloody one-piece swimming costume, worried about what you look like. Rule one. No fucking kaftans.'

'I like a kaftan,' Beth says.

'No, you hide under kaftans, sarongs, sundresses. Beach cover-ups? Have you noticed, they don't have those for men? Men never have to cover up. They can let their bowling ball paunches and hairy cracks hang out for the world to see but women are never allowed the same luxury. They tell us we have to hide.' This is the Lucy we all know and love – the little sister powerhouse energy. 'You're all fucking beautiful. You've given me nieces and nephews, used your bodies in the most marvellous ways, you've all endured so much. And for god's sake, we're in a villa. There'll be no one about. So please, get your tits, your yonis, all your bits out. Get the sun on them. That's rule two.'

'And are you going to help me put aftersun down there when I burn and it goes all pink and crisp like bacon?' Meg asks, grinning because behind Lucy's forthright ranting, there is only love and wanting to raise us all up.

'Always. I'll buy cucumbers and we'll stick them in the freezer,' Lucy tells her. 'I'll get a big one for you, I know you like girth.'

Meg flares her nostrils trying not to laugh. 'Well, maybe we'll trade that for the night trip you have planned to Shagaluf, I don't mind saying that I really am too old for that shit.'

'We can negotiate,' Lucy says, mischief still dancing in her eyes as she winks at me.

I laugh to myself because looking at all this family, all this banter, all this shared history in front of me tells me this holiday may be exactly what I need.

And with that, a waiter appears at our table.

'Two fried breakfasts?' We all look down as he pushes them in front of us. I look down at two shrivelled bits of bacon and catch Beth's eye over the table as we all burst into fits of uncontrollable giggles.

Charlie

'STAG! STAG! STAG! STAG!'

The chanting is all quite ritualistic and gets louder, more offensive to families on other tables whilst the man of the hour, the intended, the stag, downs a pint messily, slams the glass down on the table and puts his hands into the air, swirling his body around like he's hula-hooping without a hoop, all whilst wearing a very snug and ill-fitting Hulk costume.

It really is a shame that the stag happens to be Max, my brother.

'I am so sorry...' I whisper to a family of four near us. 'Can I pay for another round of coffees maybe?' I feel they would take me more seriously if I wasn't dressed like Aldi Iron Man.

'Iron Man has a beard... and a moustache,' the young boy at the table tells me, judgementally. I don't know how to tell you this, kid, but I shaved mine all off after I broke up with Krystal.

'I know. I apologise for not keeping it more authentic. Thor is in a wig if that helps, that's not his real hair.' This gets a rise from the kids that seems to calm their parents, given the amount of swearing and sexual anecdotes flying around. At this time of morning, I'm not sure anyone needs to hear about the time Dave had a threesome at Butlin's with a couple of lifeguards.

'Who's getting married?' the mother asks.

I point to my brother. We really should have invested more money in that costume as the Velcro is giving him issues and the fake muscular trousers make him look like he's got three massive testicles hanging in between his legs. 'He's my little brother.'

'And the Avengers theme?' the father asks. Was decided on a WhatsApp group chat. It went to many polls, of many terrible suggestions from lederhosen to Smurfs to Baywatch lifeguards until we settled on Avengers because of my brother's infamous teen years where he dyed his hair bright green.

'Was not my idea. My idea was normal clothes at the airport so we'd stand a chance of actually getting on the plane.'

The dad smiles. 'To...?'

'Mallorca,' I say. You see both of his shoulders drop with relief to know they are on a flight somewhere else, away from us stags.

'Batman is also not an Avenger,' the little boy tells me, annoyed by the amateur nature of how we are representing these superheroes. I mean, there's also a man in a black leather catsuit and fake boobs dressed as Black Widow. I hope he's not clocked him yet.

'I know, right?' I say, shaking my head. 'Again, I'm very sorry for the interruption to your morning.' The dad looks at the crowd of men in fancy dress and puts an arm around his boy. It's a look that says: I did that once and now I have this, and I really don't mind it that much. I smile to see it.

Two giant green hands suddenly land on my shoulders. 'CHARLIE!' Max yodels. Lordy, he's bladdered. I hope we can get him on the flight. He hugs me from behind as I try and shuffle away from the family of four. I didn't encourage the drinking; that was all his friends who seem to have been drip-feeding alcohol slowly and intentionally into his bloodstream since we arrived.

'Maxi Pad. Just slow it down, man,' I say, as he wraps his big green arms around me.

'You never call me Maxi Pad anymore, Chuckles,' he says, pouting. 'You're such a good big brother. I am so glad you're here.'

So am I. I hadn't planned on it. I'd been thinking of something sedate like golf and a curry for this stag do, but the plans evolved and I find myself here because I don't trust many of Max's friends. Max has had the same friends since school; they've played football together and graced local pubs and nightclubs with their collective presence. I'd be alright if I knew half their names but for years, they've all gone by the same nicknames that are either versions of their last names (Wrighty; Coops) or just passing observations that seem to have stuck. I always thought Hawkeye across the way was called Gareth. I only found out last year, his name is actually James. He just looks like Gareth Southgate and it stuck.

'Pace yourself. Please,' I beg him.

'I promise,' he says, burping under his breath.

'TONY STARK! You handsome bastard!' a voice bellows from behind us. Oh, it's Andy. Also known as Captain America but for the longest time, also known in our family as the Flanker, mainly because he likes rugby, it rhymes with wanker and we liked having a codename for him. Andy got married two years ago, has two kids but still acts like he's single. It's like the wife and kids are an inconvenience to him so he continues to go on monthly golf trips, raves and stag dos. If I was a betting man, I would probably put a solid grand on the fact he cheats on his wife too, which is why him and me are never likely to be mates. It always surprises me that Max still hangs out with him or thinks that there are any redeeming qualities there.

'Steve Rogers, a pleasure.' He even has his hair smoothed back to add to the smarminess. 'So, are we ready for this? The water in Mallorca don't taste like it oughta because I tell you my friend, it's going to taste like beer and sambuca. Am I right?'

I think this is what the young people refer to as ick. 'As long as we deliver this lad back to his fiancée in one piece and with eyebrows. I'm on a promise to Amy,' I tell them.

'BORING!' Andy bellows. 'Coops has also found that strip club, mate. It's going to be wild,' he says, putting a hand up for Max to high-five. I'm glad to see my little brother joins in with some reluctance. 'I see that look, Charlie boy,' Andy says. 'You of all people need a lap dance and a bit of fun. Max has already told me you broke up with that tattooed bird.'

I look over at Max and fake a smile. I'm not sure you can call it a breakup when you've only been out for three months but I'm glad the news has circulated so quickly.

'Yes, I'm single and ready to...'

'Get knobbing,' Andy says a little too loudly, waving his arms and shield in the air.

Have a break? Feel the sun on my face and get a decent tan. If I'm honest with myself, I'm not sure I was properly heart-broken after Krystal. I was more disappointed that I'd wasted time on a relationship that wasn't up to scratch, and that finding someone to share my life with was proving harder than I thought. She also has my phone charger, though she says she doesn't. So, mean and a thief.

'You don't have much luck with the ladies, do you Chuckster?' he gloats. 'What happened to that dancer you went out with? She was fit, should have locked her in.'

'She didn't want a family,' I say plainly.

'Minor details then,' he says laughing. To him maybe but quite a dealbreaker as it turns out to others. 'You're just too uptight, mate. We'll find you a señorita to bob about on your dick and loosen you up a bit. Ain't that the truth, Maximus?'

Even Max puts a pint glass to his lips at this point to hide from the crassness of it all. I don't really know Andy's wife but feel a wave of sympathy for that poor girl.

'Next round's on Gareth, I reckon. Oi! Spiderman, get your stingy webbed fingers in your pocket and get the pints in!'

I look over at Spiderman who from what I can see is just wearing themed pyjamas. Those are fleece. He'll die of heat exhaustion. Meanwhile, Andy heads over to a group of women who also appear to be on some sort of hen do, eighties themed and raucous, they all wear penis necklaces and are as half cut as the rest of our group. He leans against a table to introduce himself, posing with his shield. Utter twat.

'Don't do that, Chuckles,' Max tells me, as I half prop him up next to a pillar in this badly lit fake pub.

'Do what?' I ask innocently.

'That face. I know you look down on Andy. He's a good friend.'

I laugh under my breath. 'When you were nineteen, that good friend once left you on the night bus.'

'He was drunk,' Max says defensively.

'He left you, took your girlfriend home and shagged her. You cried. For days.' He played Coldplay love songs on repeat. I had to force him to turn them off and get in the shower.

'Bros before...'

I put a hand to the air. 'Don't you dare repeat that line in front of my face or I'm going home.'

We both laugh. We share the same eyes – bright blue, just like Mum's, and they shine a little too brightly sometimes in that we always expect the best from people and put far too much trust in them.

'I'm not saying don't have fun this weekend but if he's a twat, I will drown him in the hotel pool and make it look like an accident.'

'He's got kids,' Max says. I scrunch up my nose at my gold-hearted little brother. He's always been loyal to this bunch, which speaks volumes about him really. I look around; maybe they're not all that bad. I guess they're here to help celebrate him and his impending nuptials. Kudos too to the lad in the purple face paints dressed as Thanos. That is commitment to the cause.

'Do I have to wear this the whole time?' I ask him, changing the subject. 'It's synthetic. In the heat, it's asking for trouble.'

'I'm not quite sure. Wrighty has the mankinis in his carry-on.'

Oh good, there's more than one. 'Not sure there's one big enough for me,' I inform him.

Max shrugs. 'Yeah, don't flatter yourself.' He wraps his arms around me again. I'm not sure what all these men feel for Maxi Pad, but I love him, genuinely. I won't say that out loud because I'm not drunk yet but I'm here for him, always. I pull out the unfortunate wedgie situation that seems to have formed with my outfit. Damn this one-piece malarkey. How do women handle these? Most likely thongs but I don't think Iron Man would tolerate that. How do I pee in this?

I glance over at Andy, right in the thick of that hen do now and perilously close and intimate with one of them. 'Avengers!' I shout across the room, a half-formed idea in my head. 'I think it's time to assemble.' Everyone in costume roars and I'll admit, I didn't think I'd feel so powerful saying those words aloud. I angle my phone for a selfie, ensuring that old Captain America, with his arm on a lady's waist, is fully in frame.

'Hulk! Smash!' I order, and everyone poses. Perfect. Time to get that on social media and tag the crap out of it.

'Excuse me,' a girl says as she pushes past me, heading for the toilets. She wears denim cutoffs, Crocs laden with charms, sunglasses on her head. Full holiday mode activated.

'Sorry... my bad, wasn't looking.'

She looks me up and down at the sorry state of my costume. I know, I know, it's not even a full mask. It's elasticated. I mean, she can talk though. I think that's a UB40 T-shirt she's wearing. That's a bit sad. I didn't even realise they were a thing anymore.

THREE

Suzie

'¡Hola! ¿Señora Callaghan? Bienvenida a Mallorca.'
 'Sí, gracias. Encantada.'
 '¿Usted habla español?' she asks excitedly.
 'Solo un poco.'

I have a feeling that another reason why I've been invited on this holiday is that I have some ability in conversational Spanish that may help during our time here. The sisters stand behind me, Lucy to the back to hide her party girl face, hoping all these Spanish words are positives. The lady in front of us is in a linen dress with a blazer, and a name badge. Rosa. She's tanned, her hair slicked back, looking very different to those of us who've endured an early-morning flight and the joys and hassles of navigating our way over here in our hire car through dusty amber roads, flanked by rocks and trees, nearly taking out a whole herd of unmanned goats on the way.

'There are six of you, only?' she asks.

'Yes,' interrupts Meg. 'I was the lead booker. I am sorry we were *tarde*. There were *cabrónes* on the road.'

'CABRAS,' I say. Goats, as opposed to bastards.

We're lucky that makes Rosa laugh.

'Then let me take you around the villa, tell you about the key codes and show you where the linens and controls are,' she says politely to Meg.

We probably should follow, but instead we stand by the side of that pool, gawping into the space in front of us. When the gate pulled back, we were mesmerised but as we walked out over the stone paths to take in the views and the size of this place, we realised this was not just any villa. This was some slice of paradise, hidden away in the mountains. Through groves of orange trees smelling sweetly of jasmine, the paths led down to a traditional looking stone house, shutters to the windows, guarded by yew trees and encircled by a giant patio with tables, chairs and an outside cooking space. Beyond that, there's a perfectly azure pool, surrounded by white sun loungers and parasols. All you can hear is the trickle of water, and a few birds tweeting their welcomes; you can almost hear the sun beating down on us, baking the floor. And the view. It's like a long deep exhalation, you can see sea, sky in all directions and just feel it all repairing your soul. Even Lucy is lost for words.

'Well, feliz cumpleaños, señora, and we really hope you all enjoy your stay at Villa Sueños,' Rosa tells us, returning with Meg. She looks at our party curiously. I'm hoping it's not the UB40 T-shirts. 'There are no men?' she asks.

'No, it's a women's only holiday,' Lucy pipes up proudly, putting her arm around Grace.

Rosa looks over at us, blankly. 'Oh. That is fine. I do not mean to... I don't know the word... *No pretendo juzgar.*'

My Spanish is basic so I just nod back. I think she said something about lights but I'm hoping she's also left us a manual.

'Are you expecting other visitors? Maybe from town?' she asks curiously.

The sisters look a little confused but mostly look at Lucy who is a fan of bringing in strays and one-night stands. Still, the theme for the weekend seems to be womanly bonding so I'd assume she would know what is appropriate. We all shake our heads, assuming any outsiders is possibly against the rules of our rental.

'Then enjoy... ladies. Actually, there's some items in the bathroom that you might find useful,' she says, a little tentatively.

'Gracias por su ayuda,' Meg tells her.

Meg's been on Duolingo. I know because she told me on the plane. The accent is a little off but she's tried and Rosa looks impressed she's made the effort at least. She takes her leave as we all stand there in different states of shock gazing at this place that will be home for the next few days.

Grace turns towards the sun silently, letting it beat against her face, Beth removes layers as the intense heat starts to hit, draping them over her trolley bag.

Emma looks around, silently, her eye catching the big mega barbeque and outdoor dining area. 'Meg, this is too much. How much did it cost you? We should be chipping in?'

The other sisters look to Meg in agreement and curiosity. 'Danny booked it as a gift. He had a contact. I mean, it's my fortieth and I don't splurge enough on myself apparently.'

Lucy heads to the pool, kicking off her shoes and sitting on the side to dip her feet in. 'And this is why I've always liked Danny.'

I think about the gesture, booking a holiday for someone when you're not even going on the holiday yourself, acknowledging that they are deserving of something this grand, this special. I see Meg look around the place, floored by it but unable to wipe the huge smile from her face.

'Is this private enough for your yoni sunning then?' Meg jokes.

'It's perfect,' Lucy says, standing up to take off her T-shirt and shorts revealing she had her bikini on the whole time. Some of us really know how to prepare for a holiday. She jumps into the pool squealing with delight, splashing Emma slightly who would probably normally be angry but instead smiles broadly. Beth takes off her trainers and socks and dips her feet in, stepping into the shallows, the relief on her face clear to all. 'Take it all off, Beth!' her sister commands.

'I haven't got any swimmers on?' Beth complains.

'You have a bra and knickers on, it's practically the same!' Lucy yells, as she comes over to attack her, like some sort of overexcited shark.

'Well, now the kids are being entertained. Let's get some drinks, I'm gasping,' Emma tells me, putting a hand to my arm so we can explore. The other sisters disperse as Emma and I stroll inside towards the reprieve of cool stone floors and ceiling fans. Inside the décor is minimalist, large sofas by windows framed by gauzy curtains that let in a cool mountain breeze, and an open-plan kitchen with a fridge bigger than the moon.

'IS THERE A PUMP IN THE HOUSE?' a voice booms from outside. I stick my head out of the window to see Lucy has opened her bag poolside and seems to have brought a large inflatable unicorn with her.

'How did she...?'

'Fit that in her bag?' Emma asks. 'Oh, she got me to carry her clothes. Which is actually fine as she's mostly brought bits of string and vest tops to wear.'

Emma opens her bag in the lounge area and takes out two large bottles of sunscreen and after sun. I love the priorities of both sisters but also the differences. Emma was the one who had space for me in London when I first moved back and I bunked in with her family, including husband, Jag, and three daughters. Behind all of Emma's practicality is amazing amounts of heart and I felt that in spades when she took me in.

'You know, we haven't caught up since you moved out of mine,' she says, as she unpacks more provisions for the kitchen, including a fully stocked medical bag. All praise the doctor in the family. She heads for the fridge, filtering through cupboards to find two glasses, pouring us both some water from the ice machine attached to that giant fridge. 'How's the new place?'

'Different. I'm slowly making it my own.'

'I'll come over one day to check it out. And how are things besides that?' she says. Before the lovely Jag, Emma was once married to one of the biggest arseholes known to the planet. He was an awful man but she recovered, she rebuilt. Maybe out of all the sisters, she's the one who knows how it feels to be in my position.

'I'm getting there. The good days are starting to outnumber the bad ones,' I say, honestly. 'I got an email from his mum the other day though, he got her to do his dirty work for him.'

'Coward,' Emma says.

'That's what I thought.' This particular email was full of condescension, lots of references to her golden boy and then a parting shot at the end about my lack of trying.' I didn't reply. I've barely replied to any of Paul's random emails and texts. The fact is I held that man up to the sun and it's like he's doing his best to continually rain all over our relationship, cloud my opinion and turn all that light into dark. I just don't see how we'll ever come back from that so I just move forward, refusing to look back.

She pulls a chair up to the solid wooden table and urges me to sit down. 'You are a wonder, you know. I'm in awe of your strength, your cool in all of this. How you've started afresh and got a new job, but how is everything, really?'

I take a deep breath as she says those words. Of course there were tears, this raw and potent mix of pure fury, sadness, shame, three months ago. But I think those emotions are starting to ferment into something else. It's not even bitter anymore. It's something that sits better in my bones now. All I know is that running away helped. I deserved better.

'I'm here. That's all I know for now.' It's a cryptic answer to a question I'll never really have the answer to. But she gets it. Sometimes to just still be standing is enough.

'Well, if you ever need to process the big emotions then you know where I am.' She pulls me in for a hug and then sits back to scan my face. 'Little Suzuki. You've survived it all with more fire than I ever did. Aunty Bea would be so proud.'

I pause for a moment to hear her talk about my mum. She passed seven years ago and these girls looked after me then too. God, she'd have castrated Paul in his sleep. She was a single mum and all she was made of was fire and steel. It pains me not to have her here but to know how much of her flows through me now. I swallow hard to process that, looking away to almost escape the emotion. 'You've not called me Suzuki for a very long time,' I say, trying to divert the conversation.

Emma laughs. 'You were our little sidekick. So loyal. Always so happy and unfazed by life, you still always remember our birthdays, you're just lovely to your core. You're even nice to our mum and she's hard work.' I laugh but grip her hand, grateful. She looks up at me earnestly. 'Reclaim that main character energy, that's what the kids are saying these days, yes?' she tells me. I smile. 'Keep being you. Don't let that shitting prick take away everything that made you the person that you are. Promise me.'

'Emma, you swore...'

She laughs. She's not the swearer of the sisters. She's not even in the top three. 'There are no kids around. I swear when the moment deserves it. Maybe I've changed.' Or not, I think, looking over at her bag where I know everything will be in packing cubes, labelled and pressed.

'You'll be on the unicorn next,' I tell her.

'Only once you have.'

Emma downs her water and then gets up to inspect all the drawers and cupboards in that kitchen, all stocked with beautifully patterned china, champagne flutes and a coffee machine.

I dwell on Emma's words; there was no other way to be after Paul's betrayal. I don't think my mum would have settled for anything less than sticking up for myself and getting the hell out of there but Emma's right – there are big emotions, the main one being a real fear there that in running away from my past, I don't really know what the future looks like. I sit down and look out at the view. Maybe I'm right though, it all starts here for now. I can picture the next few days, coffee on the big sofas with a book in hand as the morning sun comes up. All in my pants obviously as Lucy doesn't want us to cover up.

I stand up and examine the modern art on the walls, brightly coloured in yellows, greens and hot pinks. However, the longer I look at it, the more my eyes seem to deceive me. I thought it was a series of brightly coloured circles, but could they be something else? Are those nipples? No, they can't be. Pervert. I laugh to myself, feeling a little surge of joy that I can still find things funny. I turn to point the nipples out to Emma but she seems to be hovering over the dishwasher, reading a note on the counter.

'Hun, what does the word *juguetes* mean?'

I pause to sift through my basic Spanish knowledge. 'Jugar is play. Possibly toys?'

'Why would you put toys in a dishwasher?' she enquires curiously.

'I don't know but do these circles in the photo look like...'

And with that, there's a sudden squeal from upstairs as Grace pokes her head over the balcony, laughing so hard I fear she can't quite breathe.

'I can't bloody believe it! I'm calling him now. Oh my life...'

We hear Meg's voice echoing from one of the bedrooms as Emma and I head up the grand spiral staircase to investigate, watching Grace literally lying on the floor still in hysterics. As we open the door, Meg stands there, on her phone not knowing whether to laugh or cry. 'Seriously, Danny. What do you mean you didn't know? Surely they should have mentioned it? We could have brought our kids here!' I don't hear her words though. All I can see is the giant swing hanging from the ceiling in the middle of the room.

Emma looks at me and then back at Grace. 'What the hell? Is this in every room?'

Grace can hardly control herself. 'LUCY! BETH! Get out of the pool, you have to see this!' she bellows over the balcony. She turns back to us. 'There's a pole in my room. What do you guys want? The rotating bed or the room of mirrors?'

'Noooo,' Emma says aghast. She walks over to the swing and examines it closely. 'I don't want to think how many people have used this? We'll have to go into town and get some bleach.' I'm too shocked but I have to side with Grace here, this is mildly hilarious.

'Danny, this isn't funny. How can we sleep on these beds knowing what goes on here? I could catch things.'

'Chlamydia,' Emma mutters under her breath. 'Herpes, BV, ringworm.' She goes over to a wardrobe and opens it to see racks of sex toys, arranged like one would hang guns and ammo. She puts her hand to a mouth like she's just found a dead body. 'Oh, god, this is what that note in the kitchen meant. Don't put the toys in the dishwasher...'

I look over at Grace now and can't stop laughing. Those were likely nipples in that painting downstairs so I'm not a pervert at all.

Meg has moved into the bathroom. 'For the love of God, Danny. There's a rack of strap-ons in here.'

And my more muted laughter suddenly erupts. 'Oh my, that's what Rosa meant when she said there were items in the bathroom. When she questioned why there weren't any men. It's because she thought we were all...'

'On a lesbian sex holiday...' Emma says, nodding her head and looking like she might pass out from the shock.

'Who was this contact? You go and ask him how this is all cleaned. Lucy is in the pool. God knows what could swim up her bits,' Meg's voice echoes through the walls. 'Did you know? I bet you knew. This is the sort of thing you'd find funny. What do you mean? Didn't you look at the pictures? You always look at the pictures. There's a whole drawer of butt plugs.'

Grace really can't breathe now as Emma goes to sit on the edge of the bed, not realising it's a water bed and falling right into it, the waves making her bob around, unable to find her feet. 'Oh my god!' she screams. 'Get me off this fucking thing. I can't...'

Grace and I would help if we weren't doubled over in laughter. Turns out Emma really can swear if she needs to.

Charlie

'NA-NA-NA-NA-NA-NA-NA-NA-NA-NA-NA-NA!'

Christ. I'm trying to work out if I can get the coach driver to slow down so I can roundhouse kick Andy off this vehicle. I reckon everyone who's not a part of our stag do would hail me as a hero because this impromptu chanting/singing is not what we all need at this time of morning.

Maybe focus on the sight of leafy palms, sandy beaches, blue skies and mountains zipping past the windows, and just try to imagine Andy, conductor of the world's crappest boyband, isn't here. I really don't want to hear club classics as sung by a group of twentysomething young men. I want late nineties chillout if possible. I want to feel that deep relaxation of knowing you're somewhere else in the world, you're on holiday, you've escaped. I don't want to have to make constant backward glances to the back of the coach to a group of older men tutting and rolling their eyes. I reckon I could take Andy on. He's not Captain America anymore – the cabin crew made us change as Max's Hulk outfit made a small child cry. But in fact we look far worse now. Some of us (me) had the good sense to pack a change but the rest of us are just wearing cobbled together items from people's cabin bags. Coops is in a polo shirt that's two sizes too small so it clings a little too much to his shapely frame. God help the lad who didn't have time to take off his purple face paint. Andy is literally in a rash guard and swim shorts, bopping from seat to seat, the music blasting from his phone. The bus slows down but brakes suddenly so Andy loses his footing and stumbles, dropping said phone. I look at the driver in the rearview mirror and catch his eye. I saw that. Well done, that man.

'Playa del Sol. The Playa del Sol hotel,' he says in loud annoyed tones.

'YES LADS! This is US!' all the stags cheer, as we stumble off that coach and I try to do some damage control with the other coach passengers with mumbled thank yous, explanations and my hand to the air in an apologetic wave.

'Gracias, siento mucho el ruido,' I tell the driver as I disembark. I slip ten euros into his hand and he looks at me strangely. I don't know if it's the fluent Spanish or the crappy tip but he nods silently.

'¡Suerte, señor!'

Good luck. I think I might need it.

I step off the coach where the lads have already made their loud and boisterous entrance into the reception. We booked a package holiday to keep the costs down and this meant many things: a cheap early-morning flight but a cheerful all-inclusive party palace hotel. We are here for the unlimited drinks, the beach access, and the foam parties. I have a feeling it will be a bit of a shagfest with hangovers, house music and a bit too much half naked ass on display but at least we're abroad. Even if this becomes debauched and ridiculous, just being near the sea with the mountains in the background feels like a massive weight off my shoulders. The air already feels and smells cleaner but there is something about the heat simmering in the air, the sun in the sky, that feels energising. I close my eyes, enjoying the prickle of it on my skin.

'Let's have it, lads!' Three seconds of serenity. That's all I got there. I spy Andy through the doors, still pissing about whilst Max does his best to check them all in. I head over to him, the coolness of the reception air a welcome break from the heat, laughing at Max as I know he still needs his fingers to count.

'All good?' I ask.

'Yep,' he says, a little blurry eyed. From downing pints in the airport pub to cheeky cans on the plane, I can see the constant drinking is starting to take effect. 'We can't get in the rooms until three but they said they can store our bags and we can hang at the pool until then, grab some lunch, head to the beach?'

'Check out the talent,' Andy says, eyeing up some girls who have just come out of the breakfast buffet in an assortment of tiny shorts and cut-out swimsuits. I grimace at him slightly. 'I say we head to the pool, have a dip, get them Estrellas in?' Andy announces to everyone. There are cheers and murmurs of approval. I look at Max still sorting the paperwork and directing bags into a cupboard next to reception. Or maybe he could help his mate rather than thinking about where his next drink is coming from? How am I going to do three days with this man? I've already wanted to shove him out of a bus, now I want to drown him.

I put a hand to Max's back as they all disperse to the gardens of this well-landscaped hotel and its large winding tropical lagoon style pools.

'I've got you, bro. Here, you deal with all the signatures and key cards. I'll do the bags.'

He smiles. I spy a black trolley bag marked with Andy's name. Maybe it's the lack of sleep, but an evil whim overwhelms, and I slip it into a trolley headed out towards the airport. Sorry, not sorry. I can hear him out by the pool area, still singing like a howling dog. I turn to Max leaning over the reception counter, looking like he's struggling.

'You still with me?' I ask him.

He holds his head in his hands, scrunching up his hair. 'I shouldn't have drunk so much at the airport. I think that, mixed with the heat, has got me...' he says.

I prop him up and then turn to the receptionist. 'Disculpe, señorita. ¿Tiene usted agua?'

She reaches under the desk to a small fridge and pulls out a bottle of water.

'Down this now before any more alcohol. Did you eat anything?' I ask him.

He shakes his head, holding the bottle to his lips and gulping it down.

I sigh. 'It's like I've taught you nothing over the years.' I reach into my backpack and dig out a cereal bar. 'You can have that.'

'Yes, Dad.'

The receptionist looks at us curiously. '¿Padre?'

I shake my head, laughing. 'Hermano.' Christ, I hope she doesn't think I look that old. There's only five years separating us. She smiles and looks over at Max who is a whiter shade of grey. 'Señor Max, if you are feeling unwell then I can maybe find a room for you. I can't accommodate your whole party but I can give you the one room?'

'Really? Eso sería increíble,' I tell her, getting my Spanish out again to try and seal this deal.

She looks at her screen and nods. 'Room 345, you can use

the lifts to the right here. But your friends will have to wait,' she says, side-eyeing them.

'Gracias,' I say, flashing my best smile.

'Max? Max?' He looks at me over the tops of his sunglasses. Oh dear, I know that look. It's halfway between throwing up and passing out. He did this to me halfway up some stairs before and I couldn't deal, so had to just leave him there with a pillow and a blanket hoping he wouldn't slide down in the night.

I prop him up against me and shuffle him towards the lifts, trying to drag two bags along with me too. 'I owe you one, bro,' he whispers. 'I should have eaten,' he says, cereal crumbs spitting out the side of his mouth.

'I should have forced something down you at that pub. Some bacon or something,' I say, realising that I am carrying his body weight. I push him into the lift where he collapses into a corner, curling into the fetal position. He looks about twelve, partly because he's always had a baby face but also because he had to borrow someone's SpongeBob SquarePants swimming trunks that he's wearing with a tie-dye T-shirt and some trendy bright blue rimmed sunglasses.

'Can you make it to the room? Or do you want a piggyback?' I ask him. I don't know why I've offered this. This was perhaps an option when I was fifteen and he was ten but I don't know if I can carry him now.

He pushes himself up and clings to my back like a koala, wedged between me and the side of the lift. This will all be in the legs. His head nestled on my shoulder, he mumbles in my ear, 'I wonder what Amy is doing. Do you think she's also drunk? I love her so much, man.'

I didn't realise he was this wasted. The philosophical end of the drunken spectrum. It's good to hear him talk about Amy like this though. They were childhood sweethearts and, despite my reservations that maybe he hadn't lived enough, they stood the course and she's a sweet girl who looks out for him. She's at a spa in Bucharest this weekend and I am hoping she's got better friends and just living her best life with some mud packs and an infra-red sauna.

'I know you do. Please don't throw up on me.'

'I won't.'

The lift stops. This is the test. I can carry five bags of shopping at the same time, I reckon I can do this. I straighten my legs and lean forward to take his weight. 'Oh my dicking hell. How heavy are you?'

'Rude.' He places his head on the back of my shoulder. 'Can we get room service?'

I look up momentarily to look at the floor signs, kicking our bags along as we go. 'Shall we get chips?'

'You know me so well.'

'I'm your brother, that's part of the job description. Get that key card ready. I don't have enough hands.'

He holds it up so I can see it. In this heat, the carrying of another human is really not great. I have a newfound respect for people who carry things. Sherpas, camels, horses. I count the doors, sweat starting to form around my temples. I feel a shot of hot air around the back of my neck.

'Max, did you just burp on me?'

'Just be glad you can't smell it.' I feel his body convulse.

'Don't you dare, don't you dare.' I can't have this stag do start with steaming hot sick down the back of my neck. I pick up the speed, counting the doors. 340, 341, 342, 344, 34... This feels like an awful relay where the changeover has to be perfection to avoid disaster. Max waves the key card at the sensor. 'Go go go,' I shout like an army major, plonking him down by the entrance. He storms into the room, heads to the bathroom and then I hear him throwing up violently. I look in and he's clinging onto the toilet bowl, a look of sadness yet relief on his face. Thank god. I drop the bags, put my hands on my knees to steady myself, my T-shirt sticky on my back. And then I look up. I frown. Why are there shoes in this room? And an open suitcase? An older woman stands on the balcony with what looks like a butter knife in the air, petrified. I put my hands to the air to show I come in peace.

And then the screaming.

'INTRUDERS! POLICE! HELP! WE'RE UNDER ATTACK!'

The noise is coming not from her, but from inside the bathroom. I look in, and in the bath, another woman, completely naked, pelts bottles of free toiletries at Max, then holds a showerhead directly at him as he cowers in the corner, the bath mat his only defence.

FOUR

Suzie

So despite the sex villa that we seem to find ourselves in, and Emma and Meg dousing a lot of the contents of the house in disinfectant and insisting we boil-wash all the linens, there is already something quite magical about being here in Mallorca. The villa is in a gorgeous position and my room overlooks towering cypress trees, fields of almond blossom, little white buildings like polka dots on the landscape. There are no clouds, not even a sliver of white in the sky.

And Lucy may be right. It feels good to just stand on the balcony wearing very little and feel that heat, that sun on my skin, to stretch my arms above my head and just let everything go. Despite everything that's changed in the last months, I am here, I am alive, I'm going to have a killer tan when I leave and my bed rotates, which will be an interesting experience. I hope I don't get too dizzy.

When the disinfecting was done, we left the villa after Meg conned Danny into buying us a meal to make up for his booking gaffe, so we've indulged in a feast of tapas, steak and bottles of smooth Rioja at a beautiful spot near the beach.

'Una botella màs por favor,' I ask the waiter, who bows his head, smiling. I've lost count of the number of bottles we've had so far tonight but the waiting staff in their white shorts and matching polos don't seem to mind as it's going to considerably add to their profits. Flamenco music is piped tastefully throughout, fairy lights and vines hang off the rafters off this outdoor space and a cool breeze takes the edge off the humidity. It's just a hundred yards from the beach, where I can see the inky sea meet the sky, punctuated by lines of rocks. After a day of travelling and surprises, it feels like the perfect end to this evening, and it warms my heart to see all the sisters dressed up, glasses in hand, laughing over age-old anecdotes and banter. I curl my feet up in my rattan chair, holding a glass to my lips.

'I am still sleeping on a sun lounger. I'll drag it in the house if I have to,' Emma says, as the evening winds to an end and she feasts on the glorious Balearic cheeseboard in front of us.

'But you made us boil-wash everything,' Beth says, her feet dangling from her chair, cradling her glass. 'I can't believe you made us do chores on holiday.'

'Plus, the chances are, in a house like that, they've had sex on the sun loungers too. Kitchen table, bath... nowhere will be safe. Not even the floor if you think about it,' Lucy tells her.

The sisters all laugh as Emma flares her nostrils.

'The rental car will be safe,' Meg explains with a grin. 'You could sleep in there. I could disable the alarm.' Even though Meg was furious earlier today, you could hear her argument with Danny descend into laughter, into a space where the anger couldn't exist anymore, and I thought it a wonderful thing. That's relationship goals if ever I saw them. She now sits there, her hair tousled, with dangly earrings and a patterned maxi dress, and it's a joy to see her smile so broadly and appear so relaxed. 'Can I just say though? I love this. I was quite unsure what I wanted to do for my fortieth but this... this here... this is perfect.'

There's a momentary silence, and I lean back and let the ambience wash over me. This is pretty perfect and I feel honoured but incredibly lucky that I've been let into their circle, that with all that's happened this year, I have had family reach out and invite me into their fold. I rest my head on Lucy's shoulder and she kisses my forehead.

'But...' Lucy interrupts. 'Your actual birthday isn't until two days' time, so we have time to plan, put an itinerary in place.' There's a twinkle in her eyes that matches the very cheeky two piece she wears that leaves little to the imagination. I keep seeing the waiting staff angle themselves to get a decent look. 'Because, this is lovely and everything, but we are having fun too, yes?'

Meg looks at her curiously. 'We have very different definitions of fun.'

'Party catamaran?' Lucy asks.

'No,' Meg replies.

'They have a nineties one that plays all your old-lady club classics. I've seen the pictures. There are people your age, in case you thought it was all young people.'

Meg doesn't reply.

'Cliff jumping?' Lucy suggests. 'How about a euphoric dance experience in the mountains?'

Grace puts a hand on hers to indicate she needs to stop talking.

'I could be down with that. What is euphoric dance?' I ask curiously, sitting up.

'I knew I could count on you, Suze. It's freeform dance where there are no steps. It's like a form of meditation.'

'I can do that in our villa with a Bluetooth speaker,' Meg argues, frowning. 'I don't want to dance around a load of people I don't know.

'I haven't come here to do days of staying in the villa, eating patatas bravas and drinking sangria, you know?' Lucy says, grumpily.

Emma puts her hand in the air to let us know she's come here to do exactly that.

'But seriously, you're forty,' Lucy continues. Meg wrinkles her nose to hear her enunciate the forty so clearly. 'No kids, no husbands. If there was ever a time to tick something off your bucket list then this is it. Come on, there must be something you want to have a go at. Something that involves an element of risk.'

'That villa is a health risk,' Meg says, saluting her. 'Luis over there also told us this cheese is made with raw milk. That's risky enough for me,' she says, popping a bit in her mouth with a slice of fig.

Lucy does not look impressed with her. 'Come on, the Meg I knew, in her twenties, would hate this, you know? Beth tells me you used to have one-night stands, you'd host legendary London parties. That story where you turned a night bus into a nightclub from Oxford Circus to Hackney...'

Meg stares her down. 'Lucy, you better not be suggesting I have a holiday fling.'

'No. I'm just telling you to have fun, live a little. I don't think you're brave enough anymore. I dare you.'

I watch this strange stand-off between the sisters. It's triggered something in Meg, who has enough alcohol in her system to be insulted by this comment but also rise to the challenge.

'You dare me?' she says, taking a large sip of wine.

'Yeah...' Lucy says immaturely, and I can see her mind whirring. She looks towards the sea. 'Right. All of us now. Let's go skinny dipping.'

Beth chokes a little on her wine. 'Hold up now, this was between the two of you. Why have the rest of us got dragged into this?'

Emma shakes her head whereas I look out at the sea, the twinkle of fishing boats drifting about, the moon shining brightly, illuminating the crests of the waves. There's a little part of me that knows that's how most shark attack movies start, but I quite like the idea of the coolness of the water, running with the sand between my toes, doing something out of my comfort zone. I put a hand in the air. 'I'm in.'

Lucy high-fives that hand. 'The cousin has spoken. Look how brave and magnificent she is.'

'She's got nice little boobs that don't need a bra,' Beth says, gesturing towards me.

'And you've got nice big ones that will keep you afloat,' Lucy says frankly.

'Well, I will be the voice of dissent and say it's illegal, there's the likelihood of all sorts: sharks, jellyfish, flotsam...' Emma lists.

'Flotsam...?' Grace says, trying to stifle her laughter, fanning herself with a napkin. 'I'm in, I'm bloody melting in any case.'

Meg still maintains eye contact with her sister who won't stand down. 'If I do this then none of your stupid euphoric wellness dancing and party boats.'

'It was a catamaran.'

'Same thing.'

'No, it isn't.'

There's a moment of silence then Meg downs the last of her wine and claps her hands before rubbing them together. She raises her hand. 'Luis, la cuenta, por favor.' Luis nods in reply. 'We're going swimming.'

'EMMA! Look at you with your shaved foofoo!' Lucy announces to the shore as Emma charges at her to shut her mouth. 'Who's going to hear me? The fish?' Lucy tells her.

We're all drunk and, it would seem, naked. I'm not sure when I was last naked with these girls, but I think it may have been in the late nineties one summer's day when some of us were little and running through sprinklers in swimming costumes and jelly shoes. Now we've found this quiet little cove, dotted with rocks, the buzz of lights from resorts and buildings in the distance. Is this legal? Who knows? But nothing has changed, the humour, the joy is still there.

'Oh my god, don't make me laugh. I'm going to piss myself,' Beth whispers drunkenly.

'Save it for the sea,' Grace tells her.

Well, maybe something has changed – our bodies have changed and evolved – but I love how the mums in the group have been encouraged to not care, to run wildly across the sand and jump into the spray, fuelled by freedom and Rioja.

'You good, cuz?' Lucy asks me, as I watch Emma folding her knickers and placing them on her dress, stumbling towards the water with Meg, cackling as they go.

I look out onto the sea and up at the stars, stretching my arms into the air. I've never felt readier. I pull down my knickers and out of sheer drunkenness, lunge and get ready to swim, Lucy joining me as she pings off her thong.

'I've never seen your arse up close and... girl, I'd kill for that,' she says, peering round. She puts her hand out. 'You look pensive. You're not thinking about Paul, are you?'

'I wasn't,' I say defensively. I realise as I say it – the whole evening, Paul's not even crossed my mind, and that is the beauty of being here with these girls.

'Is he lingering, like a bad smell?' she asks, analytically. I laugh under my breath as sometimes that's exactly how it feels, how he wafts in and out of my mind.

'Occasionally. But get me out in the sea. Let's exorcise his demons.'

'Amen.'

She smiles at me and we run towards the sea, laughing and screaming as we go. As soon as our feet hit the water and we get waist height, we shriek with laughter. The water is a relief and I dive in to feel the full effects of it all. Never mind, Meg, I don't think I've ever swum naked before and there is something about it that's completely liberating, the water cocooning me, the taste of salt against my lips, the light of the moon reflecting off our faces. I look over and see Beth floating in a massive star shape, looking up at the stars.

Meg screams, 'Oh my god... oh my god...' she says, reaching down, splashing around in the water. We all freeze. It's the sharks. She reaches down and pulls up a dark bushel of seaweed, throwing it away from her.

'Thank God, I thought that was your muff,' Grace says. And we all laugh, a bit delirious with joy. That sound is almost medicinal. I want to say that aloud. I want to thank them all. This holiday isn't about me at all, so I won't do it, but the truth is that this – getting our boobs out and being together, the cousins allowing me to be a part of this – is healing, is making me remember how to really laugh. I will always be grateful to them for that.

I lean back and look into the sky, thinking about a future that looks more like this. Main character energy, Emma said. Let's remember what Suzie Callaghan used to look like. What she loves. She used to laugh like this everyday.

'Shit, shit, shit...' I suddenly hear a loud whisper, and I tread water again, looking out for the girls. Is this seaweed based or have the sharks finally come for us? However, as I look up, I see Meg and Emma treading water staring towards the beach, where there's the sound of male Spanish voices and erratic flashlights piercing the dark and quiet.

'Is it the police? Oh my god, we're going to be arrested,' Emma says.

The sisters all encourage her to be quiet. 'Maybe they haven't seen us. Those could just be piles of clothes that someone's left there,' Grace whispers.

'But what if they take the clothes?' Meg says. 'I'm not going back in a taxi, naked. We've got to say something. Suzie, what are they saying?'

I try and listen in. Oh, shit, 'Peligroso. That's dangerous and... shit. My Spanish isn't great. I can't... guardia. Is that a guard? Police?'

And that is when it all goes a little mad. As soon as I say the word 'police' we hear a dog barking from that beach and for some reason, convinced that we are all going to rot in a European prison and never see our families again, we all panic swim in different directions, the sounds of different exclamations and screams filling the air. *He's taking the clothes! My phone is in there! I can't go to prison! I'm too young to die!*

However, my panic reads slightly different. I'm a teacher, I work with young people and I've just got a brand-new job. I can't get caught naked on the beach. If I get arrested for public nudity then that's not good for me. I have rent to pay. I'm supposed to be starting anew. So I swim sideways towards some rocks jutting out into the sea. This might be very dangerous but I can catch up with the girls when it's all died down, when Lucy has sweet-talked them round, she's good like that. It's Meg's birthday and she's reached a landmark age, there must be special dispensation for that. There's one of those party hotels across the way where people must be naked in the water all the time.

I attempt a rough freestyle that helps me keep an eye on what's happening. Don't drown. That would be an awful way to start the summer. Just keep swimming, keep kicking, keep afloat. Don't get eaten by jellyfish. Just...

'¡Señorita! ¡Señorita! ¿Estás bien? ¿Puedo ayudar? ¿Estás en apuros?'

I look up and see a figure standing on the rocks, hollering at me, waving his hands in the air. Is it the police? I think he thinks I'm drowning. I'm not. I try to wave at him to turn around.

Please don't jump in after me because I'm just really quite fucking naked in here.

Charlie

'Ooh, flowers and wine. A girl might think you're trying to get in our knickers, young Charlie,' the lady says, as she stands there by her hotel room door.

I flash my best smile at Meredith who I've seen far too much of today when she was standing in the bath, naked, attacking my little brother with bath products. As it turns out, the hotel computer had Meredith and Sue in another room, so it was all a big admin disaster – not our fault at all – but our mother raised gentlemen, so to ensure they both felt safe and unthreatened by us, this felt like a nice gesture, in case we bump into either of these ladies at the omelette station tomorrow.

'It's just to say sorry again for the intrusion earlier. I'm very glad the hotel got it sorted and offered you some compensation.'

'They're giving us a free dinner at the fancy pan-Asian place downstairs. We're heading down there now. Apparently, they set things on fire and chuck bits of meat around,' she explains with a wink. I have an unfortunate flashback to this morning but try to wipe it from my mind, grateful that Meredith is now wearing clothes. She's fully embracing her inner zebra in a black-and-white print dress and some fluffy pink mules. She's had a few days on us so her tan is glowing through the creases in her decolletage. 'How is your brother, is he OK?'

'He's having a night off. Such is the way of the stag do that he didn't pace himself.'

'Well, do give him our best and please apologise to him again for throwing all those things. I guess we'll see you around.'

I feel a lump in my throat as she scans me up and down. Meredith, no. I'm just being nice. 'I am sure you will.' She winks at me and I immediately jog away from the doorway back towards our room, a tad unnerved that we're only five doors down from her.

'I'm back,' I say, opening the door to the room to find Max exactly where I left him, in bed with a bin beside him and a six pack of bottled water. On the television, he's watching an action movie from the nineties in Spanish, his naked torso curled around the pillows. He can barely turn his head to acknowledge me.

'I got your supplies,' I tell him, handing him a flimsy blue-striped plastic bag. 'Paprika Pringles, Fanta Limón and red liquorice vines because... well, because...'

'You're the best...'

'I know.'

'What did you tell the lads then?' he asks me.

'I told them they were all tossers and that you didn't want to be their friend anymore,' I say, nicking one of his sweets and kicking off my flip flops before sitting on a chair in the corner of the room, facing out onto the balcony. The room might be the saving grace on this trip – it's bright, clean and away from the others, with all those little things that one normally gets excited about on holiday like a very tiny kettle and shower caps that I'll never wear. Outside, the hotel has come to life with a foam party in the pool. A pulse of house music resounds through the walls. I close my eyes to take it all in, enjoying the feeling of the warm air against my face.

'No, you didn't,' he mumbles, unconvinced.

'I told them you were violently ill and so you'd give tonight's foam party a miss. Let's just get you well enough for tomorrow. I want at least two litres of water in you by the morning. Deal?'

'Deal.' He looks over at me sheepishly. Naturally, after Meredith and Sue raised hell and accused us of breaking into their room, there was mess to clean up and not just the mess that came out of Max. I had to negotiate (in Spanish) with all the staff and convince them that my brother and I were not common criminals looking to mug two middle-aged ladies. But there were room changes, having to manage the idiots outside, one of whom managed to get severely sunburnt in only two hours, and then playing nurse for the Hulk here. In short, I am knackered and hungry as hell. I steal a couple of Pringles.

'I feel bad, you know,' Max says, looking at me. 'You don't have to babysit me, I am twenty-three now. I won't play with the hob. Go and have some fun. Are the others at the foam party? Why don't you join in?'

I give my little brother a look. In my current mood, it's a no. All my instincts tell me to stay here, entertain the stag and also ensure he doesn't die on foreign soil.

'Or the strip is just on the doorstep. There's a street market, I researched it. They do churros and there are fellas with big pans of paella. You love paella.'

I shake my head. 'Or I could get room service. I could watch this with you. Protect you from Meredith and Sue. I think the flowers were too much though, they think we like them.'

Max retches a little again. He takes a sip of water. 'I don't want both of us wasting our holiday in this room. Please. Just go for a walk or something. Have a beer in the bar. You've earned it.'

I go over to him and put a hand instinctively to his forehead.

'I'm hungover, you idiot. Not ill.'

I look at his sad dehydrated little eyes. 'Maybe I'll go for about half an hour. If you think you're going to throw up...'

'Call you?' he asks.

'No. I don't need to hear that sound any more today. Just use that bin. I can't deal with this hotel hating us as much as they do already.'

He salutes me as I put my flip flops back on and grab my phone and wallet. Is this the start to the holiday I wanted? No. By this time, I thought I would have had the sun on my back all afternoon and be a couple of chapters into my book with a beer in hand, but at least it's still warm, the sky is clear and starry and I can try and find some food.

I head down to the lobby where the overspill from the restaurant and the foam party converges as guests scramble to get taxis into town. In short, it's badly dressed chaos that smells like cheap aftershave and suncream. I head outside into the hotel grounds, passing two people snogging on a sun lounger wrapped in hotel towels. Christ, I think they're doing more than that. This isn't the place for me. I walk through the pool area, away from the lights and the deep house beats towards the sea.

It's funny how, growing up in London, any proximity to the sea feels like a luxury, an escape. We rarely went abroad when we were younger, but we went down to Cornwall, to the Witterings, big sandy beaches that felt so different to the built-up city. The sea always felt new, energising, like possibility.

I walk past folded-up sun loungers, closed parasols and pedalos and inflatables all chained up for the evening, taking off my flip flops as I hit the sand, rolling my feet through it, smiling. I should have stopped off to pick up a beer though. I walk, inhaling deeply, grateful for the peace, the evening heat warming but not unbearable. The beach seems to be sectioned off by some rocks but they're a perfect place to stop, collect my thoughts. I have my phone and my AirPods; maybe I'll listen to a podcast. I don't care if that makes me old. Should I be surfing in foam with wanky sunglasses, grinding against a girl in a bikini that's held together with a few knots? Maybe not. And for a moment, I think of Krystal. Not just her. I think about Gemma and Adele and the disaster that has been my dating history in the last four years. They haven't even been epic romances, just a catalogue of bad fits and poor judgement on my part. Gemma was the sort of girlfriend who'd follow me to the barbers to make sure they were cutting my hair right, and Adele was lovely until I realised how much time she spent falling down TikTok conspiracy wormholes and just how firmly she believed the pyramids were built by giants who had huge cats as pets. I'm starting to give up on ever finding someone to share my life with. Not that it makes me sad, I have a lot in my life to make me feel fulfilled. But, on a holiday like this, I realise I've become the sensible one. Have I forgotten how to have any fun? I am fun. I hope.

I settle down on a rock and put my AirPods in, but after a few minutes of listening to my podcast, I notice some splashing and, like some aquatic life nerd, I feel a flurry of excitement, wondering if it's a seal. I get my phone out to zoom in for a pic and then I notice it's an actual person. A woman? Shit. I put my phone away. I refocus my eyes. Is it ridiculous that for a second I think she might be a mermaid? It's dark. She's got more nerve than me. Is this a thing? Night swimming? Her stroke isn't natural, a little panicked. I hope she's alright. I'm standing now and I'm wondering if she's seen me because if she has seen me, I'll look like a pervert. I need to say something. I wave.

'Señorita! ¡Señorita! ¿Estás bien? ¿Puedo ayudar? ¿Estás en apuros?'

She stops swimming to tread water and turns towards me. This is good. It means she's not drowning. She doesn't answer immediately.

'¿Es policía?' she shouts.

She thinks I'm a policeman?

'No, no soy policía,' I say to reassure her. 'Estás a salvo conmigo.' She remains in the water, staring at me.

'Espagnol?'

'Sí.' I can speak Spanish.

'Towel? ¿Una toalla?' she asks.

'No.'

She mumbles something under her breath and I can't quite hear it but I hear the word 'merde'. That's swearing. That's French.

'¿Eres francesa?' I ask her.

There's a pause. 'Oui, je peux parler français.'

I guess I can switch this up.

'Oui. Yes. Avez-vous besoin de mon aide?'

I'm being a gentleman and offering my help but she looks at me like I'm stupid. Her hair is all slicked back and her eye make-up smudged from the water. What if she's a pirate on the run? I can't quite tell if she understands me.

'Avez-vous des vêtements?' She's asking me for clothes. To make some sort of life-saving device? I don't quite get where she's coming from and I only have what's on my body.

'Pourquoi?'

She looks confused and slightly fed up. 'I'm naked. I don't have any clothes.'

'They what?' I say, struggling to hear her. Why is she changing to English now? She swims a bit closer.

'Mi ropa, mes vêtements – GONE! Je suis naked.'

Oh. She's starkers in the sea. I don't quite know how to answer that. I look around the rocks and don't see anything that she may have left here. Which brings me back to my mermaid theory. How did she get in there then?

'I... I... Do you want me to look for your clothes?' I shout out randomly in a mixed foreign accent trying to keep up with the strange multilingual flow of the conversation.

'Non, no. They're in... Another playa... Don't worry.'

There is a moment where we both just look at each other trying to work out what the solution is. I see her bottom jaw starting to tremble with the cold. 'You should come out. You're cold. Let me help you.'

I step down on to the rocks to offer a hand but she puts her hands in the air.

'I'm naked. Get back, amigo. I don't know who you are. You could be some random Spaniard who's going to take advantage.'

I am slightly hurt by the suggestion but also secretly pleased

I could be confused for a native. 'Look. It's me or drowning from exhaustion. How about I take off my T-shirt and leave it on this rock and then I'll turn around and you can come out and put it on.'

'You'll give me your T-shirt?' she says, curiously.

'Well, it's that or the shorts. You can decide.'

I see a smile that she's desperately trying to keep in. 'OK. But if you turn to look then I will scream. I know stuff.'

She is a pirate. I put my hands to the air to surrender, removing my T-shirt awkwardly, not before backing away and turning to look at the beach. I hear her pulling herself up onto the rocks and then the sound of her wet footsteps.

'OK, señor. You can turn around.'

As soon as I turn, it feels like that gameshow at home where people meet each other for the first time naked. I do go to the gym but hello, lady who's just emerged from the sea, this is my bare chest and those are your legs. The night air is dim and lit by lamps on the beach but all I see are her big brown eyes, a petite frame and a face framed by wet raven hair. She's very pretty. I shouldn't stare. She desperately tries to pull the T-shirt down so it doesn't get inappropriate while I breathe in ever so slightly, not sure whether to tell her I've only been here for a day which is why I'm so under-tanned. She's still tugging the T-shirt down as far as she can so I cover my eyes to help her feel more comfortable in the situation. I hear her laugh.

'Gracias. Sincerely gracias,' she whispers, shivering slightly. She tilts her head, but I don't engage, my eyes darting in different directions, anywhere but directly at her. She looks like she's wondering what on earth I might be doing. 'Are your eyes OK?'

'It's just... nipples,' I say. I said that out loud, didn't I? And in English because I don't know what the Spanish or French word is for nipples. It's just never come up. Until now. And they are really up. She grabs at the material so it doesn't cling to her. 'I just didn't want you to think I was staring and being weird.' I should stop talking about nipples. I'm grateful she's not kicked me in the cojones and run away, stealing one of my favourite T-shirts.

'Maybe if I looked at your nipples now, we would be even,' she suggests, laughing.

'Be my guest,' I tell her, standing straight and pushing my chest out a little. She stares at them, for a good three seconds. I try not to be too self-conscious. I'd never really considered them before now. 'Are they OK?' I ask her.

'They're your nipples. Maybe you should ask them,' she says, grinning.

'Are you telling me to talk to my nipples?' I ask her.

She laughs again and I'll admit to quite liking that sound. I think I might draw a line at talking to my nipples in front of her though. She stands there shivering. The night air can't be doing much to warm her up. 'Look, this might seem strange but can I make an odd suggestion?' I ask her.

'The fact I'm wearing your clothes and staring at your nipples isn't strange enough?' she asks me.

'You need to move around,' I tell her. I simulate such movement in the form of some keep-fit dance moves.

Again, she laughs. In terms of first meets, I really am excelling here. 'To warm up,' she says, jogging on the spot.

'Exactly. Or you could roll around in the warm sand...' I suggest.

'I could do what now?' she says.

'Se rouler dans le sable...' I repeat. I look at the smirk on her face. 'Oh, shit. Not like that. I meant like the sand is warm and you could roll. On your own.'

'Like a meerkat,' she asks.

We both burst into laughter and she stumbles a little on the rocks. I put a hand out to steady her. She grabs it, another cold, wet hand lying on my bare warm chest and looks up at me.

Whoa. The physical contact catches us both off guard and we pause for a moment. We're touching. She realises this and lets go of my hand. I walk her over to the safety of the beach.

'I will feel incredibly self-conscious if you're going to watch me roll in the sand,' she says, trying to break the tension. 'At least tell me your name, kind señor.'

I pause to have a think. Señor. I'm Spanish? I like that she thinks I could be, and maybe that's why I don't correct her. I guess I have been putting on a very strange accent. Plus when you've just pulled a stranger out of the sea who has a bizarre story about why she's naked then you have to be a tad apprehensive. She could report me for being some weirdo at the beach eyeing her up. 'Carlos...' I blurt out.

'Enchantée, Carlos,' she says, looking back at me.

'Et comment vous appellez-vous?' I ask, in what I will assume to be her native language.

She looks at me curiously, glances away briefly, then smiles and holds out her hand to shake mine. 'Aurelie.'

'You were speaking a few languages out there. You're French?' I ask her.

She hesitates to answer. Did she not understand? 'Je suis française.'

It figures. Plenty of fish in the sea, isn't that what they say? Lucky you, Charlie, to catch the most beautiful one out there. Yet she's French. Not that I have anything against the French but practically, that's a fish living many oceans away. I look into her eyes and smile. She smiles back and it's a bit of a killer to see her face relax, the curve of her cheeks glistening. Maybe I do just need to let go, take a chance, have some fun. 'Do you know what else would warm you up?' I tell her.

She tilts her head to the side, her eyes widening.

I put my hands up in the air. 'Un café?'

She smiles and nods.

FIVE

Suzie

Right, work with me here. I wasn't quite sure what I was doing. One minute I was swimming for what felt like my life and my freedom, then the next I was by some rocks conversing with a strange Spanish man who could have been either friend or foe. He started speaking Spanish, so all my Spanish went out the window. I thought he might murder me. He thought I was French so I spoke a bit of every language – just trying to work out a way to get out of the sea without him seeing everything.

As the conversation progressed, I panicked and kept talking with a bizarre French accent and when he asked my name, I had no idea what to do. I didn't want to give my real name in case he was an undercover policeman, and I also wanted to protect myself, so I became Aurelie, standing in an oversized Stussy T-shirt trying desperately to pull it down so it became a dress. Aurelie was the name of the French penpal I had when I was twelve. She had a dog called Bijou and her favourite colour was brown, which I always thought a little odd.

'What are these called again?' I ask him, stuffing another fried doughnut in my mouth.

'Bunyols,' he tells me, miming an action that suggests perhaps I have to dust a little icing sugar off my chin. I smile, wiping my mouth with the back of my hand.

When we got off the beach, we managed to find a strip of shops with a food market and I watched as he ordered these fried doughnut balls expertly, trying to catch every word. I also watched as he haggled with a souvenir shop and got us both new wardrobes. I don't know what we look like to outsiders but I now sit here in a hooded beach towel that is supposed to make me look like a mermaid, usually the remit of five-year-olds. It has Mallorca written across the hem and it's teamed with matching flip flops. He's wearing a brand new lilac Mallorca T-shirt complete with palm tree and seashells. We look like we're big fans of this place. I turn to him on this bench, our little street food picnic separating us, as we look out on to the sea, the neon buzz of bars and shops behind us.

'I must pay you back for this when I find my clothes and my phone,' I tell him.

'No importa,' he says casually. His accent feels a bit stronger than before but my lord, the multi-lingualism is quite impressive. Stop it, Suzie. You've just met this Spaniard. You have no idea who he is. I don't know how to be more French but I put some accents on words to keep up the illusion, grateful that we've worked out our common ground is English. 'You feel a little more warmed up?' he asks.

I nod and take a sip of my café con leche. I'm still trying to work Carlos out. I don't think he's a threat or a dick but blimey, he's quite good looking. Close up, his eyes are bright blue and his hair is brown and tousled, a dimple to his left cheek as he smiles. I've also seen his chest and it's not awful. I don't know what awful is really but I did date someone called Maz once who had a lot of hair. He used to comb it. Bonjour. Remember you're French. He keeps looking over at me and I have flashbacks to the beach, the moment where I emerged from the sea, him with his top off. The absolute cinema of it, the way that could have turned into something mildly erotic were it not for all that nipple talk.

'Lilac is really your colour,' I say. 'Compliments your...'

'Nipples?'

'My thoughts exactly,' I say laughing.

'Look at us. It's just holiday vibes. I should have bought a bum bag.'

'One of those big straw hats,' I add.

'I mean, we can go back...' he suggests. 'She liked me in there.'

'It's because you're...' I don't know how to put this. He gives off good energy. It's warm and likeable. I didn't get everything he said, but he was polite and complimented her and held the step ladder for her when she had to grab my towel off a high shelf. 'Spanish?'

'Maybe,' he says, biting into his empanada he bought at the market. 'So tell me, little mermaid... how are we going to get you home? You said you're staying at a villa.'

As warm as the man's energy is, I'm also wary of giving him too much detail.

'Yes. I got separated from my group.' The thought suddenly strikes me that maybe I should have spent more time looking for my cousins or worried about their whereabouts. I think they made it to shore. I just hope they're not all in a prison cell waiting for me to bail them out.

'Do we know any telephone numbers?' he asks me. 'I can lend you my phone if you need to call them.'

'Is it awful I don't know their numbers? C'est terrible,' I say, throwing in some French to actually go along with this charade.

'No one knows numbers these days. Do you remember the name of the villa? The road? Maybe we can get you a taxi?' he tells me. But there is something in me that doesn't want this little bench date to end. I just want to sit here for a little bit longer, with this random Spaniard. I don't know how to tell him that without giving him the wrong idea because this moment with the palms and streetlights hovering over us feels like a very calm antidote to the panic of half an hour ago. 'Whenever you're ready, no pressure.'

'You're very polite,' I tell him.

'Isn't everyone?' he asks.

'You'd be surprised,' I tell him, thinking immediately of Paul. 'You're respectful of my personal space, there's the way you lent me your T-shirt to protect my modesty...'

He shrugs. 'The fact was I was very warm. I was going to take it off anyway. You did me a favour. It looked better on you in any case.' I can't quite take the compliment and look away for a minute to avoid the intensity of his eyes, to resist the temptation to tell him I'd quite like him to disrespect my personal space. I can't say that out loud. 'But I was raised right, you can blame mi madre,' he says, smiling, looking out towards the beach. 'So, Aurelie... where in France are you from?'

'Nice.'

'Nice,' he replies. 'That was an awful joke.'

'I hear it all the time. Yourself? Where do you live in Mallorca?'

He pauses and I can't tell if he wants to share that information with me. Crap, he's married or something, isn't he? I may be crossing a line. He's just a nice man who helped me out, and it's nothing but a good reminder that despite what the universe has delivered to you of late, those sorts of men do exist.

'Palma. I am a teacher.'

Do I tell him I do the same? I won't. I've already really distorted-slash-abandoned the truth by telling him I'm French. I'm not sure how I extend this lie. It's fine. He's a random

Spaniard and I'll probably never see him again. Maybe I just have some fun with this. 'What do you teach?'

He frowns momentarily before answering. 'Yoga. I go from hotel to hotel and do classes.'

'Wow. You must be...' Don't say bendy, don't say bendy. 'Zen.'

He laughs and I smile at the sound. Being back on dry land, I feel the warmth of that Balearic heat again, but I can also feel that I am warming to this man, and a need to try and sit a bit closer to him.

'Do you have any recommendations for my holiday then, Carlos?'

'The markets in the plazas are great. That church is one of the oldest in Mallorca. You have to try traditional paella.' He says paella like a Spanish person. 'There's the beaches, walks in the mountains. It depends what you're into.'

'What I'm into?' I ask, blushing.

'What do you want from your holiday? I see you like the risk of a naked swim.'

'It's just the group I was with, *mes cousines*, we wanted to be more spontaneous. I wanted to let go a little.'

'Why?' he asks me earnestly, leaning into me to show interest in my story as opposed to be leary. I allow our knees to touch slightly and feel a spark from the contact.

I shake my head. 'You don't need the details. But there was something very freeing about the water. I would recommend it.'

He smiles. 'Oh, I do it all the time. It's what we Spanish do. It's good for the...'

'Bunyols?' I say holding up another fried doughnut.

He chokes a little on his drink and laughs. I like making him laugh like that. I put the bag out to offer him another doughnut and his fingers brush mine as he takes one. The touch makes the breath tight in my chest. He turns to me and smiles that warm smile again. I need to try and trust this feeling – it feels too magnetic, too right. Even if I am wearing a mermaid hooded towel.

'OH MY GOD!' The silence is suddenly broken by Beth and Lucy running towards us, fully clothed, hair wet and matted. 'GET AWAY FROM HER!'

Oh, shit. I suddenly realise how this must look. I'm sitting on a park bench with a man I hardly know, in clothes that must make it look like I may have lost my goddamn mind. A man I only know as Carlos who teaches yoga. Lucy practically launches herself at him and he falls to the floor as she tries to twist an arm around his back. 'FUUUUCK...' he yelps.

'Lucy, NOOOO!' I yell, trying to pull her off. 'He's cool. He's a nice Spanish guy who helped me. He's cool, he's cool.'

Carlos taps out against the cobbled stones, and she lets him go as he rises to safety.

'His name is Carlos.'

Both sisters watch him curiously as he stands there circling his arm around. 'Les cousines?'

I nod. 'Oui.'

I turn to Beth who's trying her best to work this out. Why is he speaking French? Why am I wearing this towel? 'Where did you go?'

'I swam away in the other direction, and when I looked back...'

'Oh,' Lucy says, gathering herself off the floor, still keeping one eye on my new Spanish friend. 'Turns out they were just fishermen. They didn't want us to get caught in their nets and scare the fish away. Lovely fellas actually. Meg's getting some massive prawns from them but I think her tits got those for us. God, we were bloody worried about you. Grace is sobbing. We thought you'd drowned.'

I see Carlos laughing but he must also be clocking Lucy's strong London tones as she embraces me tightly. 'So, are you all from France then?' he asks.

Beth and Lucy look at me. Did I knock my head? Did I possibly swallow too much seawater?

I try to silence them with my eyes. 'Yes. We're all from Nice. But Beth and Lucy spent a lot of time growing up in London,' I explain. Beth looks like she's smelt a really bad fart but I can see that Lucy gets the assignment. Lucy was made for assignments like this.

'Oh, bien sûr. But j'habite à Nice. Je m'appelle Lucy.' That would perhaps sound more convincing if it didn't sound like she was reciting it for an exam.

Carlos casts his eye between the three of us before landing on my gaze again. I don't know how to continue this, how to keep talking to him to see where it goes. I can tell from the way they're looking at me, at Carlos and at each other that the cousins also realise they've interrupted something.

'We have your clothes if you want to swap...' Beth says, holding up my dress and lacy knickers.

Carlos looks away. 'Or you know, to protect your modesty, maybe just keep what you have on for now. I feel I've seen far too much of you this evening.'

'Likewise...'

Beth's jaw drops, Lucy can't hide the massive smile on her face. I glare over at them when Carlos' back is turned.

'Well, maybe I can return the T-shirt to you tomorrow. I can wash it first,' I tell him. 'And repay you...'

'For?' asks Lucy.

'His kindness,' I say firmly, killing off her assumptions.

In the corner of my eye, I see Beth elbow Lucy hard in the ribs. Please don't laugh, please keep this going. For me. 'Look, Carlos, we're staying in a villa in Santa Posa. Maybe come and see us tomorrow, come and get your shirt and have some brunch with us. A thank you for looking after our cousin,' Beth suggests.

Lucy nods. 'A très bien idea, Beth. Where's your phone, Carlos?' she asks. He holds it aloft and she takes it from his hands, holding it up to his face to unlock it. 'I'm putting a pin in your maps. Come for midday. Bring some swimmers. Comprendez?'

'Oui,' he says, an eyebrow raised.

Lucy's phone rings. 'Zut alors, it's Meg,' she exclaims as she goes to answer it. 'It's fine, we found her, she's OK. I'd actually argue she's more than OK.' I feel my cheeks redden. 'A taxi? Yeah, we'll come find you.' She hangs up. 'We have to go. See you tomorrow, Carlos.'

He waves, smiling. Beth and Lucy start walking away while I linger, unsure what it is I want to do. I think I want to stay. 'Tomorrow?'

'Tomorrow? Why not?' he replies.

I laugh. Exactly. Why not? Why not have a drink with a good-looking man who's bought you bunyols and has dreamy blue eyes. Take a chance on him, Suzie. Let go. Just remember your name is Aurelie. I lean over and kiss him on the cheek, putting a hand to his arm. His lips are perilously close to mine, his skin is warm, inviting. Kiss him. But instead I stand there, that energy between us clear, almost intoxicating.

'Merci beaucoup,' I mutter.

'De nada.'

He smiles as I turn and catch up with my cousins, looking up, asking myself why all the stars in that clear midnight sky suddenly seem to be winking at me.

Charlie

'Hola, me llamo Carlos,' I say into the mirror, unconvincingly. Max watches from the balcony and laughs.

'¿Dónde está la biblioteca, Carlos?'

'Up your arse, I believe.'

Max laughs as he bites into a croissant he stole from the breakfast buffet. He's better now and I'd like to think it was my story of having found a naked woman at the beach that brought him back from the dead. A beautiful naked French woman. But then, like I always do, I complicated the situation by telling her my name was Carlos and now I'm about to have brunch with her whole family. She didn't really go into who would be at the villa. Just the cousins? There could be dozens of them. Europeans usually have very large families.

'So explain to me the moped?' Max asks, as he packs his bag. Today, like the adult teenagers they are, the stags are off to a water park to bomb it down the slides. I've been given a bye as long as I join them for dinner afterwards in Magaluf at an all-you-can-eat ribs and steak place.

'I need to keep up the pretence that I'm Spanish. If I show up in a taxi or hire car, it will look suss,' I explain.

'Instead you'll just look like a pizza delivery boy,' he jokes.

I scrunch my face at the insult and he watches as I try to style my hair. In this heat, it doesn't seem to be playing ball. I also don't know what look I'm going for. I take off my T-shirt and try a white linen short-sleeved number.

'How fit was she?'

'She was very pretty.' I sigh. Her eyes were bright, the sort that looked sweet, kind but alive. Given how much I saw of her, I keep going back to her eyes, a kiss on the cheek, feeling the warmth of her breath against my skin.

'Charlie boy has a crush.'

'Piss off. Make sure you pack your sunscreen and some arm bands,' I retort.

'Make sure you pack some johnnies,' he jokes.

I throw a T-shirt at him, but there was something there last night that I can't quite get out of my mind. I've been rational and put it down to being on holiday, the unique way in which we met, the heat, the different location... But last night, did I think about what it would be like to kiss her? I did. I may have thought about more. That's not me at all. Charlie is sensible, he's respectful, he's never had sex on the beach before because one of his pet peeves when he was little was washing sand out of his trunks. But I guess you can meet someone and the spark can be strong, they fill some space in your mind, and then they are all you can think about, your mind wandering to what could happen... I look at myself in the mirror. Aurelie. All I can see is her wearing my T-shirt, stood on the rocks, seawater dripping off the edges of her hair, the curve of her lower thighs. Stop it, Charlie. Get a grip. You don't even know her last name.

In theory, I had different visions of the moped and how I might look arriving at the villa on it. I thought about a few buttons undone, sunglasses on, riding along a coastal road, the sun on my face, looking really fucking sexy. Instead, I realise all that hair styling was for nothing. I will have helmet hair, I'm sweating balls and Spanish drivers are a mix of lawless angry Mallorcans and hire car drivers trying to remember to drive on the right side of the road. And goats. No one told me there would be goats.

So by the time I arrive at the massive wooden gates of this villa, I'm wondering if I should just turn around. Anxiety is already high with the very vague plans we've made and I'm not sure if any illusions that I planted yesterday of being a cool and capable Mallorcan are now evaporating with the giant sweat patch that is my back. I hover over my scooter as I look down at the map on my phone. Is this it? I peer through the slats in the gate. This is not a party palace hotel by the beach, this is a sophisticated villa and it's huge. I mean, she is French. She was likely to be far too classy for some bar on the beach specialising in fishbowl cocktails. The gate suddenly slides back and I stand there, desperately trying to tousle my hair.

'Are you Carlos?' a woman says as she approaches me,

dressed head to toe in white. Shit, not cousins. It's a cult. She lowers her sunglasses. 'Je m'appelle Emma. Enchantée.'

'Enchanté,' I reply politely. 'Is Aurelie here? You must be one of her cousins?'

'I am,' she says, scanning my outfit, smiling broadly.

'This place is incroyable. Are you renting? Do you own it?'

Emma pauses as I crane my neck to the roof admiring the stone architecture, peering around to see the azure calm of the pool.

'It belongs to Aurelie's father's family. He is in champagne,' a voice interrupts.

I recognise this cousin from last night – Beth – but today she wears a vest top and patterned trousers. She comes over to greet me. 'We are French, we do the double kiss,' she tells me, putting a hand to my shoulder. She looks at me, scanning my face. 'This may sound strange, but have we met before this?'

'Before last night?' I ask her.

'You just look like someone I may have met, possibly? I'm terrible with names,' she says.

I shake my head. Is she suspicious? She knows, doesn't she? Have I not made my accent thick enough?

'AURELIE!' The moment is interrupted by a shrill voice inside the villa. We all turn to look at it. 'THE SEAMAN IS HERE!' a voice booms from inside. My eyes open widely as I wipe sweat from my brow. I am the *what?*

Emma closes her eyes. 'You'll have to forgive my sister. She has a terrible command of the English language.'

Lucy – the one who wrestled me to the ground – suddenly appears on the drive, her eyes on the moped. She skips excitedly along the hot stone towards me.

'Too much,' Emma says out of the side of her mouth, thinking I didn't hear that.

'Je ne sais pas what you may mean? ¡Hola, Carlos!' she says, pulling a basket bag over her shoulder.

'Bonjour... you said brunch last night. Did I get the time wrong? You look like you may be going somewhere?' I ask them as I see another cousin emerge from the villa, craning her head to have a look, also dressed as if she's heading out, with a cloth bag on her shoulder. There are so many of them.

'Oh well, Lucy invited you over but we forgot we've booked other plans,' Beth explains.

'Plans?'

'A euphoric dance workshop,' Lucy says excitedly.

'And as you can see, we're euphoric,' another cousin tells me. 'Meg... bonjour.' Meg feels like the matriarch cousin. Her look and tone are a bit more judgemental.

'Bonjour... so we're cancelling brunch?' I say despondently, unable to keep that feeling from flooding my face. I also ate a light breakfast so am starving. 'That's cool. I don't live far. I can...'

'Oh no!' Lucy interrupts. 'We're going out but Aurelie is here. You guys just... have some brunch, chill, use the villa, explore the rooms, you know?'

The other cousins go quiet as I stand there trying to figure out this little welcome party. I don't know whether to be scared or amused. And then, she appears. Aurelie. It's bizarre to see her in daylight but everything I remembered about her is still there, the big brown eyes, the sheen to her dark hair, the way her smile creases the sides of her eyes. She wears a white vest top and short skirt over a bikini. I look away for a second to hide the fact I'm so excited to see her.

'Carlos,' she says, coming over to me and leaning in for the double kiss. She smells amazing. 'You found us then?'

'I did. And I found all your lovely cousins too. Are you sure you can't join us for a drink before you head off for your dancing?' I suggest.

'Non,' says Lucy confidently. 'Or we will be late.' She opens the doors to their hire car and pushes one of her sisters in. 'Maybe we can catch you later though?'

'I am sure. Lovely to meet you...' And with that a car door slams shut, windows winding down to wave us goodbye. '¡ADIÓS! AU REVOIR! ARRIVEDERCI!'

And in a flutter of activity, the car reverses in a cloud of dust and they're gone, leaving Aurelie and I standing on that driveway.

'They're really subtle,' Aurelie says, smiling.

'I thought so,' I say, laughing. I catch myself looking at the curve of her shoulder, tanned and smooth, and have to distract myself. I probably shouldn't do that by rubbing my hands over my helmet. My moped helmet, obviously. Be cool, Carlos. We start walking down the pathway to the villa. 'So this place... it's amazing. Emma told me your family works in champagne?'

'Did she?' she says turning towards me. 'Yeah, champagne. It's been a family thing for decades,' she says nodding.

'Fancy.'

'It is. Can I get you a drink?' she asks me, anxiously.

'It's a bit early for champagne but I'll take a water if you have it,' I tell her.

'There's juice as well, or wine, Coke, tea, coffee...' she nervously lists every beverage in the house.

'Water is good,' I say, smiling and trying to reassure her. I put my helmet and belongings on the kitchen table, standing at some open windows that look out to a view of mountains, sea and sky. I take a deep breath to drink it all in. This is not like the balcony of my hotel at all. 'What are the bedrooms like?'

There's a notable silence as I say that.

'Oh, I meant... I'm just nosy. Nothing more...'

'Umm, they're great. Just... not as great as this view though.'

She appears beside me, two glasses of water that she places down on a coffee table.

'It's a pretty awesome view, eh?'

I turn to her. It is. 'So I am the seaman, am I?' I say, as we both look out of the window. 'My English is not so great, like a sailor?'

'YES, exactly like that...' she replies, trying to stifle her laughter. She looks over at me and blushes immediately. 'I don't... I mean... today... this... it's just... thank you... I don't know how to do this...'

'How to do what?'

And that spark, that energy just sits there again. It's a rare thing that chemistry, that heat. It can just ignite in a flash, and I think of the sum of all last night's moments – holding her hand, brushing my fingers against hers and the warmth of her breath on my cheek – and without hesitation, I put a hand to her waist and pull her into me. Is this too much? I hardly know her but there is a deep intense need to touch her. She looks at me. I think she feels that hesitancy too but she leans in and kisses me gently. A kiss that intensifies, draws me in. She puts a hand to the back of my head, before pushing me down on to the sofa and straddling me. I reach around to take off her vest top, pulling down the material of her bikini to run my tongue along her nipple. The reaction it makes is almost addictive. I want her to make that sound over and over again. She unbuttons my shirt, keeping eye contact the whole time but kissing my chest, working her way down, pulling down my shorts, until she has me in her mouth. I lose my breath. I run my fingers through her hair, my spine straightening, moaning loudly. *You lied. You do know how to do this. You really do.*

SIX

Suzie

I have a sex headache. It's the heat. I've lost too many electrolytes or maybe need a transfusion. I need a Lucozade. I'm not sure how sex works like that sometimes. One minute, you're just standing there taking in a view and having to wing it that your family are in the champagne business and the next a man you only met last night is sucking on your nipples and fingering you on a sofa until you come so loudly and freely that you're worried you scared the mountain goats.

I blame the cousins. Lucy most of all. Last night, she came back here and even though we were all tired and drunk and needed to rinse the saltwater out of our hair, she sat us down outside and prepared us. Suzie needs this. The man is hot and there is an opportunity here for us to make this Spanish wanger happen for her (her words, not mine). So, she gave all the sisters back stories, she made us practise accents and she made me give them a brief conversational lesson in French. We role-played into the early hours, which is not the sort of role-play I think this villa usually sees.

And I guess it worked because I've not had an orgasm like that in years. One where your mind is clear and intent and in that moment. There was intensity there, a dance where we seemed to know all the moves and we were focused on getting as much pleasure out of the experience as possible. There was no one watching, no expectation, no boredom, no minds wandering out of the room. We were both there. I attempted positions I've only managed when drunk. I did things I usually only do when I've known someone for years.

I think I might be experiencing some sort of shock now; I can't rub the smile off my face. I stand there and do an uncoordinated excited dance, my fists clenched. He's passed out on one of the sun loungers, swim shorts on, face down and in a deep state of slumber. Did we just have sex in the pool? We did. Suzie Callaghan, you had a sex in a pool. You had your legs wrapped around his neck, you were lying against the stone poolside and he did this thing where he licked the inside of your thighs until he got to your clit, your toes grazing the coolness of the water, and you had nothing to hold on to so you grabbed on to him.

I don't know what to do. I don't know who to tell. I want to tell the cousins I didn't need to do that euphoric dance workshop. I'm doing it here. The sun bounces off his back now, beads of sweat and pool water in the shallows of his shoulder blades. I want to lick it all off. Holy balls. Who are you, girl? You are not this person. You're usually a bit more measured when it comes to sex. You're careful. I put two hands over my mouth again to hold in the fact I want to scream with joy. Hydration. Hydration. Pull yourself together. We haven't even been in a bedroom yet. It's the house. It must be the effect of the house. They probably spray pheromones through this place to make people super randy.

I go and rest my forehead against the fridge door, unsure about what to do. This is what I needed. Holiday sex. I needed to indulge for a change, have some mysterious, no-strings sex with a stranger and just feel alive again, recharged. Hence the whole French charade and being someone else. Maybe that's half the attraction. That person out there doing things isn't me. It's Aurelie who's French and liberated and has no sexual reservations. Aurelie has had sex with beat poets and artists, she's that sort. In Paris. In lofts. She smokes French cigarettes, lives off endive and good coffee, and wears a beret without looking like a twat. I really should just light up a cigarette now and sit here with oversized sunglasses and a pout looking nonplussed about life. *C'est la vie, non?*

I get two tins out of the fridge and head outside, perching on the edge of the sun lounger where Carlos sleeps. I put the tin to his back and roll it slowly.

'That's cold,' he mumbles. 'But keep doing it.' I smile as he rolls over, his hand immediately going to my waist. 'Hey.' There is a peace to just sitting here with him.

'You look...'

'Drained?'

I laugh. 'Tired.'

'Make sure I don't bake in this sun, s'il te plaît.'

Just his singular hand on me makes every cell in me sing. But no, get it together, Suze. Hydration before you both pass out with the exertion. He sits up so his face is inches away from mine. I scan his face, feel the warmth of his skin next to mine.

'How's it going, mermaid?'

'I'm good.'

'Just good?'

'I'm hot.'

He smirks. I don't quite know what this is. I've been in relationships before that started with good hot sex, but it never lasts. Flames can't burn that strongly forever. They just fizzle out. Because people have to get up, get dressed and stop to eat, to drink, to pay the bills, to live their lives. Suddenly, an intense sadness fills me at the thought that this will have an end point. I wouldn't be able to move to Spain, he wouldn't move to England. I'd have to tell him I'm not French, that I lied. Momentary joy brought down to earth with a big complete jolt. Why am I thinking this far ahead?

'All OK?' he asks me, his bright eyes concerned.

'I think I'm just in shock. That was...'

'Please be a good adjective.'

'Magnífico.'

He runs a hand through my hair and kisses my forehead, a moment of complete tenderness after the frenzy of the sex we just had, and I pull him into an embrace. But what if I want to keep him? To get to know him better? How does that work?

My thoughts are interrupted by the main gate of the villa opening and the cousins returning in their rental car. Carlos looks me in the eye and smiles. The bubble has burst, but maybe it's a good thing to have a break from all that intensity.

Lucy is the first to appear, peeking her head down to the pool and waving with both hands. '¡HOLA, AMIGOS!' she hollers, running down to greet us. I know her game. She looks around for signs of sex but we are both fully clothed again, just sitting by the pool having an iced tea. He made me come three times though, Luce, I want to shout into the sultry Spanish air. 'Well, this is lovely. Did you both have a *lovely* afternoon?'

I look over at a clock in the kitchen. It's coming up to four o'clock. I bite my lip to think that at least three of those hours were spent having some of the best sex I think I've ever had. She sees the blush in my cheeks and smiles, clapping her hands. 'We brought home some amazing seafood. We're probably going to barbeque it, you're welcome to join us, Carlos?' she suggests.

He sits up, stretching his hands up over his head. 'Merci for the invitation but I have to get back for a family thing.'

My heart drops when he says family. 'My brother,' he says

reassuringly. 'But maybe tomorrow. I don't want to take you away from your cousins tonight. Maybe we could...'

I nod. 'Do something?'

'Something,' he says, a cheeky twinkle glinting in his eye. 'Tomorrow, the beach where we met. Maybe about eleven? Unless you have plans with your cousins?'

'We can spare her for a couple of hours,' Emma tells him, watching with a grin.

Meet him at the beach where we met? It's the holiday equivalent of meeting under the clock. Sex I can do but romance I can't. It'll see me get attached. This is a one-off holiday fling, I tell myself, putting those barriers back in place for protection. Is this wise? I see the other sisters emerge from the house as Carlos stands up.

'Do you want to have a shower? A quick dip to freshen up?' I ask him quietly.

He turns to see the sisters watching. 'I think I'll make a swift exit to escape...'

'The Spanish Inquisition?'

'Good one...'

I hover over him as he collects his belongings, pulling his shirt over his shoulders and downing the rest of his drink. *Don't go.* I can't say that. That will give the game away that you have zero French cool. Let him go. If he doesn't come back, this will be something to imprint into my memory forever, at least.

I walk him to his moped by the gate.

'Aurelie, that was...'

I sigh and he laughs. He leans over in what I assume to be a kiss but he whispers into my ear, softly. 'I can still taste you.'

I may die. I have no words. He kisses me on the cheek and then with equal amounts of charm and machismo rides his moped away as I try and prop myself up on that gate. Fuck me.

'OI!' a voice suddenly pops up. I jump back into reality.

Lucy's face suddenly appears from behind the gate. 'What was that he just whispered to you, I couldn't quite hear it?'

I smile to let her know she'll never know. 'The "oi" is not very French by the way. You're like a cat, you know. Where were you hiding?'

'Behind that tree...' She points to show me where Grace has also been hiding.

'Someone had some sex, didn't they? I know sex face when I see it,' she exclaims, nudging me and linking her arm through mine. 'Did you try that mermaid position I was telling you about?'

I shake my head, not quite knowing how to explain what just happened.

'We're not all like you, Lucy,' Grace says, shaking her head in disapproval.

'And that is where you're all failing in life,' she says. 'Look at that smirk. Was he good? He looks like he had moves. The moped is a bit cheap but I liked the sunglasses, the linen. Good schlong?'

I cover my face to hide the blush, refusing to answer.

Grace rolls her eyes. 'I hope you had fun. Emma just wants to know where you had sex so she knows where she can safely sit. You look...' Grace scans my face as I drop my hands.

'Orgasmed out,' Lucy says.

'I was going to say you have a bit of colour in your cheeks...' Grace continues.

'That's the sun,' I jest.

I return to the pool where the remaining sisters have already cracked open a bottle of red. I collapse onto a sun lounger, burying my face into the towel where Carlos was laying. Don't inhale like some saddo. Don't fall for him, Suzie. It's too soon. Don't be that person.

'Well, we want details, dear cousin...' Meg says. 'Because I had to go stand in a field and pretend I was in some deep trance state of ecstasy while some woman clanged on a bowl. We need to live vicariously through you.'

I laugh but in some sort of strange delirium, I kick my legs around like a toddler unable to control their emotions. I can hear all the sisters laughing. 'Magnifique. Chef's kiss. All the superlatives.'

They all sit there quietly, beaming.

'I'll need more than that,' Lucy says, getting comfortable on her sun lounger.

'You know there's a moment between two people where it's just...' I can't find the word and growl instead. They all nod. 'And then it's just clothes flying off and just plain old-fashioned...'

'Rutting?' Meg says. Lucy howls with laughter.

'That is an awful word, Meg,' Emma argues. 'That's what sheep do.'

'No, I get Meggers here,' Lucy adds. 'Sometimes it's primal and hot and grabbing and all your reservations about your body just go out the window. That's some hot sex.'

'He knew where my clitoris was. He knew what to do with it,' I continue.

There's a sharp intake of breath around the pool. We all know that's not an immediate thing. The pressure, the movement – that can take months, sometimes years to teach. I may be spoiled for life now if I have to compare any sexual experience to that, ever again. My head is still spinning. I take a large gulp of wine.

'It's the Europeans, they're just educated differently,' Beth says. 'You know, when you see him next, just ask him again if he went to college in London. I have a feeling I know him from somewhere.'

'He does look a bit like that bloke from that medical show – the Italian one...' Grace adds.

'Maybe,' Beth says, having a brain wave. 'But if I can say, the ass was on point.'

Emma even nods in agreement at that point. She smiles at me. 'What?' I ask her.

'That there is the Suzie I know. Look at that glow,' she says.

'It's the sun,' I reiterate.

'We've all been in the sun, honey. We're not glowing like that,' she says, winking at me.

'So, how was the dancing?' I say, trying to take the focus off me and the events of the last few hours.

'Absolutely bonkers and shit. Some wild bird in tie-dye wanted to look at my chakras and drugged our tea,' Meg says.

'Hold up,' Lucy argues. 'That was not drugs. It was coca leaves.'

'It's cocaine. I Googled it,' said Emma.

'And went against the camp rules by getting a cellular device out...'

I lie back and listen to the sound of them bickering. I like it, it breaks the silence, takes me away from my thoughts. My most indecent thoughts. I look into the sky, at the sort of blue you don't get anywhere else. It's untouched, it shines differently and I immediately think about his eyes. The eye contact. Eyes looking right into me while I orgasmed over him, like he wanted to really see it in me. Lordy. I gaze up into the blue, trying to make sense of what just happened but there's not a cloud in sight. Just sky for miles and miles above.

Charlie

'Would you look at the mammaries on that specimen?'

The table all turn their heads towards a girl heading to the toilets. All except me. Andy could say that the building was on fire and I think I would just sit here, sipping on my Coke and staring at this hot sauce bottle. I seem to be in some sort of sex trance.

What the hell happened this morning? Sex is usually something that happens after a couple of dates. There's a build-up, space to plan and take stock of what's happening. One minute, we were taking in the view and the next, we were having quite extraordinary sex. Sex that was sweaty and visceral and that I can picture so clearly in my mind now that it's horribly arousing, which is probably not the reaction I want sitting in an all-you-can-eat ribs and steak joint surrounded by twelve other men. I blame Carlos. I blame Carlos for all of it. He gave me the confidence of twenty men, the ability to think I could do anything. The man had rizz, swagger, charm in buckets and spades. Maybe he's not me at all. Maybe it was just an out-of-body experience.

'I once tapped a bird with double GGs. I tell you, like bloody airbags, could have rested a pint on them.' Even Andy's absurd and frankly unbelievable stories can't touch me now. I feel like I'm in a state of enlightenment, calm, serenity. Aurelie is beautiful, sweet – unlike anyone I've met before. Maybe that sounds premature and ridiculous when we've slept together just once, but there is something addictive about it. I remember that I'm seeing her again tomorrow and cannot stop from grinning.

'Are you going for the ribs too?' asks a waitress in a tiny denim skirt with a toy gun poking out her holster. Tonight's restaurant of choice is a dimly lit cowboy-themed joint on the main Magaluf strip. It's meat heavy with cheap alcohol and it also has a bucking bull to the middle of it. It's loud and raucous but a least a distraction from having to think too hard about this day.

I look up. 'Yeah, please. And the baked potato option. Thanks.' I hand my menu back to her.

'Oi, oi, Charlie boy. Don't fancy your chances there then?'

Andy says, checking her out with all the subtlety of a sledgehammer given that she's still taking orders around the table.

'Please excuse him,' I tell her.

'I'm paying her a compliment,' Andy says. 'It's not that deep.'

I frown and lower my voice. 'Well, it is. You're making her feel uncomfortable and that she's there solely for your gaze. How are the wife and kids?' I snap.

The table goes quiet except for the waitress who can't seem to stop smiling. She nods at me, thankfully.

'Oh, lighten up, you wanker. It's just jokes. At least I get some. Maybe you should do the same?' he replies.

I did, this morning, three and a half times to be exact. Around the same time that he apparently tried going down a water slide standing up and split his calf open. Remind me to get some saltwater on that.

'Actually, Charlie did hook up with someone today,' Max pipes up from the end of the table. I stare down at him. Not information I really wanted to broadcast but I can see that look on his face that says he can see I am going to rain down on Andy in a second and ruin the mood. We haven't even got our nachos yet. 'How did it go, Carlos?' he winks.

'Very well.' I mean, I think I might be suffering from severe dehydration and I had to stand in a lukewarm shower for ten minutes just to calm down afterwards but I've got that feeling in my legs like they might give way and that to me is a sign of good sex.

'You're not marking a report now, Charlie? Details?' Max shouts from the end of the table.

'She's French. Her name is Aurelie.'

'Oo là là. Oui oui, baguette,' Andy says. I'm immediately riled he gets to comment on this.

'I'll see her tomorrow at some point between the boat party and the quad biking,' I tell them.

'Oooooooh...' the stags all coo in unison, taking the piss.

'Oh, shut up. It's just a thing. I don't know where it will go.'

'Holiday fling, innit?' one of Max's mates, Wrighty, pipes up as he sups on his pint.

I take a sip of my drink too, but I'll admit, it makes me feel a little sad that today was just that: a bit of freeing incognito sex, a hook up, a one-night type of liaison that I'll remember fondly in years to come but really doesn't have much substance beyond this week. She's French. The geography is way off. It feels like such a waste of good chemistry.

'My mate Steve had a fling with a girl when he was in Greece. Brought her over and tried to make a thing of it. Married her and everything,' Wrighty says. I marvel at how he can tell this story but also down his pint at the same time.

'So it worked out then?' I ask him.

'God no. They had mad sex but she was a bit of a loon. She set fire to his car once so he couldn't come down the pub.'

'Oh,' I reply.

'Yeah, holiday romances rarely have happy endings. Most of the time, it's someone wanting a green card, gold diggers, or the passion fizzles. It don't translate to reality,' Wrighty continues. 'It's sun, sea and unlimited sex versus grey, bills and who's going to take out the bins for the rest of your lives.' If I ever needed a reality check, I think I may have just got one here from Wrighty who's at least three pints deep. He looks up from his drink, a worried expression on his face. 'You didn't give her any money, did you?'

'I bought her a hooded towel and some ten-euro flip flops,' I recount.

'That's a shit gift. And she still slept with you?' Wrighty laughs.

The problem is I don't think she's like that at all. I hate to think I'm the exception but there seemed to be something there, maybe even beyond the sex.

'French birds too. They blow hot and cold, you know? I wouldn't go there myself. Hard work, mate,' Andy adds.

I nod, disbelievingly given all his obvious worldly experience with women.

'But... you know... if it is something then I am sure you could make it work,' Max says, coming to sit at my end of the table to hear more. Little Max who's getting married soon so he's loved up, and in a space to think anything is possible. I like hearing his comments. Maybe there might be something worth exploring at the end of all this. I think about the feeling of her lips pressed against mine. I really hope there might be. Maybe tomorrow I'll find out.

'RIGHT, COWBOYS! YEE-HAW!' a DJ's voice booms over the loudspeakers. 'WE NEED OUR STAGS AND OUR HENS AND OUR COWBOYS AND COWGIRLS TO COME AND TAKE ON THE CHALLENGE OF THE BULL. WHO WANTS TO GO FOR A RIDE?'

Christ alive, we've not even eaten yet. This restaurant is full of parties like ours and a roar fills the room as everyone seems to be here for the meat and to get tossed off. A mechanical bull, that is. Andy being Andy starts rattling the tables and then gradually starts a chant of Max's name that reverbs around the room. Max, Max, Max. He's in a T-shirt and shorts so hardly dressed for the occasion but he stands to his chair, firing fake guns. I have to laugh. Maybe after such a poor start to his stag do yesterday, the man has to have his moment.

'We have a young man there? Stella! Head to that man over there!' A woman rocks up with a cowboy hat and a microphone so he can make a fool of himself in front of the whole restaurant. 'What's your name?'

'I'm Max.'

'And what brings you to Magaluf, Max?'

'I'm getting married and this is my stag do.'

The whole restaurant explodes into cheers as the fellow

stags make unfortunate rutting noises. I can't help but smile and get caught up in it.

'Ready to ride, Cowboy Max?' the voice asks.

'YEE-HAW!' he yells, as he heads over to the mechanical bull to the middle of the restaurant. Stella, his stablehand, has a water gun in her hands and fires something into his mouth. I am going to hazard a guess that is not water. Max takes a long shot and then punches the air. The stags all get out their phones as he straddles the massive creature and it slowly starts to rotate. I laugh to see him so ridiculously excited but really wish he was wearing a long trouser.

The DJ starts to play 'Cotton-Eyed Joe' (there wasn't really an alternative) and the restaurant start to clap and cheer along. 'A reminder today that if Max can hold on for at least two minutes then we will pay for his dinner tonight. Can we maybe speed that baby up?'

There's a look on Max's face that I've not seen since he was a kid when he'd be on a bike going down a hill very, very fast. The bull starts to swivel and buck in a number of different directions but the lad can hold on. That comes from years of me being his brother, times when I've pushed him down hills on makeshift sleds. I look on as the stags clap for him.

'COME ON, MAX!'

'YOU ABSOLUTE UNIT!'

But I look down at my watch. Surely it's been two minutes already? Why is it spinning so quickly? Hold up. Max, I think you should let go now.

'MAX! LET GO!' I yell but he sits gripping on for dear life.

'Shit,' a voice booms out from the DJ booth. 'Can someone get Diego? I think it's broken again.'

Panic fills my face. The bull is broken? My little brother is on it. Could it explode? I have to bring this boy home to his fiancée.

'MAX! JUST LET GO!' I yell, but he doesn't listen. In fact,

he clings to the thing for dear life like a bear cub. I'll personally pay for the dinner if we have to. I clamber past some of the crowd watching, past a table where everyone just stares in horror, clinging on to their drinks. Yes, protect your pints.

'Sir! ¡Señor! You can't go on there!' Stella shouts at me. I push her away, landing on the inflatable cushioning. God, there's smoke coming out of that thing.

'MAX! YOU HAVE TO...'

But he does. He lets go, screaming as he does and flies towards me, crashing into me so that we both land on the floor of the restaurant. The room spins, voices fade to nothing until the whole room goes black.

SEVEN

Suzie

'Are you sure he said eleven? You were there. There wasn't any way he could have said something else and I misheard because of his accent?' I ask Lucy, panicked, on the phone. I know it was dark but I am here at the beach where we first met. I'm by the rocks. The beach is a little busier by day but it's definitely the right place and he's definitely not here. Maybe he meant the plaza where we shared bunyols? Maybe it was further up where we walked under the stars half naked? I look at the clock on my phone. It's 11.45am. 'Unless he meant the nighttime. Spanish people have siestas, don't they? Maybe his body clock is different? Do you think he's OK? Maybe he crashed his moped?'

Lucy can hear the panic in my voice. 'Oh, honey. I'm so sorry.'

Because this was always going to be the other option. He was just some man I met who scored his shot and that was always going to be it. On an island like Mallorca, in the summer season, pretty scantily clad women like me are ten-a-penny and he's probably moved on to someone else. I'm just part of a body count. What an awful phrase. I hope he hasn't given me anything. It's probably why we never traded numbers or last names. I thought it added an air of mystery and spontaneity to proceedings but maybe it was his way of putting some space there so I couldn't track him down. As memorable as it was, perhaps it was always destined to just be a one-off thing.

The heat bears down on me now, my shoulders singeing slightly from having stood here for forty-five minutes, waiting and hoping, in a little yellow sundress with a swimming costume underneath. God, I even re-shaved. I let myself imagine scenarios where I was on his moped, holding on to him tightly, scooting past cliffs and beaches to the themes of a softly melodic cinema soundtrack. I'm a bit of an idiot for thinking that far ahead. I really am. I kick off my shoes and dip my feet in the foam of the tide, watching as my toes sink and the water buries my feet. This beach is busier now, filled with sun worshippers, families with kids building sandcastles; there are sun shades covered in browning palms and the sand is bright, almost white. There are people jet skiing, screaming with glee, the waters crystal clear, smaller islets and the surrounding mountains in view. It's not the calm, dimly lit oasis of our first meeting, but the coolness of the water, the sand under my feet feels soothing at least.

'I'm by the pool but I can come down there now? We can go for a drink? For lunch?' Lucy asks.

'No, don't do that. It's Meg's birthday dinner tonight. I feel bad enough being away. I'm just having a mini dip and then I'll come back. Do you guys need anything in town?' I ask, trying to hide my disappointment.

'We're good here. Oh, maybe some boxes if you can find them though so we can transport food and stuff. Danny has been in touch with the agent and they're going to move us to another villa. He's seen pics of this one this time.'

I smile. It may be exactly what I need. Then I won't have to sit in that place for the rest of the week re-living every place Carlos and I had sex, feeling like a fool. Feeling gutted.

'Just come back when you're ready... and Suze?'

'Yeah...'

'I had a feeling about him. I thought he was different. I'm sorry. Screw him and his complete lack of manners. Actually, screw men. Come back here and you can have an hour alone in one of the sex rooms. I won't judge.'

For the first time this hour, I laugh from my belly. 'Love you, Luce. See you in a bit.'

As I hang up, I look down at my phone. Why didn't we swap numbers? I don't even have a last name, a name of his yoga company. I put Carlos into Facebook and filter the city down to Palma de Mallorca. Crap. That's like putting the name John into a city like Bristol. Do I just sit here and scroll through them? What about Carlos-Yoga-Mallorca? A search result comes up with something and my heart suddenly flutters out of my chest, but the picture is of an older-looking man with tight grey curls who does retreats in the mountains and has taken a vow of silence.

I walk along the foam for a bit until I get to the rocks where we first met. Two kids skip along the rocks, while some social media influencer type sits there with a selfie stick possibly trying to vlog and take photos. I perch on a rock and take a drink out of my bag, looking down at Carlos' T-shirt which I'd laundered and hung out to dry in the sun, ready to return to him. I guess that's mine now. If I'm being honest, we didn't talk that much. We traded in banter and really didn't swap much in the way of proper, getting-to-know-you conversations. All I know is that his favourite colour is green, he can't whistle and he has a scar on his left buttock because he once sat on a barbeque skewer. All the important stuff then. Maybe I just misread all the signs like I normally do. Or maybe he's just an asshat who followed the needs of his penis, as opposed to his heart. And for a moment, I think of Paul who did the same thing. I really know how to choose them. I just need to keep moving, don't I? It's worked so far. Focus on Meg's birthday. Maybe I should just get naked in the sea now and see if any other good-natured men want to fish me out. I sigh deeply, putting my face up to the sun to take in the heat, the light. Things were brighter these last few days, Suzie, and let's keep them that way. Thank you, Carlos, for that much.

Right, I need to head back. I pick up my stuff, sliding a shirt over my shoulders and trudge through the sand, past palm trees and towards the relative cool and shade of the streets, heading to the market and arcades that Carlos and I went to that night.

'¡Hola! ¡Hola, señorita!' a woman says, accosting me in the street. I vaguely recognise her in her crumpled T-shirt and floral apron. I look up. Her shop looks different by day but she points to a mermaid towel hanging up and points to me. That is me, I was the mermaid.

'Sí. ¡Hola! ¿Qué tal?'

'¿Señor? ¿Dónde está el guapo?' I smile. I know what that means in Spanish at least. Where's the fit fella? How do I say we had a mega shag but now he's left me for dust? I shrug my shoulders, not really knowing how to communicate that he's vanished. She sees a sadness in my eyes and beckons me into the shop. 'Para usted,' she says, handing me a fridge magnet. It has a little map of Mallorca and a lizard on it. I smile. 'A veces los hombres pueden ser unos cerdos.' I nod. I think she said something about pigs so I agree. I hold it to my heart as she puts a hand to my face. 'Bonita, bonita.'

'Gracias, señora.'

She waves maniacally and I have no option but to do the same. In the day, this street is achingly brighter. The heat radiates off it, leaving a thick mist of dust in its wake. I weave around slow-moving taxis and mopeds until I get to a street corner and see a man frying bunyols on the corner under some palms.

I walk up to him, smiling. 'Hola señor, doce bunyols, gracias.' The man with his weathered skin and crooked smile nods, placing them in a paper bag and sprinkling them with sugar. I don't know how he's standing over hot oil in this heat, but well done. 'These are super delicioso,' I tell him, and he laughs. I hand over my money, putting the bag aside for the sisters. Fried doughnuts will make things better. I look up and down the roads thinking of the best way to get back to the villa, and then realise the best way is probably to head to the nearest hotel and grab a taxi. Playa del Sol looks cheap and cheerful and, from the looks of it, there's a heavy flow of people so hopefully it means I'll be able to get some transport from there. I dart across the road and head inside for a slight reprieve from the heat. It's buzzing with activity but the cool white floors and fans are a welcome escape. Even so, I'm glad we've ended up staying somewhere quieter as I can't imagine Lucy sunning her yoni anywhere near here. I wonder what the new villa will look like. I just want somewhere to read. Instead of searching out distraction sex, maybe I need to go more cerebral. Meditate, drink iced coffee and finally get through the new David Nicholls in my bag. Literature and sunlight will soothe my soul. To hell with men. Being nosy, I peer around this hotel for a moment though. The buzzing buffet, a child running through reception with a massive inflatable tyre, two women in matching leopard print sarongs fanning themselves on the sofas, complaining about the heat and the fact their flights have been cancelled. Again. Outside on the lawn, I notice some sort of aerobics class happening. Rather them than me but a thought suddenly strikes me. He taught yoga in hotels. Maybe? I go up to reception.

'Hola.'

'Hola señorita, how can I help?'

'I... I took a yoga class here a few days ago with a man called

Carlos. Brown hair, about six foot, and I was just wondering if he did other classes I could join in,' I explain. I hope that was convincing enough and she doesn't ask to see a key card.

'Carlos, you say?' she says. My heart skips a beat in my chest. 'Our yoga instructors are called Santi and Ana. Are you sure you might not have been mistaken?' My shoulders drop again.

'My mistake.'

'We have a man called Carlos who plays in the flamenco trio. But he's not six foot tall. He's also fifty-five.'

'Then not him, I really am sorry. I must have got confused,' I say. I turn quickly to mask my embarrassment but bump into the person behind me in the queue, his leg in a cast and trying his best to hobble around on crutches. He winces as I walk into his leg. 'I'm so sorry, I'm so sorry. God...'

The man senses my frustration and immediately stops, seeing my distress. 'Look, it's OK. I mean it's broken anyways.'

I stop to look at him and his cast where someone has drawn an unfortunately large penis and signed it Andy. At least someone is having a worse time of it than me. 'Geez, broken? How did you do that?'

'You don't want to know, it's slightly embarrassing.'

'I once took out a tooth by tripping up the stairs,' I say pointing to one of my crooked front teeth.

He laughs. 'My brother and I were in a bullfight.' I don't know whether that's a joke or not as I'm sure it's important to be morally opposed to such things so I laugh politely. 'It's my stag do – stupid really. I'll now be spending the rest of my time here showering in a plastic bag and talking to travel insurance people.'

'Ouch. How is your fiancée going to feel about this then?'

'We may have twisted the truth a little and told her we fell down an open lift shaft,' he says through gritted teeth.

'Well, good luck then... Here...' I say, reaching into the

paper bag in my basket. I unravel the paper bag of freshly fried doughnuts. 'These are called bunyols. You need one more than me.'

He seems taken aback by the gesture and balances on the one leg to take one. As he does, I notice his eyes, bright blue like someone I know. Or knew. Or didn't really know at all.

'Are you OK?' he asks me, thoughtfully. Maybe he can see the slump returning to my shoulders.

I give a small smile. 'Yeah, I hope you get to enjoy the rest of your holiday.'

A friend suddenly appears, strutting up behind him, and looks me up and down. 'Oi, oi, Maxi Boy. Even though one leg's broken, glad to see the other two work. You alright, babe?' he says to me, leching in his dayglo shorts and football top.

'Yeah, no. I'm good, thanks,' I say, my nostrils flared widely. Even though I am sad and all my hope and self-esteem is in the gutter, no.

'Your loss, beautiful. Mate, taxi is here to take you to the hospital to see your bro. Quad bikes at five. You think you'll be up for that?'

'Well, obviously,' he says in return, exasperated.

I furrow my brow at this mate's stupidity, trying to hold in the laughter. What happened to his brother? How is he getting in this taxi? Is his mate coming with him? My bleeding heart wonders whether to help him but I look at my phone. Meg's party starts soon. Maybe that should be the priority. Having put my trust in a complete stranger and nothing coming of it, maybe it's safer to just head to those who love me without condition. I put a hand to Max's shoulder. 'Look, take care...' I say, leaving a gap for him to introduce himself.

'Max. And you?'

There's no point lying anymore. Being Aurelie was nice for half a day, but it's time to leave her behind. 'Suzie. Hope you and your brother get better soon.'

'I hope so too.'

Charlie

'¿Señor? ¿Señor? How are you feeling?'

Like something is sitting on my head. I open my eyes to blinding white lights, white walls, perforated ceiling tiles and those blinds that we have at work in the office that always get tangled up. This feels like an awful dream.

'Charlie! Charlie, mate! It's me, Max.'

I completely open my eyes and look down to see my legs under a lemon yellow blanket, the sound of a machine beeping in the background. I see Max next to the bed beside a shorter lady with her hair slicked back into a bun.

'Who are you?' I say in a weak voice.

'It's me, Max. I'm your brother,' he says, the colour draining from his face.

'Who?'

'Oh god, has he forgotten me? Is this some sort of brain injury?' he cries, panicked.

'I'm messing with you, you idiot. You're Max Shaw, my brother. Birthday the twentieth of January,' I say, trying to force a laugh. Instead, my throat feels dry, my eyes heavy.

'Sense of humour still intact then,' he tells the nurse, as he throws his body over mine to give me a massive hug. I drape an arm over him to return the gesture.

'Señor Max, be careful with the leg, please,' she says, concerned. 'Señor Charlie. I am your nurse, Elena. I'm going to go and get the doctor. It is good to see you up.' Elena leaves the room as I try and sit up a bit more to take in my surroundings.

'The leg?'

'Fracture in the tibia. I've got a cast,' he says. I glance down to have a look at the large cumbersome cast on his leg. I'll hazard a guess that the person who drew the large penis and exceptionally hairy balls on it was Andy.

'Insurance?' I say, my practical head still on my shoulders.

'I'm on it. Amy has been helping out too. Brooke and Sam were worried. They were wondering whether to fly in?'

I shake my head. 'God, no. I'll be fine. I am fine, no?' I ask, still straining to focus.

Max holds his phone in front of my face and plays a video of the event, obviously filmed by one of his ever-faithful stags. In my faint memories of the incident, I thought I was being heroic and an excellent brother but really as I scramble on to the inflatable, I look like a toddler learning to walk, falling on my face and then trying to get to my feet again. Then Max is thrown off the bull, and I gasp to see us both flying through the air. It's like that whole Avengers thing manifesting itself. The crowd scream, we land with the biggest of thuds, but unlike Iron Man and Hulk, we don't get up. 'Holy fuck, are they dead?' says the person behind the camera. I can't wipe the look of horror from my face that someone has caught the whole thing on camera.

'Well, when I flew off the bull, you took most of the force of my fall. We totally missed the bouncy castle bit. They've done some scans. You really were out cold. They reckon you've got a concussion, and they did a small operation to fix your wrist yesterday. They want to keep you in for one more night.'

I look down at my wrist bandaged up and in a cast. I'm lucky that Andy and his graffiti has not got to that yet. My mouth and throat, however, feel like they've been attacked by razors.

'Well, that's my tennis career buggered,' I say.

'I hope that's not your wanking hand,' Max says, attempting to get some humour out of the situation.

I try and laugh but the movement hurts, everywhere. And I'm starving and need a wee.

'Tell Brooke and Sam, I fine. I'll call them later.' However, a thought suddenly strikes through me.

'What's the time?' I ask Max.

'It's just after lunch. Are you hungry?'

I feel something in the pit of my stomach but it's not hunger. It's panic that I will have missed Aurelie. She would have gone to the beach and I wouldn't have been there. She'll think I'm a flake, an idiot, that I just used her for sex. Have I missed this chance? Because I got involved in an accident with a mechanical bull? Max can see the confusion in my eyes.

'Are you alright? Are you having a fit or something?' he asks.

'The French girl. I was supposed to meet her...'

'Well, not now,' Max says. 'Oh man. Sorry about that.'

I look up at the ceiling thinking about all that hope, all that potential, all that spark is just gone. It can't be, can it? I had plans. I had researched a beach with sea caves and put down a deposit for kayaks. I don't have anything to go on. Oh God, we didn't swap numbers, socials, anything. A rare thing in today's age but I think we both liked how relaxed and mysterious the whole thing was. Or maybe she didn't want me to know? God, she has a boyfriend, doesn't she? Or maybe it was only ever supposed to be this holiday fling situation where we didn't get too close. We did get close though. Yesterday, that was as close you can get to another human being.

'Do you have a phone, Max?' I ask him.

'Yeah, do you want to call her?'

'No, I can't.' My head is starting to hurt. I see a cup of water on my bedside table and reach for it.

Max reaches forward. 'Hold up there, let me.' He reaches forward and puts a straw into my mouth.

'Get on Facebook and search for Aurelies who live in Nice,' I tell him, my voice raspy and dry.

I see Max's fingers slide over the screen. 'Charlie, there are hundreds of them. Do you want me to go through them?'

'No.' I try and think about everything she ever told me. Meg, Emma, Beth, Grace and Lucy. Did I get a last name? I don't think I did. I don't even know what she did for work. I know her favourite colour is yellow, this was her first time in Mallorca, that when she was little on holiday, she buried her dad's car keys in the sand and they couldn't get home. All the important stuff then. But then I think I can remember the name of the villa. There might be a pin in the map still. I close my eyes. 'Where is my phone?'

'I don't quite know. Your belongings were in a plastic bag.'

Remember the name, Charlie. Come on. I close my eyes and think about the sign next to the wall. Dream. Sueños.

'Villa Sueños in Santa Posa. Can you Google it? Is there a number for whoever rents it out? A management company?'

Max scrolls through his phone, side-eyeing me to ensure I haven't completely lost my mind. 'Yep, I think I have one. Do you want me to...'

'Yeah,' I say immediately, not really knowing what I'm going to say. Max dials the number and a person picks up after three ring tones.

'¡Hola! Palmera Property Management, this is Rosa speaking. Can I help?'

'Hola. Me llamo Charlie Shaw. Hace poco visité una villa que ustedes cuidan en Santa Posa y esperaba ponerme en contacto con las personas que lo alquilan. Me dejé algo allí.' My Spanish is hurried but I just want to get in touch with Aurelie and all her cousins, make sure they know I wanted to be there, I wanted to meet Aurelie and see her again. I am not that guy.

'¿Cómo se llama la villa?' she asks me.

'Villa Sueños. Era una familia Francesca.'

Max looks at me confused. 'I've told her to get a message to the French party who rented the place.'

The lady hears me mumbling in English. 'Señor, your name

is not Spanish. Can I ask about your connection to the house?' Rosa implores.

'I was a guest. I was only there the once.'

She pauses. Is she laughing? 'And can I ask what you left at the villa?'

'My... shirt.'

She pauses again. 'Well, Señor Shaw. If you give me a telephone number then maybe I can pass something on.'

My phone is not here. Shit. I look at Max and repeat the digits of his telephone number. As I do I realise, the jig is up. Aurelie will see the UK codes and realise I'm not Spanish. I could extend the lie but then maybe now is the perfect time to just be myself. She may run a mile when she knows, but at least I would have tried. At least I wouldn't have lost her forever.

'Señor Shaw, you say a French party? Not English?'

'Non. Definitely French.'

'OK. I will pass that on.'

'Muchas gracias, señora.'

I close my eyes. Please, please, please. I should get Max to go down to the beach to look for her but then I look down at the cast. Maybe I should go. I could get a taxi there now and explain myself. It's a good story and I have the scars and cast to prove it. I try and sit up and feel something inside me creak.

'Mate, can you just...' Max says, putting a hand to me telling me to sit down.

'But...'

'But it's just one girl, that you met once,' he says, frowning. I see a look of sadness and complete fear fall across his face and realise I've not considered how awful this must have been for him, for me to have been in hospital. This might go down in history as the worst stag do ever. 'When you were on that restaurant floor and wouldn't get up, I seriously thought you were dead.'

'What a fucking place to die...' I mutter.

'Don't joke. I've been in this hospital for twenty-four hours now. I've not slept. I can't even take a proper crap with this thing on my leg.'

I try not to laugh but I see the panic in his expression and immediately feel guilty that I made him so worried. 'Where are the rest of the stags?'

'Where do you think? They're quad biking in three hours and then they're off to a strip club.'

There's a real look of disappointment in his face and I don't think that's from missing out on the evening's entertainment. He puts his head down by the side of my bed and I pat it affectionately. 'Did you keep a vigil?'

'Obviously. I even went to the chapel and lit a candle.'

'Really?'

Max laughs. 'Of course not. I got crap from the vending machines and watched another nineties action movie without subtitles on that chair.' He points to the corner of the room. I am curious as to how many paprika Pringles one person can eat. 'How have you remembered my mobile number after all these years?' he asks me.

'I know all three of your numbers by heart. It's my job.'

'I don't know yours.'

'Because you don't love me as much.'

He smiles at me. There is something about hospitals that will always strike fear into both of us but I'm glad that we've both come out of this relatively unscathed. My wrist starts to hurt and I wince to move it.

'Do you need any painkillers?'

I nod.

'I'll get Elena on it.'

'I'm also very conscious that it's a bit airy downstairs,' I say wriggling around in my paper dress.

'Pants?'

'Yeah, that would be good. Maybe a drink, something fizzy.'

'Anything else from the hotel? I'll find your phone.'

I stare out the window of the hotel where the blinds mask the tops of some palms poking through, letting me know I'm still on holiday, a brilliantly aqua sky in the background. Please let that message get through. Please don't let this be another classic episode in Charlie Shaw's failed love life. I put my head back on the pillow, trying to get comfortable.

'I started reading some book I picked up at the airport. David Nicholls. I think it's in my rucksack. And maybe something sweet. Like a doughnut or something?'

'Buñol,' Max says in a forced Spanish accent.

'Look at you speaking Spanish.'

'Your influence is finally rubbing off on me. Laters, bro.' He looks at me staring out the window. 'I'm sorry it didn't work out with that girl. I really am. Was she fit?'

'Super fit. She had eyes like… chocolate buttons.'

'Poetic. Wordsworthy.' He stops to study the emotion etched in my face. 'Do you want me to scroll through those Aurelies? Did you get a picture of her?'

I shake my head. All I have is what I can remember in my concussed brain. I scan through every bit of information she shared with me. I don't even know how long she was staying or what airport she flew in from. I didn't even know her last name. Maybe I could research champagne estates in Nice. LinkedIn? But at what point does this turn me into a stalker?

'It's cool. Let's just hope she gets in touch, eh?'

'Yeah.'

PART TWO
LONDON, SIX WEEKS LATER

EIGHT

Suzie

'I'm afraid you can't park there, Miss. Are you new? Are you staff?'

For a moment, I'm hoping this man thinks I'm young enough to look like a student, but I realise he's also implying that I could be a stranger here to kidnap a child. I must be staff. I have a coffee cup, smart shoes and a mild look of terror lining my face.

'I am new and staff and I'm so sorry, my parking is dire.'

We both turn to look at the car and it's a good thing I don't teach maths because my angles are all off.

'You're not drunk, are you?' the man asks me, laughing. 'With this lot, I wouldn't blame you.' He snarls at the students walking through the gates with their blazers and collection of Nike rucksacks and sparkling new school shoes. I look down at the tape measure hanging from this man's belt, the scruffy paint-stained polo shirt and then up again to the huge smile. It immediately puts me at ease. 'Site supervisor, my name's Mark. This place is reserved for Trevor, the lab tech, because he's got a dodgy hip. Go round the back, near PE, and park there. You'll thank me because you won't get caught up in all the traffic later when all the parents come to get their little darlings.'

'That feels like a trade secret you don't tell everyone, Mark.'

'Yeah, Fred in Science can wait in a queue for all I bloody care,' he says, winking at me. 'Have a lovely first day, Miss...'

'Callaghan. Suzie Callaghan.'

'I dated a Suzie once,' he tells me.

'I thought you looked familiar,' I joke.

He chuckles. 'Oooh, we've got a lively one here, you'll fit in just fine.' He laughs. 'Oi! YOU! Get off the gate and walk in like a proper human being.'

I get back in my car and do exactly as I'm told. The first day of work never gets any easier; having to muster up all that confidence, present all the positive facets of your personality and pretend to know what you're doing. I've done this for six years now since leaving university and I love the spark of it, every day being different and sometimes hilarious. But teenagers are unpredictable and unforgiving beasts. It's not even like walking into a lion's den. It's like walking into a room of very unimpressed cats who may attack, may engage with you but most likely will sit there and think you're not all that. I am also conscious that this school is in South London, and about one thousand students bigger than my last, smaller Brighton-based school. These are bigger and cooler cats. I gather all my bags and teaching paraphernalia and get out of the car to hear a voice echo through the playground.

'MISS CALLAGHAN!' It's Beth, standing excitedly next to her Fiat Punto.

'WHY, HELLO, MISS CALLAGHAN!' I shout back.

A child who looks like a new Year 7 given the size of her rucksack, looks at us petrified before scurrying away. What is this school? Why do the teachers have the same names? At least my first day at Griffin Road Comprehensive will be all the better for having Beth here.

I walk over to her and embrace her tightly so she can feel all my fear and worry. 'I was going to call to see if you wanted a lift in?'

'Oh no, I was on school runs. I haven't even had breakfast. How are you? How are you feeling?' She may not have eaten anything but Beth's jollity is everything here. She was a teacher before me and she's never let the job faze her. I like that she strolls in here with her New Balance, a couple of cloth bags and her hair bundled into a bun, ready to take it all on.

'Nervous.'

'Don't be. You have me. You look so posh, by the way. How has your tan lasted?' she asks.

I went formal today with a polka dot dress, tights and boots, and a trench. This level of style might not last throughout the year but today is about impressions. 'I went to Marseille for a last-minute break.' People mock us teachers for our extended holidays but that six weeks in summer is all about the recharge, getting ready to be able to give ourselves so fully to the intensity of the school terms. After Mallorca, I packed in as much as I could to recharge but also maybe move on from Paul, from Carlos. I tiled my new bathroom, I read five books, I learned how to paddleboard and I went to Marseille and ate steak-frites at cafés while the sun was on my face.

'Not Nice then?' Beth jokes.

I nudge her in the ribs as we take the walk into school. 'We don't talk about that anymore.'

Oh, Carlos. You will forever be my big summer crush. Yes, I feel a lot of sadness in my soul that he was not the person I thought he could be, but some of that has been replaced by happiness. I was enjoying being able to replay secret memories of him in quiet moments of my day, fuzzy sun-drenched images of him standing by a pool, completely naked. I had that.

'Did you meet anyone in Marseille?' she asks me.

'Dozens of people. You know, I shagged a mime artist called Jean-Luc.'

'Did the face paint get everywhere?' Beth enquires. 'Was he good with his hands?' She mimics the actions.

We giggle together and I'm relieved that I can look back at all of that Mallorcan madness and laugh now. Beth walks me through the main reception of the school, a light-filled atrium, covered in glass and GCSE art. Primary-coloured sofas are angled in different directions and there's also a motivational poster that I think might be the school motto. I remember a time when school mottos were Latin phrases but nowadays, they seem to be born out of people sat around a table and collating polls out of buzzwords. Creativity, Respect, Authenticity, Pride. I read that again. They know the anagram of that is CRAP, right? I try not to laugh.

'Are you telling me there are two Miss Callaghans now?' a lady at reception asks us.

'Yes, Claudia. Double trouble,' Beth replies.

'God help us.' She laughs. 'Love, your security and printing pass is here. There's a pack waiting for you in HR.'

I did come in one day in August to prepare some resources and take a tour but it's wondrous how full the school feels with the children here. We head out to a large courtyard where children crowd around phones, laughing at TikToks and catching up after six weeks apart. I see a couple of them staring at me, clocking the new kid on the block.

'Miss... you're back...' a kid says to Beth and puts a fist out. She stares at it and reluctantly gives him a fist bump back.

'Where else would I go, Josh? I need to get you lovelies through your GCSE. Make sure you don't mix up your alliteration with your assonance. Good summer?'

'Is what it is, eh? Who's your mate?' he asks.

'Mate? Believe it or not, another Miss Callaghan. This is my cousin, she teaches French.'

He eyes me up and down, nodding his head at the information that we are related. 'I take French, innit. You're the new one.'

'Oui, enchantée, Josh.'

He looks mistrustful. 'Are you one of them teachers who'll just speak French to us the whole time? I won't do well with that, you know?'

'I also speak English.'

'Then we'll be très bons, innit?' He puts a fist out for me to bump. Perhaps.

We continue to walk through the courtyard, up some stairs and towards a staffroom, a huge hive of activity that I'm not entirely used to. In my last school, we used to just hide away in our departments. Beth glances at me and can see my shock at the manic nature of it all. 'The head started this as she thought we were all getting too cliquey.' She heads over to an empty desk space by the window. 'First come, first served. I'd put your coffee cup and highlighters down here and claim your space. There are lockers over there, don't trust the mugs, and Ed in science bakes treats every Friday.'

My brain whirrs to take in all the information. By the kitchenette, a group of men in tracksuits, who I assume to be PE, peacock by the boiling kettle, regaling each other with stories of their summers. A teacher is with the guillotine cutting up chemistry worksheets for his life. An art teacher in dungarees throws a dead plant in the bin. I listen to the chat around me. *Does this computer work? What's the new rule about trainers again? Does anyone have the key to the stationery cupboard? What time is briefing?*

I stop to process that last question. 'Briefing?' I ask Beth.

'Oh yeah, first-day briefing so the head can calm us with positive mantras and most likely tell us that they've changed all the locks. It is in,' she pauses to look at her watch. 'Five minutes. Come...'

I put my bag on my new desk, take off my coat and tag along beside Beth, trying to memorise routes and get a feel for people's faces. It will be totally fine, Suzie. Breathe.

Beth squeezes my arm to reassure me. 'And these are the cupboards where we lock the naughty kids,' she says loudly, walking past a group of Year 8s. They all narrow their eyes at her. 'It will be fine,' she says turning back to me. 'Come find me at break, lunch. I'll introduce you to people?'

I nod quietly, walking into the hall with its tiered seating and take a seat. On a screen to the front, a big 'Welcome Back' PowerPoint is up there decorated with balloons and confetti. I try to be discreet and take a seat with Beth, waiting for the buzz of people to calm down. At the front of the hall is Alicia, the school's executive headteacher. I don't know why they've messed around with senior leadership titles but I always expect these executive heads to carry briefcases. Beth has told me stories about Alicia – that someone saw a sleeping bag in her office once and she's never seen her in casual wear – but I quite like the big statement jewellery and the fact that all her deputies and associate leaders below her seem to be men. A silence descends on the room as she steps to the front in her nude heels and suit.

'So... we are back. Hello, everyone. I won't keep you. We have a busy week ahead of us and everything you need to know will be in the staff bulletin, but I just wanted to welcome the new members of staff. We have ten new members of staff joining us...'

I sit up in my chair, realising that I will be singled out in a minute. Movement in teaching these days is the norm, we are all moving to new schools to get promoted, to find a working ethos that fits. I never thought I'd be one of those people but here I am. One of the ten.

'Let's start with maths.' Crumbs, there are slides with our names. People stand up and wave as their names are announced. I really hope we don't have to say anything. No. Just standing and waving. I can do that. She gets through English, Science and Geography – the new teacher of which tells us he has a speech prepared. Alicia tells him to sit down.

'And moving on to Modern Foreign Languages. We have Suzie Callaghan who is with us after a relocation from Brighton.' Shit, that's me. I stand up and put a hand to the air whilst Beth claps and lets out a little whoop. 'For those wondering, she is the cousin of the other Miss Callaghan, which is lovely. And Charlie Shaw joining us from a school in West London.'

I was told about this. He's a last-minute hire. We haven't had the chance to meet because of this but we've both been added to the MFL Team and I know he likes a thumbs up emoji. I didn't really have the time to stalk him. I look around the room, curious to see who I'll be working alongside. A figure to the side of the room stands up.

'Come on, turn around so we can see you,' Alicia tells him.

He turns around.

What the actual.

FUCK.

I don't quite know what sound comes out of my mouth next but I yelp as we stand there, staring at each other. Beth sits up when she finds him then looks at me, her head swinging back and forth between us. Is this a prank? A really awful cruel prank? He puts a hand to the air to wave at me. I wave back.

It's him. Carlos?

Charlie

'And this is the staffroom. Don't worry about that large stain. It looks like someone died there but it was from when Jan on reception dropped a vat of mulled wine at Christmas. I also bake every Friday. It's brownies this week,' my school guide and staff buddy, Ed from Biology, tells me.

'You bake? For the whole faculty? That's impressive,' I tell him.

He laughs. 'Oh, it's first come, first served, and if and when my daughter allows for it,' he says.

'How old?' I ask, politely.

'She's one. Her name is Daisy. I'm going to be unbearable now and show you a picture.' He beams so hard that I can't deny him and he holds up an adorable selfie of him, a very curly haired baby, someone I'll assume is his wife and a ginger cat who looks less impressed. 'That's Mia – she works in English.'

'Well, that is super cute.'

'And you? Married? Kids?' he asks.

'It's complicated, but single for now.' He leads me down a staircase so we can head to a briefing in the main hall and I can get a feel for this new school I'm going to call home. I would like to say it's different but all these London schools feel the same. They're hybrids of new fancy wooden-clad buildings with flash technology and old blocks from the seventies that hide asbestos and flaking concrete.

'So, if you don't mind me asking, what made you want to move on?' he asks, trying to strike up a conversation. You seem nice and all, Ed, but I don't think we're far enough down the line to tell you the 'cock-sock' story.

'You know, the academy system isn't great – it's all money and results-driven and I just wanted another challenge,' I tell him earnestly. He nods and leads me into the hall with its pristine parquet floors and tiered seating. We seem to have snuck in through the back door and the head has already started her spiel so we take some seats to the side. Oh, they're introducing new staff. That'll be me then. I only had my interview on the last day of the summer term so it all feels a little rushed but, hey, at least I wore my good shirt.

'And moving on to Modern Foreign Languages. We have Suzie Callaghan who is with us after a relocation from Brighton.' I was told there was another new starter in the department but I haven't met her yet. We'd been added to a lot of groups where I contributed to the conversations with a thumbs up, just to show I was paying attention. I've not been told much about her but I hope she's relatively young and will let me steal her pens. I look around for her and turn my head to the person standing at the back of the room.

Holy fuck.

I turn around again.

No.

Hold up.

'For those wondering, she is the cousin of the other Miss Callaghan which is lovely.' Cousins? I know her cousins. They're also here? What sort of a twisted ambush is this? I hold on to Ed's shoulder who is a bit disconcerted by the physical contact and lean over to see the person cheering on her announcement is Beth. I've met her. What the...

'And Charlie Shaw joining us from a school in West London.'

I can just stay seated. I'll just put a hand in the air. Can I crawl out of here?

'That's you, I believe,' Ed tells me.

'It is.' I stand up and face the front so she won't be able to see me.

'Come on, turn around so we can see you,' Alicia tells me.

I turn slowly and look up, and she's the first face I see. I'm overwhelmed with relief, fear and just plain confusion. She looks at me and does a strange yelping noise like a surprised bird. And I wave.

Hey. It's her. Aurelie.

. . .

'So, call me stupid, but do you two know each other? It felt like you knew each other,' our head of Modern Foreign Languages, Lee, asks both of us as we convene at the front of the room.

I sat down after my name was announced and didn't dare look back for fear I might turn to stone. That is her, isn't it? I know I took quite a large knock to the head in Mallorca but I've been given the all-clear and the wrist is better. Maybe there was a brain bleed and she's a hallucination. But as the briefing finished and Alicia had introduced all the new-starters, I turned to see her staring at me and really not looking very impressed at all. Seriously? And now, here we are, standing literally a metre away from each other. There's no mistake – it is her.

'No,' Suzie says. 'I just thought he looked familiar. Like someone from my yoga class, strangely enough...' She looks me directly in the eye as she says it.

'Do you do yoga, Charlie?' Lee asks, surprised, in his lilting Welsh accent. 'You don't look the sort.'

'I don't. Sorry, I felt the same, some strange feeling of déjà vu? Have you ever lived in Nice?' I ask her.

'No,' she replies, a little too sternly.

Lee looks back and forth between us, trying to work out the vibe. 'Well, I am excited for the year ahead. I know you're both super new so do come and talk to me if there are any problems and maybe we should have a little meeting after school? We can meet in room C2?'

'Of course, look forward to it,' I say.

'Sure thing,' Suzie says, before he walks away and we're left standing there in front of each other, both of us at a loss for words.

After what feels like a lifetime of staring at each other, she mumbles, 'Are you real?'

A teacher walks past us, 'Welcome to Griffin Road, guys!' We both smile then return to our face-off.

'Your name isn't Carlos?' she asks.

'Well, at least it's the Spanish version of Charles. Aurelie is nothing like Suzie,' I say, slightly angry that she's accusing me of lying to her.

'She was my French penpal when I was ten,' she blurts out.

I laugh in response but she doesn't take that well. She takes my arm and I try to ignore the feel of her hand on me as she leads me to a corner of the room. The other teachers continue to filter out of the hall. She leans in whispering into my ear, unfeasibly close to me... 'This isn't funny. This is a disaster. You... You lied.'

'So did you. Actually, your whole family lied to me. I know that cousin you were sitting with. Were you all just laughing at me?' I tell her.

She covers her blushing cheeks and mouth with her hands. 'I can't believe this. I really... how is this happening? Are you hot? Is this school hot, or is it me?' She runs a finger under her collar and I follow it, looking at the curve of her neck. Yeah, maybe now's not the time. 'How are we going to play this? We're in the same department, we're literally going to see each other every day. I'll just quit. I'm so embarrassed.'

My disbelief turns to resignation. Something this ridiculous would only happen to me. I try and put a hand out to calm her down but she moves away immediately, looking around to check who may be watching. She stops sharply to look at me. 'How the hell are we going to have this meeting? How can I look you in the face?'

And then resignation turns to sadness. Is she ashamed of what happened? Did she just want to leave it there on that island? Because I think about it daily. Not the sex. I mean, I think about the sex a fair bit. But I also think of a moment where two people met for the first time by the sea. I can hear the sea, feel the breeze on my face, and smell the salt. I vividly hold that image in my mind of this little sea nymph and her big brown eyes, her hair clinging to her face, pulling my T-shirt down so I wouldn't be able to see, making ridiculous jokes about my nipples and rolling in the sand. And now that sea nymph is here in a sensible midi dress and that memory clearly hasn't stayed with her the way it has with me.

'You're looking me in the face, right now,' I tell her.

'Car... Charlie... we've done stuff...' she whispers.

I smirk and she hits me on the arm. An art teacher walks past looking very confused.

'This is not professional. This is our first day and look, I need this job,' she informs me.

'Really? But what about your family champagne empire?' I snap back.

Her jaw goes slack as she stares me right in the eye. Maybe I was wrong about her. In Mallorca, I got warm and funny. I'm now getting cold and sarcastic.

'You were the one who didn't show up? The one who stood me up,' she tells me.

'I had a valid excuse.'

'Did you get stuck in a yoga pose?' she retorts.

I stop before this gets any more barbed. I don't know what to tell her.

I spent two days in hospital and when I was discharged, I went straight to that villa to look for her because she was all I could think about. Except she wasn't there. There was a German man at the gate in gold budgie smugglers who invited me in for 'party times' but I politely declined. And I tried my darndest to look for her. I trawled through every Aurelie from Nice on Facebook, and I shed tears as my plane was taking off from Mallorca knowing I'd lost her. I told Max it was indigestion.

'Hi!' I tear my gaze from her face to see the people who've

appeared next to us. One of them is my tour guide, Ed, and the other I recognise from the screensaver on his phone. She grins. 'I just thought I'd come and introduce myself. I'm Mia. I know Beth.' She points to the other side of the room where Beth stands, knowing to keep her distance. She keeps looking at me like she's seen a ghost.

'Nice to meet you, Mia,' I say, putting a hand out that she shakes animatedly.

'Suzie,' she says, still a little hot and flustered.

Mia notices it and puts an arm to her. 'I hate it when they do those staff introductions too. Making you stand up in front of everyone like a muppet.'

'Oh, it wasn't... I mean...' Suzie fumbles.

'Can I say though? It's brilliant to have some younger teachers in the school. Ed and I were trying to work out when the next gen were coming through. And which languages?'

'Spanish?' I say putting a hand to the air. 'I think Suzie may be... French?'

'Yeah,' she says, catching my eye and half smiling.

'Well, let's see what cunning linguists you both are, eh?' she cackles at her own joke. Ed closes his eyes in embarrassment. Suzie and I don't react. At all. Not one little bit.

NINE

Suzie

'And tell me what the ending of that word might look like?' I ask the class.

'It's got another e and an s, Miss,' the boy answers.

'Can you tell me why?' I say, my pen hovering over the smartboard.

'Because it's a lady word and there's more than one of them.'

I laugh under my breath. 'Feminine noun but yeah, excellent...'

'Josh, Miss.'

'I'll get there with the names eventually. Très bien, Josh.' I think he smiled at me and that today is a win after the largest baptism by fire you could imagine. Because imagine you're being baptised in all that fire and you also have one hundred and twenty children you have never met before watching, judging and waiting to be entertained at the same time. But Josh has saved this day, so I will give him an achievement point and hope that means I will be his favourite teacher, forever. 'And with that, let's pack up, folks. Dictionaries back where you found them, please tuck those chairs in.'

The kids do as they're told. There's still a silence that descends over the room because I'm new and it's the first day back, but to be fair, I expected worse with Year 10. I wait by the door and exhale loudly, waiting for the bell.

'Long day, Miss?' one girl asks, her hair bound tightly into plaits, the skirt perhaps three inches too short. I think her name is Poppy or maybe it's Polly. There are too many names to remember, there really are.

I nod. 'First day too so I'm a bit frazzled.'

'Time to go home and get the rosé out?' Josh, next to her, says.

I laugh. 'Possiblement. How was that by the way? The class? Was it OK?' I ask, hoping their judgement about my teaching isn't too harsh.

'You're cool,' the girl says, looking me up and down.

'Anything was going to be better than Monsieur Flock-It,' Josh says.

'Pardon me?' I ask.

'It was pronounced Flock-ay,' he says, waving his hands about, 'but truth is he was French, thought a lot of himself and he constantly smelt of wine.'

'I believe that's stereotyping,' I tell him.

'Ain't a stereotype if it's the truth.'

The classroom door open, the girl peers her head around to see the class down the way, also waiting to be dismissed. I daren't look because as luck would have it, the person teaching in that classroom is the last person I currently want to look at. I could literally hear him through the walls. The low rumble of his voice, the gales of laughter from his clearly captivated students.

'Isn't there a new teacher in there too, Miss?' the boy asks me.

Please don't blush, please don't blush. 'I believe there is. I only met him this morning.'

'Jacinda says he's quite fit. He looks like that actor from that thing.'

He looks like Aaron Taylor-Johnson if she really wants to know, but I won't say that out loud. 'No comment... Poppy, isn't it?'

'It is, Miss.' She glares down the corridor at the person waiting by the door. 'They think a lot of themselves, that Spanish lot.'

'Oh, is there beef?' I say.

'Oui, beaucoup de boeuf,' Josh says, laughing. 'They not like us.' And then, in an attempt to appear cool and with it, I may rap. Like Kendrick Lamar. Shit. Please find this funny instead of cringe. There's laughter. I can do laughter if it's at my expense and I win them over. 'You down with Kendrick, Miss?'

'Of course.' Before I can do any more harm, I am literally saved by the bell. 'À vendredi, au revoir tout le monde. Have a lovely evening,' I announce to everyone, as they start to file out of the room, at least 70 per cent of the room acknowledging me as they do. Thank you, Kendrick. Like I say, small wins.

I stand there, close my eyes and exhale softly. He's in the next room. Carlos. The man you thought had got away. But he didn't. There is literally a wall that separates you. Yet he's also not who he says he is and that feels like the biggest of red flags. I guess I lied as well though. I look down at my phone to see my phone ringing.

'Holy shit balls, please tell me you're still in the building. Are you OK? This is mad.'

It's Beth. I've barely looked at my phone all day. I've bounced from classes to line manager meetings to mandatory lunchtime duties and when I did have time to eat my lunch, to my shame, I ate it in the storage cupboard in my classroom because I thought if I went to the staffroom and saw Charlie/Carlos then I would actually die of embarrassment.

'I'm still here. I'm sorry. It's been a day,' I say, trying to keep my voice down in case he can hear.

'It's him, isn't it? Carlos is Charlie.'

'Yep.' It's horrible to even admit that much out loud.

'You don't think he's some weird stalker who followed you here?' she gasps.

'Well, I didn't think that before but thanks, Beth.'

She laughs. 'I'm sorry, this isn't supposed to be funny. Also... and don't hate me... but do you remember when we were in Mallorca and I thought he looked familiar...'

'Yes...' I say slowly.

'Turns out I had met him before. On his interview day, he couldn't find the toilets,' she admits sheepishly.

'BETH!' I shriek, immediately remembering I'm trying to be quiet.

'Don't hate me. I'm so sorry. So many people come in and out of this place. And I forget things. I left my son in a shopping trolley once and nearly drove away.' I want to laugh but this all feels completely ridiculous. 'Let me come to you now, I can bring biscuits?' she tells me.

'No, I have a department meeting.'

'With...?'

'Yes. I'm going to have to sit across from a man whose...'

'Dick...'

'Do not finish that sentence,' I shriek. 'We are in a school, Miss Callaghan,' I chastise her. But all I can hear is laughter.

'I've seen him naked, Beth,' I whisper.

'And? You've not met our PE department. They're particularly feral. Let me know when that meeting is over. I'll come and give you a hug. Love you.'

She hangs up. And now all I have at the forefront of my mind is Charlie's dick, his completely naked body. In the many,

many times I've thought of him since Mallorca I used to relish that image, it used to bring me joy but now? Now it would seem that for the next academic year, I'll have a constant reminder of someone I was incredibly sexually intimate with. Like so intimate. The things that man did. A shiver goes up my spine and I try and regain a sense of normality.

'We thought we'd come in here, Suzie?' a voice comes from the door. It's Lee standing there with a notebook tucked under his arm and behind him, the figure of someone familiar. *Hi there, I was just remembering what your dick looked like.*

'Yes, please come in...' I tell them. 'Is it just us?' I ask. 'I had hoped the rest of the department would be here.'

'Oh no,' Lee tells me. 'I thought as you were both new, I could just run you a few things on the books for the half term. Just us today so you can get to know each other. You both have similar work histories so I think you'll fit together well.' I glance at Charlie, who has a big grin on his face. Yes, we've fit together before. But I drew a line. I drew a line because I barely knew the man. I didn't even know his last name let alone his professional qualifications. Lee goes up to my computer to bring up the school calendar. I sit at a desk and Charlie comes to sit next to me. Seriously? How do I sit at this table so I don't have to look at him? Is it too much to ask him to face the wall? I look up. He puts a few blue biros on the desk. They go with your eyes. Stop that now, Suzie.

'So first days for both of you. How did it go? Any feedback?' Lee asks. I'll admit to quite liking Lee and his unerring enthusiasm.

'All good. A bit of a long and hard day,' Charlie explains. I look away. Long and hard. Long and hard. I cross my legs. If he's done that on purpose then I hate him. 'And I mostly did refresher lessons and basic stuff today but we're working from the in-house grammar booklets?' Charlie continues. 'And all the stuff on Teams?'

'Yes, helps to be on the same page,' Lee adds. 'You, Suzie?'

'Some nice classes. I just need to get off...' I glance at Charlie and see a smile creep across his face, '... early so I can go home, plan, prepare, get up to speed on a few things. I'd like to redecorate my classroom, is that OK?'

'Marvellous. Yes, please – go to town. Whatever you want. So I've made a handout of important dates you need to know. Charlie, can you give her one?'

We both freeze. Oh. Give me a handout. Yes, he can do that. He slips me one. Not like that. God, why is my mind deep in the gutter?

'Well, some other things on the calendar already. Charlie, mucho gracias for signing on for the Seville trip at half term.'

I look over at Charlie. How come he gets to go on a trip already? Not fair.

'But before then, speaking mocks, I'm afraid.'

'So soon?' I ask.

'Blame the exam boards. So some oral practice is required all round. Everyone's skills will be a little rusty,' Lee continues. I can't react because if I do then I will look like a child.

'How do you normally prepare for oral?' Charlie asks, completely poker-faced.

'We encourage lots of practise at home, with their peers. Actually, maybe both of you would like to run the club?'

'There's an oral club?' Charlie asks, completely straight-faced.

I can't talk. I will have to, though, at some point, so I don't look professionally inept.

'Mainly for the older ones. That would be a lovely thing for you both to collaborate on. Maybe I will leave that with you? Could you prepare some resources maybe?'

Charlie tries to catch my eye. Collaborate, that's something he and I have done before. Orally. Don't think about that at all.

'I can do that,' Charlie says. 'I have some great lessons built around oracy.'

I need to contribute here, don't I? 'I tend to use a lot of online stuff,' I add, my mouth completely dry. I look over and Charlie has written a note in his book. ORALLY RHYMES WITH AURELIE. He underlines it. I glare at him. 'Just so students can model the right sounds. I'll share some links.'

Lee stands there at the front of the room, smiling. 'You see... this is what this department needed. A bit of youth and energy, some new ideas. Two openings perfectly filled, in my opinion.'

Charlie puts a hand to his mouth to cover his smile.

'That's very kind of you to say,' I reply, proud of myself for keeping it together enough to respond so maturely.

'Well, let's bang the rest of this out. HR just want me to go through the performance review clauses on your contract and to make you aware of the FAP...' he says, turning to the screen. Charlie tries to catch my eye. Do not do that. Please. I can feel him next to me. Literally that same energy I felt when he was walking next to me at that beach. When we shared a bench on that plaza. When he leaned into me and told me that he could still taste me. This is both unfair and really bloody confusing. I can't seem to balance the two realities. How am I going to share class data with him when I know I've made jokes about his nipples, when we've both lied to each other. This doesn't feel like the foundation on which to build anything, let alone foster a collaborative working relationship.

'Sorry to interrupt, Lee...' Charlie puts a hand up in the air. I sit up straight in my chair. Is he going to say something about us? Does he have a need to give full disclosure as professional courtesy? Don't do that. Especially when I've not really had a say in that information being divulged. 'I just wanted to check how long this meeting will go on for?' he says, looking at his watch.

'Oh, it'll only be another half hour. I won't keep you from your family. Don't worry, we like you to be able to maintain that life/work balance.'

As soon as the words leave Lee's mouth, that energy that once lay between Charlie and I fizzles to a damp squib. *Family*. Family? I turn to him slowly. Carlos has a family. That explains a lot.

Charlie

In truth, we all have families, otherwise none of us would be here, right? But as soon as the words left Lee's mouth, I saw all that humour and light leave Suzie's body. I saw judgement. I saw someone who didn't want to hear my explanations. Instead, she did everything she could to continue chatting to Lee and to avoid me. She literally threw me out of her room afterwards. If she'd asked me to stay though, she'd have heard that I have a damn good explanation for everything. I didn't meet her at that beach because I got into an accident involving a mechanical bull. I do have a family; one that I am responsible for too. I see them now through the misty window of this restaurant, Brooke trying to persuade her brothers that a selfie is in order. She poses with the trademark pout and peace sign, takes a few and then chastises them for their efforts. I'm not surprised. Sam's hair looks like he's just rolled out of bed. Or maybe that's the style. He looks like a very tired llama. I'm trying to think when I last washed that hoodie.

I push against the door to enter. It's a Wednesday so the place is quiet, a large 1 and 5 balloon swaying to the middle where our party of four is sitting. They all cheer.

'Late much?' Brooke says, as I take off my coat.

'Some of us have to work in the real word, sis.' She replies by sticking her tongue out at me. 'Sammy boy, happy birthday.' I hand over my gift bag to him, ruffling his hair.

'That's an awfully small bag for a PS5,' he tells me.

'It's from me and Max,' I say, as I place my hands on Max's shoulders.

He puts his hand in the bag, pulling out a pair of AirPods instead. Like I needed more ways for him to ignore me. I see something that looks like a smile creep across his face. 'You're very good big brothers.'

'It has been said,' Max says.

'Cheapo here got me a Gregg's gift card,' he says, pointing at Brooke.

'Ungrateful. I thought it the more useful gift, given you're half sausage roll,' she retorts, sticking her tongue out at him. Max hits her over the back of her head. I stare at both of them to cut it out. 'First day back went OK?' I ask Sam.

He shrugs his shoulders. 'All a bit mid, truth be told. Having your birthday on the first day back feels like a very cruel joke too.'

'And Brooke, how was college?' I ask her. Brooke is the only one attired for the evening in a dress that's perhaps too brief, her blonde hair and make-up styled well. I never quite know how to tell her as her older brother though that she doesn't need any of it.

'I've got a timetable but they're talking about universities. I've got some dates for open days, can I book those in? Also, can you help me with my UCAS statement?'

I nod, as she studies my face. 'You look battered. How's the new school?'

Max pushes a beer in my direction and I take a very welcome swig on it. 'You've gone South London, I thought it might be marginally posher?' he tells me.

'Not by much really... the school is fine. I just...' I look over at Brooke, who gives me her full attention now. Brooke is the mirror image of our mum with that cheeky look in her eye that was always keyed in to gossip and wanting to know what was going on in people's lives. But it was empathy through and through. She puts her hands on my shoulders and rests a chin there. 'I bumped into someone I didn't plan to see there.'

'Was it that sus bitch, Krystal? I thought we got rid of her?' she adds.

'No, it's someone I met on holiday. Is that weird?'

All my siblings look at me curiously now. We went on a group holiday, camping in Devon. It was pretty quiet unless I'm referring to one of those pheasants who tried to get in our tent.

'Hold up, Mallorca?' Max asks, sitting up straighter in his seat.

'Pray do tell, big brother. You never shared this story with me,' Brooke says. I never shared because sometimes I am not sure how much I'm supposed to share with an eighteen-year-old sister who usually criticises the cut of my trousers and a fifteen-year-old brother who is far too young to hear about the details of my dating and sex life. I'll maybe give them an edited PG-13 version.

'It's a girl I...' I cough. 'Hooked up with in Mallorca and...'

'WHOA!' Max says a little too loudly so a table across the room jump as they eat their calzone. 'The French bird? How the hell?'

'Charlie "hooked up" with a French bird?' Brooke repeats. The looks on my younger siblings' faces read absolute horror.

'Was she fit?' Sam asks. Brooke hits him round the head with her napkin. 'It's my birthday and that is a pertinent question.'

I'm mildly impressed that Sam has used such a big word there. 'I guess,' I reply.

'Max, was she fit? Nice?' Brooke asks.

'I didn't meet her. What the hell was she doing at your school?' Max asks. The garlic bread arrives and all our hands go in so we have snacks to take in this little story.

'Oh, so it turns out she's not a French bird called Aurelie. She's a French teacher called Suzie.'

Max opens his mouth to take in the drama. 'And just out of sheer coincidence, you're both at the same school?' I nod slowly so we can all take that in. 'But didn't you give her a fake name too? You'll love this...' he tells the younger two. 'He told her his name was Carlos.'

I need say nothing ever again to my two youngest siblings because that rouses enough hilarity in this room to last them for a whole year. 'Breathe, Brooke...' I tell her as she struggles for breath.

'But why?' she asks.

'I have no idea anymore. We'd been speaking Spanish, and when she asked if I was Spanish I... I think I thought I was being mysterious, protecting myself, maybe?'

'Carlos?' Sam says in a thick Spanish accent, so we can get more laughs out of the situation. 'That's a better gift than the AirPods. So what are you going to do? You gonna carry on shagging?'

Brooke gives him a dirty look again. 'Samuel!'

I wince, remembering how everything transpired today. 'I don't think she was too happy to see me. We'll see how it goes.'

They all look at each other curiously. Yes, it's another instalment in the adventures of my love life, where the path of true love darts in many different directions. Did I ever dream of bumping into Aurelie/Suzie again? Of course. Maybe not in those circumstances, where I was ambushed on my first day in a new job. I imagined it might be on a random beach somewhere, perhaps a stylish café where my hair looked good. Now, I just get a sense of embarrassment and shock from her, to the point where I don't really know what to do.

'I need a mental image here,' Brooke says. 'Who does she look like?'

'Your girl, Sofia, from *Outer Banks*,' I suggest. Just more beautiful?

Brooke's jaw drops. 'That's quite hot, and kudos for the *Outer Banks* reference.' I had to bond with you somehow, little sister. 'So really this is quite cute, no? It's giving romance,' she says, whirling her hands around in front of her.

Sam pretends to retch whilst Max laughs in between sips of beer.

'No, hear me out. Maybe this is the universe's way of giving your little hookup a second chance? What were the odds of the two of you Londoners meeting up in Mallorca in the way that you did? And then meeting again. Both of you having applied for jobs in the same department, in the same school. I know I only got a 6 in Maths but the odds are pretty mega.'

That thought may have crossed my mind. What indeed are the chances of this being serendipity at work? The energy between the two of us being so strong that we were brought together again, like human magnets. The stars aligning, the universe screaming that we belong together. Perhaps. But then I've seen too much of real life to know that's not how it always works.

'You watch too much shite on Netflix,' Max tells her. 'Maybe Charlie will realise they're meant to be and he'll chase her across town and they'll declare their love for each other.'

'At the airport,' Sam adds.

'In the rain,' Max jokes. 'While a flash mob dances in the background.'

Brooke sits there sullen. 'Well then I'll have to teach Charlie the moves, you cynical twats,' she says. 'I just want our brother to be happy.'

I smile at her and nod my beer bottle in her direction. I am happy, kiddo.

'CHARLIE!' a voice suddenly interrupts from across the restaurant and the owner, Enzo, appears in his trademark white shirt, black trousers and shiny black loafers, coming over to say hello. I stand up to give him a hug while he pats my back hard, the sort of slap you'd use to release catarrh. 'Sammy, fifteen? I want to see some ID, young man.'

'I don't have any. I'm only fifteen,' he mumbles.

'I am JOKING!' he roars. 'How is everything? Have you ordered? I'll send someone over. Love you, kids. You have a nice evening, yes?' We all smile at the familiar volume and nature of his cheer but as he walks away, I slide away from the table to follow him to the bar.

'Enzo,' I call to him.

'Yes, Charlie. You are looking so smart? Are you still doing the teaching?'

'I am, started a new job today,' I tell him.

'Then it is a double celebration. I will send more beer to the table. How can I help, my boy?' he says, putting an arm around me.

'Did Max bring the cake?' I ask him.

'He did, it's around the back. I'll bring it through with the desserts?' he asks.

'As per usual,' I say. 'Thank you.'

He takes a minute to step back and look at me, putting his palms to the air. 'You're a double for your father, you know? It is astounding.' I take a deep breath and smile back. 'He and your mama would be so proud of you, you know? The way you are raising your siblings, the way you keep the family together.' The comment would be all the more heartrending if he wasn't slapping my cheeks at the same time. 'Beautiful boy.'

I look over back at the table. The option was that or shipping my ten- and thirteen-year-old siblings to my aunt in York. Brooke would have hated me forever. I don't know if I'm doing a good job. I don't know how my parents would feel about any of this this, but I think they'd like the fact we are still together, celebrating all our family birthdays in the same restaurant they used to take us to. I'll start tearing up if he doles out any more compliments so I pat Enzo back on the cheeks.

'Love you, Enzo,' I say.

'I love you more, Charlie boy.'

'Can I see the cake?' I ask him.

'Sure thing. I was bit surprised but Max said it was the last one in the shop. He thought it would be funny.'

Oh dear. I know Max's sense of humour. Please don't be rude. He beckons me to look beyond the bar at the mermaid cake below, complete with shells for boobs. I laugh under my breath. 'It's perfect.'

TEN

Suzie

'Dans la photo, il y a un grand chat.'

'That's right, there is a big cat in the photo, or we can use the word, un lion. Because it's a lion,' I tell the student.

'The French for lion is lion?'

'Well, not quite, try a 'lee' sound at the front. Like the town?'

The student looks at me blankly.

'Or we can stick with big cat, which is accurate.'

They nod and continue to look down at the picture. This afternoon is the first of my Voice sessions, my newly named club where students can come and practise their language skills after school. It's a decent turnout but I think that might be because I've bought biscuits and made posters on Canva on which I deliberately avoided the word oral for obvious reasons. The only thing missing is the other teacher who was supposed to be 'collaborating' on this project and who has been decidedly missing from this working relationship. Do you know how he's been answering my emails about this? With a thumbs up, which is the same sort of apathy you expect from a teenage boy. It tells me volumes about his character but then since last week, when I found out about his 'family', I'd already cast my assumptions. And in reality, it sucked because in my head, Carlos was some perfect man, someone I had put on a pedestal, and now all the layers are being peeled away to reveal someone who is work-shy and lazy. A smidge of internet snooping helped too because what did I find? A selfie of him with a kid. Charlie looked younger and the boy was about ten but I guess that could have been feasible. He would have been super young when he had him but, in reality, Charlie was a padre. This meant that there was possibly a girlfriend or wife out there. It explained a lot, too much, and lodged a huge seed of disappointment in my guts. There are some dynamics there which complicate matters. I don't want to break up a family or be a secret holiday fling. I don't want to be with a cheat. I've seen enough of that this year.

'Oh god, I'm so sorry. I'm so late, everyone. I got held up in a pastoral meeting and... I'm... oooh, biscuits...' Charlie enters the room like a whirlwind, placing his coat over mine, which strangely annoys me, and chucking his rucksack to the floor. He searches the room for me and does a weird salute action as his hand grabs two biscuits at a time. Two. Greedy and late. 'Where are my Spanish kids at?'

A table at the back of the room all put their hands up and he walks over to them, his hands going to the resources on the table. Yes, I made those laminated vocabulary support prompts that they are using. I made ones in Spanish too as I didn't want kids to miss out. Charlie sees them and turns to me.

'You bought Nice biscuits,' he says.

Is that it? Seriously? Is that how you are entering into this conversation with me?

'I did. They weren't for you. The Hob NOBS were for you,' I whisper so it's out of earshot.

He breaks into a smile. I wasn't being funny. I was trying to offend him. Instead, he puts a hand to his chest.

'I'm sorry I was late and I haven't really bought into this. I will be better, I promise. I will contribute. It's just been a killer first week.'

I try not to react but smile and return to the kids I was working with. We're just very different teachers. Organisation and preparation is my bag, and I guess when you have a family then your time and priorities are shaped differently. From what I've seen, Charlie is a run to the photocopier five minutes before the lesson kinda teacher, his worksheets all in Comic Sans, my personal teaching bugbear. That said, the kids really like him, which is annoying. He has a good teacher voice which I occasionally hear echoing through the walls and down the corridor, he calls the kids 'amigos', and I hear him playing his class random Spanish songs like '*Despacito*' which isn't on the curriculum but I will assume keeps the kids onside.

'Miss, how do I say annoying?' a student asks me.

Charlie overhears this and looks at me.

'Oh, you can say agaçant? Or my favourite is embêtant? Who are you talking about?' I ask the student.

'I'm preparing my questions about family. My brother. I want to say he cheats at games.'

I smile, my gaze returning to Charlie's. 'Then you can call him un tricheur or un fraudeur. Like the English word for fraud.'

Charlie laughs under his breath to hear that. 'Sorry to interrupt, do you know what the Spanish word is for cheat? Una tramposa.'

I feel my jaw drop a little to hear that. What did he just call me? 'Mr Shaw, I believe that's a feminine version of the word, he was talking about his brother and we're French here. You Spanish lot stay in your lane.'

There's a murmur of giggles as the kids pick up on the drama. Oh kids, if only you knew.

'My bad,' he says. 'Right, so the word for lion in Spanish is león like the restaurant with the overpriced porridge or the film from the nineties that none of you should have watched.'

'A French film...' I interrupt.

'Did someone hear something? Was it the French butting in again?' Charlie jokes.

Giggles now turn into cries of disbelief that we seem to have started a little war of languages here and I bite my lip because despite all this disdain I have for him, this is what attracted me to him the most, that little bit of electric banter that flowed so well between us.

'Miss, are you really going to let him talk about you like that?' a girl says.

'I tend to just ignore the Spanish. They're all talk, no...' I stop myself from completing that sentence.

'What's the French word for that, Miss?' an older kid asks me.

'Let's say *il péte plus haut que son cul*. He's a bit full of himself you know?' I smile.

There's laughter in the room as Charlie and I look at each other, I widen my eyes at him. He has not melted this ice yet. I'm still angry with him.

'Well, this is lovely. So great to see...' A voice suddenly sounds from the door. It's Lee, standing there, counting heads and looking at all this good work in action. He stops at a desk and picks up one of my laminated sheets. 'Mr Shaw, this is brilliant. I might steal this template for myself with all these Spanish sentence starters. Great work.' I look at Charlie, waiting for him to say something. He must say something. 'Keep up the good work, everyone.'

He disappears and I don't dare make any eye contact with Charlie in case my gaze kills him like icy lasers. I am not in the habit of outing colleagues in front of students or our seniors but I expect a little bit of professional decency. And yet again, another layer is peeled away. I look at my watch to try and hide my irritation. 'And everyone, we're coming up to four o'clock so let's start packing up. This has been so great, thank you for coming.' I look at Charlie at this point, a passive-aggressive smile plastered across my face.

The students start to filter out of the room and I walk around to collect my resources and put them away in my folder. I had hoped Charlie would have left with the kids but he lingers. I zip my folder up a little aggressively hoping he'll get the message.

'I'm sorry... I should have been a bit quicker to tell Lee that you prepared those sheets. I will correct that. That was wrong of me,' he says contritely. I look over to see the sincerity of a gaze I saw backlit by the Mallorcan sun. I need to snap out of this.

'I didn't do this for the gold stars, don't worry yourself.'

He continues to stand there, helping me straighten chairs and pick up pen lids off the floor, looking like he's actually doing some work. 'You think I'm lazy – the person in the group who doesn't do the work and takes all the credit?'

'The one who wings his way through the day and ends up getting to go on trips to Seville.'

He furrows his brow at my remarks. 'You don't know me, that's a little unfair. I am happy to contribute to this moving forward, give you your flowers for all of this.'

'Like I say, I didn't do this for the extra credit,' I say. I remove his coat from mine and start to pack up my things, pretending to look at my phone.

'Suzie...' he murmurs. Is it terrible that I hate how he says my name? That his voice is like an echo within me, that I actually respond physically to it. 'We've got to sort this out.'

I shrug. 'That's oversimplifying it a bit.' I stand still, rooted to the spot. I'd done a good job of avoiding him so far, of keeping some distance whilst I tried to work out what this is between us, but the truth is he's not the person I thought he was, and that's a little bit upsetting. I don't have enough energy or goodwill to deal with the aftermath of the failings of yet another man. Only this morning, I got another email from Paul, still trying to invade my inbox with what I now call split spam. It's him trying to start a conversation about nothing, to reel me back and I don't want anything to do with it. Or Charlie. It feels far simpler to do life alone right now. 'You called me una trampa.'

'It was all bants, Miss.'

He's trying to make me laugh. I don't like that. He heads over to the end of my desk as I wrestle with putting my coat on.

'You weren't like this in Mallorca,' he says, and I gasp, picking up a white board pen on the desk and throwing it at him in shock. Mallorca feels like a secret code word that shouldn't be said out loud.

'Oww?' he says, laughing. 'Are we not supposed to say that word?'

'It's just...' I mumble, trying to find the words. 'I just... I'd drawn a line under what happened in Mallorca,' I whisper.

'Because you just wanted a holiday fling?' he asks.

'No,' I say indignantly, finding my voice trembling a little. 'Because you never showed up the next day, you never gave me a number or a last name, so I parked it all. I'm old enough now to know sometimes men are like that. You just sleep with someone and move on. But now you're here... and you're...' I can't quite find the word. 'You're late.'

'I had a valid excuse.'

'You said that about Mallorca.'

He forces a laugh under his breath. 'Well, today I had to have a conversation with a mum about her Year 7 kid who's not settling in well and I didn't want to cut that sort of conversation short. In Mallorca, I was in hospital. Had a nasty fall, concussion and a broken wrist,' he explains.

I stop for a moment as he holds up said wrist and shows me a small scar. 'Really?'

'Really.'

'So I'll assume you're not a native Mallorcan. You were there on holiday?'

'A stag do for my brother.'

'Ouch,' I tell him. 'That part about those girls being my cousins is true. We were there celebrating Meg's fortieth.'

'The cousins who grew up in London?' He shakes his head, chuckling, and I know what he's thinking. I lied too. 'I rang the villa. I tried to leave a message but I told them to contact the French party who had rented the place so I'll guess that message never got to you,' he tells me.

'It didn't.'

We both sigh loudly and hold each other's gaze. It's clear now why our dalliance came to such an abrupt end. However, there is more that complicates this situation.

'What about your family?' I say quietly. 'You have a kid? Kids?'

He laughs. 'I thought that might have tipped the balance a little too. You didn't really give me time to explain that.'

I go silent because, next to the deceit, I can't help feeling sadness at the thought that he belongs to someone else.

He creases his brow; I assume because he's trying to concoct some bullshit story. I've been here before. 'The abridged version is that I am the eldest of four siblings. Our parents died in a car crash when I was twenty-two and I have legal responsibility for all of them, but the youngest two especially, who are eighteen and fifteen. Their names are Brooke and Sam.' He exhales then walks away from that desk to put something in the bin.

I don't have an answer. If he made that up then that is bloody impressive, but I feel a surge of emotion knowing that it's true. Is that why he lied? He has people depending on him. Now I feel bloody awful.

'Suzie,' he says, approaching me again. 'Whatever you think of me, I never parked Mallorca. I think about it all the time. When I saw your face in that assembly, do you know what it was like for me?'

'Shock?' I mumble, laughing.

'Magic. Like a wish had been answered. Like you just reappeared out of nowhere. Pouf!' I bite my lip when he says pouf because there is a hand action to match and his words make my jittery heart a little calmer. 'I get the anger, but know I never intended to lie or keep anything from you to hurt you. That's not what I do.'

Why is he looking at me like that? Why is he being nice? I'm angry with him. I laminated things. I made a poster today to which he made zero contribution. His eyes are so intensely blue I can't look away, can't speak.

'Look, we can't take back what happened. Happy to park it all if you want. We can just be colleagues with history and I will never speak of any of it again.'

'Peut-être,' I mumble.

He exudes a sad smile. 'You're not French now, you don't have to pretend to be something you're not, to feel something you don't...'

I pause. 'Oh, I was never pretending...' I tell him, before cupping my hands to my mouth.

'I heard you. I didn't think you were...' he mumbles.

Am I red? I feel like I could be a bright shade of rose at this point. And in a rush of sheer need, I walk up to him, my heart pounding to feel so close to him again. He looks down and I put a finger to his chin, a hand to his cheek and kiss him. I remember this. Too well. There are so many times I close my eyes to search for the memory of this feeling, I feel it everywhere like static, like a wave drowning me in pleasure.

'Hello! Hello!' a chirpy voice calls from the doorway and we part immediately, jumping back to see a lady in a pinafore dragging a hoover behind her. 'I am here to empty your bins and clean up. Are you staying?'

Charlie exhales gently, his gaze not leaving mine.

'No,' I tell her. 'We were just leaving.'

Charlie

Does this school have CCTV? This feels like something I should double-check for safeguarding and my professional interests. I just kissed someone on school grounds. That's not great. I mean, it's not as bad as the whole faculty seeing me on a big screen dancing around with a thermal sock on my penis but I'm new here; I think kissing in classrooms is generally frowned upon.

I can't quite believe that just happened.

And just like I can't believe that I'm here, in Suzie's flat, sitting on a very new teal corduroy sofa. And that just wasn't some random kiss. This is Suzie. This is someone I thought I had lost. This is, according to Brooke, stars aligning and the universe speaking. And we've cleared this all up. We know what happened now, there really is nothing getting in our way from being together. I felt that spark between us in that classroom, I felt it in every inch of me, that familiar banter bouncing between us, the yearning and craving for her again. It all makes sense. I look around her flat, the jaunty angles of her matching throw cushions, a few photos on a shelf, one which looks like her and all her cousins. I tilt my head to one side to look at her reading habits. David Nicholls, I read that one on holiday.

'Hola,' I say, as she re-enters the room with two bottles of beer.

'Bonjour,' she replies, smiling.

I can't quite look away from her, not quite believing that's the same naked girl from those rocks on the beach and she's here. All the little things I remember about her still remain, the way she bites the edge of her thumbnail, a little freckle just above her upper lip. She comes to sit next to me and clinks the top of my bottle.

'So, this is where you live?' Good work, Don Juan. Of course this is where she lives otherwise why would we be here? I think I might be nervous.

'Yeah,' she replies. 'It's been about three months now.'

'I like your curtains? Where are they from?' I ask her. My sexy talk seriously knows no bounds.

'Dunelm. They were made to measure.'

'What colour would you say that is?'

'I think it's seafoam,' she replies.

There is no innuendo here is there? I don't know what to do next so I turn to her, our knees touching. I need to choreograph this a little better. I take her bottle of beer and go to put the bottles on a side table.

'Could you use a coaster?' she asks me.

'Of course,' I tell her, understanding why. That's a new table and condensation would not be great for it. I put the bottles down and return to her. There was spark in that classroom, we can recreate it again. I lean forward, putting a hand to her cheek, before kissing her gently. She kisses me back. But strands of her hair graze against my face. I pull back. 'Tickles,' I say. She looks at me strangely, half laughing but goes back to kiss me, cupping her hands around my chin.

Don't get me wrong, the kissing is nice but something is different. Maybe both of us are anxious or I've spoiled this by asking about her curtains, but there's something missing. In that classroom, the words flowed so nicely, the back and forth, the anticipation of something more but that doesn't seem to be replicated here.

'Do you want to...?' I ask.

I see the look in her eyes. I kiss her neck instead, hoping it might stir something, to feel the curve and warmth of her skin under my lips. She lets out a noise. I know that noise. That noise is polite, but it's not into this. I look into her eyes trying to work her out. But she leans over and reaches over my groin area, rubbing against my crotch. OK, she does want this? Let's do this. We did it in Mallorca and we were good at it. Shall we go to the bedroom? She's unzipping my trousers so maybe we can do it here. This is a ground-floor flat. Will people be able to see in? I'm overthinking this. I'm not in the room.

I unbutton my trousers as she still kisses me, fumbling with buttons and flies, doing my best to give her access. 'Is that OK?' she asks, as she grabs on to my penis. That's always pleasant so I nod, smiling. I don't want to ask for too much. But I remember a moment in a villa where she held on to it and licked the side of it and I thought I was going to explode with desire. I close my eyes to think back to that but I should be here, now. With her.

She stops, looking me in the eye. 'Do you have a...'

'Condom? Of course.'

Is it awful that I always have one in my wallet? Is that presumptuous? I faff around with the back pocket of my trousers to get it and rip it open with my teeth, putting it on slowly and deliberately. Even this feels slightly awkward. In Mallorca there was laughter, her kissing me as I did it, doing it for me herself, watching my face as her hands glided over me.

When she sees it's on, she starts to roll her tights and knickers down to her knees. 'Hold up, I'll just take these all off so it doesn't get in the...'

'Yep,' I reply. 'Good idea.'

We both take off the clothes covering our bottom halves, in a strange and routine way like two people undressing in a changing room. I want to be tidy and not just toss my belongings around randomly so I fold my trousers and underwear neatly and place them on a sofa arm. Then we both sit there for a second, half naked. My naked arse is on her sofa and it's brand new. I don't know why I'm thinking about that. She then leans back into the sofa, putting her knees up. 'Yeah?'

'Umm, yeah?'

OK, we're doing this. I climb on top of her, trying to angle myself correctly as she pulls her skirt around her waist. Should we get more naked? I'll let her take the lead on that. I slide a hand over her vagina. Yeah, she's not very aroused. I don't know how to feel about that.

'Do you want me to go down on you...?' I ask her, sitting back.

'Or I could...' She puts a hand down and fingers herself gently and quietly, looking slightly ashamed that she's not as aroused as me. I am aroused and evidence of that is sitting between us quite awkwardly. Should I kiss her? Hum a tune? I don't know how to break this unease and it's slowly killing me. 'Yeah, just let's go and I'll get into it.'

I don't know what that means. She lies back on the sofa and I hold the base of my penis, lying on top of her, entering her gently. We both sigh at the same time. OK. Please remember how good we both were at this. Maybe we just don't have enough vitamin D in our systems. It's only about fifteen degrees outside. I kiss her, hooking an arm under one of her knees, maybe I just need to hit that right spot, get deeper.

'Maybe a little left,' she tells me.

'Me or you?'

'You,' she whispers.

'My penis or my whole body?'

'Your whole body.'

'Here?'

From the look on her face, that might be a no. I think we might both be in shock. Maybe we'd built this up too much. Good sex will do that. It will warp your sense of space and time, giving you a moment that you'll never be able to live up to. This isn't good sex. She knows it and I know it. We're too scared to admit it to each other. Is it terrible that I can hear people on a pelican crossing outside?

'You're so pretty...' I tell her, looking her in the eye, trying to give the occasion a bit more sincerity.

'So are you...' she tells me. 'That's the wrong word. This feels good.'

Not amazing, not superb, not any other type of superlative. Good. That's the word we give kids who are just coasting, who are average in the classroom. I mean, it's not awful but this isn't Mallorca.

She smiles at me and wrinkles her nose. 'This is all off, isn't it?'

I nod sheepishly, still looking at her and still inside her. 'I can't...'

'Yeah, do you want to exit the...' she asks.

I nod my head and withdraw from her, my dick just sitting there woefully between the two of us. 'You're beautiful,' I tell her. 'I want this. I've wanted this since that villa, and I can't believe I've found you again, but...' I say, hoping I sound reassuring and authentic.

'No, I get it. I want it too but there's something...'

'Missing?'

'Yeah.'

I don't think either of us are upset or offended, but more confused. We have bags and spades and great big sacks full of spark. When I return to memories of this woman, I can go hard in seconds. But what just happened there?

In my fantasies, I think about ripping her tights off with my teeth and burying my face in her. I want to fuck her against a wall and cover her mouth when she wants to come to subdue her screams. Why didn't that happen? Is it me?

I look down at my penis again, slowly descending from position. I take off the condom and reach down to pick up the wrapper.

'Tissue?' Suzie offers, reaching to a coffee table. I wrap up the condom and hold it in my hand.

She looks into space, disappointment etched in her face, then reaches over to put her knickers back on.

'I'm sorry,' I mumble.

'Christ, don't apologise,' she says, giving a shy smile. 'It was probably a bad idea. You said those nice things and then I kissed you and I think we're both just...'

'Anxious?'

'Exactly.'

I pull my pants and trousers up, doing up my top fly button. I didn't even see her boobs. 'Maybe we needed to warm up to this, go for a drink. We still hardly know each other really. For example,' I say, panicking, 'I don't know your likes, dislikes?'

'I like you. That much I know,' she says.

'I like you too.'

Even saying those words out loud doesn't feel right. Maybe we just needed to work our way up to this in the way normal humans connect in the real world. They go for dinner, coffee, they find out details about each other, their personalities link up. Perhaps we ran into this too soon, too eager to recreate a moment. But there's also a silence and I wonder if in the back of her mind she's thinking what I'm thinking: what if that moment is gone? That would be awful.

'SUZIE! You in there, girl? You got hot water? I think something's wrong!' a strong West Indian accent vibrates through the door, a hand knocking repeatedly.

Suzie grabs at her tights and throws them across the room. I straighten my shirt quickly and place the half-used condom in my pocket. The whole room is a frenzy. This is the energy we needed four minutes ago.

'It's just my neighbour,' she tells me. 'Hold up, Maureen!'

She looks all around the room to check we've not left anything too incriminating lying around and goes to open the door. When she does, there's a lady standing there in a towelling robe and a shower cap.

'Do you have hot water? I don't have hot water. I'm trying to work out if it's the whole floor, if so I'll call the management company, if not...' She suddenly sees me sitting there. 'Ooh, child. You have company. Close your eyes, boy.'

I put my hands over my eyes. 'I wasn't looking, I promise.'

The lady pauses. 'You know about hot water?' she asks me.

'I could have a look?' I tell her, realising I also have my eyes closed under my hands.

'Hold up,' she says, walking up to me. 'You're not Paul, are you?'

I am unsure whether to reply as I can sense anger in her tone. Given the fire coming off her, I'm glad that I'm not Paul.

'Oh god, no,' Suzie says. 'Maureen, this is a work colleague, Charlie. Charlie, this is Maureen,' Suzie intervenes.

'He's nice-looking, girl,' she says.

'Maureen, he's got his eyes covered, not his ears,' Suzie loud whispers and I laugh.

'Thank you though, Maureen. I appreciate the compliment.'

The room goes a little quiet though I can hear hushed whispers as they argue about something. I don't know if I should move my hands or if I should tell them it's likely a fuse if their hot water is electric. But as they stand there working out what to do, there's only one question in my mind? Who the hell is Paul?

ELEVEN

Suzie

The mattress undulates up and down, the waves rolling in line with my spine, my arms firmly by my side.

'I think it's too soft.'

I don't answer.

'No purchase, it needs to be firmer. Let me change position and see if it makes a difference.'

'It won't. You're right, it's too soft. I'll do my back in on this,' I say. I turn my face to the side to see an Asian family watching Lucy curiously as she bounces on the mattress like a cat. Probably not what IKEA anticipated when they invited us to try out their mattresses. But I guess they've never met my cousin.

'You talk about your back like you're an old woman,' she tells me, lying still for a moment and turning to her side, propping her head up with her hand. I still lie there looking at the ceiling of this IKEA, that Asian family still waiting patiently to try out this mattress we're lying on.

'Come and do Pilates with me. There are machines, we'll stretch you out,' she says.

'I wouldn't think you needed a machine to stretch you out?' I jest.

She grabs a cushion from behind us and hits me over the head. 'That's the Suzie I know and love. Come on, let's try that big king size.'

She crawls off the bed, holding two hands out to lift me up. In the king size, a couple lie there holding hands, trying out the mattress and smiling. It's all so wholesome.

'You think you're going to hold hands in bed when you're married?' Lucy tells them. 'What you need to do is practise sleeping with your backs to each other looking at your phones, ensuring there's space for a toddler to fit in between you, working out if you can get far enough away from him when he drops an absolute bazooka of a fart.'

The couple look at Lucy half smiling but also annoyed that she would want to disrupt their perfect IKEA date. They move on, Lucy happy that her words worked and she jumps on like a wildcat, landing in a star shape. 'This is why I don't have a partner.'

'Because you sleep in that position?' I ask.

'I don't want to share a space where I'm supposed to be resting.'

'Budge up,' I tell her. I slide in next to her and again feel the mattress under me as she jumps about. There's less undulation with this one. Without wanting to be too Goldilocks about it, I think this one is too firm. I roll over multiple times as an IKEA staff member in their sunshine yellow T-shirt looks on curiously.

In my haste, when I rented my new place in London, I got a really rubbish mattress from Amazon that came vacuum packed and which I swear was stuffed with the same filling they put in stuffed animals so I'm here looking for a replacement. All I knew was that I didn't want to do something like this alone, and Lucy was the answer. IKEA alone is painful for the soul; it's always filled with couples, cheekily posing in the kitchens, sitting in fake dining rooms discussing their futures. In that respect, Lucy was the best person to tag along.

'So, you started your story about the sex but you didn't finish it,' Lucy tells me, on the hunt for morsels of juicy gossip. The other reason I've asked Lucy here is she is the only person I can talk to about the confusing recent sex debacle I experienced.

I stare at the ceiling. 'So yeah, it was just...'

'Shit?' Lucy says.

I manage a whisper of a laugh. 'Shit is harsh, it's not that I didn't want to be there. I liked being in that position,' I tell her.

'What position is that then?' she asks, her eyes lighting up to be getting to the juicy stuff.

'We were on the sofa, missionary,' I explain. She nods to tell me she can visualise such a position. 'But it was nice to be there with him. Does that sound soppy?'

'Yes.' A couple walk past our bed watching us curiously. Lucy stares them down, 'Did you say you had ringworm, should we be lying on this, honey?' They walk away.

'It just lacked a bit of spark. A bit of oomph,' I say, punching the air. 'We kept talking through it, we took off our clothes very politely. It wasn't like Mallorca, it was just a bit...'

'Shit,' she repeats. I hit her with a cuddly dinosaur toy that's on the bed. 'Babe, we've all been there. I've had more disappointing shags than this place has meatballs.'

I laugh. That's a lot of meatballs. 'But what I don't get is that Mallorca was not shit. It was the other end of the spectrum. It was some of the best sex I've ever had, full stop. No notes. We were totally in sync,' I tell her, my voice lowering to a low whisper to keep it appropriate for the families in the vicinity. 'You know that sort of sex where you're in the moment, it's just...'

'Feral, primal, take me now, orgasms in your eyeballs?' Lucy says.

'Well, in so many words, yes...' I say. She howls with laughter and I have no choice but to laugh back.

Lucy sits up and crosses her legs. 'Look, we know Mallorca was good. No need to brag but isn't that just holiday sex?' she explains. 'Holiday sex is all heat and nudity, no one is wearing very much, we're all drunk and liberated and want to play out sex fantasies in the sand. Even the smell of suncream is an aphrodisiac.' She lies back again and nods. 'Yeah, if I had to list some of my best sexual experiences, they've probably all been on holiday.'

'You took a while to go through the ol' mental Rolodex there, cuz.'

'Cheeky bitch.' She sits up to look out across the showroom. 'Look at that couple over there,' Lucy says, looking at a pull-out bed across the way where the man has a paper tape measure trying to gauge the dimensions. The lady sits on it gently, rubbing her hand over the linens. 'I bet on Saturdays they come here, pick up some tealights, a new colander and think about what bed to put in the spare room. "We could put blankets in this drawer, Janet,"' she says, mimicking the man's voice. I'm not sure why he's Northern but we'll go with it. 'They'll drive home and decide what to have for dinner and then go to sleep in sensible pyjamas. Him with his snore strips and her with a Horlicks and a Mills & Boon.'

They stand there, him with his hand on his chin, turning to a bed with a fancier wrought-iron frame.

'But I bet they go to Lanzarote once a year, get to a villa and they let loose. They have sex on the deck, she gets her baps out and they probably do stuff that their three-bed bungalow has never seen before. "Oooh, Janet, put it up my bum, just like that, love."' I can't stop laughing. Janet and her husband look over curiously at us. 'So how did you leave it? Are you sexting? Chatting?'

I shake my head. That was a fortnight ago. We didn't talk about it, he didn't stay. He helped Maureen fix her hot water and she offered him a drink to say thank you but he didn't take it. He didn't finish his beer. He just said he had a lot of marking and left. Since then we've been polite at work. We've sat across each other in departmental meetings, joined in group conversations in the staffroom and waved to each other in the car park. But it feels like both of us are too disappointed to admit that we were good on holiday but under the harsh spotlight of real life, when we weren't Carlos and Aurelie, then it was really quite average and that's a horrible, horrible word.

'Well maybe that's just the end of that then. You lock in Mallorca for any time you want a wank and some inspiration and maybe just friendzone him so you can survive at work,' she tells me.

'Surely it's not that simple?' I ask her.

'Hun, I don't believe in spark, magic, all that gubbins. I think you can have that with a multitude of people. Personally, after the year you've had, I would just look at options, shag about. How is Paul the Prick anyways?'

I love how she says his name so casually but it still unsettles me. In the same way you feel when you eat a bad prawn. This was exactly the kind of thing we used to do together: IKEA. We'd walk hand-in-hand around this place and sit in fake living rooms and try out all the sofas. It sometimes still seems bizarre that that life doesn't exist anymore, that he's not here, that he opted out.

'I wouldn't know. We're not in touch,' I say bluntly, knowing it's a slight lie. The fact is I continue to keep moving, to not look back, but he's still trying to flag me down and get my attention with emails, the occasional text. It's infuriating, annoying, boring. I want to move on, not with Charlie per se, but he lingers.

'Good. You know, every night I pray that something awful happens to him. Like that girl from *Game of Thrones* who has her hitlist of people she wants to avenge. I list them all as I sleep.'

'What do you pray for?' I ask, amused.

'Oh, minor annoyances. That every time they go on holiday their luggage gets lost, herpes, ingrown hairs on their face.' I laugh. 'Am I putting Charlie on that list then?'

'Nah. Leave him be for now,' I joke. I continue to look up at the IKEA ceiling with its silver aircon vents and messily wired ceilings. I wonder if I'm sad because it wasn't just sexual spark, it was conversation and laughter and feeling completely at ease with him. *Estás a salvo conmigo.* That was what he first said to me when I was bobbing around in the sea trying to work him out. You are safe with me. I felt that, whether it was in his arms or sitting on a bench with him eating bunyols. It's a hard feeling to ignore or throw away. It's sad that this might be the end of all that.

'Ummm, the idea is that you try the mattress and move on,' a cross-looking lady says, hovering over us with her husband. 'You and your girlfriend have been on there for far too long, just having a chat it would seem. It's rude and inconsiderate to all the other customers here.'

Lucy puts a hand to my shoulder, looking around the couple.

'I'm so sorry, is there a queue?' she retorts, then turns to me. 'I think this one is a good choice, honey bear. When we're scissoring, I think it'll give us some good leverage.'

I close my eyes, trying not to laugh. The woman's husband doesn't know where to look. 'Lawrence, LAWRENCE... go and get a member of staff.' The woman drags her husband away towards a person in a yellow shirt.

'We're going to get thrown out,' I tell Lucy.

'And...? What a story for the ages. My nieces will love it. Meatballs first though, yeah?'

I smile. I haven't even picked a mattress yet but maybe we can loop round through this labyrinth for refreshments. As I stand, I look over at Janet and her husband buying their sofa bed. They sit on the mattress together, laughing, his arm around her as he kisses her on the forehead, her eyes closed.

'It's those two over there...' the angry woman's voice screams out.

Yeah, we better loop round.

Charlie

'Is this your boyfriend then?'

Brooke turns to the tour guide and then back to me and starts making very swift retching noises. 'Oh god, no. He's my brother, eww!'

I also scrunch my face up at the insinuation. The guide either thinks I look young or that I'm some older man after a teenager and all of it just gives ick factor. To try and reinforce the point, I shove Brooke in the arm and she pushes me back.

'I'm sorry...' the tour guide tells us, resplendent in a yellow university campus T-shirt. 'Do you still want one of these?'

'Yes,' Brooke says, 'I think that's compensation for the trauma you've just put me through,' she says, grabbing at the tote bag on the table and peering inside, not before taking one for me too and handing it to me.

'Brooke, no...' I tell her as we make a very swift departure from the foyer. 'I'm too old to be carrying a bright yellow tote with #TOTESFUN on it.'

'You're not old, and there are free phone chargers in there so suck it up,' she tells me, hooking an arm into mine.

Today, we've ventured over to a university open day in East

London. It's involved a trek to some Instagrammable food van and a shoe shop to look at vintage trainers, so I hope the university thing wasn't a ruse and education is at the forefront of Brooke's distractable mind.

'So what are we looking for?' I ask, skimming through a brochure in my hand. I scan the room and it's a mix of parents looking earnest and enthusiastic, and confused kids being dragged around being sold the dream that this could all be theirs.

'Cute boys and coffee shops with seating, no?' she tells me.

'You could have just gone on forums and YouTube for that sort of information,' I tell her.

She grins at me with big giant teeth. 'I joke. I'm so funny.'

'According to you...'

'There's a talk in psychology at eleven thirty and I want to check out some accommodation and the people on the year abroad scheme,' she says, showing me a note on her phone where she has it all planned.

Brooke is our mum, from the desperately curly hair to the way she cheerleads everyone in her life with her unwavering positivity. In a house of three boys who sometimes deal with life in flatulence jokes and sweatpants, she's made us presentable to the outside world, ensuring we have some female influence in our lives.

'Your nose looks so nice since I did that face mask on you, you know?' she says, putting a hand to my chin and examining my face. She also spends her weekends preening me in the absence of having other females in the house to share these rituals with. My pores are far more refined for the experience.

'I have also been seeing the benefits,' I say, to which she smiles broadly. We join a stand where someone is talking about the student union and the many club nights they have here on a weekly basis. My heart pangs to hear that information; I miss nights like those with their two-pound pints, but it's also because this is part of my little sister's future. It's a mix of fear and pride.

'Is this what Warwick was like then?' she asks me.

'Warwick was lovely and green and a little university campus isolated from the world, this is...'

'Grim?' she asks.

'Quite the opposite. You're in the thick of it, you can go to a club night and then head for salt beef bagels, five minutes that way. I think a city university is more your jam,' I tell her.

'Are you calling me some rowdy city type?' she asks, laughing.

'I'm saying that you need somewhere that will keep all of this entertained,' I say, pointing at her up and down. And close to us, but I don't dare say that aloud. Brooke leaving home would be a big shift in our dynamic. When Max moved in with Amy, it was only fifteen minutes down the road and he's still a huge part of our lives, but Brooke going will leave a massive gap. I wonder how Max will cope. I also worry for my pores.

We wander along a big hall with tables set up for societies, student finance and volunteer schemes and I see her face light up as she takes it all in, wanting to be a part of it.

'You never told us what happened with that girl from your school, by the way?' she says, as she saunters along, stuffing flyers and free chocolates in her tote. I thought we were supposed to talk to these university people before we take their freebies. Maybe not.

'Nothing,' I say, reluctant to give too much away, knowing that ultimately she's my sister and some of the detail of my last sexual encounter with Suzie can be kept from her.

'Really?' she says, disappointment in her voice. 'But the way Max tells that story, you cried when you came home from holiday thinking you were never going to see her again. He said you texted him every day for two weeks to see if she'd got in touch. You must have been happy to see her again.' I turn to

Brooke and pull a face. 'What? Max and I have coffee dates in the daytime when you're at school. He tells me things. I'm helping him plan his wedding.'

'I was not crying. I'm a little scared of flying and had indigestion.'

She raises an eyebrow. 'Liar. You're a big old softie. You cried during *Inside Out*.'

'That was a sad film,' I argue.

'We were in a cinema. You scared the children,' she tells me, laughing.

She reaches into her free tote to find sweets and rips the packet open, carefully deciding which ones I'm allowed to have. 'So the French teacher is a no-go then? It was all sounding so promising.'

'Well, I think all that promise was based on a one-off experience. Now that I'm working with her and seeing her in an everyday light she's...'

'Proper minging?' she says.

'No.' She's still attractive to me physically but the incident from a few weeks ago haunts me. It makes my penis sad and I didn't think my penis could have feelings like that. Why didn't it work? There was some conversational run-up to it all, the back and forth was flowing, it felt like it was still there, but in the harsh light of the real world, it didn't seem to work. Neither of us showed up. I shrug, hoping I look unbothered. 'Maybe it was just a fling, the spark sizzled out in Mallorca. Mistake to think something like that could have translated over here.'

'Translated,' she says, pointing at me. 'I see what you did there with your words.' I laugh, watching as she dismisses a person trying to tell her about the board game society. 'But it seemed like the stars aligned, no?' asks me.

'Sometimes I think fate just has a funny sense of humour. It saw me having uninhibited holiday sex with a stranger and thought, hey, wouldn't it be funny if you bumped into her again?'

Brooke pulls a face. 'Too much information, brother. I don't need to think about that. Were you one of those awful Shagaluf types who did it in the club toilets?'

'What do you take me for?' I say slightly offended. 'I had classy sex.'

'Like with a bow tie?'

'And a monocle.' I can't go into the sex, at least not with my little sister, but it was only respectable in that we did everything in private.

'So there's no chance that it might work out?' she asks me.

I see the hope in her eyes, the dream of a big romantic happy ending. I like how she wants that for me.

'I think the moment may have passed. So sorry to disappoint your visions of a YA Netflix series...'

She shrugs her shoulders. 'And is there anyone else interesting in this school?' she asks me curiously. The problem with Brooke is that she takes an unhealthy interest in my love life and always has done. When she was sixteen, she signed me up for My Single Friend and in what felt like some dodgy romcom plot, she spoke to several women, auditioning them to be my wife, writing under my profile that I always wore good shoes. *No old man loafers on this one.* That said, she was also the one who suggested I ask out Krystal when really I should have understood our incompatibility from the start and given her a wide berth.

'You know, Brooke... maybe this is the universe's way of telling me to take a break from dating. Focus on my career for a bit.' The look she gives me in reply is not impressed. 'I can spend more time with Max. We can do boy things like get season tickets for football and...'

'Eat kebabs every night and fart on each other's pillows.'

Her sullen reply makes me smile, but it also makes me

realise something. 'Brooke, are you always so intent on setting me up with someone because you're worried about leaving us without a woman in the house?'

'No,' she says sternly, before secretly smiling. Busted.

'We will cope without your all-knowing, all-graceful female presence. And we will miss you intensely but I promise we will continue to do all the good things you taught us to do.'

She looks pleased that we'll miss her. It will be strange not to have her around but not to the point where I should be simply replacing her.

'And I'll print a really big picture of you and put it on the fridge,' I tell her.

'That is a such a good idea. You can look at it every time you're about to think Peperami and chips is an acceptable dinner,' she says, hooking her arm into mine and resting a head on my shoulder. We walk past someone else who hands her a leaflet for free STD testing. She takes one and snarls, and I don't quite know how to take that.

'We never talk about your love life, Miss Shaw,' I say. She looks over at me suspiciously, and I feel like an awful legal guardian. Perhaps I should have monitored this more closely. I know there have been parties and possible snogs and more with boys, but she's never brought a boyfriend home, I've never had to console her over a broken heart.

'That is classified information. State secret.' She leads me out of the hall, through to a university corridor, following a map in her hands closely to avoid the conversation.

'I ask this out of concern as a brother and an adult but are you a...'

She puts a hand to the air, closing her eyes. 'No!'

'I could have said anything there?'

'Still, no. You're my brother and this line of questioning is wholly improper.'

'Alright, Jane Austen.'

She laughs but it dies down and she looks pensive as she continues walking. 'Here's a question for you. Do you sometimes find it hard to get close to people when we've been through what we've been through?' she says, out of the blue.

I slow my pace as I digest her words. 'Oh, Brookie.' There's a fiercely confident young lady here, but I guess it masks the turmoil she must feel not having our parents around. I suddenly feel guilty that I haven't picked up on it.

'I get worried about loving someone but losing them too. It feels safer sometimes to just…'

'Be alone?' I ask, my heart breaking a little bit.

'I'm never alone though, really. I have my boys.' I hug her shoulder as she says it, trying to not show her that I'm tearing up.

'Brooke, you have one of the biggest hearts out of anyone I know, it would be a fucking shame not to share that with someone,' I tell her.

She stops in her tracks outside the doors to a large auditorium. 'That was cheeseballs, Char. And also you swore. You're such a terrible influence. It's a miracle I turned out so well.'

'It certainly is,' I say beaming. 'Can I go on My Single Friend and find you a man?'

'Hell to the no, to the never,' she squeals. 'If you do that I will go to your new school and tell them about the cock-sock thing.'

'You wouldn't…'

'I will find the footage. I'll put the stills on mouse mats.' I push her and someone looks at us bizarrely, wondering whether to step in. She puts an arm around me instead.

'Hate you,' she says, pouting with a ridiculous kissy face.

'Hate you more. Now tell me why you pulled that face when that man gave you that STD flyer.'

'It's because I have crabs. Big fat ones…' she tells me with a serious face.

I scrunch my nose. 'Lovely.'

TWELVE

Suzie

I fucking love laminating. There is something immensely satisfying about placing the paper in the plastic pocket and the slightly acrid smell it makes as it passes through the machine to become all glazed, shiny and wipe clean. I don't know why anyone would need to wipe clean the months of the year in French but maybe it's because they're so turned on by the standard of my laminating skills. I laugh to myself as I think this and then realise how sad that is as this classroom is empty.

Ever since Lee told me to decorate my classroom and make it my own, I've thrown myself into it and let my crafting fetish loose onto the walls, my desk and basically every part of my room where I can stick something. It felt like a project to stick my teeth into because I wanted this room to feel like my own but I also just needed distraction. It's been a tumultuous six months or so. From leaving Paul to coming to London, to Mallorca to Charlie and a new job, I've not really come up for air. So this is my way of finding peace and throwing all my good energy into something primary-coloured and orderly. I go over to my stationery trolley and place a stack of biros into a pot. As they all fall into place, I feel a shiver go down my spine, that is a good sound. Again, it's a little sad that that's where I get my kicks now. From super-hot holiday sex to fun with pens.

'You absolute motherfrigging donkey...' A familiar voice echoes through the wall suddenly and I jump a little. God, it's like he knows I'm thinking about him. It's not a good tone or volume but I do laugh a little at the word donkey. My mind races – what is he talking about? I've only ever used that turn of phrase for a photocopier or students. It's four fifteen so at least he's not talking to actual kids. I hear some fumbles in the room and something falling. It doesn't sound loud enough to be him. Maybe I'll just leave him be. That's the safer option. We've managed to avoid each other thus far quite successfully. The new school term has hit us both for six, which has helped us to avoid any sort of management of our relationship.

'Seriously, I hate you... you cocking piece of...'

I go over to my door and look through the panel of glass at the top. I see something fly out of the next-door classroom. Was that a shoe? Don't go out there. Stay in here where it's safe and keep laminating, Suzie. Colour-code the highlighters. Label your drawers. But I ignore my own advice, open my door and edge down the corridor towards his room. This is just me ensuring a colleague is safe. He may have been attacked by a dictionary or something and could be bleeding out. As I approach the room, I hear a Bluetooth speaker blasting out music and peer round the doorway to see Charlie stood on one of the desks, no shoes, trying his best to hang some Spanish flag bunting on to his ceiling tiles. He seems to be tangled up in it like a Christmas tree and I'm not really sure how he's achieved that. He reaches up, revealing a slice of stomach. I shouldn't look at that.

'Hola, ¿señor? All OK?' I call up to him. He sees me at the door and freezes for a moment. I don't know if it's because he has a hole in the big toe of his sock or because I'm clearly struggling not to laugh. 'It's looking very Spanish in here,' I say politely, looking up and around at the badly hung bunting and the massive Spanish flag that he's hung at the back of the room, in the same way one would hang curtains in student digs. On one wall, he's stuck on a lot of Spanish style fans, the ones with lace that your nan would bring back from Malaga as a souvenir, a very sad-looking novelty tea towel and a picture of a Real Madrid shirt printed out on A4 paper obviously meant to give the boys of this school aspirations for how they could use the Spanish language.

'No, it's not. It looks like shite. Remind me to stop buying all my teacher stuff from Temu,' he says.

I try my best to hold in my laughter. I think the sombrero on his desk may have been stolen from a Mexican restaurant.

'Was the swearing loud?' he apologises, dropping down from the desk he was standing on, and readjusting himself.

'Quite loud,' I say, putting the sombrero on. 'I thought I'd better check to see if you were OK.' He smiles and I panic a little. 'Do you wear this to teach Spanish, then?' I ask him, taking the sombrero off again.

'Au contraire. I make the naughty kids wear it as punishment and we all laugh and point...'

'Really?'

He shrugs. 'No. I just thought I could hang it somewhere.'

I smile. His room is a little different to mine. Dictionaries are piled like mountains at the front of the room, the pens, glue sticks and highlighters are all in one big box so you have to lean in and pull out what you want, like a lucky dip. I hope there aren't scissors in there. Around his monitor are Post-it notes with little reminders to himself about things he has to do. I spot one that says DRINK MORE WATER. I look up at the bunting and the unevenness of the hang makes my eye twitch.

'Your bunting is wonky,' I point out. 'Do you need a hand?'

'Will the kids notice though?' he says, a little defeated.

'No, but I will every time I walk past this room,' I smile. 'Give me a minute.' I head back to my room to get supplies and return. As I do, Charlie looks at what's in my hands with an eyebrow raised. 'Is that a...'

'Stationery caddy...' I tell him. It's a purple storage box for all my pens, pins, glue and tape. He'd better not be mocking this because this is one of my few sources of joy. He's laughing, I can tell. 'The problem with your bunting is that you're trying to hang it with Blu Tack. We need... pins...' I say holding them up into the air. I unzip my ankle boots, take them off and climb on top of a table, hitching my midi skirt up to my knee. He watches me curiously. 'I'm not doing this alone. Come on...'

I smile as he steps up on top of the table opposite mine and I reach up to attach a length of string to the ceiling tiles. 'I'm not sure if this meets with Health and Safety standards, Miss Callaghan,' he tells me, trying to unravel bits of Spanish flag.

'I've done worse. In my old school, I had to hang my own blinds once, nearly fell out of a third-floor window,' I tell him.

He laughs, skipping across to my table to meet me. He's very close to me now and I'm aware of his face, just centimetres from mine. He also has very good pores. I put two pins into his hand and he jumps back across to his table. 'It's already looking miles better,' he says, fixing the strand in place and looking up. 'Tell me honestly though, are the fans a bit naff?' he says looking over to the wall as one of them falls off.

'Yeah? I mean you could do an adjective word bank there? Some grammar stuff?' I suggest.

'Perhaps,' he says. 'That might be a project for further down the line.'

'Is that tea towel used?' I ask him, looking at the slight grubbiness that's more apparent now I'm closer up.

'Only once or twice. But look at the front with the Madrid

stuff and the bull, the flamenco, the pictures of the tapas. I want kids to come in here and immerse themselves in...'

'Patatas bravas.'

We both look at each other and grin. It's the lightest flicker of banter but I don't think I can go there, not now. Instead, I look up. At least the bunting is straight. 'I have a staple gun for that flag if you want?'

'Now that sounds fun,' he says, jumping off the desk. I let him follow me into my classroom and his eyes widen as he comes through the door. 'Holy shit, seriously?'

I don't know whether to feel embarrassed or proud but I confess I like this part of my job – the laminating, the organising, the creativity. 'Did you make that Eiffel Tower yourself?'

'Out of tin foil and a Sharpie,' I tell him. I went home and laid it out on my kitchen table. I coloured it in while I watched Korean soap operas and attached fairy lights to it for authenticity.

'And your baguettes. They have faces?'

'Yes. They have outfits too.' I decorated baguettes with faces, Breton berets and gave them speech bubbles with essential phrases for giving opinions and justifications. He stops to take it all in. If ever there was a reason to just stop any romantic interest in me, this is it, right here and now. I am slightly unhinged and unfunny when it comes to decorating my classroom. Half the kids won't get it but it will keep me amused at least. I look at him and can see he's suppressing a smile.

He wanders over to my desk and goes through my pen pot. 'And you name your pens?'

'Yes. It is proven that if you name your pens then it's more likely they'll be returned to you.'

He stops, trying to hold in his laughter. 'Are you mocking my baguettes?' I joke.

'Never,' he says, those blue eyes far too intense again. And then he exhales gently, grinning, almost as if to compose himself. He walks over and I put my staple gun in his hands, our fingers brushing momentarily. Does he feel that too? Am I imagining this?

'I'll remember to return this.'

'It's all good. Come knock whenever you need help.'

'Will do, Suzie.'

I don't know what we do now? Should we hug? I don't quite know so I put a hand out to wave to him but I put it a little too high and he comes to high-five it. I panic and move my arm, and he ends up putting a hand to my shoulder. We freeze, his hand resting there. I flinch but when I look up at him, I read a softness in his eyes, his hand doesn't move.

'Suzie...'

A jangly ringtone suddenly pierces the moment and I literally run to my desk to answer my phone. I look at the caller. Paul. I stare at the screen for a really long time. No, not now. Not ever.

'Don't you want to get that?' he asks me.

I look up at Charlie and sigh. 'It's just spam. Let it ring.'

He pauses as my ringtone keeps sounding. 'I'll leave you to it. Merci beaucoup, Mademoiselle.'

I don't know what to tell him. It's like the wiring in my brain is all tangled. My phone still glowing on my desk tells me that much. 'De nada, Señor Shaw.'

He walks away, leaving me standing in my classroom, turning to look back at me one last time.

Charlie

'Oh, he's a little angel. He would never do that, he's such a nice boy. You must have mistaken him for someone else,' a teacher in the staffroom mimics. 'No, your kid's a gobby, disrespectful twat, sort him out.'

I must admit, I do like the staffroom here, the sheer bedlam of this large space, the way I can lose myself listening to all the different conversations. It's been a super quick way to learn who the troublemakers are, who's dated who, and all the quirks and personalities of the different members of staff. There are the swearers (hello, History), that one teacher who thinks he's down with all the kids, the cynics, the Diet Coke addicts. I especially like Kim in art who told me she labels her milk as breast milk so no one will steal it. My staff buddy, Ed, invites me here every Thursday for a catch up which usually involves some sort of cake. The man wasn't joking. He can bake and that Mia girl he's married to is super lucky.

'So Seville soon?' Ed asks, passing his Tupperware over my way. Today it's some sort of rhubarb and custard crumble slice and it's bloody magnificent.

'Yep, the school trip beckons. Pray for me,' I say.

'I will get my rosary beads out.' I like Ed. He is very dry but has kept to his word with this staff buddy thing and regularly sends me emails. I hope that whatever length of time I spend here, he may become a friend of sorts. I just need to learn how to broach that without looking too keen. Asking someone to be your friend is almost as hard as asking someone out sometimes. We're not in a school playground. I mean, we are but not like that. 'Who else is going?'

'Lee, Fraser from German and then Jackie from HR and her husband, Mark?' I inform him.

'Mark the gatekeeper. He's good value on a trip. We took him to the Science Museum once and he spins a good yarn. On a one-hour coach trip, he managed to tell the kids he was once in Fleetwood Mac, scored a winning goal for Borussia Dortmund in the seventies and once got arrested for stealing a zebra.'

I laugh but the truth is I need a Mark, I need this trip. I need a break from the emotional chaos I've felt since seeing Suzie. Even though school trips are usually anything but peaceful, and jam-packed with activity, it will be the escape and distraction I need.

'And how's everything with the Year 8s now? Sorted?'

He speaks of a class I have on Tuesday afternoons straight after lunch when they've consumed what can only be a full bag of sugar each.

'Reset my expectations, changed the seating plan, threw one out the window...'

'Scare tactics like that are a winner. Light beatings always help too.'

I told you. Dry. I smile. 'Noted.'

'Oh, I spoke to Julie on data and she'll send you an email. And you asked about detentions. It's basically up to you and your department.'

'I tend to set mine on fish-and-chip day in the canteen since that gets them even angrier,' a voice intervenes. It's Beth, Suzie's cousin, who to be fair I haven't spoken to a lot since I arrived here. She's kept her distance and I don't know if this means she disapproves of me. She helps herself to one of Ed's cakes and sits down on the lime green sofa to join us. 'Carlos...' she says, in my direction.

Ed laughs. 'Of course, you know Beth because...' He waggles his finger around between the two of us and I look curiously over at Ed, who it would seem has terrible poker face. He realises and suddenly appears apologetic. 'I'm married to Mia and Mia thrives off gossip and she and Beth are in English and all they do over there is just chit-chat. Slackers department, really.'

Beth narrows her eyes at Ed but turns to me awkwardly. 'Sorry,' Beth says. 'We haven't had a chance to chat.' I wonder whether I should be afraid. I can't read her look. I can imagine all those cousins are quite a protective force to be reckoned with. 'I just can't believe it's you in this school. That bloke from holiday. We were all starting to think we hallucinated you because of the heat and now you're here. You honestly had no idea who she was? That she was a teacher?' she asks me. 'I mean what are the odds, Ed?'

'Minuscule,' he replies.

Her tone sounds suspicious and I have no idea how to counter that. 'How much has Suzie told you about me then?' I've only been in this staffroom for a few weeks but I know far too much about people I don't really know. I know there's a maths teacher called Zoe who's getting married next summer and that Robert in Science has an awful time with his ingrown toenails.

'Well, your name isn't Carlos. It's Charlie.'

'This is true.'

'You're not good at decorating your classroom,' Beth adds.

'That is also not a lie.'

'And you've stolen her best stapler.'

'LIES! It was on loan, I am no thief.'

Ed laughs but Beth can't keep eye contact. I realise that beyond these small details she knows far too much about me. If we rewind this, this is the same person who I met on a bench in a Mallorcan plaza, the same person who saw me after I'd had sex with her cousin and she most likely heard all about that sex. It was a girls' holiday – I saw the empty wine bottles in the kitchen, and their brazen unsubtlety when I first arrived at the villa. Suzie most likely spoke about my penis, all the moves, all the positions. My face goes a little hot at the thought of what Beth knows, and how much Ed and Mia know as a consequence.

'Do you like her?' Beth asks me. The question catches me off guard, but I like how she doesn't beat around the bush.

'Why? What has she said?'

'She's said things,' Beth says. In an instant, I realise that if Suzie spoke to her cousins about the good sex then it's likely she's told them about the bad sex too, which is a tad mortifying.

The way Beth has flared her nostrils at me lets me know the answer to that question. I'm not too sure I like the fact this has been broadcast. I've told no one for the shame of it. How was it described to her? Was this done for laughs? Ed looks between both of us. *Mate, you're married. You're safe. I bet no one in here has gossiped about your sex life.*

'Things...' I repeat.

Beth realises that maybe she's given too much away. 'Well, it wasn't Suzie. It was my sister, Lucy. Suzie told her what happened and...'

'So, it's a family discussion, is it?' I ask. I really hope this isn't on a WhatsApp group. Or they were at least kind about my penis.

'What happened then?' Ed asks casually, biting into another one of his baked slices.

'Oh,' Beth says, looking at me, knowing the only honourable thing to do in this case is lie. 'They went on a date and it kind of... fell flat?'

I don't think I like her intonation at the end of that.

'That's a shame,' Ed says, kindly. 'Is it the stress of the new job?'

I wave my hands about. 'No, no, no... not flat like that... just the chemistry was a bit off.'

'Oh, then I apologise,' Ed says, then frowns. 'But from the way Mia described it, didn't you two have pretty acrobatic sex in Mallorca?'

Beth chokes a little and I feel my face heat up again. I am starting to wonder how much Suzie told people about our little dalliance. I don't mind good reviews, but how does Ed know to use the word acrobatic?

'Well, it wasn't Cirque de Soleil but... yeah, we had a nice time in Mallorca.'

'But since meeting here?'

'No somersaults.' Not even a forward roll, mate. But despite how that went, I see the spark. I feel it when I stand next to her on a desk, smiling, putting up bunting, jesting at the way she names her pens. But then I think back to her flat, I think of the way she flinched when I touched her shoulder and I have no idea what's happening. It's like doing a forward roll but ending up facing the other way and not knowing how you achieved it.

'She also told me about your family situation,' Beth says a little more sincerely, and I tense up. Ed doesn't seem overtly curious so I will assume he's also in on this as they both give me tight-lipped smiles to show their approval of my character. Joke about bad sex, good sex and anything you like about me, but the fact they've gossiped about the saddest part of my life and my siblings hits a protective big brother nerve. Beth can tell this doesn't sit easy with me. She nudges Ed who offers me more cake. I don't turn that down. 'I'm sorry. That was insensitive of me.'

'Please don't apologise,' I say, dusting crumbs off my trousers. 'Your cousin likes to talk though, eh?'

Beth immediately sits up to defend her cousin's honour. 'No more than any girl would, when getting advice from family and friends.' That's fine but I hope she knows that I've told no one. Not even Max. I was gentlemanly, discreet. I kept all of the emotion and confusion to myself. Beth can sense I'm not too impressed by Suzie's inability to do the same. 'You've got to understand, she's fragile. She's had a super tough year.'

I pause when she says this, realising that Suzie has not told me any of that. I've just seen a sweet, confident woman with absolute no backstory whatsoever. Then I remember the name Paul was mentioned in her flat. An old flame perhaps?

'Are you saying I was a rebound thing?' I ask, trying to dig for more information.

'No,' Beth says resolutely. 'Not at all. I'm just saying she doesn't need another person to mess her around. Do you know how sad she was when you weren't there at the beach to meet her?' I shake my head. 'I was there. After Meg's birthday dinner, I saw her on her phone looking up Carloses who lived in Palma. She got to page ten on the Google search. You don't do that for people you just want to shag and never see again.'

I don't know how to reply to that. Since we've reconnected, I just can't recalibrate how I feel about any of it. The spark just yo-yos so much, it either burns bright or not at all and I don't know what that means.

'She is a good person, Charlie. Just in case you thought differently,' Beth says, trying to remedy the situation.

'I'd like to think I am too. Just in case you also thought differently.'

Beth tilts her head, her eyes narrowing as if she's still trying to work me out. Ed picks up on the awkwardness, sitting between us, his eyes shifting as if realising the energy has changed. It's then we're rudely interrupted by a hand reaching into Ed's Tupperware of baked goods.

'Steady Eddie. How goes it? What have we baked today?'

I look up and see one of the PE fraternity. I've not had the pleasure of meeting anyone from PE yet but I can already tell from the way he's nicknamed Ed, the over-tight shorts, dayglo white ankle socks and two-hundred-quid trainers that this man might be a bit of a helmet.

'Oh well, they weren't for...' Ed mumbles, but the man doesn't listen and puts his dirty mitts in the tub anyway. Ed rolls his eyes.

'Look at the little napkins. He's so fancy. I'm Tommy from PE, mate,' he says, turning to me. 'And you are?'

'Not your mate. I'm Charlie.'

Tommy laughs even though it wasn't a joke. 'You're new in languages, aren't ya? You and that fit new girl, what's her name?'

As soon as he says that something runs through me, a feeling not unlike white-hot fury rising in my stomach. 'Suzie, her name is Suzie.'

'Rhymes with...'

'Yeah, no...' Beth pipes in. 'She's my cousin, Tommy. Don't go near her or I will...'

'Attack me with words?' he jokes. 'Ooh, the English department have the Macbeth daggers out again.' Beth sits there glaring at him and it has absolutely zero effect. 'I'm pretty sure she's an adult and can make decisions for herself. Maybe I'll send her a cheeky email and ask her how she's settling in? See if I can be of assistance,' he says, riling her even further. That feeling in me builds until it runs through my blood.

'What was your name again?' I ask him, coldly.

'Tommy.'

'Rhymes with wanker, eh?'

He stops, side-eyeing me, realising I wasn't joking before. I clasp my hands together, leaning over, exhaling gently to keep my calm. 'Why don't you jog on over to your corner of the kitchenette there and go have a plank or something?'

I don't know where this alpha energy has come from because he does have impressive calves in those shorts and looks like he'd probably be able to take me in a fight. But there is one thing I don't deal well with and that's bullies. Tommy looks me up and down and I shrug my shoulders.

'You shagging her or something?' he asks casually.

Well, at least he's one of the few who doesn't know my whole story. 'Doesn't matter if I am or not, you don't talk about a woman like that. Ever. Not in front of me at least.'

Ed's eyes widen when I say this, Beth bites her lip to keep her laugh from spilling over, I brace myself, because in reality I have no idea who this man is and whether he's going to invite me outside for a fight. And when I say brace myself, I mean clench really hard, in case he does decide to punch me here and now.

'Alright then, amigo.'

'See you, capullo...' I say back. 'That's a more colloquial term for amigo.'

He shrugs. I don't think he knows what colloquial means. He'll never know *capullo* is a term for a dick. I hope he finds that out in Benidorm one summer holiday. He scrunches his face at me and walks away. As he does, I glance at Beth and Ed, who are looking at me and smiling. 'What?'

'I liked that,' Ed says, grinning. 'I have stories about him. He's generally not a nice person.'

'Yeah, I could tell.'

It pains me to think that Ed ever suffered under Tommy's cruel hand but maybe this is a chance for our bromance to flourish. *I've got you, mate.* However, I also wonder why I jumped to Suzie's defence so quickly, feeling territorial, jealous, protective, unwilling to let her move on so quickly, especially into the arms of someone so heinous. I don't want to imagine her with anyone else and again, confusion eats away at me. I take another of Ed's cakes.

'Do you cook the rhubarb down first, Ed?' I ask him, trying to change the mood.

Ed smiles. 'Yeah. With a bit of butter, ginger, brown sugar and cinnamon. You should try my muffins.'

I laugh under my breath. 'Stop flirting with me, seriously. I mean, you're married...'

And Ed and Beth laugh. Beth's expression softens and she gives me a little side smile. I nod at her. *I hope you tell Suzie and your sisters about this, I really do.*

THIRTEEN

Suzie

I used to have a friend who worked in the City, some bigwig in accountancy and corporate bollocks, and she used to talk about how at the end of a financial year, they would all literally live in the office. They'd order in food, lay down sofa cushions on the floor and just stay in that space until the job was done. The way she spoke about it always sounded horrific, until I became a teacher and that became my reality for the majority of the academic year. I love how people think that as soon as the bells goes we skip out with the kids, hand-in-hand, head to our cars and drive home in time for a four o'clock gameshow and a cup of tea. The reality of modern teaching is that we're usually here late. We occasionally bring work home with us but the truth is it litters our brains, our hard drives and it never leaves us because it is more than just a job; it's young people and as much you don't want to admit it out loud, you care about them, you want them to do well.

I watch now as the microwave in the small kitchenette in modern foreign languages circulates with its familiar hum. New start, new school, and my mission this year was to not let work follow me home. We get it done here, even if that means staying a bit later, though the dark has settled outside, half the lights in the school are off and there are only a handful of vehicles in the staff car park. The microwave pings and I open the door, looking longingly at my ham and mushroom tagliatelle in its pale green plastic container. This is a monster marking evening and I have email admin to sort too, so I have come prepared, I have brought food, snacks, I've kicked off my ankle boots to walk around in my UGG slippers and also in some sort of act of womanly rebellion, I have taken off my bra and popped on a hoodie. If I am going to do this right, I am going to be comfortable. I pop my pasta into a bowl and carry it back to my classroom. I should have brought a dressing gown but then they'd have caught me on CCTV and they'd have had to do a welfare check for my mental health.

I get back to my classroom. It's been a long afternoon of meetings, data entry and lesson planning and now this is the final piece of the puzzle. I look at the clock. It's five thirty-two. I'm going to give myself one hour. I put on my headphones, crack open a can of Rio, take a sip and go to process my personal emails first. I really need to unsubscribe from mailing lists, don't I? I've won something on the lottery though. I click on the link. I've won £1. Whoop-de-doo. As soon as I see Paul's name, I sigh, my shoulders slumping, and I pause until my eyes go fizzy and I have to look away. Isn't it strange that I used to see his name on my phone or email and melt with excitement. Now, it's like a fly hovering over a picnic. Seriously, piss off and find someone else to bother.

That said, I have to admire Paul's persistence. At first, he would send text messages that got progressively longer, ones where you'd have to press 'read more' and then spend an eternity scrolling down. They then turned into emails. Paul is no wordsmith so it was just long vague apologies where one minute, he'd say how sorry he was, the next he'd try to blame me for the relationship ending, gaslighting me into thinking that I was at fault, that I'd imagined it all. It was all desperate words from a desperate man because I think he thought he had time to talk me down, to balance his affair alongside our life and have it all. It all came crashing down pretty quickly when I found out, when I ran, when I left him.

I click on the email.

Suzie,

No 'Dear' to start it all off. Alright then.

We can't go on like this, can we? Before anything, we were friends and I don't think this is how friends treat each other. Why are you being like this? I don't know what to do with a lot of things here. Shall I sell them? You have Vinted? Maybe you should sell them? I still love you. I think we should at least try and give this another go. I've said sorry.

I wince a little at just how terrible he is at emoting in the form of words. Not that I need long reams of poetry from him, admitting what an idiot he is and how I'm the love of his life, but it's how he can go from Vinted to sorry in one mere sentence. You could have at least written a poem about that:

> Can we sell stuff on Vinted?
> So we can be minted?
> I maybe should have hinted,
> That I was a twat.
> I'm sorry about that.

I really am in the wrong career. I should have been a rapper or a greetings card writer. I feel nothing when I read his messages now. I used to dread getting them but they're just a way for him to manipulate me and have the final word, make me feel some element of guilt for what's happening. *Well, you know what, Paul. No. Your feelings in the aftermath will never be my responsibility.*

I don't know what else I can do to make you forgive me. Your mum would hate that this is happening.

I stop reading. *Don't you dare make reference to my mum. Ever. She'd have hated you for this. She'd have thrown you in the sea.* I move the message to the folder where all the other ones sit. The last one was a particularly lovelorn note where he told me he went to a bench on the pier and cried the other day because he saw a seagull and it reminded him of the time one stole a doughnut out of my hand and it was the funniest thing ever. Romance, right there.

It's a good feeling to know that any hold Paul had over my feelings is diminishing, that he has zero power in this situation, so much so that I toast myself, holding my tin of Rio in the air. Well done, Suzie. Paul is becoming a memory, a dot in the distance the more time passes, and I made that happen. My mum would actually love that that is happening. Actually, do you know what this needs? This needs me to get up out of this chair and leave my pasta for a short while. This deserves a dance. At least a light sway, because this is what Chappell Roan on my Spotify playlist and this moment deserve. I get up and sway around my desk, smiling to myself and singing along softly. Then I turn and see a figure standing in the doorway. I jump out of my bloody skin and shriek.

'What the...!' Fizzy tropical drink flies through the air and on to the carpet and I jump in a strange configuration that looks like I'm fighting with the air. 'Charlie?'

He also leaps back to hear me screaming and then stands

there with a faint look of horror in his face. I pull off my headphones. Oh. That could be the fact I've chosen to wear slippers at school. He processes my appearance, eyes creased with confusion, maybe even pity.

'Have you...' he mumbles, '... moved into your classroom?'

'Oh... no. I just like to be comfortable when I'm marking,' I say, trying to normalise my madness completely. I look over and see my bra hanging off a school chair and hope he hasn't clocked it.

'Marking... that's what this is. Oh, please don't stop on my account,' he says. I notice him looking at my dinner, my purple pens lined up in a row ready to mark. There is a look of amusement on his face that he's caught me in the act and it makes me blush.

'Why are you here?' I ask.

'I left my wallet in my classroom,' he tells me. 'I saw your light on and heard movement so I thought I would come and say hello.'

'Hello,' I tell him. This isn't fair. *You get to see some slummy dishevelled version of me whereas you've gone home. You don't even look tired, just effortlessly cool in a hoodie and trainers, that twinkle in his eye shining through. Damn you.*

'Marking?' he asks.

'Year 11 speaking assessment prep.'

'Snap. Except I do mine at home. Sitting down. With a pen,' he jokes.

I laugh and turn down the music. 'Can you not tell people you saw me in here? I'm a little embarrassed.'

He scoffs quietly to himself. 'Well, unlike some, I am very discreet.'

I pause for a moment as he says that, curious. 'Was that a dig?'

He stands there wondering whether to engage in this

conversation. 'It seems that a lot of the staffroom know quite a lot about me... us...'

I shake my head, mortified. 'Well, it was never my intention to be gossipy. I was confused. Beth knew quite a lot already,' I say, hoping he can read my authenticity.

'I know how staffrooms work. I don't mind it when you talk about me but just not my family, that's all.'

I don't reply but just study his intensity, that sense of protectiveness which shows the depths of his character and is wildly attractive.

'I'm sorry.' He smiles and continues to look at me, nodding. 'And to talk about us was wrong too. I mean, there's nothing to really say, is there?'

'Ouch,' he replies, feigning pain, holding a hand to his heart.

I half laugh. 'I think we both know that something's... lacking here.' Nope, that's made it worse. 'That's the wrong word... Not you lacking, just both of us...' I need to stop talking in teacher talk. Inadequate, special measures, below standards.

He nods slowly. 'I get you. Maybe it's the universe telling us we had our moment in Mallorca. It was always going to be impossible to recreate that,' he says plainly. And as he says the words out loud, I understand completely but I can't help but feel my heart deflate. I remember when I found out about Paul. That felt like someone had ripped my heart out of my chest and stamped on it with a heavy boot. This feels like a heart swollen with hope, with curiosity and we've pierced a small hole in it so it all seeps out slowly.

I can't read him at all. Was that just as painful for him too?

'I was thinking the same,' I say, trying to cover my feelings. 'We can still get along as colleagues though, right?' I ask him. 'Try and salvage a working relationship out of this?'

'I think that's important. With your lamination skills, you're the sort of person I need to keep onside,' he says, with a sad smile, and my heart breaks a little at him trying to lighten the mood again.

'I love laminating,' I say, sounding a bit like a loon. 'Aren't you off to Seville on Friday?' I ask, because as a colleague I guess I should try and make polite small talk.

'Yeah.'

'Well, if I don't see you before then, have fun.'

'I'll try,' he says, his eyes still exploring the room, this situation. 'Promise me you won't stay here too late, yeah? It's dark outside, be safe, take care of yourself.'

'I'll try,' I say, with a grin. And with that, he does a strange salute in my direction and walks away. I don't move. I just try to take it all in, a painful feeling swelling in my chest. I'd like to think it's indigestion from classroom dancing while eating a ready meal, but it feels more like deep-set disappointment wrapped around my heart, squeezing it so very tightly.

Charlie

'So I've created this booklet that allows you to magpie some phrases for your speaking assessment and build your own answers. Try and keep it fresh, interesting. I don't want... *me gusta la escuela, es muy interesante...*' I say it in a deadpan London accent and I'm glad it gets a laugh out of the class. I don't mind these Year 10s, they're curious and all seem to be engaged. There's Viraj at the back of the room who needs to remember his book and sometimes I think Tyler is asleep but I've had worse classes. I had one lad who once jumped out of a window to escape my lesson. Ground floor, in case you were worried.

'Sir, what time is the coach leaving tomorrow?' someone asks me from the back of the room.

'There's a letter that should have gone out with all the timetabling, Viraj, but I believe it's a seven thirty meet outside school.' They all reply with groans of disbelief to have to roll out of their beds that early. It's been a long six weeks to start off the autumn term. A new job was always going to take its toll but you see it in the kids too. After a long break in the summer, their brains struggle to keep up, they're tired and moody. I see it here but also with Brooke and Sam who presently have all the charm of very angry squirrels.

'Sir, did you say you lived there before?' a girl at the back, Lola, asks.

'I did my year out there at university so I'll take you to all the bars I used to go to...' There's a sharp intake of breath. 'You really are very gullible, eh?' I say, laughing. Yes, let's have a tour of Mr Shaw's Spanish escapades. In this building, I went to a rooftop party, smoked a lot of weed and then had sex with an Italian tourist who never called me back.

'Will it be hot? Will I need a coat?' someone else pipes up.

'It will be a balmy twenty degrees. Tell your folks to pack you a hoodie and a light waterproof.' I look out the window. The weather here has turned to grey and overcast, the clocks will go back soon and the days will be dark and depressing. Another reason to get a dose of sun before that happens. I hear the classroom down the hall explode into noise and pop my head out to see what the commotion is. Suzie's French lot are like this, they always seem to be having fun. If ever I glance in there, she's got them playing games, writing stuff on the white board and engaging in a lot of partner work. Colleagues. That's what we are at the moment after our conversation a few days ago, back when I caught her camping out in her classroom. Suzie senses me snooping and waves at me. I put a thumbs up to ask if she's OK and she replies with the same gesture. We're colleagues. This is what we do now. I think she thinks I'm one of those nosy neighbours complaining about the noise. I return to my classroom, frowning.

'All OK, Sir? Don't worry about them. It's the French lot, Sir. They're just idiots,' Lola says.

'Bad classroom management from the new teacher,' Tyler says. Oh, he is awake.

'She seems OK though?' I tell them. 'What's the tea? What have you heard about her?'

I don't know why I ask this question. I don't care. I really don't. A line has been drawn. The universe has brought us back together again but it was obviously so we could add some zest to this department. She could bless the kids with her organisational prowess and I could bestow upon them my conversational charm.

'The tea?' Lola asks, giggling.

'Yes, Lola... ¿Qué es el té?' I say, trying to keep things Spanish based.

'Do I have to answer in Spanish?' she asks.

'No.'

'Well, then Josh said she's sound. She knows Kendrick Lamar,' she tells me.

'Like actually knows him? That's impressive?' I say, a little shocked.

'Of course not. But she rapped in class and they thought it was funny.' I stand there pondering whether I need to do the same. I only know that bit from the song where I can shout out about A-Minor, but I don't think that's a good line to repeat to children.

'And how would you know what Josh thinks?' Viraj asks her, teasing.

'Shut your hole, Viraj,' she snaps back.

'Hey, we don't swear in my classroom. Only in Spanish,' I say, trying to de-escalate the situation. They both smile. 'So, Josh, eh?'

'We've been snapping each other, Sir. It's all it is,' she says innocently. 'What's the deal with the French lady then, you interested in her?'

I hope my panic doesn't show in my face when Lola asks me that. I was. I was very much interested in her. But it's done.

'She seems nice but I don't think I want a relationship at present. I'm focused on my career, my wellbeing,' I tell the class, hating myself as I say the words aloud and hear how shit they sound.

'Boring,' Viraj says.

I look over at him, peeved, though I agree with him.

'Sorry, Sir... Aburrido...' he replies, and I grin at the audacity. 'Maybe we can find you a Spanish girl in Seville?' he suggests.

'Really? Like that fit Spanish girl in *Outer Banks*,' another kid pipes in.

I stop and smile to myself, shaking my head. 'Or maybe I can tempt you all with some authentic chorizo.' I shouldn't have said that out loud, eh? And with that the bell sounds and they all gather their belongings. 'Señores y señoritas, I will see you tomorrow, bright and early, please do not lose these booklets! I spent a lot of time making them!'

They all exit the room to a chorus of adiós and hasta mañana as I stand there, taking a big deep breath. There's much to do before tomorrow. Bit of lesson planning here, going back via the shops to buy some travel deodorant, packing and making sure Brooke and Sam are safely deposited at Max and Amy's while I'm gone. It will all be good. I know it's a school trip and a lot of the time will involve herding children and ensuring they're not drinking, having sex or indulging in recreational drugs, but to me, it will also be a second homecoming of sorts. A return to a place where I was allowed to be young, carefree before the worst of life events interrupted all of that.

'Sorry, were we noisy?' a voice says, appearing at the door. I turn to see Suzie standing there. She seems to wear a range of maxi dresses these days with colourful trainers. Not that I've been noticing, of course I haven't. She tucks her hair behind her ear.

'As long as they weren't taking the piss, you know? We colleagues have to look out for each other,' I tell her, offering her some strange salute. I shouldn't have done that. I'm making this weird.

'Half term, eh?' she says, continuing the conversation from a distance.

'Yeah, do you have plans?' I ask her, hoping it doesn't sound too intrusive.

'Sleep and binge-watching all the TV I've missed in the last six weeks? I might even do something crazy like laundry.'

'Super divertido,' I tell her.

'Bien sûr.'

I can't help smiling when I hear her speak French. Bonjour again, Aurelie. That was fun while it lasted, eh? Maybe that's the remit of our jobs, we role-play and read out scripts all the time as the kids try and work out what we're saying. Maybe it all became real life for a while. If anything, it just shows how good we are at our jobs.

The moment is suddenly overtaken by thundering footsteps on the stairs and Lee appears, a little frazzled, like he's being chased, hopefully not by the students.

'Thank monkeys for that. I thought I may have missed you. You're still here...' he says.

'Me?' I tell him. 'Yeah, the bell has only just gone.'

'No, Suzie,' he says. He clings to a desk to steady himself. 'Fraser... downstairs...'

'Wasn't in today. Is he OK?' Suzie asks. 'Is it something serious?'

'Oh god, no... daft prick dislocated his shoulder playing

pickleball. How on earth does a person do that? It's basically badminton with children's rackets,' he says, almost a little angrily. 'But he was due to go on the trip tomorrow and now we're stuck. We have to take another adult to balance the ratios otherwise we're screwed. The trips team are pulling their hair out and the parents will lose their shit with us if we cancel.'

We both stand there, taking in all that information. I don't even know what pickleball is, has he made that up? 'Could we ask a parent?' I ask.

'The safeguarding is the problem. So, I am literally just here, begging you to come on this trip, Suzie. I don't know if you have plans or a holiday booked...'

'She was just planning on doing laundry,' I say, out loud.

Suzie looks at me and smiles. 'Doesn't it leave tomorrow though?'

'Yes, seven thirty,' Lee says. 'We'd just have to switch the names on the flight bookings. I'm asking too much, aren't I? You're new, I don't want you to feel pressure to do this. Do you even have a passport?'

'How long is the trip?' she asks.

'We get back Monday.'

She nods then turns to look at me before asking Lee, 'Who else is going?'

'Well, there's me, Jackie from HR... her husband, Mark in site maintenance and Charlie here.' I put a hand to the air. Yes, I am going to Seville. This might be the killer here, eh? We've done a really good job at being grown-up and levelling out what this is so I understand if you want to give it a miss. But there's a little voice inside that is really hoping she says yes.

'My Spanish is a little rusty,' she tells Lee.

'Mark only knows how to order beer,' he replies.

She stops for a moment to think. 'I guess, ¿sí?' she says. 'Is that cool with you, Carlos?'

As soon as she says that name I laugh. Are we doing this? Because universe – I don't quite know what you're playing at but this feels like a U-turn. It feels dangerous, risky and I quite like it.

'Yeah. I'm very cool with that.'

PART THREE
SEVILLE

FOURTEEN

Suzie

'Miss, are those Gazelles? Those are fire,' Lola tells me, as we all get on the plane, Lee to the front trying to direct people to the right seats. I look down at my red suede trainers and smile.

'Thanks, lovely. You managed to find something to wear?' I ask her. When Lola arrived at school, she basically showed up in a crop top and cycling shorts claiming Mr Shaw had told her it'd be really hot and she wouldn't need much. Mr Shaw disputed this fact quite sternly but it didn't make up for the fact that all she had in her bag were shorts, crop tops and bikinis.

'Yeah, Mr Shaw made me wear his hoodie. Does it look crap?'

'It looks warm at least.' It's actually Nike and vintage-looking so she does look quite cool. Well, to my twentysomething eyes at least. She continues down the aisle in her UGGs, socks and polka dot trolley bag. The mention of Mr Shaw's name makes me peer around from my aisle seat looking for him. Why am I here? Why? I had a whole season of *Reacher* cued up for half term and had planned how many episodes I was going to watch per day. I was going to laminate more things for my classroom, see my cousins. I guess I'll still have time for that, but school trips are always draining, eventful, not the reprieve from school life I need. I tell myself I'm here because of my bleeding heart; I didn't want the kids to miss out and a whole trip to be cancelled. But then there could be another reason why I'm here. Him.

'Ladies and gents, please keep to the seats you've been allocated. No swapping. This really is for your own safety,' Lee shouts. A couple caught in the melee look at him. 'Obviously not you, madam, I meant the teens. Ah, Señor Shaw! You will be sitting here with Señorita Callaghan...' Señor Shaw. That would be him and that señorita would be me. We both look at each other. It's the most I've looked at Charlie all day. We've managed not to converse much so far. We sat on different parts of the coach to the airport, we were allocated our own kids to herd and check in, we were even ushered into different security queues. Maybe this doesn't have to be a trip where we are anything more than colleagues. However, this? This is a possible problem.

Charlie freezes in the aisle, hovering over the seat.

'You... There are people behind you...' I tell him, as a queue starts to form, blocking the way. He hesitates then puts his bag in an overhead compartment and I stand to let him squeeze past me to his seat. There's no easy way to do that with the people waiting. I don't really want to put my back to him so he'll brush against my arse, so I let him face me, hands in the air, and he slides himself past me, his face just inches away from me. This is not ideal. I just smile so the kids don't think it's weird. Breathe, Suzie.

'I can swap with Mark, if it's easier?' he asks me, still hovering around his middle seat.

'I don't think we're allowed. It's a safety thing and if the kids see us swap then they'll want to swap and then...'

'Bedlam,' he says.

You can do this, Suzie. We are adults. We have been super professional in how we've herded the children this far. It's a three-hour flight, we can literally just nap, plug in a podcast, read. It could be easy to just ignore each other again for this short time, and then throw ourselves into showing these kids around Seville, helping to improve their conversational Spanish and broaden their cultural horizons.

'So, kids... I don't want to have to remind you that there are expectations on this plane. Any disruptive behaviour and we will...'

'Sell you to the Spanish,' Mark shouts. Some of the other passengers look at each other, worriedly.

'Well, we won't, Mark, but there will be severe consequences,' Lee continues. That sounds worse. The plane starts to quieten down, air hostesses walking up and down the aisles closing overhead compartments and checking seat belts before the plane starts taxiing away from the terminal. A few of the children cheer. I try to focus on them so I won't notice Charlie next to me. Across the aisle is some fifteen-year-old I've never met before in a full Nike tracksuit and some pretty swish Air Force Ones. Well, we're now going to be best mates for the next few hours.

'Do you have one of those emergency card things?' Charlie asks me.

I turn to face him. I reach around in the pocket in front of me, pulling one out as I see him scanning it and looking at the flight attendant teaching us all how to put a lifejacket on. I like how he's paying such close attention. 'You good?'

He nods. 'I just... every plane is different. It's good to know things.'

'Things?'

'Emergency exits. Like, those lifejackets have whistles. That's useful.'

I bite my lip. 'How many times did you have to do the fire safety course at school when you started?' I ask him.

'Passed first time, I took notes,' he tells me.

'Nerd,' I say, surprisingly casually.

'You?'

'Twice,' I say, I lie, it was four. I clicked through and didn't anticipate the surprise questions at the end. 'I was morally opposed to some of the questions though. That one that asks you to leave children in a burning building if they refuse to come with you? I didn't like that one.'

'So what would you do?' he asks, curiously. 'You'd put your life in danger?'

'I'd carry them all out on my back. Emerge a hero, of course,' I tell him.

He laughs, opening a bag of Maltesers and offering them in my direction. The idea was not to engage with him as much, don't talk. Don't look at him, even. However, Maltesers are my kryptonite. Maybe just a couple so I don't appear rude and maintain some civility between us. I can do this. Just ask very general questions, don't go down that dangerous Mallorcan road again. I take a deep breath as the plane stutters towards the runway. 'You managed to get everything packed and sorted in time then?' he says, keeping the Maltesers packet there in case I'd like more.

'It was a bit rushed. I probably haven't packed enough pants but I'll survive.' Why am I talking to him about my pants? It's the quickest I've ever packed, going to the back of my drawers to find my summer clothes and then realising I had to self-wax and shave and get my body summer ready in one night. 'It's actually quite exciting.'

'Exciting?' he says. I side-eye him. We don't go there anymore. He and I.

'The last-minute nature of it,' I explain. 'I've never been to Seville.' I look down at the sinews of his forearms. I shouldn't really be looking at those. He reaches down to his bag stowed under the seat in front and pulls out his phone and a notebook. It looks old, weathered but covered in stamps and stickers.

'You... journal?' I ask him, admiring all the pretty adornments.

'Nah, it's... I spent my year out in Sevilla. This was my diary that I wrote during my time there, all the little notes I made about the language. I used to eat oranges, peel the labels off and stick them on here. Everything from observations to addresses, telephone numbers...'

'... Of all the señoritas you bedded?' That was maybe not the right thing to ask.

He shakes his head. 'Of all the friends I made. Here, this man was called Pablo. I lived in a flat above him. He was sixty-five, his wife made exceptional gazpacho and he still sends me a Christmas card every year.' He offers me the book to look through and I study all the notes made with such care and attention.

'It's very *English Patient*,' I say, looking at some of the sketches and notes. He looks over at me and furrows his brow. 'Sorry, niche reference.'

He pauses then shakes his head, dismissing the idea. 'Where did you have your year out?' he asks.

'Guess...'

He shakes his head and grins. 'Nice?'

I don't answer but smile. He roars with laughter and I see some of the kids arching their heads over to have a look. I turn back to flick through the pages of this journal that speaks of someone who loved his travels, who loved the culture, the city. When I hand it back to him our fingers brush against each other and I try to ignore the charged feeling I get when my skin touches his. I don't trust that spark anymore. I try and change the subject. 'Lola said you gave her your hoodie?'

'Yep, it was question of her modesty over my warmth. I just

hope she gives it back. I've lost too many good hoodies to thieving girls over the years,' he moans. 'Keep eyes on her.'

I smile. 'Are you cold?'

'Nah, it'll warm up by the time we get to Seville.'

We both pause to take in what those words mean, as the plane gets to the start of the runway, engines growling to a start to summon up the power to take off. He holds on to both of his armrests, fists clenched around the corners of it, taking heavy deep breaths.

'Are you alright?' I ask.

'Nope,' he says a little too quickly. I can physically see him gulp as the plane starts to pick up speed.

'Charlie,' I whisper. This explains the attention to detail with the emergency cards. 'It's the safest way to travel, you know.'

'That is a myth. The safest way to travel is to walk.'

'You'd rather walk to Seville?' I tell him. 'You'd get there in time for Christmas.'

'No, I'd get there for November. I'd walk quickly.' He closes his eyes but smiles.

The plane picks up speed, until that moment when we are slammed back into our seats, the force lifting us slowly into the air, the windows rattling lightly. I'm different, I've always liked that feeling, that charge down the runway, the roar, the anticipation. And then you're floating. The world is behind you. I turn to Charlie – every part of him tense, strained – and I put my hand over his. I squeeze it tightly.

Charlie

'Sir, you told us that it would be about twenty degrees, it's bloody boiling!' Viraj says, stripping off his tracksuit top and tying it round his waist. It's not just him, it's our whole group who stand there outside the youth hostel on the pavement, stripping off their layers to escape the heat, admiring the blue skies and the sun shining like a beacon above us. Hola, sunshine, how I've missed you. Over by the coach, I notice Suzie, taking off her hoodie to reveal a vest top, sunglasses on and looking up to the sun to absorb the warmth. It's a pose that triggers a bit of déjà vu so I quickly look away. Suzie is here on this trip. It's fine. She's here because she's a good professional who wanted to save the trip. She's not here because of me. She's not here because of me. She did hold my hand when the plane took off because I have an irrational fear of flying. And then she had a little nap and her head landed on my shoulder. That wasn't out of choice. That was because I was next to her and the physics of the situation meant her head leaned towards me. I close my eyes. Did her hair smell nice, though? Yes, it did.

'You can have this back now, Sir,' Lola tells me, snapping me out of my trance and throwing my hoodie at me.

'Thank you kindly, Lola,' I say, marvelling at how she is immediately the most suitable person dressed for this heat.

'And this is Señor Shaw. Say hello, Sir!' she says, immediately sticking her phone in my face.

'¡Hola!' I say, waving into the screen. 'Is this some sort of vlog, Lola?'

'Of course.'

'A perfect time to practise your Spanish skills, ¿sí?'

'You're so funny, Sir!'

I watch as she heads into the hostel and I hand out the rest of the trolley bags in the hold. I can do this. Keep my distance, respect the boundaries as a work colleague. I feel the sweat running down the back of my T-shirt, starting to run down my brow. The hostel is in the heart of the city, and the drive over was less scenic and more roads of low-rise industrial estates, palm trees and fast-food places; the children all marvelling at the fact there was a McDonald's here. Arriving in the city involved entering rabbit-warren-style roads, our coach fighting against the narrow Andalucian streets. I always liked that, the lack of tarmac, the rustic feel of the streets, old ladies dragging trolley bags along noisily with their shopping, people sitting outside cafés casually, legs up on seats, everything slowed down because of the heat, the vibrant sound of Spanish flitting in and down the streets like birdsong. And then we got to our hostel: a satsuma-coloured building with cast-iron balcony railings at each window. Mosaics spell out the language school name and street number and I look up to see that building reach into the sky, the orange perfectly set against the bright blue. The street is crowded with cars and the heat radiates off the cobbles. It's familiar and drenched in sun and I inhale deeply to let that heat enter my body.

'Gracias, Señor,' I tell the coach driver.

'¡Suerte, Señor!' he says, grinning broadly to see all the kids gathering in the foyer of the hostel. That's what the last bloke said on a similar coach in Mallorca. Stag do or school trip. I don't know what the lesser of two evils is but if anyone gets on a mechanical bull here then they are on their own. I walk towards the hostel where Lee and his plastic pockets of registers and organisation stands in the foyer. He takes a long drink of water and tries waving his hand in the air.

'Señores and señoritas, I know we are all tired but let's sort this out and then we will leave you alone to find your rooms before we have lunch and head out. Young man, can you put your shirt back on please? You are not a football hooligan. I am giving you keys. Do not lose these keys! And no arguments about the rooming, please.'

He goes through a list of names, calling them out in fours, directing them towards dorms as the crowd of fifty children gets smaller until there is only the staff standing there by the desk.

'Who the hell is that annoying one with the buzz cut and the earring?' Jackie from HR asks. 'Anyone want to trade? He's so gobby.'

'Trade you for Kyle with the flatulence problem,' Mark says.

Lee goes through his folders once again, chatting to reception as Suzie stands there quietly. 'Who do you have?' I ask her.

'Mostly girls. Lola...'

'She's a nice girl. If you need a conversational in then ask her about Josh.'

'From my French class, Josh?'

I nod. Don't look at the sweat pooling around her collarbone.

'So, guys. The room situation... um... err...' from his hesitation, I am not quite sure what he's hinting at. It'd better not be sleeping bags as my back won't cope with that.

'Don't tell me it's bunk beds,' Mark says. 'You know what happened on the ski trip.'

'What happened on the ski trip?' Suzie asks.

'Mark got drunk, fell out of one and took out a tooth,' Jackie, his wife, explains, rolling her eyes.

'You two have a double bed because you're married...'

'I'm in with our tour host, Jorge and then... I know this is awkward but because we thought Fraser was coming, the other room is a bunk bedroom for you guys,' he says, looking at myself and Suzie.

We both freeze, looking at Lee. I can almost hear the universe pointing and laughing at us. 'I know this is awkward but there's no other room. I don't want it to be awkward. If you'd like to stay at another hostel nearby, we can try and find you a bed elsewhere, in an all-female dorm? Or we can put you in with some of the girl students,' Lee says, looking at Suzie.

'Or I could go so you'd be with the group?' I offer. This is mildly ridiculous. First the plane and now this. I think about what Brooke said about the stars aligning. How the stars may have tripped Fraser up at pickleball to facilitate this situation and to now be pushing us in a hostel room together. It does feel like the stars were not in her flat that day though to witness the very awkward sex we had. I don't know what they're trying to tell me.

'Bunks?' Suzie asks.

'Again, not ideal but it is ensuite.'

Suzie looks at me again, almost a little suspiciously. I have no idea what she's thinking.

I put my hand up. 'Look, ideally we should probably stick with the group because of the ratios and sharing the responsibility of all the kids. But I don't want this to be awkward. I can leave the room when you want to use the toilet, get changed or have a shower. You get to choose the bunk too. Maybe we give it a night and then see what happens?'

'Can I go on top?' she asks, biting her lip, looking down to her feet to stifle her giggles. I hope no one heard that gulp leave my throat and hit the pit of my stomach like a rock.

'Whatever the señorita wants,' I reply.

We both stop and look at each other. I can't quite breathe.

'Then that is perfect. I am so grateful. So regroup here in an hour? Does that give everyone enough time?'

I nod as Lee hands me a key. I turn to Suzie. 'Ready, roomie?'

She smiles as we head up the staircase towards our dorm, both of us saying nothing to each other. I should break the silence, shouldn't I? I can bring some humour to it. *You don't snore, do you?* Come on, Charlie. Talk about the heat. Or maybe don't. I get to our dorm room, putting the key in the door.

As I push the door open, I see there's a wooden framed bunk bed to the corner of the terracotta tiled floor, a window that frames the houses of the street across the way and a white gauze curtain waving in the breeze from a fan in the corner. I walk in and Suzie follows me.

'You wanted to go on top?' I ask, facing her.

That was not the line to open with. I can't do this. I'll go and sleep outside or something. Because she's an arm's length away and all I want to do is kiss her. My breath gets heavier. Why is this so tense? Charged. Hot. She doesn't reply, she just looks at me with her lips parted gently. Kiss her, Charlie. I take one step towards her.

'SIR! SIR!' The moment explodes with fierce knocking on the door. 'THERE'S NO AIRCON, SIR! WE'RE ALL GOING TO DIE!'

FIFTEEN

Suzie

'YOU AREN'T GOING TO DIE!' I shout through the door, frustrated, desperate and supremely confused. Because I think we were about to kiss. Me and Señor Shaw. And maybe do more. On our bunk bed. Possibly. Charlie smiles, his shoulders fall. With relief? He walks past me and opens the door.

'Hola, Viraj. ¿Qué pasa?' he asks. I walk over to a leather armchair and sit down, kicking off my shoes and socks and sitting in the path of the fan in the room, feeling the lukewarm breeze on my skin. There really is no aircon. It also looks like I'm going to have to make my bed. Cool down, Suzie. Now is not the time to get overexcited with kids outside and in a bunk bed. That frame doesn't look sturdy enough. It might squeak. Stop imagining yourself having sex in it. Don't look at him. It's like trying not to look directly into the sun.

'Sir, there's a sign saying they don't operate the aircon in the autumn and winter to save the planet. The planet? What about me, eh? I'm calling my mum,' Viraj moans.

'To tell her what? It's too hot in Spain? You'll survive, it gets cooler in the night. Think of the polar bears.'

'So I can feel cold?' he says, confused.

'No. Because you'll be saving them by not using the air conditioning. Just sleep with the fans on. You'll be fine.'

'I'm still calling my mum. What's your room like? Do you have aircon?' he says, peering round the door. He catches sight of me and then winks at Charlie. The boy winked. This is not a good idea. None of it. Because he is going to go now, tell all his mates and it will be all anyone can talk about. 'Go away, Viraj. Go and find the ice machine in the communal kitchen.'

'There's an ice machine?' he says, jogging away.

Charlie laughs, closing the door and then resting his head against it.

'And so it starts...'

He turns to see me, sprawled in that chair, trying to keep cool. He stops, tentative, but then comes over and sits on the edge of the bunk bed opposite me, taking off his trainers and socks too and putting his feet on the cold tiles.

'Water?' I ask. He nods and I throw him a bottle that was on the side table. He catches it perfectly, opening it and taking a few sips. I watch the action of his throat swallowing, the sweat tousling his brown hair. He then turns to look at me.

'Barcelona, two years ago. A kid managed to buy alcohol from a 7-Eleven and used his suitcase as a sick bowl. I had to buy him a brand-new wardrobe,' he tells me.

I can play this game too. 'Skiing in Les Arcs,' I challenge him. 'A group of boys set fire to a mattress and threw it out of a window.'

'Ding ding ding,' he says. 'The lady wins this round.'

We both laugh and for a moment it feels strangely comforting to have something in common, beyond this weird energy that exists between us. The laughter fades and he leans forward, looking down at his hands.

'I don't quite know what's happening here...' he says, a little confused.

'Neither do I,' I reply.

'We're colleagues. We decided that much, right? We just sit across tables now and compare data.' I smirk a little and he shakes his head at me. 'Why do you think it worked in Mallorca and not in London?' he asks me, earnestly.

I hold my bottle of water to my head. 'Who knows? Maybe it was the role-play thing? Maybe it was because we could be different people.'

'I was Carlos. Carlos would know how to decorate a classroom, and write things in notebooks, not Post-it notes plastered over his computer. Carlos is never late for things.'

'Aurelie wouldn't make her own Eiffel Tower for fun, she wouldn't eat microwave pasta or wear slippers at work.'

'We could role-play our way through the trip?' he says, with a cheeky look in his eye.

'Because, you know, the kids wouldn't talk,' I reply.

He laughs and I like seeing the shape of his eyes change. 'Also, and no offence, but I found being Carlos...'

'... bloody tiring?' I say.

He laughs again but then leans back on the bed, smiling, watching me. 'There's something here, isn't there?'

I nod.

'So maybe we use this time to get to know each other. Hi, I'm Charlie.'

'Suzie,' I reply.

'Is that short for anything?'

'No. Are you a Charles?'

'God, no.'

'Excellent to meet you, Suzie.'

I feel the air lodge in my throat as he says my name aloud. My real name. I move around on my seat and exhale loudly. He then looks me straight in the eye. That bright blue gets me every time. The way he doesn't relent makes me bite my lip. 'I have a question. Do you think about Mallorca, what happened?'

I nod.

'What part do you think about?'

I'm not sure what he's asking me. Is it the part where we first met? Or was it in the shop when he asked me whether I wanted a mermaid or a llama towel? But then he takes off his T-shirt. I bite my lip, taking in those shoulders again, his stomach.

'Hot, are we?' I ask.

'Very.'

'I think I remember something.'

'Tell me,' he whispers.

I take a deep breath, shifting around again to mask my arousal, feeling a specific memory in every part of me. 'It was when I first took you in my mouth...' I say, feeling my cheeks glow. I see his breaths get heavier, he loosens his flies, slowly unbuttoning them, his hand reaching inside. '... I could feel you get harder, every time my lips moved up and down over you.' He leans back on the bed and he's all I can see. I put my hand down the elasticated waist of my trousers, my other elbow on the armrest, the edge of my thumbnail in my mouth. I feel my nipples getting harder under my top. 'And then it was that moment of putting a condom on you, taking off my underwear and then climbing on top of you, sliding on top of you, that first sensation of feeling you inside me.' I put my hands in my knickers and stroke myself, watching him get more and more aroused.

'You felt incredible,' he moans, closing his eyes briefly.

'Open your eyes, look at me,' I tell him.

He looks over at my hand.

'Tell me what you remember,' I ask, my hand sliding over myself more furiously.

'You did this thing where you'd glide over me, slowly. I remember licking your nipples, that sound you made when I had them in my mouth, not quite a moan, like you were a little surprised, a laugh.'

I shift back on that chair, feeling the leather sticking against my shoulders 'The way you lost control after that. You flipped me over and hooked my legs under your arms, and you slid deeply into me.'

We hear the footsteps of kids running up and down the corridors. I put a hand over my mouth to control my moans. I look over and he smiles at me.

'It was all very, very...'

'Very...' I gasp.

I think about the way he slid into me, the motion, being completely lost in him, feeling so deeply aroused and being in that space where I could scream with pleasure. I could tell him how hard I wanted him to fuck me, how I gripped on to his shoulders and pulled him into me. I feel the tension, the pleasure build inside me. I watch him put an arm down to steady himself. This is not professional. All that separates us is a door that I hope can't be opened from the outside. I want him so incredibly badly. I want to hold on to that bunk bed ladder and have him pound me until I scream. Suzie, who even are you? This is... this is... I watch him lie back as he comes, the motion rippling through his back, making his neck clench. I can't hold it in any longer. I clasp my hand tightly over my mouth to muffle the sound of my orgasm. I... I can't. I don't know. What is happening? I've not even opened my bag yet. I've not seen the ensuite. I laugh, loudly in relief, in satisfaction, feeling the pulses of pleasure roar through me. When I look back at Charlie, he lies there, staring up at the underside of the bunk bed, speechless.

'Did you?' he asks me.

'Yeah.'

He sits up, sweat making his chest and stomach glisten, a glow to his cheeks, trying to regain his composure. I've never been more attracted to someone in my life. Charlie. Not Carlos. Just him. And as all the emotion I once felt for him comes flooding back, it transfers to the right person, maybe, the one in front of me.

'That was...'

'Hot,' I tell him.

He nods. 'Very...'

'Just...' There's something wrong, a proviso, a problem? Maybe he doesn't want this? Maybe it's too soon, too quick? 'Viraj is right. We need aircon. It's too hot to be doing that for the next three days.'

'Three days?'

'Yeah,' he says smiling at me.

Charlie

'Whoa, someone is thirsty...' Mark says as he watches me down my Coke on the rooftop terrace of the hostel, a beautiful spot draped in fairy lights that lets us drink in the view of the spires of old churches and brightly coloured terraced houses, neighbouring rooftops draped in plants and terracotta plant pots. The sun sits low for five o'clock and the students all sit there, lounging around on white plastic chairs, posing for selfies and posting it all on their IG. We've just dragged them round the largest Gothic cathedral in Europe and filled them to the brim with churros so with the early start, the hope is that they're going to pass out really quickly and we can start hydrating properly with Estrella. This is all very thirsty work. I notice Suzie laughing with the students in the corner of that rooftop. Incredibly thirsty work.

'I'm going to have to go down the pharmacy and get some talc for my bits,' Mark announces to the teacher group that involves a very confused Jorge, our tour leader.

'Mi cojones are very sweaty,' Mark explains to him. 'Mucho caliente.'

We all need that image removed from our heads, immediately. Jackie shakes her head. 'Because we all wanted to know that, love,' she says, burning with embarrassment.

'You love it, it's romance, all that intimacy,' he says, winking at her.

'Romance is flowers, chocolates, you buffoon,' she says, blowing him a kiss.

I smile at both of them, headed over to grab another drink, taking two tins and walking over to Suzie. I can do that now. I think. There have been times in the last few weeks when I would see her in the staffroom and walk away, going to sit in my car during lunch sometimes to avoid bumping into her. I was confused, embarrassed. But what just happened in that hostel room? It was Mallorca again. It was balancing on the edge of that bed and watching her legs straighten as she came, her body giving in to the moment, beads of sweat resting in her decolletage. It was so incredibly intense. After that happened, there was another knock on the door. We had to go through the fire drills, so we redressed, splashed water on our faces and tried to look like we hadn't had the most ridiculous orgasms within ten minutes of stepping into this place.

After that, we headed out almost immediately, surrounded by teens; the only eye contact we had was over Christopher Columbus' grave. None of the kids knew who he was, which is fine because history is not my department, but Suzie knew, I knew. We both knew. And maybe the most ridiculous thing is that all this tension has been built without even touching each other. It feels like lightning in a bottle, electric – if I were to touch her, I'd implode. Or to put it simply, my cojones would not cope.

'Un coca para la señora?' I ask as I approach her, sitting on a white stool surrounded by all the students.

One of the boys giggles because he is a child and I give him a look as I thought I was being quite smooth. 'You thought I was offering Miss something else?' I ask him.

'Nah, Sir. I heard Coca-Cola, definitely,' he jests.

Suzie narrows her eyes at me and takes the drink, putting the cold tin next to her forehead. The heat here is different to Mallorca. Over there, you have the sea and mountain breezes but in Seville, the air is thick, it's balmy and it sits there like syrup. I look over at Suzie's shoulder, the way the strap of her top rests on her collarbone. She changed before into a white sundress. I watched as she stripped and rolled it over her body before posing for me, cheekily. I lean against the ledge of the roof, still keeping my distance, loving being able to just watch her.

'There's a lot of laughter coming from this corner?' I ask the group.

'We've been filling Miss in on the school gossip. Do you know Miss Swift in maths?' one of them asks.

'I think I do, we're in the same house,' I say.

'Well, last year she got it on with one of the cover teachers and he was a bit younger than her, you know. One of the Year 11s reckons he saw them copping off by the bike sheds,' he continues, eyes wide open.

'I like stories like this, tell me more!' Suzie says, her arms propped up on her knees. Don't look at her knees.

'Do you know Mr Rogers in science?' a girl asks.

'Ed?' I say. There's an inhalation of air as I say his real name to the crowd. These kids do think we just live at the school and have no identity, don't they?

'Well, before Ed married Miss Johnson...' they all look at me expectantly to reveal her name.

'Her name is Mia,' Suzie interjects.

'Ed was with some maths teacher who did the dirty on him. Now she's at another school and we heard she got fired for having an online sex sesh with someone's dad when she was supposed to be doing a parents' evening,' this boy speaks at about seventy miles per hour and Suzie and I laugh to hear him so enthused by all the hearsay.

'So what's your goss?' a voice pipes in. It's Lola who seems to be in her element now her clothes don't look so out of place. 'You're both super new, I bet you both have stories.'

I glance over at Suzie. I don't think those stories are suitable for this young audience.

'Ooh, two truths and a lie!' one kid suggests.

'You what now?' I ask.

'You give us three things about yourself, two of them are true and one is a lie and then we have to guess which one's the lie,' he says, rubbing his hands.

There's a group of about six to seven kids here, all waiting. Suzie laughs and looks over at me. 'Well, I am twenty-six. I'm an Aquarius and I learned to speak French from my childhood friend who happens to be Timothée Chalamet,' she says, earnestly. The children all roll their eyes and giggle.

'I think the idea is that the lie is marginally believable...' I tell her. She laughs, tilting back her head.

'Well, I am twenty-eight, I once fractured my wrist in two places after an incident with a mechanical bull. I have a brother called Maximus.'

The children all sit there, trying to work it out. 'Why were you on a mechanical bull, Sir?' someone asks. 'Like one of them bucking bronco things?'

'Yes.'

'But why? Are you a cowboy?'

'Yes. But I gave up the Wild West to come to London and teach you neeks Spanish.'

They all laugh whilst Suzie looks at me, trying to work it all out. 'It's the Maximus thing, I reckon,' she guesses.

I shake my head. 'I'm twenty-seven. My dad was a big fan of the film *Gladiator*. We just call him Max now though.'

She smiles.

'What *Gladiators*, like that show where they wear the leotards and have the muscles?' someone asks. How have we let them all down so badly? Again, not my department. 'What's your real name, Sir?'

'Charlie. And Miss is...'

'Suzie.'

It's like we've told these kids our passwords.

'What about a middle name?'

I smile. 'It's also a bit random. It's Rafe. But spelt like Ralph.'

'Like the boy from *Lord of the Flies*?' a lad asks. English department representing well here.

'Yes but no. On their first date, my parents went to see a film called *The English Patient* and they named me after one of the actors in that film.'

Suzie stops for a moment when I say that out loud, and I wonder if she's thinking back to what she said on the airplane. That was a coincidence, right? She looks over at me, smiling.

'Are you both single then?' Lola asks.

'That's a very personal question, Lola,' I reply.

'¿Estás casado, señor?' she asks again. I now feel obliged to answer because she has asked me in Spanish.

'Sí,' I watch Suzie stop for a minute. 'Mi esposa es Camilla Cabello,' I answer. They all moan. 'You all laughed when Miss said Timothée Chalamet taught her French.' I see Suzie smiling, taking another sip of her drink. 'Anyways, enough about us because I think we should all be asking Lola how it's going with Josh.'

That corner of the rooftop all cheer teasingly, pushing Lola's shoulders. I hate to shift the focus on to her but I need to avoid the awkwardness of talking about marriage and relationships with Suzie in the vicinity.

'Sir, that's a very personal question,' Lola says. 'I can't believe you.'

'I know Josh,' Suzie adds. 'I teach him French. He's lovely. Are you two a thing? How long has it been going on?'

'We've been talking for about three months.'

'That's quite a long time,' I add. 'Do you really like him?'

'This is the thing, Sir,' a girl interrupts. 'They only talk on Snapchat. They've never actually spoken in real life.'

Suzie and I look at each other, smiling. 'So what do you do when you bump into each other at school?'

'I say nothing. He says nothing,' she replies.

'They're too nervous, Miss,' someone interrupts.

'I'm not nervous. It's just that it works nice on Snapchat, that's all.'

'And when we say chatting,' I enquire. 'It's all PG, yeah... above board?' I ask, putting my safeguarding hat on.

'Oh yeah,' Lola replies. 'My parents would kill me otherwise, we talk about school and what we might do at college, gossip and swap memes. He's well funny.'

A boy in the group scrunches up his face in disgust but Suzie and I smile at the sweetness of it all, we know what teen relationships can look like and how they can be rushed. God, we know rushed, but here's something where two people are taking their time and getting to know each other and these are the foundations every relationship should really be built on.

'So why don't you talk to him? You could call him now?' Suzie suggests.

'NO!' Lola says. 'Not with you spoons standing around.'

'Or maybe go on a date?' I tell her. 'Go for coffee? Maybe go for a walk?'

The young people look at me strangely. You guys still date,

no? Or do you just snap and do interpretative TikTok dances for each other?

'That sounds like a perfect date...' Suzie interrupts.

'Or...' Lola says. 'You can all leave us alone. It will happen. I just... I'm scared.'

'Of....?'

'That he won't like me when he gets to know the real me. What if I'm better on text? What if he thinks I'm an idiot? I'd have to be close to him, actually touch his hand. I don't know how to do that.'

Suzie and I look at each other, smiling knowingly. 'Then maybe you just take a chance. Be brave, go for it, right?' Suzie looks her in the eye, holding her drink aloft so Lola can clink it against hers.

'Maybe,' she says. 'Miss... you never told us if you were married?' Lola asks.

She hesitates then searches for my face, still learning against that ledge, the city landscape still behind me and the warmth of the evening sun on my back.

Before she can answer, the conversation is suddenly interrupted by someone putting a Bluetooth speaker on. This feels like one of the songs Brooke blasts out in the kitchen when she's making a mess. It might be Charli XCX but I won't say that aloud in case the kids crucify me. Yet I'm grateful it has some sort of beat.

'Everyone,' Lee shouts out. 'Other people are also staying in this hostel. Please can we make good choices. Do not repeat some of these lyrics.'

'But they're in English, Sir, no one will know what they mean!'

It would be useful if Mark and Jackie also listened to this advice as they get up and start swaying. I marvel at how they're not even drunk unless they've been knocking it back already in their room. A few of the kids get up and start to dance, shouting out the lyrics, hanging drinks in the air and swaying.

'Come on Miss, Sir...' Lola shouts, live streaming it all to someone, somewhere, on her phone.

Suzie comes up and stands next to me on that ledge, leaning back. She holds her face up to count some of the stars peeking through then looks at me. I think we're supposed to be stopping this from getting out of control but it's hard to resist the memory they're creating on this rooftop drenched in sunshine that will stay with them forever. We normally don't see our teenagers so joyful.

'Do you want to dance?' I ask her.

She laughs. 'The children would talk.'

'I'm not talking slow dancing, tango style...'

'Oh, you're going to do a flamenco for us, are you?' she jokes.

'We wouldn't even have to touch...'

'That seems to be our thing at the moment,' she says, grinning. I look down, trying to hold in my laughter.

'This isn't really dancing,' she tells me. We look over at the kids, who are basically jumping with their arms around each other. 'It's more... letting go... euphoric dancing,' she says, laughing to herself.

I give her a look as she shrugs her shoulders and invites me on to that dance space. And I laugh as she starts to jump around, throwing shapes, her hair swinging and backlit by the Sevillian sun. I don't think she's a very good dancer. I'm not sure I care.

SIXTEEN

Suzie

'It's midnight. I don't care if other Spanish people are up. Go to sleep,' says a beleaguered Charlie in the hallway. What are you doing with that shaving foam? Give it here? No, put it down.'

Contrary to what we previously thought – that the early start would have made these kids super tired – it transpires that dancing and too much Coke (the drink) on the rooftop has turned these kids into whirling swirling overtired child beasts. This hostel is going to hate us, they're going to tar us English all with the same hooligan brush. It's been like this for the last six hours so this also means Charlie and I have barely spoken, let alone touched or had the time to do anything remotely steamy.

'Please put some clothes on, why are you in swimming trunks? Where are you going?' I can still hear Charlie trying to control them and herd them into their rooms. 'I will ring all your parents. All of them, look at me! I'm holding my phone.'

I lie back in my top bunk and try to rest for a little bit, grateful for a night breeze coming through the window. All the staff are rotating patrol duties so I try to think of ways to calm them down when it's eventually my turn. Cough medicine? An attempt to block all their WiFi/data signals? Money? I scratch at my left ankle. Urgh, I'm also getting bitten. I scratch that itch again and reach down to feel a red bump. Not just one bump, it's a little cluster of them. Some Spanish mosquito has had a feast. I'm calling him Miguel. The little prick. I turn on my phone torch to try and look for him and give him a good piece of my mind. But as the light hits my ankle, I look at the bites and my face creases up. I don't think those are mosquito bites. A quick Google images search confirms my suspicions and I do some sort of strange spasm-like movement in the bed, crawling towards the slide so I get down and out of here. The bizarre jumpy seizure like dance continues on the floor, just as Charlie enters the room. He stands there for a moment, watching me.

'God, not you too. Is this still part of your euphoric dancing?' he enquires.

I am suddenly conscious that I am in my pants and a vest top.

'No,' I say, shimmying in my discomfort. I lift my leg a little in the air to show off my bites. 'I'm getting bitten. I think my mattress has bed bugs.' I continue to do my dance as he tries to pretend he's not smiling.

'Are the kids in bed yet?' I ask.

'No, Mark has taken over. He's already threatened to throw someone's suitcase out of the window so we shall see how that goes.'

I am listening but also have my phone out examining up and down my legs with the torch from my phone.

'This is a strange way to present your legs to me,' he says. 'Lighting them up like this.'

'Do you think they're in me? Are bed bugs like nits? Do they cling on?'

He continues to just stand there looking at me in disbelief. I am not a biologist. I teach verbs.

'I think they live in the bed which is why they're called...'

'Bed bugs...' I repeat, slowly. 'Why are you laughing at me? They might be in your mattress too. There could be an infestation...' I whisper. I'm not quite sure why. Maybe I don't want the bed bugs to be offended.

'That's a sexy word,' he says, poking his tongue out, trying to lighten the mood. 'Are they itchy?'

I nod, reaching down subconsciously to grate my fingers over the bites. 'Sit down on the edge of my bed,' he says. I do as I'm told while he digs through his bag. He then comes to kneel down in front of me and puts out a hand.

'I'm going to touch you now,' he says, a cheeky look in his eye knowing that we haven't done that yet. The touching. 'Give me your ankle.' I hold it out and he cups it gently, running his fingers along the bites like he's reading braille. I feel that touch everywhere and shudder again, feeling it run up and down my spine. 'I think with bed bugs you have to suck the poison out?'

'Really?'

'No.' He strokes his fingers up and down my foot and ankle and looks me in the eye. He reaches down for a jar of ointment. 'They went for you. You must be tasty.'

'It has been said.'

'I'm rubbing some Tiger Balm on this. It will calm down the bites and help with the itching,' he says, using his index finger to rub the balm over the bites lightly in circular motions. He's good at that but we knew that already. I remember a moment next to a swimming pool where he was exceptional at that. I try and steady my breath. He then leans over and kisses my knee. 'This poses a very serious question, you know?'

'It does?' I ask.

'Where on earth are you going to sleep tonight?' He rests his hands on my knees and looks up at me. It's started again, hasn't it? All of it. This tension, feeling so incredibly turned on every time he's close to me.

'Your mattress might have bed bugs too,' I tell him.

'Maybe if we sleep on it together, our combined weight might scare them off,' he suggests.

'Is that a scientific method of prevention then?'

'Yes.' He kneels up. 'We can do this as fast or as slow as you want though? We can top and tail, I can sleep on the floor if that would make you more comfortable?'

I shake my head, appreciating his good manners. I pat the space next to me. 'Let's share.' This is the moment, right? Lying on the same mattress, a singular pillow and a shared space where we can have sex. The sort of sex we've craved all day, we can recreate Mallorca and I can feel him inside me, I am aching to feel him inside me.

He takes off his shirt and I look at the outline of his shoulders. He comes to sit next to me, our bodies not quite touching yet. 'What a day,' he says, his eyes heavy, exhaling loudly. He rests his head on the pillow and invites me to curl into him, to rest in his arms. I find a space, our legs meeting and he finds a space just above my hip to rest a hand. I feel the warmth of his breath on my neck as he goes to kiss it, just below my hairline.

'I like this,' he says, sleepily. And I will admit to liking it too, to feeling safe in his arms, like this is a good place to be. I adore the feel of his skin against mine.

'I hope you don't snore?' I whisper. 'Or steal the covers, not that there are any covers. It's basically a sheet.' I should stop talking because I think talking is what killed it last time. The fan in the corner of the room still rotates and the breeze is still soothing, making the curtain dance around the window. 'Do you think if we move around a lot it may just crush all the bed bugs?' I ask. It was a bit of unorthodox way to initiate sex but I'm hoping he finds it funny. I can literally feel his groin pressed up against me. I think about him slipping my knickers down, sliding his fingers over me, me putting a hand to his chin, as he whispers absolute filth into my ears. Charlie still hasn't answered. Instead, his lips are against the back of my neck but I can feel the steady stream of him breathing against me. 'Charlie? Are you asleep?' I don't know why I ask this because if he is asleep then he won't answer. I know what's in his shorts is asleep. But I don't mind. I like this, quiet space where the energy just lets us rest for the moment, it lets us become entwined in each other. 'Sleep tight... don't let the bed bugs bite...' I laugh at my own joke. I'm half glad he's not conscious to hear that.

'Ummm... yeah... wha... no...'

Oh no, maybe he did hear it. 'What was that, Charlie?'

I don't think I can cope with a sleep talker, I'll think him possessed half the time.

'Put the shaving foam down.'

Well, maybe he isn't possessed. I giggle quietly. In this in-between sleep, he also rubs his feet together. It makes a strange noise like he's trying to start a fire. I smile and close my eyes, feeling like I'm at peace, like I could fall asleep very, very quickly.

Charlie

Max always tells me there's a test to know if you really love someone or not, and that's when you wake up in the morning, and the sight of them and the smell of their morning breath doesn't completely scare you. With his fiancée, Amy, he says it happened when they first went camping together in the New Forest. In his own words, Amy woke up looking like the Gruffalo. She swore profusely at how cold and rainy it was and then got out of her sleeping bag, threw a hoodie on, opened the tent up and ran into a bush to go and have a wee. He said he lay there, laughing at her and knew he was in love.

I look over at Suzie now and see her curled up on the bed like a little kitten. Her dark wavy hair is swept over her face so she just looks like a massive hairball with a body, her knees curled up towards her, those red bumps on her ankle still visible. She also drools when she sleeps. I woke with a very wet arm, assuming it to be sweat but no. I just laughed and inhaled her hair which smelt vaguely of sweat and coconut. It felt like I was just where I needed to be.

I head over to the window and peer out on to the street. The kids eventually crashed and with any luck they'll sleep in. Outside, the twilight hangs in the air, a few cyclists and people shuffling up and down the cobbles, a cooler air sweeping through the window that is mildly refreshing. One thing I always liked about Seville was that the sun rose and set late so it felt like the day was framed perfectly. I slid out of bed about half an hour ago to calm myself down in the shower. Is this because I woke up with a raging hard-on? Yes. And it didn't feel like the ideal way for her to wake up, feeling that in her back, thinking I'm obsessed with sex. I'm just obsessed with her. Enough to want her to wake up comfortably and not feeling mortified that she left my forearm sticky with her saliva.

I hope this works. I hope she won't hate me in a few seconds. I squat down next to the bed. 'Suzie? Suzie?'

'Huh, shit. What is it? Is it the children? Are they still fucking up?' she moans. I laugh as she tries to clear the hair from her face, a line of dried drool leading down from her right lip. 'Maybe we can call the police and they can just arrest them all,' she says, her eyes still closed. 'Is it my turn to go and patrol the halls?'

'No... it's about seven in the morning.'

She still hasn't opened her eyes. 'Then why are we up? I thought breakfast wasn't until nine.'

'I had an idea,' I say, bending over and kissing her elbow, the one curled and supporting her face.

'You're a morning sex person, aren't you?' she mumbles. 'I like you but I also like sleep. Come back to bed.'

The invitation is tempting but I'm hoping she might be open to the alternative too. She stretches out in bed and I see a slice of stomach and the curve of her pelvic bone as she does. She picks at the corners of her eyes. 'I must look a state?' she says sheepishly.

'It's just a bit of sleepy dust...' I say.

'What did you call it?' she says, smiling.

'What do you call it?'

'Eye bogeys,' she says, laughing.

'That's...'

'Gross?' We both laugh as she smacks her gums together, trying to wake up. 'What was this grand idea then that involves us being up at this ungodly hour?' she asks, finally opening her eyes.

'Fancy a walk?'

'Did you just say walk or wank?' she says, smiling. 'I'm still half asleep.'

'Walk...'

She finally focuses enough to look me in the eye, cradling my chin, kissing me gently on the forehead. 'Just so you don't have to smell my morning breath,' she tells me. 'Will this walk involve coffee?'

'It will.'

'Then let's do it.'

'Eres más feo que una nevera por detrás,' I say, as we walk along the banks of the Guadalquivir river. 'Which means you're uglier than the back of a fridge.' She bends over laughing, cradling her coffee. 'You asked me about my favourite Spanish phrase and that is it... I learned it here.'

Having Suzie beside me on the cobbles, making her laugh, being able to hold her hand feels intensely right. It reminds me of our first moments together in Mallorca, but this feels a bit more like a date rather than the stars pushing us together. This feels like it's on our terms. She's also wearing knickers and I have a shirt on which helps settle the mood a little. Suzie wears her hair in a ponytail, teaming it with a short denim skirt, a white camisole top, her red trainers and a light white shirt that she leaves open. If anything, this feels like a date in disguise and I can't stop from grinning widely, hoping this isn't putting her off. I bite into one the pastries we picked up on the way here, licking the icing sugar off my lips. The river is still, the palms painting dark silhouettes into the sky. On the other side, the brightly coloured buildings are illuminated by the streetlights. There's still a warmth to the streets, even without the sun in the sky, and there's the promise of heat ahead when it comes up. Cars and mopeds speed past us as the city starts to stir slowly.

'And it was just the one year you were here?' she asks me.

'Ten months in the end, they let me finish those last two months in London.'

'How come?' she asks.

I pause. 'It was around the time my parents passed away so I had to go back. Extenuating circumstances.'

She's quiet, pensive. We've not spoken like this before. We've dealt in banter and surface talk that hasn't really been that meaningful I guess. 'You did explain it briefly once. I am sorry you had to go through that. I will assume it was unexpected?'

'Car crash,' I say, not before sipping my coffee to not have to think about it too much. It's quite hot and scalds my tongue. 'After that, life took a pretty sharp turn. Sam was only ten at the time so I…'

'Did a truly amazing thing…' she tells me. I don't reply immediately because I hear that phrase a lot. Mainly from relatives, Sam's teachers at school and Enzo at the Italian on the high street, but the truth of the matter is that I wouldn't have not done it. And it's an impossible job to be a sibling and a pseudo-parent. We eat a lot of omelettes and pasta because my cooking still isn't great and I let them on their phones too much. I have no idea if I'm getting any of it right. 'Tell me about them, your siblings.'

I veer off the path of the riverbank and get her to cross a road for me, back towards the city. 'Max is twenty-three. He's an electrician, he's very loyal, occasionally a tool but in the best possible way.' She laughs. 'Brooke is last year of college and wants to go to university to study psychology, she's loud and argumentative but a heart of gold. And Sam is big on skateboarding and a really good artist. He's a kind, soulful kid. I wish he'd wash his hair more.'

She remains quiet, giving me the space to speak, nodding thoughtfully, and I wonder if this is scaring her off, quelling all those flames of desire to hear my life laid out like this. But maybe it's important she knows everything about me.

'And Max is the stag?' she asks me.

'Yeah, he's marrying a woman called Amy. I know it's young to be getting married. Twenty-three. I worry about that sometimes but they're cute together. She's good for him. I think it works.'

Again, she's quiet but continues walking next to me as we enter the gates to a park, the walkways still dimly lit in the twilight. 'So being a teacher? Was that your decision or...?' she asks me.

'It fit in with my degree, my life at home. It turns out I'm not awful at it,' I reply. 'What about you? Your family?'

She pauses. 'It's just me. No siblings. My mum passed away seven years ago. I never really knew my dad. All I have really are my cousins.'

'Beth and the famous cousins. I know them,' I say, trying to show her I'm listening, that I care. 'I'm very sorry about your mum.'

'Well, you know what it's like? To lose a parent, an anchor of sorts. She was a wonderful woman, I miss her a lot.'

I reach over and hold her hand, giving it a light squeeze, my heart swelling to know exactly what she means. I try to read her vibe as we walk; she seems serious, even a little sad as we walk past heavy metal railings and grand white buildings that shine through the twilight. 'And why teaching?'

'I had some vague naive notion that I could make a difference. Now I think it just fuels my stationery fetish. I make a mean flashcard,' she says.

She doesn't offer more. We cross a final road towards the Parque de María Luisa, dodging scooters and cyclists. Beyond the park gates, a long sandy walkway extends beyond us lined with trees, the sort of dark green tropical plants that always make you feel you're miles away from England. 'You do know where we're going, yeah?'

Literally, yes. I don't know in the other sense of the word. I nod. 'This is my favourite place in Seville.'

'Why?' she asks.

I smile but I don't tell her. It's pretty, for sure, but the truth is my parents came out to visit me while I was here and this is the spot where I took my last photo with them. 'You'll see.'

I glance over at her, still sipping her coffee and I can't read how she's feeling. We could have been having quiet morning sex in a bunk bed in a hostel; instead I went for the option where I just spilled my guts to her, telling her all about my complicated life journey. I am miles away from that brooding Carlos who swaggered into her life. It's just me, Charlie. Clutching a bag of pastries, wearing my New Balance that my seventeen-year-old sister brought me because she says my taste in trainers is cheugy.

We continue walking past the trees lining this path, past early-morning joggers and a few tourists with big cameras until the buildings start to come into view. She stops and stands there for a moment taking it in. 'Plaza de España,' she says, under her breath.

I used to come here a lot because it was so regal and magnificent, and one of those places where you can remind yourself the world is bigger than that small suburb of London you grew up in. It's the way the ornate stone building sweeps around the plaza, the cavernous arches, the patterns on the stone courtyard before it, the way a canal sits in front of it, still and dotted with Venetian style bridges, adorned with mosaic and glazed ceramic features. She walks up to a parapet, placing her hands on the stone as I watch her. I like seeing her reaction in her eyes, the wonder and shock. 'We're supposed to be coming here later,' she says.

'I know, I just thought it would be nicer to see it without fifty kids in tow.' I look down at my watch as the sky starts to lighten, the streetlamps surrounding the canals turn off and, just like magic, the sun peeks through over the top of the buildings. It casts the whole place in an amber glow. I turn to look at Suzie. Is that a tear in her eye? She reaches down for my hand, our fingers grazing past each other, the softest of touches until she turns to me, facing me, her eyes scanning the outline of my face. Our faces are barely touching but she closes her eyes, breathing gently. Yes, this was planned. Waking her up early, walking her over here, looking up the sunrise times so we'd be here at just the right moment. I wanted us to have some time to talk, to understand each other, to not let the heat consume us. Our lips finally meet and the feel of them pressed against me is surprisingly soft. She tastes like icing sugar.

I cup her face with two hands, the energy building as she presses herself against me, my hands moving down to her waist, and, with the light of the sun behind us, it feels like electricity.

She stops to catch her breath, her eyes closed. Then she looks over her shoulder. The plaza is still relatively quiet, a few tourists milling around. I know what she's thinking. She looks out to the park, taking my hand, and leads me down a sandy pathway, until we're hidden away by bushes and a stone gazebo draped in greenery. We smile at each other. We can't do this back at the hostel, not in the way we want. But this might work. She goes to kiss me again and I move my hands to her lower back, taking her shirt in my clenched fists. I remember this feeling so well, so intimately. I back her into one of the pillars and move my kisses lower across her neck and stomach, reaching down to her skirt until I'm on my knees, my hands reaching around to her butt, reaching to press her against my face, moving her knickers to one side, to taste her.

'THAT IS A SUCH A LOVELY TREE!' she suddenly shouts. At first, I wonder if she's talking about my erection but then she leapfrogs over me, leaving me on my knees. 'I think it might be a... what tree is that?'

I look around swiftly and then turn again, pretending to tie a shoelace that I don't have. Shit. I need to stand up. 'It looks like an oak, darling? Maybe a... beech?' I don't know anything about bloody Spanish trees but I do know a group of very curious Korean tourists stand in front of us. They wear broad-rimmed hats and carry selfie sticks. A tour guide looks at us and shakes her head, smirking. 'Y pensabais que la temperatura solo iba a subir más tarde.' I shake my head at her, chuckling, as the group walk past us, one lady taking a picture of me. I'm hoping she didn't take that at an angle that lit up my semi.

Suzie turns around, her face in her hands. 'Oh my god, oh my god,' she says, resting her head against me. 'What did she say?'

I put an arm around her. 'And you thought it was going to get hot later in the day...'

And she laughs, this full-bellied loud laugh that rings around the park and makes a few pigeons fly away, and I laugh back, holding her next to me as the sun starts to make its ascent and the sky shines bright blue around us.

SEVENTEEN

Suzie

'Miss, Miss... this fish ain't looking at us?'

'It's because he's Spanish, innit? He don't understand us.'

We need to get these kids out of London more or at least develop the curriculum to teach them fish don't have a language. I think. They just speak Fish, don't they? I look over at them, their little faces all backlit by the aquarium lighting, marvelling at getting up close and personal with these strange creatures in the Acuario de Sevilla.

'Look at that big bastard shark!' one of them yells.

'Language!' I yell back, trying to herd them in the right direction. I look around the tunnels of this place and see Charlie up ahead with his group, a pale blue neon light over his face, laughing with his teens and talking about how something is 'muy grande'.

After the Plaza de España this morning and being caught out by a group of Korean tourists, we headed back to the hostel drenched in some sort of halcyon radiance, walking down cobbled streets of quaint shops and cafés, hand-in-hand, my head rested on his shoulder. It was a silent walk of knowing looks, stolen kisses and an understanding that we'd shared a moment, we knew each other a bit more intimately and the seeds of something were planted, growing. Before it felt so frenetic, and it felt good to have seen him more clearly for a while, to have heard him talk so affectionately about his family life and how he cared for his siblings. I wondered how much to share in return. When do I bring up Paul? But I think I was almost scared to – afraid of polluting the intimacy we were creating, the love he expressed for his family, with the complications of my messy life. Maybe that would come in time. It felt right to protect that moment of calm. Until we got back to the hostel that is, and all the students started getting up for breakfast.

'And this is the Estrella de Mar Roja,' Jorge our guide, tells us. I like Jorge's calm. You sense he's been around lots of these school groups before and little seems to faze him. He's an older man with a rucksack, sandals, socks and a sunhat with a strap. 'In your native English, I believe it's called a red-knobbed starfish.'

Naturally, this results in quite a few sniggers among the group as we proceed to the next tank.

'Señora, why do the children always laugh when I say this?' Jorge asks me. 'It is confusing to me. Are they laughing at me?'

'Oh no...' I tell him. 'It's just, in English, knob can be a word for...' My limited Spanish means I don't know the word so I point down.

'Vagina?' he says in shock.

'Oh no,' I say. 'What you have?'

'Pene?' I will assume he's not talking about the pasta. I nod.

'Oh,' he says, horrified. 'Well, hopefully, it is just that fish.' He smiles, walking up to the children again. 'And you all know our good friend Nemo here but this blue fish is called a doncella rayada – in English, a slippery dick.' I walk away again, trying to hold in my laughter.

We did the Plaza de España with the students this morning, a different place under the throng of tourists with their tour flags and desperation to record everything, but many a picture was taken and sent home so worried parents can at least believe we're trying to introduce their kids to some culture on their time abroad. Bocadillos in the glorious leafy park for lunch followed but now, the peace and cool of the aquarium is a welcome break from the sun and all the kids telling us constantly that they're too hot.

'Do you happen to know the name of that fish, señora?' I recognise his voice immediately and smile in that dark room, as I feel his arm graze against mine. That feeling that soars through me when he's near is like being recharged.

'I'm not au fait with fish, I'm afraid,' I inform him.

'Well, this silver one is usually found in the shallows of the North Atlantic, in reefs. He's called Swim Shady.' I laugh a little too loudly at that. 'I can't take credit for that joke; that was some kid called Jack over there.'

'I'm disappointed in you, scrounging jokes off the kids like that...'

'And there was you thinking I was actually funny...'

But he is. He is so many things that I'm slowly falling for, so much so that I'm almost too scared to voice it.

There's something about his honesty, the fact he wanted us to go for something as simple and cleansing as a walk to begin the day together, the fact he wants to rewind from all that heat in Mallorca and not just jump into all that passion and physical attraction so blindly. Most men would do it differently, they would let it dictate a relationship, overpower it. I knew someone like that. I don't think I've ever met someone like you, Charlie, and that scares me a little.

'Keep an eye on Thomas, by the way,' he tells me. 'He keeps

asking me what fish in here can be used to make sushi,' he says, laughing. 'I worry that sandwich at lunch wasn't enough for him.' I giggle again as his hand brushes against my back and rests there for a moment. I ache for it to be there for longer. He leaves me again to re-find his group. 'And look at that shark, muchos dientes,' he tells them. I find my gaze following him, watching his figure disappear into the darkness again and he turns to smile at me.

'When are we ever going to need that, Sir?' someone complains.

I walk ahead, stopping in front of a big tank of corals and tropical fish, a ray floating past with his tiny mouth, possibly smiling at me. Next to me stands Lola who, instead of looking at the fish, looks down at her phone. I glance over and see she's talking to Josh and they seem to be trading in fish emojis, which I hope isn't some teen code for sexting. She sees me peering over. 'That's a bit rude, Miss. Looking at my private messages.'

'I was looking at nothing,' I lie defensively. 'I was just surprised you want to be looking at your phone instead of all this aquatic sea life.'

'It's just fish, innit? My dad has a tank like this at home.'

'With sharks?' I say, pointing to one that swims past us.

She narrows her eyes at me, shaking her head. There's big teen energy that comes off this one and I suspect she doesn't find me too amusing. She looks over at me. 'Miss, can I ask a question?'

'Is it related to fish? I don't think I know that much about them.'

'No, it's about boys.'

'Josh?' I guess.

'Kinda. I just... I like him. I can talk to him for hours sometimes but I'm not too sure if I want a boyfriend right now,' she says. I smile to think about the innocent thrill of a relationship, the long conversations with someone you've just met. That said,

I'm impressed by the head on this girl too, for being able to cope with the idea she can survive without a relationship or a man defining her.

'That's fair. You can focus on your schoolwork then,' I tell her.

'Yeah, you sound like my mum,' she says, unimpressed.

'Well, if you have to find out if Josh is for you then perhaps you need to talk to the boy first.'

'This is true,' she says, slightly suspicious that I've remembered that detail. 'That's going to be mega awkward at school though. Like, I just go up to him one day and say hi or something...'

'Yeah, can I borrow a pen? Isn't maths rubbish? What have you got for your packed lunch?' I suggest.

'Packed lunch chat? Yeah, you're telling me you've not got much rizz, Miss...' she says, laughing.

'Be brave, jump into the water, fully clothed,' I tell her.

'And what if he's a shark?' she asks, looking out into the tank. I think that same shark is circling us, watching. And for a moment, and quite bizarrely, I think of Paul. I think it's the beady soulless eyes.

'What if he hurts you? You punch him in the nose and swim away, quickly and far away,' I say plainly, still looking at that shark.

'Alright then, Miss...' she says. 'Gracias.'

'You're welcome.'

I notice the students I had responsibility for have walked ahead, through to another room with more tanks and I pick up my pace to catch them up as there seems to be an open rockpool where a guide is letting the kids touch the fish. Where is that Thomas kid? Do we have eyes on him?

'Podéis usar uno o dos dedos,' the aquarium guide says, and the kids gawp at him cluelessly.

Charlie stands to the front of the group, flaring his nostrils. 'Did anyone get that?' he asks.

'Something about two?' a voice shouts out.

He sees me at the back of the group with my students. 'He said to touch the fish, you can use one or two fingers.'

'That's what she said,' a boy shouts out.

'Yeah, less of that Jack,' Charlie says in resigned tones, as I look down and laugh rather unprofessionally.

'Acariciadlos, suavemente. A los peces les gusta con suavidad,' the guide shouts out again.

Charlie closes his eyes. 'Stroke them gently. The fish like it gentle.'

Again, the crowd of kids roar with laughter and I have no choice but to join in. They all line up in a reasonably orderly manner and take it in turns to stroke rays and pick up urchins. When I get closer to Charlie, I still have a rather puerile grin on my face.

'Sir...'

'Miss...'

'Did you want a stroke?' he asks. 'It's quite the experience.'

'Really?'

'Is it wet?' I ask.

'Well, that is a stupid question, they are aquatic animals that live in the sea,' he jokes.

The aquarium guide looks at both of us, slightly confused that I would ask if the fish would be wet. Is this woman an actual teacher?

'I wouldn't mind a stroke of something different perhaps?' I say biting my lip, the last student out of earshot and Charlie's eyes widen.

'Later? I promise,' he says.

However, the aquarium staff member standing there in between us, who we assume can't speak any English interprets that dirty talk a little differently. 'You want to see something diferente?' he asks me. We both turn to him, wondering what he's going to suggest, and he opens a door and reaches into a tank. Different could mean many things, no? Maybe something benign like a mussel or a turtle but what he pulls out is the biggest motherfucking crab I've ever seen. His legs lengthy and gnarled, pincers the size of adult hands, the bugger looks like he has seven tentacles coming out his mouth. I can't talk to see it. But someone can. He doesn't quite talk, it's more a high-pitched shriek.

'But señora said she wants to stroke...' he says, laughing heartily. 'Yum yum yum...'

I laugh as he makes the noise coming towards Charlie.

'Get it away... get it away...' Charlie says, flapping his arms around, still screaming and backing away from it, into me.

'Charlie, CHARLIE! I'm too close to the...'

Edge. Of the rockpool. I lose my balance as he backs into me, my arms flailing, feet coming off the floor. And the last thing I feel is me grabbing on to him, and a massive splash as we both fall in, together.

Charlie

'Well, at least it wasn't one of the children so there will be less paperwork,' Lee tells Mark and me as we sit there on the rooftop of the hostel, taking in some beers in the last of the Sevillian light. The group all laugh at us as I sit there nursing my pride and my wounds, because I got an urchin stuck in my thigh that had to be removed. I can't tell what's worse. The fact that children filmed the episode so that might be the basis of our school notoriety until the end of time or the fact the aquarium, desperately apologetic for scaring us with the giant crab, gave us free annual membership and T-shirts to take home.

I watch Suzie wearing hers now, her hair freshly washed, letting the last of the sunlight and heat dry it and I hold a bottle of beer to my lips, feeling pleasantly drunk, remembering the moment when we both got back to our room today and realised the first port of call was to have a shower.

'Do you want to go first?' I asked her, not wanting to assume anything.

'We could go in together?' she suggested.

'Saves water. You could check me for algae.' It was not my sexiest talk but it made her laugh, and she came over to me and kissed me gently. I ran my hands over her shirt, damp and matted to her back, and removed it, planting kisses on her shoulder, up to her neck. She smelt a little like chlorine and tinned tuna but I didn't tell her that. All I know is that one minute we were half clothed, the next we were naked and it was all achingly familiar, the curves of her, the softness of her skin, the second where she stopped to look me in the eye, biting her lip, before...

'I don't think I've ever heard a scream like that before,' Mark chuckles.

I snap back to attention. Did he hear something whilst we were in the shower? My throat is dry thinking of how the foam dripped off her breasts, the pertness of her nipples, and I backed her onto the wall of that shower, slipping my erection into her, an arm under her knee, the sound we both made when that happened, the way we both recognised the pleasure immediately. I adjust myself in my chair. It'll be all the kids talk about now if people heard us. 'Scream?' I ask, clearing my throat.

'The crab,' Mark tells me.

I relax back into my chair, relieved, bringing myself back to that roof space. 'Well, it was fairly sizeable, Mark,' I argue. 'The claws could have had my eyes out. It could have speared my bollocks,' I say in all seriousness, watching as Lee bites his lip trying to control his laughter.

'And that would have likely eclipsed every school trip story I have in my locker, and I've been on twenty-four of the things.

Remember when we brought that Spanish teacher back without any knackers because some crab went for him,' he jokes.

I look around to see everyone doubled up laughing and realise I can take a few jokes about my possible death by mutant crab if it produces this kind of mood. However, I think it also may be the effects of this 7-Eleven sangria finally kicking in after a very long day. I look down at the empty bottles around us.

'More drink, folks?' Lee says, not waiting for us to reply but disappearing to procure some more bottles.

No one tells you about this part of the school trips for teachers. It's great that everyone thinks we're so committed to their kids' education and sacrificing our time to safeguard them, but really we're here for the monumental piss-up, to blow off some steam and get to know all our colleagues properly. And when I mean properly, I've already learned that Mark likes a tight short and he has a tattoo of a maraca-playing cactus on his left shin. I know Suzie likes it when I run my tongue along her pelvic bone. I close my eyes for a moment to think about that and steady myself.

Suzie and Jackie don't sit with us. They sing along and dance to the music on the Bluetooth speaker we've stolen off one of the kids. Suzie's teal aquarium T-shirt is tied in a knot at her waist. There's something sweet about her mistimed dance moves, all joyous and happy, her bare feet skipping across the tiles. It feels like I'm seeing an unedited version of her. In my head, when I was thinking about that French girl in Mallorca, I'd romanticised her to the point of idolising her. She was this perfect mermaid who I had incredible sex with, who became the object of my fantasies when I was in the shower at six thirty in the morning. But there is something deeper in getting to know someone like this, in seeing them singing along and not quite knowing the words to a song, in having them drool on your arm when you sleep next to them. In how they also show you consideration and care when you tell them the deepest, most personal details of your life.

'Someone's got a crush, eh?' Mark says, resting his hands on the back of his head and leaning back in his chair.

'I have no idea what you mean?' I reply. 'I'm just looking at them dancing and find it hugely entertaining.'

Mark laughs. 'Yeah, right. I know loved-up eyes when I see them.'

'That would be sangria, mate,' I say, holding my glass up to the air. 'So tell me, how long have you been with Jackie for?' I ask, trying to change the subject.

'Thirty years,' he answers proudly, looking over at his wife as she quite awkwardly twerks against the ledge showing us all that she might not be wearing a bra.

'And how did you meet?' I ask him.

'Oh, it was a club in Camden. We were interesting people before we settled down with kids and became boring school fuckers,' he says, laughing. 'You'll like this story. We was at a Britpop club night, there was me looking like some wanker in a tracksuit top and a mullet and there was Jackie and her mate, Lisa. Anyways, we got talking, they needed a place to crash so they came back to my house share in Bethnal Green.'

'Smooth...'

'You'd think. Her mate passed out on the sofa but Jackie and me spoke the whole night, conversations flowed like the Carlsberg. We didn't sleep together but I thought, you know what, I think I've met the girl I'm going to marry... and you know what I did the next day? I was so sure of it that I went out and got a tattoo of her name on my left bicep.'

'Mark... that is undeniably one of the loveliest love stories I've ever heard...' I tell him, genuinely moved, but punching him in the leg.

'Oh, it would be, except I got the names mixed up in the club. I thought her name was Lisa. So here...' he tells me, pulling up his sleeve that reveals in a rather lovely cursive font the word *Lisa* and I spit out my sangria in laughter. 'Yeah, you can laugh now.'

I bend down to look at it more closely. 'Didn't you think to cover it up?'

'God, no. Jackie thinks it's bloody hilarious and that's probably why her and me get on so well.' We sit there bellowing with laughter. 'Take a punt, mate. She seems like a nice girl. But her name is Suzie, just in case you thought it was something else.' I smirk. He will never know what he just said, will he? 'Jackie! Oi! BABES!'

Jackie shimmies over, drunk and uncoordinated. 'Why aren't you dancing, you boring twat?' she asks her husband.

'Because it'd show everyone up, you know?' he says, winking at me. 'I'm tired and need a shower. Let's turn in.'

'Already? It's only eleven?' she moans.

'Only eleven? Normally at this time you're sparko. Come on, bird. You can sort an old fella out.'

'Around the kids?' she replies. 'How rude.'

'I'll show you rude.' Whilst I don't want to really picture what they're talking about, I do smile at the ease of the banter, the way her eyes twinkle when she talks to her husband. That's spark too, isn't it? Mark turns to me. 'Right, I'm giving you a segue, young Charlie. Don't waste this. I'll cut off Lee in the foyer so he doesn't interrupt you,' he says saluting me.

I salute back. 'But...'

'Name your first child after me, please?' he says, winking at me, his wife pulling him off the plastic chair with both hands. 'You sounded like you were hauling up a sack of potatoes there...' he tells Jackie.

'Ain't that the truth though?' she jokes, and they put their hands around each other, staggering away.

I smile and then look over at Suzie, who hasn't even realised they've gone and is continuing her manic rooftop dance, the fairy lights catching her hair swinging around her face. I'm not sure what to do. Do I join in? I'm not sure whether to show her that I'm a bit of a shit dancer too. She finally looks over and around, confused that she seems to be alone.

'Where did everyone go?' she says, coming over to me, glowing with perspiration, her cheeks rosy from the sangria.

'Bed, I think,' I reply. 'It's been a long day.'

She drags over a plastic white chair and sits opposite me. 'Look at us matching in our T-shirts.'

'We look good in teal,' I say.

'Keeping it real in teal, like a Spanish seal who is très gentil,' she says, half rapping, putting her hands into strange positions.

I laugh, watching her shoulders continue to dance in time to the music. 'You are arseholed.'

'I'm not!' she says, offended. 'I'm on holiday, it's kind of allowed.'

'Except it's kind of work.'

She shrugs. 'You're drunk too. This sangria is 11.5 per cent so if you're not drunk, you're lying.'

I will admit this is the reason I've stayed seated. If I got up, I may have just fallen over like a felled tree. 'How are those bed bug bites?' I ask her, looking down at her ankle.

'Surprisingly numb. Either that or the bed bugs are now a part of me,' she makes a face that I think is supposed to resemble a bed bug, putting her fingers to the top of her head like antennae, sucking her lips in.

I laugh because I'm inebriated but because she really is quite funny. 'Don't do that, you're giving me trauma from that crab we met before,' I tell her.

She laughs, her body curled around that seat and the light hitting her face perfectly. 'Do you want to hear my best crab joke?'

'You have a best crab joke?' I ask.

'What did the crab call his daughter?'

'I don't know.' Yet I think I have an idea.

'Michelle,' she says, laughing, her nostrils flaring. It's only funny because she's laughing so much as she says it. So much so that she falls off her chair. I double over laughing with her as she lies on the floor, unable to control herself.

'Is it bedtime?' she says, putting her hands out for me to pull her up. I think it might be. Don't fall over, Charlie. As we pull each other up to standing, our bodies bounce and press against each other. Normally, that sort of action would lead to tension, a moment of intensity where we'd be drawn into each other, searching for a kiss. Instead, we both still seem to be in hysterics, her hands around my neck, me laughing so uncontrollably that I let out a little snort. This makes us laugh even more. We stumble to the stairs, draped around each other, Suzie giggling then putting a finger to her lips.

'You'll wake the children,' she whispers.

'Ssssshhh,' I say.

I slip on a stair and catch myself just in time on the handrail. She comes down to help me, hooking her hands under my arms. We venture down the corridor, her creeping like she's a Grinch as I try to hold on to the wall to control myself. When we walk past Mark's room, the effort of not laughing might kill us though. As from beyond his hostel room door, we can hear sounds. Sex sounds. And a bit of light slapping?

'C'mon, Jackie. Give it some welly...'

Suzie falls to the floor, rolling around, tears of laughter streaming down her cheeks, while I almost have to crawl past the door, like a bloody army soldier undercover. By the time we get to our room, we can hardly communicate for fear of being heard, and our faces are a shade of lilac. I fumble with the key to let us into the room and we roll in, not totally wasted, just warm and fuzzy, in a state where everything is fucking funny. I stumble to the bed and lie there face down, watching the gauzy white curtain float and dance in the low lights of the room.

Suzie stands by the doorway. This is when she should slide over and make her move, isn't it? But instead she dances over, her hands make cycling motions to a song I can't hear. It's not sexy and we both know it. I giggle and she falls into the bed, next to me, resting her head on my shoulder. We lie there on the mattress, taking in the twilight, and catching a breath.

'It's been a good day, Charlie,' she tells me.

'It has,' I say, putting my arm around her. 'I think you peaked with your bed bug impression.'

'My favourite bit was the part where the Korean lady filmed you going down on me in the park,' she mentions.

'I did nothing of the sort. I just slipped and found myself there,' I tell her.

'So clumsy. I'm glad I was there to break your landing,' she says, and again we burst into laughter. She puts a hand over mine and interlocks her fingers. 'We had sex before.'

'In the shower...' I remind her.

She cups her hands over her mouth as we both bring the memory of it back into view. Thinking of a movement so fluid, the water flowing down her cleavage, the sound of her moaning in my ear. I am not sure it would look like this if we attempted it now.

'Are we too drunk for this, Charlie?' she asks. 'I don't want to take advantage.'

'I'm fine. There was fruit in the sangria. So basically it was just like fancy squash.'

'Vitamin water, really,' she continues. 'I might be a bit...' she says, putting her hands out in different shapes like she's still dancing.

'Handsy? I would encourage that.'

'I would too!' she says excitedly.

We both grin and then there's a moment where we look at each other and just find ourselves. Her lips search for mine and we laugh, in between smiles. As I pull her T-shirt over her head, she gets tangled up and it covers her face like a veil. 'Can we just do it like this?' she says, a head of teal staring back at me and I laugh again. I kick off my shoes and they fly across the room knocking over a bottle of water that I apologise to, of course. And then we kiss, balancing our bodies out on that single mattress, lying there together, desperately trying to unclothe ourselves, me doing some weird dolphin kick to get rid of my boxers and her using her feet to move her knickers down towards her ankles. And there are elbows in the way, a point where I find an especially ticklish spot on the underside of her upper arm and kisses that involve way too much tongue but I like it all, the messiness of it.

I then balance off the edge of the bed to find a condom in my backpack, tearing the wrapper off with my teeth, lying back to put it on. She starts humming to pass the time as I pull the rubber over my sheath.

'Are you singing...'

'Lady Gaga? I think I am,' she giggles, turning to face me, propping her head up with her hand. 'You scrunch your face up when you're concentrating,' she says mimicking me.

I nudge her with my elbow and she giggles before kissing me and slowly manoeuvring over me, angling her body to glide on to me but then sitting up and then bumping her head on the upper bunk. She laughs and falls into me and we both lie there just wrapped up in each other. And this is not what I imagined. As I roll her over and she opens her legs a little wider, she looks at me and puts a hand through my hair. And I'll admit, I didn't imagine sex with her looked like this. Back in the summer, I always thought the sex we'd have again would play like a movie. A roll around on a sunswept beach, the light hitting us at the right angles and orgasms in slow motion, like they're under a filter. This isn't perfect. It's messy and unrehearsed. Damn it, it feels a little sloppy. Moments of unfettered pleasure coupled with a very real laughter. I put her arms over her head and run my tongue along her neck. 'I like this,' I mumble into her ear, thrusting deeply into her, witnessing her arousal in the shapes of her back and mouth. Her lips taste like sweet red wine. Her eyes look deeply into mine. Searching.

'Yeah. It's OK, isn't it?'

'OK?'

'C'est magnifique...' she whispers.

And there's a feeling in my chest that's not some burning, aching passion that's fiery and uncontrollable. It's something I feel deep in my body, a warmth running through my veins, a feeling like everything around me is glowing. It could be sangria or maybe it's me getting swept up in this, falling. In love.

In you. And just you. Suzie. Not that other French girl I knew once. God, I can't even remember her name.

EIGHTEEN

Suzie

I wake the next morning alone. No Charlie. Just me, lying here in this hostel room, wrapped in a sheet, a teal aquarium T-shirt next to me, the inside of my mouth dry and furry like a hamster has been bedding inside it.

The fierce morning light shines through those gauzy white curtains and I panic for a little knowing I have a professional responsibility for some children in this place. Did I sleep in? Where's Charlie? I then worry about the sex. We had sex. This was not a huge surprise. It was headed in that direction, but last night felt different. I felt like myself with him and that's because the sex wasn't some slick operation, it was real. It felt like we could get everything wrong and we just laughed through it. And it was amazing to feel at ease, like I can lie there, and smile and chat and then have a mega orgasm halfway through all of that. I mean, I sang Lady Gaga. I've not done that, like ever.

But maybe that's why he's not here now? How do I check if he's in the top bunk? Shall I kick the mattress? I think about it but then I get worried it might dislodge some bed bugs who'd come to find me and my sweet blood.

'Charlie?' I loud whisper. Nothing. Shit, maybe he went to another room to escape me? I sit up on the edge of the bed and adjust my eyes. Maybe he got a glimpse of me this morning and it scared him off. I reach over to the side table and down a small bottle of water, thinking about the day ahead, herding children. Must get up. I stumble to my feet and make my way over to the bathroom, having a wee and then heading into the shower. This will heal my head, wake me up and get me ready for the day. I stand under the showerhead and let the hot water hit my face, a memory flooding back of us showering together yesterday after the aquarium, the moment where he backed me onto the wall with such urgency. But then I also think about last night. Last night was messier. I think about all the potential ways in which I may have embarrassed myself last night. Maybe he woke up sober and had some flashbacks from the rooftop dancing. I run some shampoo through my hair, rinsing the suds away and then get out to dry myself, wrapping myself in a white cardboard-feeling hostel towel, the terracotta tiles cool under my feet.

When I get out of the bathroom, I dig through my trolley bag to find clothes for the day, slipping some knickers on, looking at the teal shirt and wondering if I should just wear it for shits and giggles. It would at least keep the children amused especially as a certain aquarium video of ours has gone viral. I've had texts from Beth because even she's seen it. I glance down at my phone, picking it up to scroll through messages and photos. Besides all the texts welcoming me to Spanish phone networks, naturally, the cousins are all very keen to hear about Seville and what has transpired. Lucy has even set up a group chat: Suzie's Seville Sex Chat.

> Bet you a tenner they've done it already.

> On a balcony, with some flamenco music in the background.
>
> It's a school trip, I doubt it.
>
> I reckon she's taking the bull by the horns.
>
> Got her hands on his chorizo.

I laugh to see the discussion in full flow.

> You realise I am in this chat?
>
> SUZIE! We're just here because we live for the drama? What's happening?
>
> A lady never tells. My lips are sealed.
>
> I BET THEY'RE NOT!
>
> LUCY!
>
> You were the one talking about his chorizo!

I send a line of laughing emojis and a picture of a Sevillian sunrise, no other notes, and leave them be as I know that last time, they were less good at being discreet about my sexual escapades.

I then scroll through a few more photos. Random photos taken on the coach where we caught Mark asleep with his mouth wide open, stained-glass windows, giant olives the size of marbles, group pictures of kids throwing up peace signs, and a singular selfie of two people in Plaza de España, drenched in a golden glow. I stare at the picture, lingering over his arms draped around me. All that light. It's all I can see. I close my eyes to think about what it all means, what it *could* mean, when suddenly a text pings out of my phone.

Paul.

> We really need to talk x

Maybe it's the shock of seeing the notification of that text against the backdrop of Charlie's photo, maybe it's the shock of hearing anything from him while I'm here, hundreds of miles away from each other, but I throw my phone up in the air in surprise to see him invade this space and then struggle to catch it with my slippery hands, watching as it falls to the terracotta tiles with the sharpest of sounds. Shit shit shit shit. I bend down to pick it up, swearing at my own clumsiness, shards of the screen on the phone. It's dead. It won't switch on. I squat there in shock. Wanker. Look what you've done now.

'Oh dear, what happened here?' a voice says from the door. Charlie stands there in denim shorts, a white linen shirt and trainers, sunglasses hung over his buttons and two coffees in his hand. He rushes over, putting the drinks down to help. 'Careful, you've not got shoes on.' He goes down to my level, an eye on the towel still wrapped around me and a thigh on show, waves of dark brown hair still damp and clinging to my face. He picks at little crumbs of glass, pulling a face to look down at my phone.

'That'll teach me to check my messages when I've just come out of the shower,' I say, blushing but perhaps for all the wrong reasons.

'It happens. I can ask around, see if we can get it into a phone shop to get it repaired?' Charlie says.

We could but that text would still be there. It feels nice to just remain in this little bubble of ignorance. 'Or it can wait. Might be better to have a digital detox, we leave tonight anyway.'

'Are you sure?' he asks, scanning my face, a hand over mine. I don't think he can read the emotion. I don't care for Paul anymore, but I still feel like I've just been revisited by a ghost and not in a nice way, like in a horror film where he's just appeared at a window when I was least expecting it.

'I just feel like a prize idiot,' I say, slipping the phone into a pocket of my bag.

'You're not. Would a coffee make things better?' he asks. 'I also found a churros place. Look how long this is...'

I smile, my eyes widening as he pulls out an abnormally long doughnut from a paper bag. 'Kids meet for breakfast in five, so hurry,' he tells me, and holds it to my mouth. I take a bite, nodding that it is indeed very tasty before dropping my towel to get changed. He doesn't flinch. He just watches my naked breasts as I stand there in my knickers, pulling my shorts and bra on and settling for that teal T-shirt, drying my hair with my towel.

'Whatcha looking at, señor?'

'Just... you.'

I smile as I turn to the mirror and haphazardly apply some make-up to my face. I see him through the glass as he takes a seat on the leather armchair and sips at his coffee, his legs crossed, a reassuring smile when our eyes meet. It makes me a tad giggly but I'll admit to also feeling a little pang as Paul sits there in my thoughts. Paul who never bought coffee. Paul who probably never looked at me like that and I just never realised. I shouldn't compare. Do I tell Charlie about him? He's been amazingly honest and forthright with me about everything in his life, but this feels like it would spoil a moment. To bring Paul up now just after sleeping together would feel a little distasteful. Perhaps it can wait, all these details can reveal themselves further down the line. I don't want to overload him.

'It is a shame though,' Charlie says.

'What's a shame?' I ask.

'You're going to have to reapply that lip balm in a bit.'

'Why?' I ask, turning to face him.

He approaches me, swooping in and makes it all better with

a hand to my face and a long lingering kiss, a chance to melt in his arms, feel his body against mine and realise that this is more now than just a coincidence or a one-off, this could mean something.

'Morning,' he tells me.

'Morning,' I say, our foreheads touching.

'Shall we do this?'

I don't quite know what he means. Today or tomorrow or the next day? I'd consider it all if he wanted it too. However, there's a sudden knocking on the door and the sound of Mark bellowing that it's time for breakfast and we part, opening the door to find a sea of kids headed downstairs.

'OI OI!' Mark clamours, winking at Charlie, who looks mortified at the lack of subtlety around the children. 'How are you two drunks this morning?'

'Were you and Miss drinking?' a voice pipes up from the crowd.

'No?' Charlie retorts. 'Never. Alcohol is not good for you, at all.'

'We're very good, Mark. Did you have a good night?' Charlie and I look at each other, a flashback coming to us of having to tiptoe past his room because of the pretty vocal sex sounds we heard last night.

'It was alright. When in Rome, you know?'

'Except we're in Seville, you plonker,' Jackie says, appearing behind him, sunglasses and a colourful kaftan top on, her hair a light frizz. He slaps her on the bum and she shakes her head at him affectionately to almost say he can but she's also hungover and he needs to watch himself.

'That's romance that is, Charlie boy,' Mark tells him.

I laugh because he's right. Until I see their room door ajar and something hanging from the bunk bed frame. Is that a fan of some description? Maybe a fly swat? Why do they get one?

Until I realise there's something next to it. That's a whip. Christ alive. Mark. You old romantic, you.

Charlie

'PLEASE CHECK THROUGH THESE ROOMS, EVERYONE! I do not want you on that coach telling me you've left your phones on your beds,' Lee shouts out into the corridors, as our Sevillian trip comes to an end.

It's been a busy day of going to the Royal Alcazar, me admiring the Moorish architecture and beautiful ceramics, the kids less so. *My nan's got these tiles. It's very hot, Sir. Why didn't they build this palace with air conditioning?* After that there was a wander around the shops and markets so the kids could practise their language skills, an exercise in crowd control and making sure they all bought items that were at least legal and avoiding, as Lee reminded us, a repeat of Paris three years ago where a group of lads bought PSG shirts from a man on the pavement and ended up being arrested. As we are in charge of our own sets of kids, I've seen less of Suzie – maybe more from a distance, under an arch, laughing with her group, picking out souvenirs. Snapshots of someone I can see a little more clearly now.

Our room door open, she packs the last of her things, zipping up her bag. She's changed out of her summer clothes into leggings and a hoodie tied around her waist preparing for the autumn chill that awaits us when we go home. I look around our room, it has all the simplicity of a basic university dorm, stucco walls and the furniture all doesn't quite match compared to that fancy villa in Mallorca. But I'm starting to think I prefer this, maybe this is more me. Maybe this is a better memory to hold on to.

'Ready?' she asks me, rising to her feet and dragging her bag along.

I nod, but I also feel nervous. We're leaving a holiday again, leaving the sun behind to go back to school and normality. Maybe we've laid a better foundation this time round, but there's something in the pit of my stomach that's laden with worry. Back in England, we have the worries of my siblings, work and a thousand odd kids getting in the way of anything happening. This is still in its infancy. For all that can go right, there's also plenty that can go wrong. I linger by the door.

'Can anyone tell me what the Spanish is for key?' Lee announces to all the kids, collecting keys and trying his best to organise this chaos. There are no replies. I see Lee with a clipboard trying to focus his eyes. If Suzie and I are hungover, it turns out he's in a worse state. After we all disappeared from that rooftop, Jorge persuaded him to go to a flamenco bar in town. If you walk past him, you can still smell the faint whiff of tequila. 'Mr Shaw, can you just check those rooms on the end, give them a knock.'

I stand by the door, a little paper bag package in my hand. I was trying to create a memory to mark the end of the trip. It was a silly gift I picked up for Suzie in the markets today but I guess it can wait. I slip it into the pocket in her bag and make my way down the corridors.

'Sir, I can't fit this into my bag?' a voice cries out.

I look into a room and see a girl holding a guitar in her hands. Never mind legal, it would have been good to buy something that could fit in your case.

'Do you play the guitar?' I ask her.

'No, it's for my dad. Isn't it great?'

I nod. It's super pretty but I reckon that's going in their loft within three months. Behind her, I see someone who's bought a whole hock of Spanish serrano ham, wielding it like a weapon. We will possibly have to hustle her through Customs.

'Sir, what do you think of this?' I turn around. Lola. Lola has been a pure source of comedy this trip. From constantly stressing about the state of her eyelashes in this heat to speaking to everyone in her Spanish with a London accent, there is something endearing about her. She holds up a little keyring with a golden bull on the end.

'That's quite classy, Lola.' ... and more importantly, it fits in your bag.

'It's for Josh. I'm just trying to work out if it's not enough, or too much? Maybe I should just get him some Spanish M&Ms or something. What do the Spanish call M&Ms?'

'M&Ms...' I tell her.

'Oh.'

'The keyring is cute. You realise you'd have to talk to Josh though to give it to him,' I joke.

'You're hilarious, Sir. How's things going with Miss Callaghan?' she teases, pointing a finger down the corridor.

I try and hold in a smile. 'Miss Callaghan is a colleague in my department. I don't know what you mean.'

'Smoochie, smoochie, Sir. You think we're all looking at our phones and don't notice you looking at her. She likes you, you know?' she says. 'It's kinda obvious.'

'Is it?' I say, my guard dropping for a moment.

'Well, yeah. Josh is always saying she has an eye on your room whenever she's teaching him. This trip confirmed it. There is some chemistry there. You got it on, didn't you?'

'LOLA!' I say, feeling my cheeks glow with a blush.

'OHMYGOD! There's going to be another staff wedding like Mr and Mrs Rogers. You know he proposed to her in an assembly. You want us to help you set that up? Can I be a bridesmaid?' There is far too much information there and her squealing is starting to attract the attention of other students who look on curiously, laughing.

'Slow down there, señorita. Does everyone know?' I ask her.

'Well, yeah? Viraj also recorded audio of Mr McWhippy and his wife too,' she says, her eyes wide and excited.

I try not to laugh. You are the adult and the professional here. Do not give anything away, Mr Shaw.

'You think we come on these trips for the culture, Sir?' she laughs.

'You're here to learn some Spanish, no?' I tell her. 'Didn't you enjoy the markets, chatting to the locals?'

'Ask Tyler that. He went and chatted up all the Spanish girls. We went to Bershka instead, Sir. Where do you think I got this hoodie from?'

'Bershka?'

She rolls her eyes. 'The clothes shop. It's Spanish, Sir. Miss took us. This is another reason why you should be with her. Girl knows her priorities.'

'Shush now, Lola,' I say, keen to shut the conversation down but also secretly agreeing.

I work my way down the corridor. I don't know why that lad has his belongings stuffed in two plastic bags or how that person has acquired a sizeable cuddly bear. I go into a room and also see how a group of boys have made a tower out of Fanta Limón tins. How have they got through so much in the space of just a couple of days? I walk to the end of the corridor to see a door closed.

'Señor Shaw, we're missing Tyler from that room? Everyone else seems to have vacated, can you hurry him on? Coach leaves in fifteen minutes,' Lee shouts at me from the other end of the corridor, walking away through a sea of trolley bags and excitable teens. 'WHAT DO YOU MEAN THEY WENT TO MCDONALD'S?'

I put a hand to the air to tell Lee I have this and knock lightly on Tyler's door. No answer. 'Tyler, mate? We've got to go. Are you on the toilet?' It seems to be quiet in there. His room is near the roof so I head up there to double-check if he's out there, only to find Suzie there, taking in the last of the rooftop sun.

'Hola, señorita,' I tell her.

'Buenas tardes, señor.' Her skin glows, her eyes are shining and the sunlight catches in her hair as she takes in this view for the last time. I can't look away, but I shouldn't stare at her. This will wig her out.

'I was told to sweep the roof,' she says.

'I'm here looking for Tyler,' I say.

'He's not here. He's likely asleep, knowing him. I found him earlier in the Royal Alcazar, asleep on a bench. I had to persuade security that he wasn't a tramp.'

I smile and walk up to the ledge where she stands, looking out at the Seville skyline. There is something about the skyline of a city that is pretty breathtaking, your eyes tracing the shapes of where they meet the sky. The idea that you literally feel like you're on top of the world. I put a hand out and she takes it, squeezing it tightly. 'We've been found out, you know? The kids know.'

'They know what though?' she asks, slowly.

'That we're... I don't quite know... that we're potentially... a thing?' I say tentatively, not wanting to scare her off but also wanting to admit to some feeling here. Let's try this out, this could work. We can't only just work in Spain otherwise we'd have to move to Spain and I don't think that's quite an option. I stand there and look out on to the view, mildly petrified.

'A thing?' she says, smirking.

'That's what the kids are calling it these days,' I continue. 'A thing.'

'Look at you, with all your rizz,' she jokes.

'Apparently, you look down the corridor at my room all the time in your French class,' I tell her.

'I do not,' she says defensively. 'I just sometimes glance that way, like a good colleague, making sure everything's OK. To check in.'

'Sure.'

We remain standing there, looking out as the sun sits low in the sky.

'So your thing?' she asks.

'Oh, it's my thing, is it?' I say, laughing. 'I mean, I'd like to think you were quite into my thing. Without wanting to sound presumptuous.'

She laughs. I want to make her laugh like that for a long time. I really do. Maybe we have a bit longer to define what this is but, like the skyline, it feels infinite, interesting, full of possibility. We start to hear Lee's voice echoing with some anger down the hallway and we look at each other. Maybe this can all wait. I put a hand around her shoulder and kiss the top of her head, her hair smelling sweetly, and then we turn to make our way down the stairs.

'I AM A TEACHER! NOT A VALET! CARRY YOUR OWN BAG!' we hear as we hit the bottom of the stairs.

Suzie looks at me, brushing my hand. 'I'm just going to give Lee some moral support,' she tells me, smiling.

I follow her figure as she walks away from me, snapping back into the present as I realise I was supposed to be looking for a child. Tyler. Tyler. Tyler. I look down a now empty corridor and see his room door still shut. I go over and bang on it a bit more loudly with my fist. 'TYLER! TIME TO GET MOVING!' I bet he's one of the ones who's gone to McDonald's. Lee is going to flip. Otherwise, we've possibly lost a child and that is also not great. Did we account for him? Or leave him to sleep at the Royal Alcazar? I'll have to go back and call his mother. I bang on the door again, no answer but I put my hand to the door handle and it turns. I tentatively enter the room. 'Tyler?' I turn to see him lying in his bed, huge earphones over his ears, a phone in his hand and WHOA, something else in his other hand. 'TYLER!' He doesn't move. I mean, his hand keeps going but he still can't hear me. I pick up a pillow from another bed and throw it at him, trying my best to avert my gaze. As soon as it hits his head, he scrambles off the bed, trying to hide what he's just been doing and pulling his earphones off.

'SIR! SIR! I'M SORRY!'

I face the wall and I hear him trying to organise himself. 'You absolute lemon. What the hell are you doing?' I ask.

'I was just...'

'NO! Don't answer that... We are leaving in literally ten minutes. Mr Jones is fuming. You've got to come, now.'

'I've got to...?'

'NOOOO!' I scream, trying not to laugh. 'Just... get your bags together and make sure you don't forget your... things...' I say, pulling a face. This is not funny.

'Sí. Lo siento, señor,' he says, trying to think a bit of Spanish might save him. 'Are you going to tell my mum, Sir?'

'I might need to tell Mr Jones to discuss,' I say. 'Possibly a detention.'

'For wanking?' he asks.

'For making us miss our flight. Just get yourself sorted,' I say in between desperate laughs.

'Oh...' he says. I hear him scampering about, zipping up his bag. 'I had a good time on this trip, by the way, Sir...'

I could tell. I still face the wall. I might never be able to look this kid in the face again. 'That is good to hear, Tyler.'

'Did you have a good time?' he asks me, a little too cheekily.

I pause. 'You're talking about Miss Callaghan, aren't you?' He laughs heartily. 'Hurry up and get your stuff... gilipollas.'

'I know what that means, Sir...' he tells me. 'The tour guide told us.'

'Then this trip has been a success if you ask me. Come on, let's go home.'

PART FOUR
LONDON

NINETEEN

Suzie

A thing. That's what Charlie called it. A thing and I quite like that. If things involve good sex in squeaky bunk beds, stolen moments on rooftops and falling asleep on each other on airplanes, him stroking my arm under a scratchy airline blanket, then I like the idea of a thing. Maybe that should be a new definition for the kids to use. I would like to be responsible for that and have people make TikToks in my honour.

We sit at opposite ends of the coach now and flash passing smiles at each other, in between trying to get teens not to take pictures of their friends sleeping and listening to their inaudible mumble rap where everyone seems to know the lyrics despite there not being any words. I haven't minded this trip at all but it will be a relief to deliver these children home to their parents, to forget the responsibility you have and the fact their energy levels fluctuate from apathy to bouncing off the walls.

'COME ON, MISS! DANCE WITH US!' one of them shouts.

I am not a performing monkey but I'm also game if the

moment allows. I move my shoulders up and down and everyone cheers. Further down the coach, I see Charlie laughing. But not dancing. I shake my head at him. I wonder what to suggest when we get back to school. Shall I invite him back to mine? Is that too much? I don't even know where he lives but I'll assume his siblings are there. I'd like to meet them, but that feels too soon. It's late on a Monday. Maybe I should suggest something casual. Shall we go and get a pizza? Shall we see where this thing goes? I would text him if I had a phone. Damn you, Paul. But at the same time, it's also a relief not to be dealing with that, to have had space from his constant interruptions. The coach finally rolls to a halt outside the school and out of the window, lines of cars and anxious parents wait to collect their little darlings.

'DO NOT LEAVE ANYTHING ON THIS COACH! I will not care!' Lee bellows down the aisle, and I laugh. The students all line up patiently, there are mumbles of thank yous as we all clamber off and I step outside. I already felt that burst of cold autumn air at the airport but to see the familiar buildings of the school and the dark sitting in the air, it really lets me know that we're home, this isn't Seville anymore.

'Suzie, I don't know how to tell you how much we appreciated you coming on this trip. We are so incredibly grateful,' Lee tells me, still clinging to his clipboard.

'It was my pleasure,' I tell him, putting a hand to his arm. 'And it was very well organised. Go home and have a rest.'

'And a stiff drink?'

I'm surprised his body can take on much more alcohol but he reaches round and hands me a bottle of wine in a gift bag. I return the gesture with a hug. We're family now, bonded by this experience for life and I will be forever grateful that he took on all the shouting on this trip.

'SUZIE QUATTRO!' Mark says next, as he disembarks the coach with numerous used drinks bottles and food wrappers.

'We will always have Seville,' he says, in earshot of his wife. Jackie rolls her eyes. I scan down to their slightly larger than normal suitcase wondering what other paraphernalia they have in there, admiring how they treated this school trip as their own little sex weekend away.

'How is Charlie?' he asks me, in exaggerated tones.

Jackie nudges him. 'Leave the poor girl alone.'

'I'm just curious as a member of staff in a school with limited parking. If you twos are lift-sharing now then that helps me.'

'Lift-sharing, is that what we're calling it?' I laugh. 'I'll see you after half term.'

He blows me a kiss and I watch as he puts his arm around his wife as they go in search of their car. Meanwhile, I get lost in the melee of assorted children reuniting with their parents and bags. Why has that boy got all his belongings in two plastic bags? A girl gives her dad a full flamenco guitar that he looks at curiously. Excited mums hug less than enthusiastic teenage sons. We ensure the boy who came with a full camping rucksack and sleeping bag and didn't read the packing list takes home all his things.

'SUZIE KATHARINE CALLAGHAN!' I turn to see that the voice is Beth, standing there, waving at me. Her presence is a strange relief. It's nice to have a welcome party of sorts amidst all these reunions. She comes to give me a huge hug and I fall into it.

'You're here?' I ask her.

'Oh, you stopped chatting on the group so I wanted to come here and be the first one to get the gossip, give you a lift back, make sure you were OK. Be the good cousin,' she says, studying my face. 'Hun, you're glowing. I'm so jealous.'

'That's the sun.'

'Yeah, yeah...' she says. 'Let's go get some fish and chips and catch up.' I nod because a little stop like that with conversation, normality and a bit of a debrief sounds perfect. She stops to say hello to a student who recognises her while I stand there watching the rest of the crowd disperse.

'Your middle name is Katharine?' someone familiar says behind me, carrying a similar gift bag of wine.

'I didn't want to say,' I explain, with a grin. 'My mum loved *The English Patient* too. It was the name of Kristin Scott-Thomas' character.'

'Niche reference,' he says, repeating my words.

I guess I didn't want to read too much into all those little things about coincidence and stars aligning and things that indicated that we were meant to be. Because I didn't want to sound flighty, with my head in the clouds. But there's a flash of intensity between us, a moment where I can hardly breathe to look at him, to know that we could have a future. I notice Beth looking at us from the corner of her eye.

'Do you want to...' he asks.

'Yeah...' I reply.

We can't do anything, not in front of inquisitive student eyes but yeah, I want to.

'CHARLIE!' a voice sounds from the other end of the car park and a teenage girl comes running over from a car and gives him a hug. Her hair is curly and wild and she's in a hoodie and UGGs. She's followed by a more chilled teenage boy who punches his arm in greeting. I think I know who these people are but I let them have a chance to reunite and stand back as Beth re-finds me again, threading her arm through mine and also looking on.

'What did you get me?' the girl asks.

'A shower cap,' Charlie replies.

'Seriously?' she grumbles, looking genuinely repulsed. 'Stingy git.'

There is a warmth and a humour there and I'll admit it makes him more attractive to see that look in his eyes, a look which tells me how much he loves them, how they are his home.

'Why did you come here?' Charlie asks them, grinning.

'Because we missed you?' the girl replies. 'We got the bus. Also...' she says, looking around before finding me. 'Are you Suzie then?' the girl asks me, boldly bouncing over.

I stand there for a minute feeling ambushed, Beth laughing that she was not the only one to come on down here and get a peek at the brewing romance. 'I am... You must be Brooke.' I see Charlie slightly mortified by her brazen approach, Sam hanging back looking at me from afar. 'How do you know?' I ask her.

'Oh, Charlie sent us pictures and updates and stuff.' She turns and puts a thumb up, flashing an excited face to her brother who shakes his head.

'I'm sorry about her. And this is Sam,' Charlie explains. I wave to him in his hoodie and big jeans, watching as Charlie puts a reassuring hand to his shoulder. I try and tuck my hair around my ear to make myself look presentable, knowing the hours of travel are going to make me look frazzled but I'll admit to feeling a bit emotional too. Charlie has shared so much of himself with me, he's obviously hugely protective of his siblings and he just introduces them to me so casually. These are my people. Meet my people.

'We're going to Nando's, you want to come with?' Brooke asks.

'Oh, I was going to get food with my...' I explain, pointing to Beth.

'You know what?' Beth says quickly, 'I just got a text from home and my husband's said one of my little boys isn't too well, so we will raincheck,' she says, smiling. 'Go get some chicken...' she mumbles to me.

'OK then...' I announce.

Behind us the crowds of people move on, the coach driver closes the doors and Lee puts his clipboard away in his bag, looking up to the sky and taking a deep breath. The trip is over. We are home.

'Suzie?'

I don't recognise the voice at first because I've not heard it for a really long time. Six months to be exact. The last time I heard this voice was in a voicemail telling me not to be such a bitch and pleading for me to come home. I can't quite understand why that voice is here though. Why can I hear it now, in this very moment?

Paul?

I see him come around from the other side of the bus to approach us and a feeling of horror goes through me. I can't seem to move but the sight of him seems to trigger Beth into action. 'Whoa. No. What the hell are you doing here, Paul?'

He walks past Brooke and Sam who are watching him curiously and then stands there alongside Charlie, who's grimacing, looking him up and down. I can't quite cope at the hell and agony of this situation, frozen to the spot.

'Beth is right. What are you doing here?' I mumble quietly. Maybe he's a hallucination. He looks no different to how I left him, all that time ago, in what seems like another life.

'You've ignored all my texts and emails! You gave me no choice.'

'How did you know I'd be here?' I ask him weakly, trying to move him away from the action.

'I asked around and made some phone calls. It's not like you're in witness protection.' He laughs, but nobody else does. I feel Beth's arm tighten around mine protectively. Seeing him next to Charlie is unbearably stressful, and the difference between them in every way possible shows me I was right to move on.

'I don't want to talk to you,' I tell him.

'Well, you have to...' Paul continues, his expression furious.

I see Charlie's back straighten at the change of tone.

'I have to, do I?' I retort.

'Yeah, because you're still my wife...'

Charlie

'Oh my god, I've found it. It's a group photo from about two years ago – that's her wedding. She's married, Charlie. She had a wedding. I like her dress... but this is not on. Did she really not tell you she was married? Sometimes I tell you stuff and you forget.' Brooke does very angry laps around the kitchen while she's on her phone, doing this deep dive into Suzie's life, as we pick on chicken in our kitchen.

Paul. She's married to a man named Paul. She never told me this. That's stuff you remember. She didn't wear a ring, she didn't allude to it at all. I wish I'd got Brooke in to do a proper excavation of her social media before now, but this still feels like something she should have said. Something I would have liked to have known – especially in the wake of everything that's happened.

'Brooke, sometimes he forgets to buy your yoghurts,' Sam explains. 'That's different.'

Brooke pulls a face and shows me her phone. It is indeed a picture on her cousin's profile that shows a country house wedding from about two years ago. Suzie is at the forefront of that photo with a man who I now know to be called Paul, the bridesmaids are in sage. I feel an ache of anger to see the photo. I take another wing and stuff it in my mouth. I knew something was wrong the moment Paul came into view. I didn't like the way he spoke to her or the panic and sadness in Suzie's eyes to see him. But even worse was that feeling in the pit of my stomach that this wasn't going to be as easy as I thought it would be. If they're still married, there's obviously something there to resolve. And it all sounds recent. So much so that instead of staying in that awkward face-off trying to work out if I had any place there, Brooke, Sam and I made our excuses and came back here and got our chicken delivered. I barely remember the drive home. All I can see when I close my eyes is Suzie's expression when we left. There was regret there, and a desperate silence where it was obvious she didn't know what to say. If she had, I don't think I was ready to hear it. So I walked away, listening to Beth's voice ringing through the air telling Paul what she thought of him.

Brooke still scrolls through her phone, desperately searching for answers. 'I think I've found Paul's profile on LinkedIn. He wears old-man jumpers with his shirt and tie. You're better looking than him and I know that's weird because you're my brother but if you wore jumpers like this I'd burn them. He's a Blue Harbour wanker. I bet his mum still buys his pants for him and he only wears Nike trainers from Sports Direct that are under forty pounds.'

Sam laughs under his breath but he's watching me at the same time, how I don't react. I know it's clear from my face my mind is elsewhere. I told her a lot on that holiday, I unpacked the two of them so she had full disclosure. I took her to one of my most favourite places in the world so she could share in that memory, to make space for us to start again, getting to know each other. But she didn't tell me she was still married. I realise I don't really know her at all.

'He posted a story on his Instagram about two years ago about "love being like a mountain and that they're only at the base of this momentous climb..."' Seriously, I am retching. That's the sort of man who likely has song lyrics tattooed on his arm thinking it's poetry,' Brooke says.

I love her loyalty. The way she will attack a man she didn't even meet. She just glanced at him in a car park and he's now her mortal enemy. She does it to make me feel better, I know, but I think I need a bit of calm right now, to not have the situation invade my headspace.

'Want to play *Call of Duty* in a bit?' Sam asks me. 'We can kill stuff? Would that work?'

I beam at him, grabbing his shoulder. Sam keeps it all close. I never quite know what's going on in his head. I can't imagine what it's been like for him, losing our parents at such a young age. I don't know how he processes emotion and even if he's happy at times, but I know that when it's all going to shit, we've bonded over computer games. We've logged on to *Fortnite* in different rooms before and taken on a group of twelve-year-old noobs and shut them down. The sense of teamwork and accomplishment, meeting in the landing to roar and high-five each other, have been peak moments of our brotherhood.

'Maybe later, thanks, mate,' I tell Sam. He then comes over and does something very weird. He hugs me. Brooke stops in her tracks to see it as the action is so unnatural. His arms feel like tentacles around me, he rests his head on my shoulder and I stop eating my chicken to hug him back and realise I'm tearing up.

'What the fuck is going on here then?' Max suddenly says, coming into the room with his fiancée, Amy, both of them standing there watching Sam display affection.

I blink continuously to hide my tears as Sam moves away and I look up to greet my other brother. 'Why are you here?' I ask him.

'I was told there was chicken. And big mouth there told me what happened,' Max says, helping himself to some chips and looking over at Brooke, who sticks her tongue out at all of us.

Amy comes over to give me a hug. 'Hiya lovely. She's married?' she asks sympathetically. I nod. 'Put on the kettle, Brookie. I need a tea.' I've always liked Amy, she's a veterinary nurse which explains why she likes my brother. Empathy shines out of every pore.

'But not married, right?' Max says as Brooke shows him

pictures on her phone. 'As in, she'd left him, they're separated, and I guess she had no intention of going back to him?'

I shrug my shoulders. Who knows anymore? I guess there is a story there and one that I should probably hear before I start casting aspersions over her character, but the truth is, I'm tired and it all feels too raw. I'm tired from the trip, but I am also tired of relationships and this quest of finding love feeling so difficult. I've been dating on and off since I was seventeen and nothing has ever quite stayed the distance. Maybe these three reprobates got in the way, maybe I'm just meant to walk this earth alone, like the Incredible Hulk. I look at Max and Amy now. They met when they were twenty. They dated, they bought a flat, he proposed and now they're going to live the rest of their lives together. I know it's not that simple, but it should be a lot easier than this.

'Perhaps. I just feel a little duped.'

'Says Carlos...' Max reminds me.

This makes everyone snigger, and I shrug. 'Maybe that's the problem. All of it was all built on a lie from the start,' I explain. 'Maybe I should have picked up on that giant red flag.'

'But you met again at school? How do you explain that? It's fate! How do you explain those cute photos you sent me from Seville?' Brooke tells me, her bottom lip out to voice what she thinks about all of this.

'Well, maybe fate is also throwing some roadblocks in the way and trying to tell us that this is a really bad idea. Maybe fate pushes people together, but maybe you can also make the decision to step away and decide it's not for you.'

Everyone stands around our kitchen counter, quietly swapping gazes with each other. 'You're doing it again,' Max tells me.

'Doing what?'

'Not letting yourself be happy,' he says.

They all look at each other and back at me. I put my hands up in the air in defence. 'I am very happy. Possibly one of the happiest people I know,' I say, my face maybe not communicating that emotion.

Max pushes a cup of tea in front of me. 'Charlie, I remember when I visited you in Seville. You were so happy, the happiest I've probably ever seen you. You were so carefree and you had the world at your feet. And then...'

Sam looks down to the floor and I put a protective arm around him.

'We will always be grateful for what you did for us. You took all of that on, all of it. But sometimes I see how you're stuck in guardian mode. You forget about yourself sometimes,' he tells me.

'You make being here sound like a chore. It isn't. I've given up things but I'm where I'm supposed to be. I wouldn't be anywhere else. I have love.'

Brooke runs up to me and gives me the biggest of hugs at this point. 'We loves you, Charlie. The mostest. You know that, but that's not the kind of love you need. You also need a life beyond us. One day we'll be gone and you'll be old and uncool and on your own and none of us want that. I don't want you to be the sad single uncle at my kids' birthday parties.'

I look at all of them. All that responsibility filled me with such fear. I never wanted them to feel that grief and sadness again. It felt bigger than myself and was all I wanted.

'Sad single Uncle Charlie dancing on his own in the corner,' Brooke repeats earnestly.

'I remember the time I had a really lovely girl and I let her go because you know, things got a bit complicated. They weren't quite lining up...' Max says, imitating me.

'Why have you made me sound like a Cockney gangster? Why has my voice dropped two octaves?' I ask.

'It's because you're so sad, you took up smoking in dark rooms,' Brooke adds.

'Wanking into a sock,' Sam adds.

'SAAAAAM!' Brooke says, as the rest of us burst into giggles.

'I don't mind if you date, you know?' Sam intervenes quietly. 'I don't want to hear you having sex and stuff because you're my brother and that's a bit grim, but find someone nice. I don't think it's supposed to be easy, finding someone to love, but it did sound like this might have been a good thing. Brooke is wrong about a lot of things but there've been signs...'

'Wrong about what?' Brooke asks, frowning.

'Sour cream and chive crisps?' Max says.

She doesn't try and defend herself. The man has a point.

'And do you know what I think?' Sam adds quietly. 'I think it's Mum and Dad up there, making it happen, just moving things around like chess pieces because they want you to be happy, Charlie.'

There's a silence in that room that takes hold of all of us. A tear rolls down Amy's face. Brooke holds on to Max at that point. Damn you, Sam. I go over to him and ruffle his hair, kissing the top of his head.

'Perhaps. You lot seem convinced Suzie is the key to my happiness though,' I say, in resigned tones.

Brooke smiles. 'I think you can be happy with whoever you want.'

I look over at Max who's studying Suzie's photo on Brooke's phone. 'Hold up, that is Suzie?' he asks. He has a confused look on his face, one I recognise from when he has to work out a difficult sum. He scrolls through photos until he sees a selfie of the both of us in Seville. 'I met her. In Mallorca?'

'What?' I say.

Amy raises her eyebrows. 'Babe, do I need to hear this story?'

'The day after we fell off the bull? When I twisted my ankle. She was in our hotel. I bumped into her. She... was nice. She gave me a doughnut. What's that word for it...'

'Bunyol...' I mumble.

'Yeah, that's the one...'

Brooke claps her hands together. That's another star she's throwing up in the sky shining down on us. Another way the fabric of the universe was trying to show us a loose thread and weave us into each other's lives. I have no idea what any of this means anymore.

'Hold up,' Amy says. 'What bloody bull did you fall off?' She glares at Max. 'You told me you both fell down a lift shaft.'

TWENTY

Suzie

'So this is where you escaped to, eh?' Paul asks, as we walk through the doors to my flat. The air inside is cool and dark and I walk straight in, depositing my bag and turning on as many lights as I can. In my hand is Beth's phone. Beth who panicked when I told her to leave me, so, with mine broken, she gave me her phone, her pin code and told me to ring any of the cousins if anything was to go wrong. Like some female Batmen, they'd be there in double quick time to save me.

I storm around my flat, quietly simmering in anger to myself. Why is he here? Why did he feel the need to jump into that moment and just shit all over it. I had Charlie. We had a thing. And now we might not have a thing.

'Tea?' Paul asks.

'I don't have milk,' I tell him.

'I guess just a water then?' he says.

'Offering you a drink would suggest that you're a guest in this house,' I tell him, taking off my coat and hanging it on the back of a chair.

He takes a tentative seat on my sofa. 'You have a new sofa?' he says. 'But you sent that van to come and get our one?'

'It was out of principle. I paid for it. It was mine. I gave it to charity,' I tell him.

He looks annoyed. 'So, basically, you could have just left the sofa with me...'

I don't quite know what to say, how to react. All I see are Charlie's eyes when Paul claimed me as his wife, a blank look which told me the extent of his disappointment, his confusion. But not just him, his two siblings standing there, judging me, all that damage from just the one sentence.

Paul goes into his coat pocket and pulls out an envelope. 'This arrived.' I see the name of the solicitors on the envelope and know exactly what is in his hands. 'No warning? Nothing. Just that arriving at my door.'

'I am not sure what else you were expecting?' I ask.

'I don't know what you want me to say? I am sorry. I am so incredibly sorry. It was a one-off thing. It meant nothing. I don't know how else to say this to you.'

I sit there, trying to comprehend the words that are coming out of his mouth. It's not like I've not heard them many times over the course of the last six months, but I can't believe he has the temerity to say them now to my actual face. 'What?'

'It was just a fling that meant absolutely nothing. Some girl from the gym. What we have? We're *married*. I think we can salvage this. I love you. You never left my heart. You are all of my heart.'

He gets down on his knees in front of me.

'Please, Suzie.'

'Your heart?' I repeat.

'All of it. Belongs to you...' he says, looking me in the eye.

'Paul...' I whisper.

'Yes...'

'Stop it, get up... you're embarrassing yourself,' I mutter.

'But I love you...'

I shake my head sadly. 'No, you don't...'

'You're telling me how I feel?' he says, a finger to the air. I immediately want to snap it off.

'I'm telling you that I know that everything you told me in the last forty seconds, and everything you've been trying to text and email me for the last six months, has been pure lies. That woman who used to come to our flat? I found out from our neighbour that she used to come to our house every Tuesday at two o'clock and had been doing so for the last three months. That's not a one-off thing, that's a full-blown affair. In our house, a house that we bought together, a bed that we chose together, that I slept in.'

He stutters, trying to intervene.

'And we were married. Were...' I say in a sad and resigned way, exhaling slowly. 'I loved you so very much and you broke all of it. You broke my heart. So you don't deserve to have any of it, ever again.' I flare my nostrils trying to keep in my tears because I promised myself I wouldn't cry over him, I wouldn't waste the energy.

He gets up from the sofa, pacing up and down the room.

'So that's it? Just give up?'

'Are you seriously telling me this is my fault?' I ask him.

'You literally threw some noodles at me, you packed a bag and then you left. I never saw you again. You sent that looney-tune cousin of yours to get your things. Next thing I hear, you've quit your job and you've moved to London. You didn't even give me a chance to explain, nothing.'

'My cousin's name is Lucy.' I feel a mangled fury at how he can be so casually rude about my family.

'She threatened to shit in my drawers.'

I bite my lip to hide my delight. 'Was that going to be your explanation then? That little spiel before about me never leaving your heart and all that Instagram meme philosophy?'

'We could have gone for counselling. We could have sat down and had an adult conversation. Instead, you ran away. From us, from all of it.'

I sit there quietly, my rage building to hear that I did any of this. That any of this was my fault. Because I ran to escape the absolute shame of it all. I did throw some noodles at him and then I went to a Premier Inn for a week. I spent a lot of time just crying on their very comfortable beds, trying to work out my next steps, my heart bleeding over a buffet breakfast. And in the middle of this I continued to go to work. Twenty-two faculty members of my old school went to my wedding. They danced, they ate, they gave us gifts. I didn't want to admit to them that all of it was a complete sham. I couldn't face it. So I quit. I ran.

'You can't just walk away from a two-year marriage. You haven't even given us a chance. Is this something to do with that bloke by the school bus?'

I look at him, almost unable to fathom how he's circling this back to me.

'Charlie is a colleague – a Spanish teacher at the school. And so what if we're starting something? I can date who I want. We are separated. We are not together.' I'm also starting to realise he's a million times more a man than Paul is.

'We bought a house together. We're still paying off the honeymoon. I can't be divorced at twenty-eight.'

I exhale a deep tired breath. 'Yes, you can.'

'But I love...'

I put a finger to my mouth to tell him to shush.

'Suzie...'

'OH, PAUL! Please shut the fuck up!' I snap. He sits there in silence completely still, shocked that I would dare shout at him. 'What did you think? That you would make the grand gesture of driving up the A23 and I would go, "Oh, look, it's Paul. I'll forget how he was fucking someone in our marital bed for months, forgive him and move back in and restart our marriage to save him the embarrassment of being a divorcée."'

'But...'

'But nothing! When you broke my trust, then I was entitled to deal with that however I wanted. We need to get divorced and split the house. I want nothing from you. I don't need money, I don't want a Christmas card. I could do with never seeing you again and forgetting how marrying you was probably the most expensive and stupidest thing I've ever fucking done.'

Maybe I shouldn't have run off to London. Maybe I should have just done this. It's hugely cathartic. I look down at his hand. He's wearing his wedding ring and I can't quite believe it.

He sees me looking. 'Where's yours?'

I hold up my bare hand. 'I threw it in the sea. I can't believe you showed up here, Paul. I really can't.'

I look him up and down. It's hard not to feel some level of emotion. I'm not dead inside. I stood in front of this man and made vows and we made some beautiful memories together. But now I genuinely wonder was it even love we shared? For him to have gone astray, maybe it wasn't. Now I've experienced something with Charlie that feels more like what love should look like.

'I had to try,' he says.

'To save a dead marriage?'

'It was worth a shot. No matter what you think of me, I would have given this another go,' he says, looking proud, as if this makes him the better person.

'Don't be a prick, Paul,' I tell him.

'What?' he says, looking offended.

'The end of our marriage was your fault. Repeat after me...'

He looks at me.

'YOU HEARD THE GIRL...' I turn to see Emma, Beth and Lucy have made their way into my flat using my spare key.

Emma looks at me, mouthing to ask if I'm OK, whereas Lucy may as well have horns and a battering ram as she storms inside.

Paul rolls his eyes to see Lucy, which probably doesn't help. 'Oh look, it's the cray-cray cousins.'

Naturally, this doesn't affect the sisters who stand there unmoved, the best bodyguards a girl could ask for. I think a reason that I possibly ran to them too is I knew how much Paul disliked them. He didn't like the solidarity, the noise, the power in numbers and family loyalty. I can see now that he was threatened by all of that. That it made him feel small.

'Why are you here, Paul?' Lucy asks.

'That's between me and my wife,' he says pompously.

'I'm not your wife! Christ alive, Paul. Stop calling me your bloody wife!' I shout. The cousins all try to stop themselves from laughing.

'Legally...'

'Well, legally you're a man but I've never seen a more dickless wonder in my life,' Lucy tells him.

'On paper, we are married. Shoot me for wanting to try and save that,' he tells the cousins.

'Did he actually say I could shoot him?' Lucy replies.

They both stare each other down. It's the first time I've ever seen Emma just let Lucy have free rein. I think she's quite enjoying this.

'And what happens if I refuse to sign these divorce papers?' he says adamantly.

'Then I know people who can chain you up in a room and put needles in your knob until you do?' Lucy says.

Emma gives Lucy a look hoping that might be a lie. 'It doesn't matter if you don't sign them. As long as they're served and you've seen them then it can still go through the courts. Paul...' she says, going over to sit down next to him. 'Let her go. Face up to the fact you screwed up and let her go and live her life. If you ever loved her, you'll do that much for her.'

It's a voice of reason from someone who's seen divorce close up but has come out the other end. He looks into her eyes, putting a hand to his face to almost hide his shame, the fact that his stupid words haven't worked and his pride has been taken down a few notches. I notice the tattoo on his arm with the quote from a U2 song that I once thought was romantic. They're just words.

'Well I want a proper solicitor to have a look through these papers and I'll send them on,' he says sheepishly.

'I look forward to receiving them,' I tell him. He stands up, as do I, and I don't really know how to part ways with him. He looks like he wants to go in for a hug but I hold him off with an outreached hand. 'Bye then,' I say. He takes the hand and I feel the ring against my skin. And you know what? It's nice to feel absolutely nothing.

'Oh, I'm not shaking your hand, love,' Beth says to him, as he goes to exit the room. I don't think Lucy is going to either, she's almost baring teeth at him, but Emma gives his back a sharp slap that makes him jump.

And then he's gone. I let out a huge breath. I don't quite know what that was. Was it closure? Whatever it was, it felt clarifying, like the end of a good exorcism but with less head spinning. As we hear the front door close, the sisters stand there, waiting, watching.

'How did you get here so quickly?' I ask them.

'We're good like that,' Beth says. 'Told you, like Batman.'

I stare at the walls of the flat, completely worn, tired, but thoughts of Charlie also rush in and threaten to consume me. I'd text him if I had a working phone, but maybe it's the right thing to give him a bit of space first. I hope Paul hasn't broken our thing. I really hope so.

'I can say this now, cousin, but looking at him close up again, his head is the shape of a muffin,' Lucy says.

'I know what you mean. He has massive temples, square jaw,' Beth adds.

'Yeah, your babies would have been hard to birth,' Emma tells me. 'You've possibly dodged a bullet.' She comes to sit down next to me.

Whilst I appreciate them trying to make me laugh, I sit there, a little speechless, very contemplative, trying to work out what all of this means. Lucy comes and sits next to me, her head on my shoulder.

'Do you want to stay at one of ours tonight? So you're not alone?' she asks me.

I shake my head. 'But thank you.'

'Oh...' Beth intervenes. 'And we also bought fish and chips. We hid them in the hallway because we didn't want to share them with him.'

She goes out to get them. I don't know how to tell her chips are the perfect thing to fill the gap right now.

'You girls. Thank you. Can I give you some money for them?' I ask, reaching down to my handbag and pulling out my wallet. But as I do, a paper bag falls out on to the floor. I reach down to pick it up.

'What's that?' Lucy asks.

I see a note on the bag. *Estarás a salvo conmigo. C x*

'You will be safe with me,' I say, mouthing the words quietly, emotion burning in my chest, my eyes simmering with emotion. And I pull out a little keyring with a mermaid on the end.

Charlie

I shouldn't work. Not now on a Monday night when my mind is racing and I'm overtired from the trip. But I just can't settle. Suzie is married. I can't think why she omitted that piece of information or why she felt she had to keep that part of herself from me. I want to let it go, but that still really lingers in my mind. I wouldn't have thought any differently of her. We all have histories. Just look at my life. I'm a pseudo-parent whose biggest concern sometimes is whether I've washed the school uniform in time for Monday. Like some masochist, I go to look at her wedding photo again, even though it's bitterly painful. She looks angelic, so bloody happy.

Marriages break down for all kinds of reasons but my mind starts to wonder why hers did. The husband did look like a bit of a dick. I should wake up Brooke again so she can help me stalk her. Probably not the healthiest idea I've ever had though. I know where she lives. Do I go around there and have an adult conversation with her? What if the husband is there and they're making up and having sex and saving their marriage? I don't think my heart would be able to take that. Everything felt so positive on that airplane back here. I was literally floating on air. But we have indeed landed back here with the greatest of face-plants. And here we are again, and there's no other way to describe it; I feel lost.

I scroll through my phone and look at pictures of the trip. Lee has asked for the best ones to put on the school website. The best ones are pictures of her on the roof of the hostel, backlit by the Sevillian sun, her skin glowing and radiant. But there are also group shots of us and I smile because there is something about my face that looks different. I look relaxed, and calm there. I should be stressed looking after all these children but the reality is that she's within arm's reach and that is enough for me. I find a picture where my gaze seems to be searching for her in that big group of people, like a puppy. I don't know if that's a bit sad but I can't think of a time when I've ever looked at someone like that. I find some group photos and scan through them. We may need to Photoshop one of the kids who has his middle finger up but it'll do. I open up my school email and send them to Lee as an attachment.

I don't know what to do now. I go to the fridge to find some snacks and sit down at the kitchen table. Perhaps some marking would distract me? I could open PowerPoint and plan a lesson but that all feels a little bleak at this hour and at a time when I should be on holiday mode and asleep. Maybe I should do some laundry? Maybe I should start baking like Ed from school? I look at the clock. It's two in the morning. Do I wake Sam to play *Fortnite*?

I probably shouldn't be eating cheese so late at night either but it's one of the few foods we have in the house. I could do an online shop. I could jump in my car and actually go to Tesco because there's a 24-hour one not far away. I don't think that's a sane idea either. What do insomniacs usually do? They doom-scroll, binge-watch television, have a wank? If I did that I would think of her and possibly cry. God, that would be the saddest thing of all. You know what, insomniacs have things like lavender sprays to help them sleep. Do we have any of that in this house? The beauty of this place is that it hasn't really changed much since Mum and Dad passed, so I head into a drawer where Mum used to put all those medicines and magic elixirs for when we were ill. Inside there is an old box of pirate plasters that have seen better days, a bottle of Vicks and some Savlon spray she used to put on grazed knees and elbows. God knows how long that's been there. I should probably throw it out. I used to sit on this very counter and she always used to fix me up. God, she would know what to do with this situation with Suzie. She'd be sensible and calm and fix it with words. It's what she always did. *It'll all come good.* That was what she'd say. I think about that a lot because it didn't really. Whatever faith she put in the universe was completely misguided as it took her away from us. It makes me think that the universe doesn't really know what it's doing at all. That realisation of how much I miss my parents washes over me. *You've met a girl, Charlie boy. Tell me all about her,* Mum would have said, stood at the cooker, multi-tasking over a pot of something, her ears wide open. Her name's Suzie, Mum. You'd like her, I think. She does this thing where she looks to the sky a lot, whether it's to look for stars or gazing up to worship the sun. She's a great teacher, she makes all the kids laugh. She shares her food with people, even before she's taken a bite, and she can't dance but she names her pens. She has this infectious laugh. Kind of like yours. I wish you could have met her, Mum.

I sigh deeply. They both would have known what could have got me to sleep. *A knock round the head* would have been Dad's likely solution but Mum would have made a hot drink and given me a hug. Sometimes I just miss that, a hug, that reassurance. I don't want to lose it, not now, in the lonely twilight of this kitchen, so I go back to the hunt for lavender. I head over to the cupboard under the washing machine. Quite a fair few pegs, but then I spy a bottle of lavender fabric conditioner. I open the top and inhale some of the scent. I really am losing my bloody mind.

The silence is suddenly pierced by the sound of my laptop pinging to tell me I've received an email. Is there a part of me that hopes it's from Suzie? Possibly. Maybe it's Lee telling me not to email him in the middle of the night. I'm not sure I can even blame the one-hour time difference here. I pray and hope it's not some parent telling me their kid left their toothbrush in Seville and asking me if there's anything I can do.

I go over to the computer, my eyes blurry, not really recognising the email address. I click on it. Oh. I sink into the kitchen chair and read on.

From: paulyboy5048@gmail.com
To: C.Shaw@griffinroadschool.com.uk

Hello Mr Shaw,

You don't know me but my name is Paul and I got your email address from the school website. I am Suzie Callaghan's husband. I think we may have met briefly at the bus when I went to pick up Suzie this evening. I could see that you were surprised to see me there tonight and I thought it was important you know the truth about her.

The fact is that eight months ago, Suzie left me. We lived in Brighton and we were very happy together. We have a house, we've been married for less than two years and we were talking about having children. All I know is that she just left, she ran away from our life and disappeared. I don't think a sane or nice person does that. Have you met her cousins yet? They've had something to do with it, I'm sure, and they've blocked all my attempts to get in touch with her. Now, she's sent me divorce papers and I have no idea what to do. I am broken without her. I've been at the doctors' because of the effects on my physical and mental health. Maybe the warning signs were there. She never changed her name to mine. She was just using me. I don't know someone who just leaves like that without facing their problems. My family were so worried about her. She's completely ghosted us.

I thought it was important you know this information to see what sort of person she is. Why did she run away? Sometimes I worry it's because of money or something she did at her school but that's not how you treat people. I guess she didn't tell you I existed because you looked shocked when I called her my wife. Think why she did that. Seriously, if you two are involved in any way then I would reconsider it. What other lies has Suzie told you? I'm learning that she's not a good person – selfish, manipulative and just thinking about herself. Give her a wide berth.

I am sorry to tell you like this.
Paul Glass

TWENTY-ONE

Suzie

There's something very calming about a school when it's empty and there's not the noise and clamour of all the children. The buildings feel large and spacious, like you're walking through a museum or a grand hall when there's no one about, and it's nice to feel the scope of the place without someone chucking their lunch through the crowd. I don't know why I've gravitated here. I needed the space but I also just needed to do stuff, do something. I've not been sleeping since we got back on Monday night; my thoughts are plagued by Charlie and what he thinks of me. I got my phone fixed yesterday and I did text but he's just left me on read, making me think he wants some space from the situation. Either way, being in this strange limbo makes me feel incredibly lost. I had someone incredibly special and he's just floated away from me. I don't know what the right thing to do is, and my heart can't quite take the pain of it.

I'm trying to work but I can't seem to sit still at my desk, so I get up to see who else may be around, meandering over to the staffroom. I notice it's empty bar one person who's commandeered a table and is sorting and guillotining a range of handouts. I recognise her as a maths teacher, the one the kids were talking about on the trip. The one who may have copped off with another teacher by the bike sheds. She sees me and puts a hand to the air.

'Ah, another sucker in over half term...' she says, taking a sip from her coffee cup. 'I've just boiled the kettle in case you need it.'

I smile and go over to her desk to admire her paperwork. 'Well, it was this or sorting my sock drawer. I don't think we've been formally introduced. I'm Suzie Callaghan by the way.'

'Zoe Swift from Maths,' she tells me. She seems nice, warm and I like her big earrings, the effortless way in which she carries herself.

'Beth's cousin? French Suzie?' she suddenly says, excitedly.

'You guess correctly...'

'Then it's a pleasure. I adore any Callaghan. My kids occasionally look after Beth's boys.' And just like that, I already am a big fan of Zoe Swift. 'You're the one who saved the Seville trip by all accounts,' she adds.

'Saves feels like too grand a term for it but, yes, I went on the trip,' I add.

'Don't downplay your contribution. You saved it.' She waits for a moment. 'Oh... and you were the rockpool person.'

'You saw the video?' I say in horror.

'My daughter did and she doesn't even go to this school,' she says, pulling a face. 'There was a male teacher there too. Didn't he fall as well?'

Who knows, Zoe? I have a feeling we both fell for each other in Seville. I know I did.

'He did. But we didn't get eaten by sharks, so it's all good.'

She laughs. 'That's good to hear. Terrible when those school trips end in shark attacks, so much paperwork.'

For ten in the morning that is quite funny so I clink my mug against hers.

'If you're that Mrs Swift from Maths, the kids had stories about you,' I tell her cheekily.

'Don't believe any of them. I did not have sex in a cupboard.'

'That's not the story I heard,' I tell her, laughing. 'What's your partner's name?'

'Jack,' she says with a twinkle in her eye.

'Does he still teach here?' I ask.

'No, he was cover for a while and then he moved abroad but we make it work. FaceTime is a marvellous thing. What about you? Is there a husband/boyfriend?'

I stop trying to work out how to define that situation. 'No. There isn't... There definitely isn't a husband. But... I think...'

'But there *was* a husband?' she says, studying my face and putting down her papers. I nod, emotion quickly filling my face. I don't know what to say. 'Suzie, I believe I need to make you another cup of tea.' She goes over to the kettle, taking my mug. 'Milk, sugar?'

'Yes. One sugar please.'

I watch as she quietly makes my tea and glances over to check in. She pushes the mug along the counter, getting out a packet of biscuits. 'I found these on one of the science teacher's desks. I'll replace them next week,' she says cheekily. She then beckons me over to a sofa in the corner of the room. I'm quiet, pensive, almost grateful that it looks like I'm being given the space to talk.

'So there's definitely not a husband?' she says. 'You can tell me to mind my own business if you want.'

'Oh, it's a little ridiculous. I'm new here because I'm separated. I caught my husband cheating with someone he met from the gym.' I don't know why I'm saying this out loud to someone I hardly know but there is something peaceful about this woman, an energy about her which tells me she's knowledgeable, there's no judgement there.

'My husband was having an affair with a family friend,' she tells me, leaning forward and just like that, we look at each other and know that we're connected, part of some club that no one ever really wants to join. I smile and she returns the gesture.

'How long ago?'

'Nearly two years now,' she says, but there seems to be a serenity there, like she's made some sort of peace with it. 'We were married for an age and it was messy and there were kids involved but as clichéd as it sounds, time can be a great healer. You're say you're separated. Is there a divorce pending? Where are you with the process?'

'Papers have been served. There's no going back,' I say resolutely. 'He's just being an arse, refusing to accept it. He hates that I ran away from our life, that I've started afresh somewhere else. I think he might finally have understood that it's ended, though.'

She nods like she knows. 'That's male pride, ego, control… him claiming ownership, it's very caveman,' she tells me. I feel relieved that it's not just Paul acting like this then.

'Stay strong. I'll assume you have Beth and all her wonderful sisters in your corner for support?'

'I do.'

'Hold on to those people,' she says, studying the confusion and pain in my face. 'There's more to this though, isn't there?'

'The teacher who fell in the rockpool with me.'

She laughs. 'Oh, do tell me more,' she says, tucking her feet underneath her on the sofa and waiting to hear the story. The problem with our story is that it's so ridiculous I don't quite know where to start. 'What's his name?'

'Charlie. He teaches Spanish.'

'That's kind of adorable,' she says.

'That we're in the same department?'

'No, just the way your eyes light up when you say his name.' She urges me to take another biscuit.

I put my head in my hands to cradle my angst. 'But it's got messy. I didn't tell him about my ex, my marriage falling apart. I kept it from him and now I suspect he thinks I was lying to him.' She listens intently. 'It's not that I didn't want to tell him. I just... it's not something you lead with, you know. Oh, by the way, I'm Suzie. My marriage was a complete failure and I like chicken wings. How about you?'

She giggles under her breath but I see her understanding that feeling completely. 'Is that how you look at your divorce then? A failure?'

'Sort of. We were only married two years. It's kind of embarrassing. It's a label no one wants. I don't see people going on Facebook and broadcasting these things,' I tell her.

'Oh, my sister threw me a divorce party. We had balloons and little cakes with his name on that we threw at a wall.' I laugh. Lucy would adore that. I might have to take notes. 'Look, I feel you completely. But maybe turn that feeling around. Maybe staying in that marriage would have been the failure. Maybe what you did was actually very necessary, very brave.' She reaches for my hand and I feel some level of emotion to have someone I hardly know praise me like this. 'If this Charlie is a decent sort, he'll understand. He'll know that people come with stories, both good and bad.'

'Perhaps. All his stories are good though.'

'No such thing. There must be something wrong with him?' she tells me.

I sigh deeply to bring him to mind again, to think of what I've potentially lost. 'Maybe. But he really is just genuinely decent, authentic. That sort of old-school gentlemanly charm where he checks in with everyone in the room, like he can't carry on unless he knows everyone is OK. He's very mature but not very organised, he does this thing where he makes a joke and then apologises for how bad it is, he has a really high-pitched scream and is endearingly scared of flying...' I look over at Zoe, biting her lip as she listens. I realise as I say it that everything I've listed is really what I've started to love about him. 'I just don't trust myself anymore. I thought my ex was a good human being. I guess I wouldn't have married him otherwise. But look what happened there?'

'That wasn't anything to do with you though. That was him being duplicitous, having no respect for your marriage...' she adds, and I laugh. 'You're a bit scared, aren't you?'

I nod quietly. It's the first time I've admitted it. I am confident about some things – in the way that I've moved away from Paul, how I know I never want to go back there, but there is fear there too, some worry that it's too soon, that Charlie could be another person who'd hurt me. It all sits there fighting with that energy that draws me to him like a magnet. 'I don't quite know,' I say, deep in my thoughts. 'I've jumped in, if you know what I mean.'

'And how was the water?' she asks, smirking.

'Like the clearest bluest warmest ocean on a sunny day,' I say, almost a little embarrassed to say that out loud.

'Have you taken multiple dips?'

I nod, grinning.

She laughs. 'Look at your face. Your stupidly young face. You know what I'm learning in my more advanced years? The universe throws you these people sometimes at the strangest times. You can watch them sail past and miss out, or you can reach out and catch them.'

The bloody universe again. I stop to look down at my coffee and then gaze up at this mystic woman and all her wisdom. Who sent her? Because do you know who she reminds me of?

She reminds me of my mum. The way she speaks with such clarity and heart. It's a rare and wonderful thing.

'That's good advice,' I tell her. She shrugs her shoulders. 'You ever want to have a chat, Suzie, about divorce and all its intricacies then you come and see me. I'm in Maths.' She reaches over and gives me the biggest and warmest of embraces.

'I'm in French.'

'Have you got a lot more work to do today?' she asks, sipping at her mug.

And for a moment, I know exactly what I'm going to do with this day. 'I'm working on a project of sorts. Just need to go to Art to steal some supplies,' I tell her.

'Well then, I never saw you,' she says, pretending to close her eyes. 'Just have faith, Suzie. It'll all come good,' she tells me.

I really hope so.

Charlie

'Oi, oi! Mr Shaw!' a voice yells from across the courtyard. I look over to find out who is screaming at me this Monday morning and it's Tyler. Tyler from the trip, who I saw far too much of in Seville. I'm glad he bears no embarrassment but allows me to feel that all on his behalf. I put a hand up to wave to him. I envy the kids who stroll in here without the weight of the world on their shoulders, just a rucksack, a black puffer coat, most likely no pencil case but just a lone biro and the remnants of a calculator, possibly a protractor. The sun sits low in the sky this morning and I look up, trying to feel some warmth on my face. I guess wherever you may be, it's the same sun wherever you go. I fell in love under that sun but that feeling was short-lived, conflicting. It's made for a strange last few days of half term, where I spent a lot of time moping, treating us all to takeaways and playing *Call of Duty*. Basically, I morphed into my fifteen-year-old brother. There was a point where Brooke had to detangle my hair and spray deodorant at me, it got that bad.

Now I'm back at school and I don't know how I'm going to do this. I guess I'll just plaster on a smile and get on with it. Needs must. Maybe I should go and find her first? Tell her? I'd rehearsed something but maybe it's best in an email so I can say everything I need to. I walk across the courtyard, up the stairs to my department, approaching my room to turn on the lights. At first, I don't quite understand where I am. I assume because it's so early and I'm not quite up that perhaps I'm in the wrong room, but then I look around and see that all my bunting has been re-hung, my flag sits proudly on the back wall along with a display of all the Spanish islands. I jump when I turn to my desk as there's a huge cut-out flamenco lady there. Her skirt is made up of little balls of red tissue paper. On my white board are laminated months of the year and days of the week in Spanish, there's an adjective and opinions wall, grammar tips for all the tenses. My display of badly hung fans is gone which is a bit of a relief. The kids were starting to refer to it as my OnlyFans wall. But as I walk to the back of the room, I see what could be described as a pièce de résistance, a tribute to Spanish football. Players are cut out and have little speech bubbles coming out of their mouths, with matching club shirts and colours. I go up to them all and read them, mouthing the words.

I then jump out of my skin. Some guitar music starts up in the background and I look around the room. Is someone in the room? Playing a guitar? I hope not. But I realise it's coming from a speaker under the flamenco lady's skirt. I go over to her and see she's holding a note addressed to Carlos. I open it tentatively.

Hola, Señor Shaw,

Your wonky bunting was haunting my dreams so I thought I

would come in and work my magic. There's a switch if you want to turn the flamenco music off, it's on a speaker under Carmen's skirt – yes, she has a name. I also named your pens. I'm sorry for the Pedro Almodóvar head in the corner. He's a bit scary looking, we might re-think that.

I did this for you because I didn't know what else to do to make things right. Because you are an amazing and excellent human being. All the time we've shared recently has felt incredibly special. You make me feel not only safe but seen, loved, held at a time when I thought I'd never find something like that again. To say I like you doesn't feel strong enough. I feel like we belong, like we could be everything together. I'm not married anymore. I'm in the process of ridding myself of Paul forever. I don't know how you feel about that and I'm sorry I never told you. I just didn't want to risk putting out the fire between us – to lose you again like I did in Mallorca. I didn't want you to run away when my heart has only just found you.

Mademoiselle Callaghan

I stop in my tracks, almost unable to breathe. Then a knock on the door gets my attention.

'Sir?' It's Lola and, quite interestingly, a young man with her. I smile seeing them together, in the same vicinity.

'Lola, ¿qué tal?'

'Super bueno,' she replies. 'Sir, this is Josh.'

'Morning, Josh.'

Without him looking, she points at him excitedly. I'll assume that means they're talking and there's a shine in her eyes which tells me this is a good thing. 'My mum told me to come and give you this. It's some wine and biscuits to say thank you for taking us on the trip.'

'Well, that is super kind. Gracias,' I say, taking the gift bag from her.

'What happened in here?' she says, looking around.

'Spain exploded, obvs,' Josh says, gravitating towards the football players at the back of the room.

'I've got some for Miss too, is she in?' Lola asks.

I pause. I'm almost scared to go and have a look. Not because of the room, the note and the giant flamenco dancer but because of what I need to tell her, what I need to say.

'Maybe just check her room. If not, leave it on her desk?' I tell her.

Lola looks at me curiously. 'You alright, Sir?'

I can't even begin to answer that. 'Yeah. Thank you for this, Lola. Really.'

'De nada,' she says, posing as she goes, taking Josh by the hand as she leaves the room. I hear them bound down the corridor and then a few moments later a familiar female voice sounds out, telling them how thoughtful it is and how she loves that particular brand of wine. As I hear her voice, my pulse races. I close my eyes, envisaging all of it. Seville, Mallorca and just all those meandering steps that have led us here. 'Bye, Miss! Au revoir!' I hear Lola say, as she heads down the stairs. And then I stand at my desk, waiting, hearing her footsteps in the corridor. Why is my heart beating so fast?

And as soon as I see her, I realise I've done something really, really stupid.

'Morning, Sir,' she says, waiting to be welcomed in. She's in a navy midi dress, tights and ankle boots, her dark hair swept back from her face.

'It's like a swarm of elves have been in here...' I tell her.

'Too much?' she says, hesitantly stepping into the room.

There's a silence between us as she looks at me, wondering. I take a deep breath. 'I need to say something. I...'

'CHARLIE! SUZIE!' a voice booms into the room. Before I

have the chance to tell her, Lee appears in the doorway with a young man in chinos and a very well pressed checked shirt. 'How are we all? How was the rest of your half terms? All recovered from Seville, I hope?'

Suzie looks at me, trying to work out the energy, the confusion in my face. 'So Diego, this is Charlie who you'll be replacing,' Lee says, 'And I mean, look at this room you'll be moving into, this is so fantastic.'

I see Suzie's face fall, and she glances between Lee and myself as if she can't process what he just said. Diego looks at the flamenco dancer then back to me. Now is not the time to tell this person that I did not make that myself.

'I'm sorry...' Suzie says breathlessly. 'Replace?'

'Oh, did you not say anything yet, Charlie?' Lee tells me. 'We're part of a scheme of schools in South London that take on language apprentices. Diego is going to do some training with us and Charlie is going to help out at another school for a bit.'

'A bit?' she says.

'Just the half term,' I tell her softly.

'Oh...'

Lee looks between the two of us, realising that he's broken the news before I had the chance to explain, that whatever he witnessed in Seville may have come to an abrupt end. 'Diego... come with me and I'll show you where we keep the dictionaries.'

He leads him out of the room as Suzie stands there, mute, looking a little lost and overwhelmed. I rub my face with my hands, feeling distraught to see her so upset.

'Suzie...' I whisper, watching tears fill her eyes.

She puts a hand up. 'Don't. Please. When was this decided?'

'I knew about the scheme and asked Lee about it in half term,' I admit, remembering the turmoil I'd been in when that email arrived from her ex at the worst possible time. I knew that he was lashing out, that what he said wasn't true. That he was a wanker. But it also seemed clear that it was all too complicated, that Suzie needed to draw a line under her marriage before we even tried to work out what we had. We needed space, we needed time, that was what my rational head was thinking. But seeing her now in front of me, my heart feels very different. I think my rational head might be a proper idiot.

'I got an email from Paul,' I tell her, knowing I need to be straight with her.

'An email?' she says, eyebrows raised. 'Did he... what did he say?'

'He wasn't kind about you... He was telling me to steer clear.'

She puts her hands over her face in horror and then laughs under her breath. 'Did he tell you he cheated on me?'

'No.'

'But you believed whatever crap he did tell you?' she says, her tone changing.

I walk towards her but she takes a step back. 'No. He described a girl that I didn't recognise at all. I knew it was just anger, and bitterness. But it did make me realise that this... whatever this is... it's happening so quickly. When did you leave him?'

'March,' she tells me.

'That's eight months ago.'

'So your solution, after Seville, after everything we shared together, is to back away? After everything that's happened in that time? How I've left him and rebuilt my life?' she says, her cheeks flushed.

'Because you never told me about any of it, Suzie. For all we shared, you never confided in me something that was really important.'

'Or maybe not very important at all, because he's nothing to me. You... you... are important. You...' she says, her voice trembling.

My chest feels heavy and I can't bear the look on her face as she says this. There was rationale there. In my kitchen that night, high on Lenor and heartache, it felt like the only adult thing to do. To not get swept up in this lusty, hot holiday romance. To translate that spark into something more meaningful, that would have the potential to last. To get in the way of the universe and regain some control of my life.

I take a step towards her, longing to fold her up in my arms but not wanting to overwhelm her. 'It's only until January. This gives you time to go and sort things with your ex. Draw a line under that once and for all. So we can separate out the two and see things a bit more clearly,' I explain.

She stands there in disbelief, then looks around the room. 'Then all of this...' she says.

'Is amazing...' I tell her.

'No. It makes me look like a bit of an idiot,' she replies, putting her hands to her forehead to hide her shame. 'Scrunch up that note because I'm mortified. I... I... opened myself up to the possibility of us. Of loving someone again and letting them in and you've kind of closed the gate in my face.'

I stand there completely dumbstruck. The flamenco dancer's skirt starts playing the Gipsy Kings and I bend down to flick the switch. 'I just...' I want you. Every part of you, right here, right now if time and place allowed for it, though we'd most likely get fired and put on some sort of bad teachers' list. The universe is screaming yes but I'm putting my finger to my lips and telling them to just shush for a moment.

'I can't do this again. I just can't.' Her bottom lip trembles. She bites it to try and control the emotion.

'Suzie... it's not a no. It's...' There's a touch of desperation in my tone.

'A wait and see,' she tells me. She looks me in the eyes and shakes her head. 'I think I'm done here,' she mutters.

'Don't walk away...'

'No, that's what *you're* doing, Charlie.'

And with that, she brushes past me, turning away from me so I won't see a tear roll down her face as she leaves the room. That's when I realise I may have really messed up here. I've run away from the sun. My sun.

I widen my eyes as they travel around the room and all her handiwork before they land on my pens. I look at the labels. They're all named Carlos.

PART FIVE
PARIS, DECEMBER

TWENTY-TWO

Suzie

> I reckon you just find some fit businessman in the lounge looking for a one-night stand and get busy, Suze. I won't mind. Use the room! Go incognito! Bring back Aurelie!

I look down at the text on my phone, laughing to myself. Typical Lucy. Come to Paris with me, Suzie. We'll have a laugh, get drunk and run up and down the Eiffel Tower. But wait in the hotel first because I'm stuck at work. I look at the text again. Bring back Aurelie? Maybe not, because there seems to be some company Christmas do happening here in this hotel so I am surrounded by the sort of businessmen who have tufts of hair coming out of their cuffs and earholes. That said, I think this is a very Aurelie place. It's a classy Parisian joint with its brass fittings, high ceilings and marble floors. I can picture Aurelie here, she's got a vintage Chanel bag, of course, but she wears heels with well-fitting jeans and a casual blazer without looking like a PTA mum. She has a bold lip, sips on Pastis and when a man approaches her, she's bold, cool, sexy and charming. *Tell me about you. I am not impressed. Buy me another drink.* You know she's wearing a matching set of underwear too. I laugh. Oh, Aurelie. You were super fun. Thank you for being there when I needed you most, when I needed escape and excitement and adventure. I hope we'll always be friends.

'Plus de vin?' a waiter asks me.

'Oui. Merci.'

Oh, Paris. Everything about this hotel is entirely magical and charming. It's also decorated to the nines for Christmas with its big red velveteen bows, fairy lights and Christmas trees in every corner. There's a mountain of festive patisserie behind a glass counter in reception and unlike London, it's not the same old Christmas soundtrack of raucous seventies pop hits but some traditional carol-like folk songs that waltz through this bar and just sound classy because they're in French.

I knew it would be like this so when Lucy asked me to come with her whilst she attended some auditions, I jumped at the chance for a weekend away, to wrap myself up in another place, far away from London. I mean, I'll always love London. London has in many ways been good to me and will always be home, but I'd be lying if I said I haven't been lost in these last six weeks. Since Charlie left, I've been twiddling my thumbs, wondering what the hell happened there. There were so many questions. Paul emailed Charlie. What did he say that made him put his defences up like that? It's made me hate Paul even more.

We've not been in contact. I've seen Charlie reading my messages in the departmental WhatsApp group but I don't even get a thumbs up. I've gone to message him so many times and not been able to find the right words. What if it's just not meant to be. Maybe that really was the end of it all. If it was, then what a complete and utter tragedy. Because back in October, I spent a day on my knees laminating and making him a full-size flamenco dancer out of cardboard, tissue paper and tulle. Though the more I think of it, seriously, who does that? Who crisis-manages romantic dilemmas with crafting? No one. Divorced or not, I likely killed that on my own. As the weeks went on with no Charlie, no romantic entanglements, I bounced between lots of different emotions. Sometimes I missed him, I closed my eyes to imagine him, the way he'd make me feel, laugh. But then I'd push it all away, just in case I never got to experience any of that ever again.

I now sit in the bar of this splendid hotel nursing my second glass of excellent red, wondering how to pass the time. Lucy said she'd be a few more hours and then we have plans to go to a bar, something with a terrace and men who wear stylish trousers with pleats who talk with their hands. Maybe I should go for a swim in the hotel's subterranean spa pool, hang in the jacuzzi, stewing like a teabag. I look over at all the company men who have overindulged on cheese and alcohol, their ties loosened at the collar, the overhang of their waistbands on parade. Yep, definitely not an option. I've never been less aroused in my life.

'Connards,' a woman on the table next to me mumbles. I sneakily turn to look at her. She's older, her face a little withered but she has wonderfully bright grey eyes and wears the most adorable burgundy velour tracksuit and gold trainers, her white hair slicked back into a bun. It's old-lady goals if ever I saw it. I smile to myself because she's uttered one of my favourite French insults, it's multipurpose to describe all sorts of morons, jerks and dickheads.

She sees me smiling and looks me up and down. 'Vous êtes française?' she asks me.

'Non, je suis anglaise mais je parle français,' I explain to her telling her that I can understand her.

She looks me up and down. I'm not Aurelie. I'm not classy and sophisticated. I'm dressed for winter with a fluffy jumper dress and boots, my hair dishevelled from a short nap on the Eurostar. She carries her glass over to my table, sitting next to me on my banquette, looking out on to the restaurant. 'Well, then I think I would like to come and sit with you. Then at least I would have someone to speak with about all the arseholes in this place.'

I laugh. I don't think I have a choice in the matter. 'Suzie, enchantée.'

'Henriette, enchantée,' she says, smiling at me. 'Tell me Suzie, how come you speak French?'

'Je suis prof,' I tell her.

'A teacher? Then you are crazy, we will get on well,' she tells me. I laugh. I like this lady's vibe, the fact she's drinking what looks like whisky or brandy and her belongings are all in a LV bum bag around her waist. 'And tell me, what brings you to Paris?' she says.

'I'm having a pre-Christmas treat of culture and raclette,' I say.

'Moi, aussi. I am visiting a sister who lives near here.'

'Super, non?' I tell her.

'Peut-être. My sister is hard work. It will either be a great week or I will push her in the Seine.' I laugh heartily. 'You will be able to read about it on the news. Et vous? You travel with a husband? Boyfriend?'

'Ma cousine,' I tell her.

She takes a long sip of her drink and makes a noise to signal her content at the effects of the brandy. 'But there is someone in your life? You are très jolie.'

I smile. 'Merci beaucoup. I was married but he was a...'

'Connard?' she says, finishing my sentence.

'The biggest of arseholes.'

She rolls her eyes. 'Zut alors. Men, they are either a heaven or a hell. He sounds like hell. I hope he spends the rest of his life in pain. J'espere qu'il se fasse attraper la bite dans un piege d'ours.'

I double over laughing. 'You hope he gets his dick stuck in a bear trap?'

She giggles. 'I say this a lot to people who've had their heart broken. I like making people who have been at their saddest laugh from their insides. For your ex-husband, I hope it's not just his penis, also his... how do you say... couilles?'

'Balls?' I ask.

'Oui,' she says, pointing at me, laughing. She puts a hand to my arm and I must admit, I like this lady's charm, her need to extend some sort of sisterly affection towards me. 'My advice usually would be to you know... sow your seeds or whatever you English say... but in this room, it is almost impossible? They all look like potatoes,' she says still looking at all these self-important business types that sit among us.

I grin at her accurate observation. 'Oh no, that's not for me.'

'Paris is full of men. I am sure you and your cousine can find some fun tonight?' she tells me.

I laugh. You see, I tried that once. I went on holiday and had super-hot holiday sex with a man and that wasn't the holiday fling that I anticipated. It followed me home, it confused an already very jumbled-up heart. I don't think I'll ever trust a holiday fling again.

'Unless there is another man already in the wings?' She puts her hands under her chin, waiting for me to tell her more. 'I do not have a lot of excitement in my life, humour me.'

Well, if anything it's a good story. 'His name is Charlie but...'

'He has a nice butt?' I laugh.

'It was a lovely derrière.'

She grins. 'But what is the problem with this Charlie?' she asks.

Lots. His eyes are almost too blue, he's almost too bloody nice. Trust me, I'm trying to find things, Henriette, so it'll be easier to untangle myself from him.

'I don't know what he wants, I don't know what I want,' I tell her. 'It's not been a smooth ride.'

'Because he does not take care of his man areas?' she asks, bluntly.

I laugh again. 'No, his man areas were fine. I just mean...' I smile to think of his man areas but also my favourite French phrase. 'C'est comme les montagnes russes.' She smiles. It's one of those sayings that isn't literal, *it's like being on a rollercoaster*, but it feels perfect here. How Charlie and I just keep going up and down but in our case, also left, right, upside down and just circling back. It has sometimes all felt completely insurmountable. I don't think I understand it at all.

'Aah. Is it more heaven or more hell though?' she asks. 'Men are not perfect but you are looking for that person who can take you to both, back and forth, that can make you feel everything all at once.'

She says the back and forth a little cheekily to let me know what she really means. 'That sounds like someone speaking from experience.'

She holds up a hand with a wedding ring firmly planted on her ring finger. 'Clement but, alas, he passed two years ago.'

I cock my head to one side to see her eyes fade a little at disclosing this. 'Tell me about him.'

'Oh, he was magnifique...'

I pause to hear her say that word. 'We met later in life. I guess the universe is funny that way. The timing was strange but sometimes you know in your heart when it makes sense. I was thirty-five, he was forty. He was the most beautiful soul. Also, très bien monté...'

I try and sustain my laughter as this wonderful old lady tells me how well-hung her husband was.

'What is Charlie's penis like? Tell me...' I fear the alcohol may have taken my new friend to a point of indiscretion but I'm not sure I mind too much. I sit back in my comfortable chair ready to tell her all. 'Hold on, before you start. Let me get you a brandy. Garçon!'

By the time I finish talking to Henriette in that swanky hotel bar, I am three brandies down. For her, this hasn't touched the sides, but for me, I swear you could light me up and put me on a Christmas pudding. It's a gorgeously warm drunk feeling, the sort that reminds me a little too much of sangria-soaked rooftops in Seville, but also has helped set me up for an evening of Parisian partying. Henriette is my new heroine. My favourite part of the evening was when she told me in detail about her husband's cock. It was very refined, girthy but quite hirsute. Oh, the images I had in my head.

I reach my room now looking for texts from Lucy. Maybe now is the time to just have a bath, wrap myself in towels, and see where French television takes me while I wait and get ready for whatever Paris has to offer. Room 912. I enter the room, seeing my bag and belongings exactly where I left them but someone has been in to switch on the cute tasselled lamps at the bedside, turn down the beds and leave some chocolates on our pillows. It's all very sophisticated. I head to the window and gaze out over the city. I don't mind this view at all. Paris. The city of lights. It's like standing in the middle of a Christmas tree, all lit up, the rows of lights running through the buildings and darkness, like arteries, giving the city life, heart. And at the very edge, tiny like a small pylon on the periphery, the Eiffel Tower in the distance. I'm supposed to feel big waves of overwhelming romance now, aren't I? But tonight I feel differently. I feel calm, entranced, neither in heaven or hell but just floating above this glorious city. I turn back to the room and open up my bag. I smile at the first thing I see. I should have given this back maybe, there was opportunity and chance, but it's Charlie's T-shirt. The one he lent me the first time I met him on those rocks in Mallorca. I kinda held on to it and possibly packed it subconsciously. It's one of those T-shirts that have been through the wash so many times that the cotton is aged and super soft. You can't buy T-shirts like this. And it's become my favourite thing to sleep in. I can't tell if that is sweet or desperately sad. I'll hold on to the former sentiment. I get out the T-shirt and some toiletries before I notice a text on my phone.

> Can you order me some room service? I need a snack before we head out or I'll drink and just snog random French men.

> Anything in particular?

> Cheese, bread. Frites? And extra frites?

> Done.

I pick up the room service menu, scanning the choices and dial the number on the hotel phone by the bedside.

'Bonsoir, le service de chambre.'

'Bonsoir. Je voudrais un croque-monsieur et des frites, s'il vous plait.'

'Bien sûr, Madame Callaghan.'

I smile. You know the hotel is posh when they say your name and make you feel important. That calls for more frites. 'Actuellement, beaucoup de frites?'

'Beaucoup? D'accord, et à boire? Il y a un menu à prix fixe?'

'Oh, a set menu,' I blurt out in English, a little merry, forgetting where I am and who I'm speaking to.

'Sept?'

'Oui. Un coca.' The line goes a bit fuzzy.

'OK, that will be with you in about half the hour,' the staff member says in broken English.

'Merci beaucoup.'

I hang up the phone. I look at Charlie's T-shirt and run a

hand over the slightly faded logo. I think about a time when I first wore this in the summer when the weather was warm and sultry and I had just emerged from the sea, clambering over rocks onto the warm sand. The temperature has plummeted since then. An Indian summer in the autumn gave us a touch of warmth but now I'm looking over the banks of the Seine lined with the skeletons of wintry trees, the breeze making them dance in the shadows. We really are in the belly of winter, people are bundled up in wool coats, shielding themselves from the bitter cold, scarves wrapped around their necks, headed towards the warmth of all that light. I look out the window again, watching, waiting.

Charlie

'Bonjour? Êtes-vous avec Laurent-Sabra?' a woman in a suit by reception asks me. I look around at all the other suited and booted people by the desk. 'Pour le dîner?' she asks. Oh, does she think I'm some corporate bigwig here for a function of sorts? I look at the other partygoers in the foyer, all older men in suits, and look down at my brown boots and black wool coat wondering how she got that idea.

'Aah, non. Je suis désolé?' I reply.

'Quel dommage...' she mumbles, and winks at me.

I feel an elbow to my back as Max nudges me sharply. Look at you, Charlie. The French are flirting with you. That's a lovely form-fitting red dress but the fur coat and the fact she's possibly twenty or so years older than me is completely intimidating. I don't think I've got the couilles to survive that sort of encounter.

'Merci. Bonne soirée,' I say politely, as she sashays away.

I stand there in this gloriously festive foyer, furrowing my brow from the encounter.

'I think she just made a pass, Monsieur Shaw,' Max says in hysterics. 'Go on, have some fun. I won't mind.'

I like the fact that he's given me permission but I don't think I could do that to Max, nor have the energy. Today, to make up for the fact that his stag do was a bit of a disaster, we took an early Eurostar over to Paris to attend a beer festival. I've liked the fact that Max planned it all, chose this very swanky hotel, and that like our dad, he kept our passports in a Ziploc bag. A weekend away from responsibilities and work felt very grown-up, to sip our way through tasters of golden French lagers, not watered down at all, and keeping up with our European counterparts, is the ultimate treat. Paris is like a dream. As Brooke would say, it's one of those cities that's pure vibes. Even in the cold, it's the density of it, the narrow streets, the unpredictability of what you'll find on any cobbled street corner. Will it be a quaint boulangerie, its misted windows filled with delights and baguettes just casually stacked in a basket or will it be a motorist in a retro Renault trying to kill me, swearing profanities into the air? And it's just chic, so nonchalant. Even the bollards are more slender, the railings on the windows of every ornate building are more sophisticated, the people are so damn fashionable. This morning, there was an old lady I met in the lift wearing a velour tracksuit and an LV bum bag.

'Where to next then?' Max asks, as we walk through the foyer of this grand hotel that Max has booked for us. I notice his spine straightens as he walks through here with his shopping bags. He's not just come here to get drunk with his big brother but also to splurge on gifts for Amy. Max is not like me. He's not travelled much outside of the usual holiday destinations so everything is magical and wondrous to him. I took him for raclette earlier and I'd never seen someone so blown away by a bit of melted cheese and potatoes. 'What was that place you were talking about before? To get the steak-frites?'

'A bouillon?' I tell him. 'Or any brasserie really?'

'Do we need to get there before they close?' he asks, his eyes big, possibly a little sozzled.

'Most of them never close.' Max's eyes open in wonder. We're not in London anymore where our food options after midnight are kebab vans and 24-hour McDonald's. 'We have time to dump our bags, recharge?'

'We could go in the jacuzzi, Charlie!' Max tells me excitedly as he enters the lift.

'We could.'

'I just feel like we're only here for a night, we should take full advantage. Pose now...' he says, holding his phone up to the mirror in the lift as the doors close. This is also part of the weekend, as Max has said he'll send pictures of everything to Amy. I think her photo roll must be full of pictures of me half sipping on pints. I hope she liked the comedy picture with the baguette. So like a mug, I do pose now in this lift, not because selfies will ever be my thing but because I can see how incredibly happy Max is to be here, spending time. With me. It's a different face to the one I saw on his stag do. That one looked like it was just trying to have a good time, playing the role of a stag, fear in his eyes about what would happen next. Here he just looks like happy, excitable Max. The lift doors open.

'What was the room number again?' I ask him.

'922.'

I am never quite sure what to do in a jacuzzi. I think the idea is that you're supposed to relax but, in truth, all that bubbling and extreme warmth always feels a little violent, the jets hitting spots where they shouldn't and when I say that, I mean they do rush up my arse. I move a little so it doesn't do that. Max, however, looks very excited. I hope he's not getting kicks out of this. This underground pool area of the hotel feels slightly unnatural, it's lit by pink neon lights and surrounded by ferns to make it look subtropical but really it just makes it look like a swimming pool a villain would have in his underground lair. One where the floor would open up and sharks would appear which is why I've given it a slightly wide berth. A group of ladies on some spa weekend are representing here in numbers which means they're basically wading, doing ladylike breast-strokes in chic one-piece swimsuits. Almost like the antithesis to Max with his luminous yellow patterned swim shorts that clash a little with the surroundings.

'You have a strange look on your face,' Max tells me, looking over. 'You don't look relaxed.'

'I'm just trying to remember whether it's safe to jacuzzi when you've been drinking? Does this water also smell funny to you?' I ask.

'I haven't farted, if that's what you mean?' he replies, to which we both laugh because we are brothers and men of a certain age.

'Thank you for all of this, by the way... I appreciate it...' I say. 'I just thought I'd tell you before I forget.'

Max's face lights up at the compliment. 'Well, it was more Amy and Brooke's idea. You work hard and sometimes you just don't give yourself a break.'

'I've just been to Seville,' I say, feeling a need to be truthful.

'For work, really. And we know you've had a tough year with work and...' He pauses and just stares at me.

'You can say her name out loud, you know.'

He doesn't. None of the siblings have really known how to broach that subject for fear of breaking me.

The truth was I really liked Suzie. What I felt for her, I could feel in my very core, but I think I may have also fucked that up big time. I walked away. In my stupid head, it felt like a really sensible thing to do. It felt important to test this out, to see if it could survive some months apart so we could breathe and take stock. Who does that? Where in any romance book does a hero step away from big emotions like that and say '*Waiteth one minute, fair maiden. This love is o'erpowering. I am going to leave and take stock.*' No one. So well done, Charlie for being just a little bit too mature about it all. Because I think Suzie saw my leaving quite differently. I reckon she must have seen it as me running, abandoning her, leading her on and, in the wake of a separation, that probably wasn't what she needed at all. The more I think of my poor judgement, the more cringey I feel, the more I wonder how I will be able to go back in the New Year. Because I can't stay at the school where I am. The school where I'm helping ration out pens and I have to share a room with a French teacher who day drinks. She's not Suzie. She's not even in the same arrondissement.

'Have you really not spoken since half term?' Max asks.

I shake my head. Complete radio silence. The only communication I saw coming was from the departmental WhatsApp group, of which I was still a member, so the messages I saw were from her telling the group the downstairs printer was out of toner or asking about where they kept the Year 9 listening assessment papers. They're in the 2023 assessments folder, Suzie. It's not an obvious place to look but I think they were put there by accident. I never piped up and said that though. It felt like the wrong way to start talking to her again.

'I can't read if you're angry with her. Or is that your feelings for the jacuzzi talking again?' he asks me.

'I just... a lot happened there in a short space of time. I need time to recover, work it out. For now, this is good. This is unfeasibly warm and I've read that's not good for your sperm count but time with you, just you, is good.'

He smiles, knowing that my reluctance to talk about Suzie means a steer is needed. 'Normally, you and I time involves a PlayStation or a supermarket,' he jokes.

I laugh at the memory. When the both of us were tasked with looking after our family, we used to head out with a shopping trolley and come out with lots of crisps, toilet paper and cheese. We had no clue what we were doing. It seems like only yesterday but also a lifetime ago.

'Also, I'm not sure when and how I'm supposed to do this but I also have a question for you? That was also the purpose of this trip.'

I nod curiously.

'Well, it's kind of obvious but you'll be my best man, yeah?' he asks. 'Amy's furious I've not really made a decision about that yet. Thought I'd go with one of the boys but I mean, you make sense. You are the best man I know and you know me so well, so yeah...'

I don't think he was supposed to ask that question here while our ball sacks are being pummelled by these jacuzzi jets but I smile and feel myself tear up. We certainly have moved on from just thinking we could live off multipacks of ready salted Hula Hoops, haven't we? I'm so fucking proud of him, of us. I float over and give him a hug, holding him tightly.

'Love you, bro,' he says, his head on my shoulder.

'Love you more.'

It's only then we hear a slight cough though as the hug is drawn out, and those ladies in the pool look over judgementally to see what we're up to. Yeah, not that.

Max peers over the side at them. 'Way to ruin a moment... tournez around and mind your own. Is that a yes then?'

'It's a big oui from me.'

'Probably not something you should say in a jacuzzi, bro.'

And I laugh, from somewhere in me that thought I'd never laugh like that again.

'So you didn't think to ask Andy then?' I ask Max, as we return to our room in white robes and hotel slippers. It's a comfy and swish look for us and yes, we may have taken a selfie like this too. Brooke will love that one.

'To be my best man?' Max asks. 'Hell no. Turns out after Mallorca, his wife saw some photo on Facebook of him cosying up to some girl, and she dug a bit deeper and realised that's why she kept getting thrush. They've separated now.' I try and act shocked and maybe a little bit disappointed. 'Yeah, don't be smug. I didn't ask Wrighty either because he did it for Coops last year and he said the f-word twenty-two times in his speech. They think it's why his aunt had a stroke.'

I laugh. I'll have to write a speech. I'll have to make sure he gets there on time and wears clean pants. It somehow feels like everything I've been doing for the past six years really, except I'll be doing it in a suit. I hope it's a nice suit. We amble down the corridor of this hotel, a few guests giving us strange looks. Such is the way of hotels, it's just people coming and going. It feels like a very apt place to be. We enter the stretch of corridor of our room when we both suddenly stop. A room a few doors down from us seems to be getting a room service delivery.

'Laissez-le dehors,' a voice pipes up from beyond the door.

Max puts a hand to my chest and we linger in the shadows as the porter rests the tray on a folding table outside and then leaves. That is a bold move. Anyone could walk past? Two chancers in bathrobes, for example, who have worked up a hunger after a day of drinking, slightly parched from overheating in the jacuzzi. We stare at the food, longingly.

'That is a lot of fucking frites,' Max says, as we look at the tray.

'Like almost too many. I count seven portions of chips, that's just greedy,' I say.

'It could be a family in there, you know? Fussy-eater kids?' Max says.

'But it's also late – perhaps it's sex food for two lovers who've been going at it all afternoon.'

Max laughs, side-eyeing me. 'I dare you.'

'You what?'

'Dare you to steal some chips, come on?'

'You dare me?'

'I'm just telling you to have fun, live a little. I don't think you're brave enough anymore.' I look at him, my mouth agape with shock at the insinuation that I'm a bit of a coward. 'This is like a second stag of sorts? We need a bit of excitement.'

'I hugged you in a jacuzzi? Wasn't that enough?' But he's right. Why not, eh? They won't miss some chips. Maybe I do need to lighten up. Max gets his phone out. 'You're not filming this, are you?'

'Sam will piss himself laughing... go on...' he urges me.

I tiptoe over to the door, in full-on stealth mode, looking around for signs of other guests, staff, cameras. They have condiments too. I can steal mayonnaise. I go over and pick up the bowl ever so quietly and pick up one frite, stuffing it in my mouth. I can hear Max cheering quietly.

But then the door opens.

Shit shit shit shit shit.

I hear footsteps running away as Max abandons me. God, I hate you.

I turn around, slowly, awaiting my shame, my embarrassment.

But, hold up.

You?

Suzie?

She stands there for a moment staring at me.

I stare back.

'How?' she says, confused.

'What?' I reply.

'Did you know I was here...? Have you followed me? Was this Lucy?' she asks me, her eyes darting around the corridor.

I shake my head incredibly slowly. 'No. You're here...'

'I am.'

'You are...'

A feeling, a happy shock washes over me. It's the same emotion that rushed through me when I saw her in the assembly hall that morning. When the universe decided that would be funny. It's her. How on earth did that happen? And now she's here. Again.

'Why are you... what are you wearing?' she mumbles.

I look her up and down. 'Is that my T-shirt?' I say, looking at her legs, her hair freshly washed. She's exactly the way she looked when I first met her.

'Why are you eating my chips?' she says.

And we both stand there, slightly stunned by all of it, by what bloody glitch in the universe this may be. There must be an entity out there saying you don't need space, you two. You two just need to realise that this is meant to be. We keep flinging you in each other's path for a very good reason. Just get together already.

I need to swallow this chip.

'You ordered a lot of chips?' I say, and she looks down at the food, a little surprised at the quantity of fried potato on that tray.

'So, you thought you could steal them?' she says, smiling.

'Says the girl wearing my T-shirt...' I joke.

There is complete silence between us as we try and work this out.

'Why are you here?' I ask her.

'I'm here with Lucy. She had work. I tagged along...' she mumbles.

'I'm here with Max, we went to a beer festival...'

'Room 912.'

'Room 922,' I say, pointing down the hall.

And we stand there thinking of all the beaches, the hotels, the airplanes and schools and places that you can bump into and meet people and for some reason, we keep bumping into each other like this. We keep dancing this dance where we end up back in the middle of the room together. Or outside a room, stealing her chips. I can feel a tear forming in the corner of my eye as I know that this is the moment to keep her, to make this something, something that lasts. To tell her how very deeply I feel about her.

She stands there, jogging on the spot and I realise I'm letting all the warm air out of her room.

'You're cold.'

'Maybe.'

'Do you know what could warm you up?' I say.

She blushes, a knowing smile on her face.

I put my hands up in the air. 'Un café?'

And we laugh before she catches my eye and that energy that hits is both familiar, it glows, it sparks and for one moment, it feels like it could light up the entire hallway, this hotel, the entire city.

'I'd like that very much. Could I maybe put some clothes on this time?' she says.

I shake my head. 'You look fine.'

'Says you all covered up... in your robe...' she says, trying not to laugh.

'Would it help if I showed you my nipples?' I say pulling it open.

And she laughs. Hi, I'm Charlie. Let's try this again.

EPILOGUE

Six months later

Charlie

It's too hot for this. It's that sort of energy-sapping humidity where the air is thick and molten. The sort of heat where it hurts to even eat. All you want to do is drink and put your mouth under a slushy machine, to hell with the brain freeze. I toy with the olives using a toothpick, watching as a lady next to us seems to have brought her own table fan. Can we rob her? We should have sat inside. Damn us thinking we needed to lap up the sunshine.

'It's too hot,' Suzie tells me, returning to the table.

'Why are you wet?' I ask her.

'I splashed some water on my face. I look like I'm sweating, don't I?'

'Like a very nervous tapas eater.'

'Who should have talced her bra.'

'That's a super sexy image,' I say, grinning. I exhale slowly as she sits down on the bench next to me and gently kisses my shoulder.

I pick up the last olive and put it in her mouth, my finger slowly trailing on her lip. 'Yum.' She takes a chunk of bread and dips it in the last of the oil. I very much like summer Suzie. It could be because that's how I first met her, but there is something very relaxed about her when the sun comes out to play. Her smile seems brighter, she always has a pair of heart-shaped sunglasses perched on her head, and well, she's always wearing less and that makes me very excitable.

'Did you know that it is a well-known fact that no one actually knows where tapas actually came from?' I tell her, finishing the last of the patatas bravas. 'There are legends and rumours – the famous one is that back in the thirteenth century, the peasants were getting too drunk and rowdy so the king decreed that all drink should be sold with a plate of food.'

She smiles. I guess once a teacher, always a teacher.

She takes a long sip of her sangria. 'I love how the origin stories always come from men,' she adds. 'I'm going to start a rumour that actually it was the women who created tapas. One day, the women in Spain decided they were too bloody hot and fed up with cooking so they just said sod this, you're all getting small plates.'

I double up laughing. 'Can I tell my students that then?'

'I actively encourage that,' she says, turning to smile at me. 'It really is bloody boiling, isn't it?' she says, pulling her dress away from her skin. 'This was not my best idea. We should've just stayed in and lain down on the floor.'

'Naked.'

'Mr Shaw, we're in public. Super inappropriate.'

I grin. 'Well, you can lie there with your clothes on and melt. I simply want to get naked so as not to overheat.'

'Not even underwear on?'

'Nah,' I say in all seriousness. 'Possibly just a Cornetto in my hand.'

She laughs and I smile to hear that sound and the effect it has on me, the effect it's always had on me. I love hearing her happy.

'So if I joined you and lay down there naked too...'

'A moment ago it was inappropriate...' I note. 'That's totally fine but don't come near me, I want to preserve my coolness. I can't be doing anything else in this heat.'

'I did not think that was on the cards at all. Please. You lie in your spot with your Cornetto. I'll lie a good distance away from you. I think it's prudent to avoid any bodily contact.'

'Prudent indeed. It'd be far too sweaty. It'd border on indecent,' I inform her.

'Not good for our hydration needs in this heat.'

'So sensible,' I tell her.

'You know me.'

'Far too well.'

We sit there, both grinning giddily to ourselves.

'We should go, shouldn't we?' she says. I reach for her hand under the table but as I do, I trace a finger along the edge of her thigh, lifting up her skirt slightly. She puts a hand to her mouth and takes a very long sip of drink to compose herself. I nod without saying a word, getting up from the bench, feeling the back of my thighs sticky with sweat. I look up to the sun, letting it hit every part of my face and neck, feeling it recharge every cell.

I look at my watch. 'Sam and Brooke get home in about an hour? Will that work?'

She smiles. 'Hun, it's thirty-five degrees. Straight in and out, no dilly-dallying.'

I laugh. 'But you like my dilly-dallying.'

She plants a kiss on my shiny forehead. 'Oh, I love it. Just not today,' she whispers into my ear.

I take her hand and we vacate our table, out from the shade of the pub garden parasol and into the blinding brightness of the London sunlight. There is something unparalleled about a British pub garden, it's the feeling of the grass under your feet, drinking outside, when nine months of the year, we're relegated to drinking inside, leaning on wonky tables or pressed up against other punters. When Suzie moved in with us last month, this became our local, a ritual, the tapas is a hidden extra, like a nod to Carlos, to Mallorca, to all of it. As we walk out on to the main street, a bus drives past, passengers packed on like prawns, a line of builders exit a mini-mart with cold drinks, no shirts but the all-important hi-vis vest just in case. The sun is unrelenting as Suzie slips on her sunglasses and grabs my hand. I feel her fingers wrap around mine and a thumb slowly stroke my palm. Sometimes it's these moments I hold on to the most, the ones of silence where I can walk and be in her company and just exist. We continue walking, turning into our street when a familiar sound sings through the air.

'YES!' I yell a little too enthusiastically. I watch as an ice-cream van whizzes by and stops to park about fifty yards in front of us. I pull at Suzie's arm and she follows me, an excited look in her eye too that we may be the first ones in the queue.

'Sometimes the universe just knows...' Suzie says.

'It does, doesn't it?' I smirk.

The music of the ice-cream van winds to a stop and the woman driver comes to the window. 'I know you...' she says, winking at me, with a touch too much familiarity. Suzie smirks but looks mildly confused. Have I kept this a secret from her? A secret love affair with an ice-cream lady called Madame Whippy? How kinky. But at least I kept it on brand with something mildly French.

'But not in a suit today? You disappoint me, lovely.' She glances at Suzie and smiles broadly. 'What can I get you two?'

'Two 99s?' Suzie says, looking at me. I won't say no. I turn watching as front doors open and people flood the street to come find her. Oh, to be the most popular person at this time of year. She gets our ice creams ready, looking down the street to see who may be coming her way. 'Christ, it's her again.'

I follow her gaze. 'Mrs Murray, she lives three doors down from us.'

'Always gets six Calippos.'

'But she lives alone?' I say.

'Then you tell me where she's putting them.' We both laugh, trying not to clock her joining the queue. 'Sauce?'

'Chocolate. As much as you think I can take, please.'

She sticks her tongue out and turns to Suzie. 'You the girlfriend?'

'I am,' she says, proudly. Hearing those words still make me beam from ear to ear. She's not just a girlfriend, she's the other half of me. It turns out all I ever wanted was someone to share in this life, someone to walk home with me, someone to buy ice creams with. I won't share that with Madame Whippy though. Not today.

'You lucky little minx. Mwah, I'm here all week. Enjoy, enjoy. Right, who's next?'

Suzie

'What on earth is that on your face?' I say, laughing at Charlie as the chocolate sauce seems to have formed a moustache on his lip. I lick my thumb and help him wipe it off, giving him a kiss. It's that sort of day where ice creams are going to last about thirty seconds given the heat so Charlie licks at the sides of his furiously.

'You alright there, señor?' I ask him, trying to keep in my giggles as we walk back towards home.

'I am trying to ensure no ice cream is wasted. You are just going to that place where it's inappropriate again.'

'Me? I wasn't talking to the ice-cream lady about taking on all of her sauce.'

'It got me an extra Flake,' he points out proudly.

'Shameless,' I tell him, as he bites into it, showing off. He gives me half and he side-eyes me, grinning. Is it strange that when I was married, I only saw the future. I saw weddings, houses, kids – pictures of what life is supposed to look like. Maybe the future is overrated. There's something special about living in the now, in perfect smaller moments with someone who makes you laugh so hard your face hurts, for taking each beautifully sunny day as it comes.

Charlie puts the key to the door and we let the cool air of the hallway hit us, both collapsing into the house. Charlie kicks off his flip flops and I line them up by the door, giving him a look. He gives me a kiss on the cheek to get back in my good graces. It always seems to work. We both slide our backs on to the wall in the hall, finding relief against the coolness of the brick, the floor, as he watches me lick ice cream out of the nooks and crannies of my fingers.

'That's what happens when you don't lick quick enough,' he says.

'I prefer it messy,' I say.

He laughs and nudges me with his elbow. 'Alright then,' he tells me, 'What were we talking about in the pub?' He gives me his ice cream and starts to strip off. He's not wearing much anyways so it doesn't take long to strip off his shirt and shorts.

'That's not naked,' I tell him, eating my ice cream, trying not to care.

'There's a glass panel on that front door, that's why.'

I hand him his ice cream and push myself off the floor to go into the front room, drawing the blinds, continuing to nibble at parts of my cone. As soon as I do, he drops his underwear and stands there, smiling. Moving in with Charlie might be one of my more inspired ideas. It happened last month, a sunny day in

May carrying all my boxes, when Brooke made space for my products in the bathroom, when Charlie found out I had six boxes just dedicated to my stationery and still let me stay. And it's the process of not just being with Charlie but becoming a part of this family, of slowly loving and calling this place my home where on the hottest of days or even the coldest of days, we can be us. Because it turns out hot is overrated. It's about a love that lasts through all seasons. Times where we can occasionally get naked and eat ice creams together when Brooke and Sam are out, where we can smile at each other in the mirror when we're brushing our teeth and I can hug him from behind when he's doing the washing up. I bite into my ice cream. I am naked in our living room. I don't think I care, it actually is quite pleasant given the temperature.

'Bonjour,' I say.

'Oh, we're French now, are we?' he jokes. 'Hola.'

'Spanish?'

'Sí.'

I finish my ice cream and pull my dress over my head. As he lies there, I can see the perspiration glistening around his collarbones, highlighting the shallows of his neck.

'It really is bloody warm, eh?' I say, taking off my bra. I am not quite sure why he averts his eyes but maybe it's so I can't see the smug look on his face. As I lower my knickers and kick them away, he looks me straight in the eye. 'That's a relief.'

'Isn't it?' he says. He walks over to me slowly, tucking my hair behind my ear.

'I believe the deal was no touching. This is far too close in this heat,' I say. I lean in and give him a light kiss on the cheek, letting my lips linger against his skin. 'Much too close.'

He reaches behind me and pulls me close to him, backing me on to the sofa just below the window. As he lies on top of me, I wrap my legs around him, both of us sighing together, my back straightening as he pulls me in. I will always and forever adore that feeling.

'Much too warm...' he mumbles, in between kisses and lightly pushing inside me.

'We should have prepared first. Maybe got the fan down from the room...' I say, not that I'll be the one who goes and fetches it. 'Or hydrated beforehand...'

'Maybe brought some Calippos,' he suggests. And this is what sets me off. This sex might well be the most magnificent thing but laughing with him comes a very close second. Seeing his face crease up and the sound, the feeling is contagious. 'I mean, the lady had a queue, she might still be there.' As I laugh, he pushes deeply into me to get me back. I sigh, exhaling with a giggle as I kiss the underside of his neck. 'Yes, Suzie...' he whispers into my ear.

'CHARLIE! SUZIE! You in? THE ICE-CREAM LADY IS HERE!'

The sound of Brooke's voice in the hallway makes both of us descend into giggles as we scramble around desperately. Charlie stubs his toe, I tidy my hair desperately and find a throw to cover both of us as we sit there, next to each other, trying to act as though this fleece layer is a choice on this very, very hot day. We watch the doorway as Brooke pops her head around the corner. She looks at us and then looks at the piles of clothes on the floor. She starts to shake her head, judgementally.

'For fuck's sake, it's nearly forty degrees. The NHS told everyone to avoid physical activity. You two are gross!' she shrieks.

For some reason, this makes us laugh even more, sitting there like giggling schoolkids.

'Have you put a sheet down? I sit there! I've had naps on that sofa!'

Charlie may snort at this point, mainly because she's turned around and is shouting all of this at the opposite wall. She has her big earphones around her neck, a rucksack in her hand.

'You're home early,' he tells her.

'So you're telling me when Sam or I are not at home, you shag your way around the house?'

'It was a one-off, Brooke,' I say, attempting a bit of damage control. 'It's this heat. You know how it is. It makes you do crazy things.'

'It is very warm,' she tells us.

'Does that mean I can take off this throw?' Charlie asks her.

'NO! You're so grim! I'm getting an ice cream. When I get back, I don't want to see your pants on the floor. Where's your wallet?'

'On the coffee table.'

She edges into the room to snatch it before storming off. I pull the throw up to my face to hide my embarrassment. I snuggle into Charlie and he kisses the top of my head, resting his cheek on my shoulder.

'It really is very hot, isn't it?' he tells me.

'It is,' I reply. 'Much too hot for sex.' I laugh, kicking off the throw and resting my legs over him.

He walks his fingers along my thighs. 'Never too hot. Love you.'

I take a deep cleansing breath, my heart glowing. 'Love you too, Carlos.'

A LETTER FROM THE AUTHOR

Dear lovely reader,

Hello, there! You're bloody marvellous! Thank you from the bottom of my heart for reading *Hot to Go*. If we've met before then hello again but if you're new – welcome, take a seat... it's a pleasure to meet you. I'm Kristen ☺

I hope you've loved reading about Suzie and Charlie's epic and fun-filled love story. If you like your romance with big heart, lots of laughs and a healthy dose of innuendo then do look for my other titles, and keep up to date with all my latest releases and bonus content by signing up at the following link. Your email address will never be shared and you can unsubscribe at any time.

www.stormpublishing.co/kristen-bailey

And if you enjoyed *Hot to Go* then I would be overjoyed if you could leave me a review on either Amazon or Goodreads to let people know. It's a brilliant way to reach out to new readers. And don't stop there, tell everyone you know on social media, gift the book to your mates, drop WhatsApp notes to everyone you know.

This is my first summer holiday romance and crikey, it was so much fun to write. I'm usually stuck in a dark room writing my books in a hoodie and leggings so it was lovely to transport myself to Mallorca and write a story filled with sunshine, sangria and, well, quite a bit of sex (do look up the mermaid position; I still don't know how that works). If you are reading this on holiday then I hope you have a bloody lovely time and take some of Lucy's advice – let go, embrace the freedom and please, put that beach cover-up in the bin. Use protection, of course, but get all that sun on every part of you and soak it up. Please swim up to the bar too and have a drink on me. You deserve it. Something with an umbrella and a big piece of fruit attached to the glass, please. And have a flirt with that man in the bar – why not? He could be your Carlos! Go for it!

I wanted *Hot to Go* to be many things – I wanted it to be a super fun holiday romp but I wanted to look at the spark in relationships: initial hot holiday fling sex compared to the sex and love that perseveres in relationships, and I wanted to create one of those magical love stories where everything falls into place, stars align and shine super brightly showing people they were meant to be together. You may baulk at all of that but I have a life and a relationship built around patterns, numbers and coincidences. The universe sometimes works in ridiculous and extraordinary ways when it comes to love. Even though I've been with the same man for twenty years and am cynical about love in a lot of ways, I still believe in sparks that settle into warm, glowing embers and the fact that love can also be a very magical thing.

I also hope you loved seeing all of my Bailey Universe characters again. The Callaghan girls will always be my best bitches and it was a joy and a privilege to bring them on holiday and let them have some sun and seawater on their backs (and other places). If you think I got it wrong, Emma does have three daughters now. She had another with Jag. In my head, they called her Jasmin. I love seeing Mia and Ed now too (married and with child) plus my wonderful and wise Zoe from *Textbook Romance*. You think I'm mad but I always project my characters into the future, I always see their love stories evolving in my mind and think where they may be now. Always happy, always thriving as all the best people should be. If you want to read those origin stories, just go and find them in my back catalogue. I'd love for you to meet them all.

I will leave it here. I'd be thrilled to hear from any of my readers, whether it be with reviews, questions or just to say hello. If you like retweets of terribly unfunny memes then follow me on Twitter because I'll never call it X, suck it, Elon. Have a gander at Instagram, my Facebook author page and website, too, for updates, ramblings and to learn more about me. Like, share and follow away – it'd be much appreciated.

With much love and gratitude,

Kristen
xx

www.kristenbaileywrites.com

facebook.com/kristenbaileywrites
x.com/mrsbaileywrites
instagram.com/kristenbaileywrites

ACKNOWLEDGEMENTS

Firstly, a huge thank you to all at Storm for all they do in turning my dodgy, badly formatted manuscripts with all my unnecessary ellipses into fully fledged books. My biggest champion at Storm remains Vicky Blunden who tells me to run with all my ideas, has unwavering belief in me and edits all my jokes so they sing that bit better. In a challenging two years personally, our working relationship is something I hold very dear and I will remain forever grateful to you for everything. To everyone else behind the scenes, my eternal thanks especially to Emma Rogers, and Gemma Lawrence for her brilliant narration.

I work in a school now. I only started doing a bit of cover teaching at the end of 2023 but soon enough, as is the way with me, it snowballed and now I teach a bit of French which is what inspired this book. You speak French, Kristen? Of course not! I did an A-level back in 1998 but don't tell the kids that. I can just do a very good accent and I was trained by a wonderful man called Mr Walls who I remember very fondly so a thank you to him.

In terms of inspiration from my current school, I can let you know that Lee is a real person and possibly one of the loveliest, kindest teachers you'll ever meet, currently guiding my fourteen-year-old through GCSE French. Thank you for sitting with me in a lunch hour, going through the French in this book and also letting on that like me, you also were a fan of Eurovision and *Going for Gold*. Thanks too to Emily, Julie and Rebecca who've guided and encouraged me through this teaching year. Mark, the site manager, is also very real and when he found out I wrote books, he went out and read them all and, I'll be honest, my own mum hasn't even done that. What I love about Mark is that he comes and finds me in the staffroom. He tells me about the characters he liked, the bits that made him laugh, the parallels with his own life. I hope he reads this and knows that when he does this, it makes me want to sob because, quite honestly, it's so darned lovely to lift someone up like that. Huge thanks also to my mega wonderful boss, Hayley, whose kindness, empathy and support are part of the reason I stay at that school. And to my team who presently are Åsa, Malachy, Lily, Farrina, Chris and Christiane – thank you for the daily laughs and hilarity.

I currently teach ninety kids French and, crikey, don't tell the adults in the building but we do have a lot of fun. I will put my hand up and say I really quite enjoy our raucous bingo sessions, and moments when we name the gluesticks (who's got Thierry?) or you ask me what a seal is in French. (It's a phoque, in case you were interested.) So big thank you to 7C1, 7P1 and 8C4. You all talk too much but I hope you all learned something, anything. Merci beaucoup.

I found my way into that school via my own kids. Jake, Tess, Oz and Maya – you share me with a hell of a lot of people but being your mum is still my favourite job. If you can call it that. It's very easy being your mum and every working day, I realise how bloody lucky I am and what a wonderful privilege it is to guide you through life. Thank you for indulging me with dance breaks in the kitchen, watching episodes of *Pointless* with me and ignoring all those videos I send you on Instagram.

Nick. You've not been around this past year because work took you away from us so thank you for all those texts you send me from Saudi Arabia asking me for the Amazon password. Thank you for teaching me that love evolves as much as it endures. I'm still the best thing that's ever happened to you and I am sure that you will agree.

I wouldn't write without a readership and the last five years have seen me absolutely blessed. I have some of the loveliest readers in the land – faithful sorts who read all my books, tell me I'm funny and write me such wonderful reviews, posts and messages. It is completely overwhelming to know that people get joy out of what you write, that they seek it out, and get comfort and entertainment from it. It is probably why I keep doing what I do. So a big thank you to the readers, the lovers, the bloggers, the Instagrammers, the fans. I shouldn't have favourites but my unofficial book husband is Javier Fernández Pérez aka Diagnosis Bookaholic, who is not just a brilliant and supportive blogger but helped me go through all the Spanish in this book. I loved that I could ask you to translate: 'you can use one or two fingers' and you both laughed and understood the assignment completely.

I've never thanked places before but there's always a first time, eh? London will always be my messy but perfect home. South of the river, forever. In this book, we moved the action all over the place but a special thank you to the beautiful Sevilla. I went there a few years ago and it captured my heart. Mucho gracias.

And, as always, a list of names of people whose friendship and support mean the world to me. Thank you for all that you do or have done to help me re-emerge into life again: Mike Howells, Sara Hafeez, Ola Tundun, Bronagh McDermott, Ellyn Oaksmith, Rachel Ellis, Dan Turkington and Graham Price.

And one last thank you... to Chappell Roan.

Printed in Dunstable, United Kingdom